The HEART Has FOREVER

OTHER BOOKS AND BOOKS ON CASSETTE
BY KERRY BLAIR

The Heart Has Its Reasons

The Heart Has Forever

a novel

KERRY BLAIR

Covenant Communications, Inc.

Published by Covenant Communications, Inc.
American Fork, Utah

Printed in the United States of America
First Printing: June 2000

07 06 05 04 03 02 01 00   10 9 8 7 6 5 4 3 2 1

ISBN 1-57734-647-5

Library of Congress Cataloging-in-Publication Data

Blair, Kerry Lynn, 1958-
The heart has forever / Kerry Blair
p. cm.
ISBN 1-57734-647-5
1. Baseball players—Fiction. 2. Terminally ill—Fiction. 3. Mormon women—Fiction. 4. Sisters—Fiction. I. Title
PS3552.L34628 H39 2000
813'.54--dc21   00-024113
CIP

Grateful Acknowledgment To:

Jessica Warner

I am often asked who is responsible
for the beautiful, artistic covers on Covenant books.
Now you know.

***

Robby Nichols and Joel Bikman

I didn't realize as a novice to publishing how great an effort
these talented men make in my behalf
or how much of my books' success is due to them.
Now I know.

***

Valerie Holladay

Editor extraordinaire, teacher, inspiration, and friend
How very much I appreciate her
She may never know.

***

And to Gary

If anyone around here suffers for the sake of art, it is he.

CHAPTER 1

"Wake up!"

Andi Reynolds tugged at her younger sister's arm, and Clytie's eyes popped open as she sat up in her bed. Finally! Each night for the last week Andi had tiptoed into their room after spending the evening with the dreamiest man on earth while sixteen-year-old Clytie had pretended to sleep, silently praying that this would be *the* night.

"Well?" she demanded breathlessly. "Did he ask you? Did he?"

Andi's emerald eyes glowed and she nodded happily.

"I knew it!" Clytie shrieked and threw her stubby arms around her sister, who squeezed her back. "I just knew you'd marry Greg!"

And she *had* known. From the moment Clytie had met Greg Howland, phenom pitcher for the Chicago Cubs and the fastest rising star on the celebrity horizon, it was as if she had gazed into his blue eyes but seen into his heart. She saw at once that despite his fame and fortune, Greg was as shy as Andi was self-assured and as romantic as she was reasonable. Besides which, Clytie thought with satisfaction, he was smart and funny and thoughtful—not to mention drop-your-jaw gorgeous.

In short, Greg Howland was *precisely* the man Clytie had requisitioned in prayer to save her beloved sister from a fate worse than outer darkness—eternity with devoted-but-dull returned missionary, Sterling Channing. So, while Clytie might admit that baseball spring training had brought Greg to Arizona, she would always insist that it was God who had led him to Andi. Theirs was a romance made in heaven and, despite a couple of major earthly obstacles—like Greg's ignorance of the gospel and Andi's infamous checklist-for-choosing-an-eternal-companion (which included Church membership)—Clytie had considered it simply heavenly from the start.

The biggest obstacle of all, of course, was a head injury that had almost claimed Greg's life and would surely have ended their courtship. But in answer to yet more fervent prayer, and in response to a priesthood blessing, Greg had not only been recuperating marvelously in the hospital, he had also managed to successfully court Andi in the midst of medicinal odors and PA calls for doctors.

Now reveling in the good news, Clytie released her sister's neck to fall back against her pillows with another little whoop of joy.

"You're going to wake the whole neighborhood," Andi cautioned with a giggle. But it was almost impossible to shush her little sister when she could barely contain her own excitement.

"Did he give you a ring?" Clytie asked suddenly, pulling herself quickly back up in renewed excitement. "Oh, Andi, let me see!" She leaned forward and reached expectantly for her sister's hand before shaking her head in disappointment. "Well, how could he," she reasoned, "being in the hospital and all?" Before Andi could respond, she rattled on, "Are you going to have to wait a whole year from when Greg's baptized to go to the temple? When is he going to be baptized? As soon as he gets out of the hospital? When will that be? And what about—"

"Clytie!" Andi laughed, pushing her thick auburn hair back over her shoulder. "Give me a chance to tell you what Greg said."

"You don't have to tell me anything," Clytie sighed blissfully. "I know it was just like I imagined . . ."

Andi smiled at her hopelessly romantic younger sister. An achondroplastic dwarf, Clytie was just three-and-a-half feet tall, scarcely above waist-high on the average Laurel. But what she might lack in height, she more than made up in passion and imagination. Still, Andi thought, it would be impossible for *anyone* to know how she had felt in those moments when Greg had knelt—actually knelt—on the slick linoleum floor beside her chair, enveloped her icy, trembling fingers in his own strong, warm hands, and asked if she would kneel with him one day at the altar of the temple.

Wonderful couldn't describe the warmth that she experienced when the blood finally returned—seemingly all at once—to her face and she remembered to breathe. *Marvelous* didn't adequately express how she felt when the overwhelming wave of joy left her unable to utter more than two whispered words: "Oh, yes!" And even Clytie's favorite exclamation—*awesome!*—couldn't characterize the long, tender kiss that followed.

She leaned forward to give Clytie another quick squeeze. "I promise, it was better than even *you* could imagine."

"Well, I knew you and Greg were right for each other," Clytie repeated. "I knew you'd marry him!"

Even as Andi nodded, she could scarcely believe it was true. She'd known Greg Howland for such a short time. A month ago, Andi had never heard of the Cub pitcher, despite his celebrity, and had been waiting faithfully for Sterling Channing to return from his mission. Three weeks ago, she had assured herself that her new interest in a certain star athlete was merely compassionate service. He had recently lost his brother, after all. The least she could do was to share the gospel with such a lonely young man. Two weeks ago, that young man—with the endearing, lopsided grin and heart-stopping azure eyes—had almost died, and Andi had realized all at once that her heart would surely have died with him. But God had heard her prayers—and Clytie's—and now her heart would have forever to belong to Greg.

Clytie blinked back tears at the look of joy on her sister's face. This one moment was worth everything she had done to make sure Andi ended up with the right man. But Sterling, she realized suddenly, needed someone to set him straight. He couldn't continue to believe that Andi was pledged to him or that she was merely "fellowshipping" Greg.

"You can tell Sterling that you and Greg are engaged tomorrow night at the Easter Pageant," she suggested, "when you're working together in the missionary booth."

Andi hesitated. With her head so awhirl lately with thoughts of Greg, Sterling had never entered it. But surely he didn't think she still planned to marry him. She had never really loved Sterling, after all, and was grateful to have realized it in time. And he didn't love her, either. Sterling knew that; she was certain of it. She bit her lower lip as she looked into Clytie's anxious face. Well, she was *almost* certain of it.

"I can't tell Sterling yet," she said finally. When her sister's eyes widened, she quickly explained, "You know what Greg's life is like, Clytie. There's a story in the newspaper about him almost every day. That's why we want to keep our engagement secret—at least for a while."

"You aren't going to tell Mom and Dad?"

"Well, yes, of course I'll tell our parents—and Mrs. Howland—first. Then eventually we'll start telling other family members and a few close friends."

Clytie nodded even though she didn't like the plan. As right as she knew all this was, personally she'd have told their father *last.* It wasn't that Trent Reynolds, a conservative college professor, didn't like Greg, exactly. It was more that he had an aversion to the young athlete's profession, and he was concerned about Greg's troubled background and his former association with a publicist who was now in jail on charges of illegal gambling and drugs. Besides, Trent had always favored Sterling and encouraged his eldest daughter's relationship with him. So, despite Clytie's belief that her father would love Greg once he got to know him well, she still wouldn't have put him very high on the list of people in whom she'd choose to confide the engagement. Elder Channing, however, would be at the very top.

"I really think you should tell Sterling," Clytie repeated. This time, it was Andi who nodded without necessarily agreeing. Not that Clytie could blame her for seeming to forget the suggestion as soon as it was made. Tonight, of all nights, was probably the last one to spend thinking about Sterling.

A few minutes later, Clytie lay on her back staring up at the ceiling as she listened to Andi sing softly to herself in the bathroom as she prepared for bed. Tears welled in her large aqua eyes. *They're happy tears*, she told herself, and for the most part, it was true. Clytie had loved Greg from the moment she met him. Though he had been startled when he first saw her and realized she was a dwarf, Clytie had watched carefully for his next response. She'd seen quickly that there was no pity in his stare and not a trace of disdain. Rather, the eyes that met her own were kind, soft, and sympathetic. It was unheard of in Clytie's experience to feel so quickly accepted, especially by someone as rich, famous, and stunning as baseball legend Greg Howland. Clytie had fallen instantly and irrevocably in love. He was meant to be her brother forever and ever; there were no two ways about it. And from the way he looked at Andi after only meeting her that morning, it was clear that the only one who would need the nudge toward eternity was her sensible older sister. Clytie nudged.

But even as Clytie loved Andi—and admired her—she couldn't help but envy her. Besides being of normal height, she was in college, and ASU, of course, had several advantages over high school. Even Andi's part-time job tending alligators and other tropic creatures at the Phoenix Zoo seemed exotic and exciting. It was, after all, where she had met Greg. At a particularly difficult time in his life, he'd seen her talking to another zoo employee and driving the zoo tram, and had been struck by her serene nature and innate joy. He'd ridden the tram half a dozen times and stayed to talk with her, then had come back the next morning to "adopt" all the alligators and crocodiles, pledging a ridiculous sum of money for their support—just so he could spend a few hours with Andi.

No one will ever do anything that romantic for me, Clytie sighed, remembering the rapturous look on her sister's face tonight and wondering, with another involuntary pang, if that were something she'd live her whole life without feeling. Her friends at school were always giggling together over the guys they were dating. Until recently, Clytie's part in the fun had been listening enviously and occasionally daydreaming aloud. But serendipity had changed all that. Now she had a plan.

Reaching under her pillow, she withdrew a book she kept carefully hidden and wiggled up against the pillows into the square of moonlight from the open window. Nobody but a cashier had seen her buy the dog-eared paperback, *How to Catch a Man*, the day she, Andi, and her big brother, Brad, had volunteered a few hours of time at the local Deseret Industries. She'd tucked the book under the band of her pants and pulled her sweatshirt carefully over the bulge it had created. She didn't want her two older siblings to see. Brad might tease her unmercifully, but Andi would be worse. Her older sister would smile that gentle, I-know-everything-smile and tell Clytie—again!—that it was what was inside a person that counts.

That's easy to say, Clytie thought, brushing back her long blonde hair and opening the book to the page where she'd left off reading, *when your outsides are as tall and slender and pretty as Andi's.*

Chapter 3: Forget Cupid's Arrows—Arm Yourself with Charm! she read. *You must never assume that deity has a plan to help you find romance.* Clytie paused and wrinkled her nose as she considered the author's thesis. She was absolutely certain that God had brought Andi and Greg together. And she didn't doubt for a moment that her Heavenly Father loved her unconditionally and must have had a plan to send her to earth as a dwarf. Still, her physical body was making the dating game particularly difficult, and God hadn't provided any matchmaking tips that were as clear as this lady's.

Firmly convinced that it was about time her love life wasn't confined to a library shelf marked *Romantic Fiction,* Clytie stuck her nose in the book. She had long subscribed to Brigham Young's credo: "Pray like everything depends on God, then work like everything depends on you." In the thirty-some days between now and her junior prom, Clytie intended to do both.

CHAPTER 2

From her booth in front of the Mesa Temple Visitors' Center, Andi gazed across Main Street at the "Got Milk?" sign on a bus stop and smiled. She was one girl who wouldn't have to carry her fiancé's picture around in a locket. Her love's face was already conveniently plastered on billboards in most major cities in America. And if she did want a more personal photo of Greg, she could always borrow one of her little brother's baseball cards or cut the young pitcher's portrait from the front of a box of Wheaties.

As she stared at Greg, Andi idly arranged and rearranged the materials on the countertop. With missionary-extraordinaire Sterling Channing as her partner, looking occupied was the only contribution she could think to make. She had arrived at the Easter Pageant promptly on the hour to find Sterling already in place and apparently completing the last of the missionary discussions for the young man who stood at the booth, clutching a new Book of Mormon and a picture of the Savior in one hand and a fistful of pamphlets in the other. At his bewildered and imploring look, Andi had stepped behind the counter and warmly thanked him for his interest, saying she hoped he'd enjoy the pageant. Released at last, he scurried down the sidewalk toward the long rows of seats, as her sympathetic smile followed him.

It was then, as Sterling solemnly began to enumerate their responsibilities for the evening, that Andi had noticed the billboard across the street. Immediately lost in her thoughts of Greg, she didn't notice that Sterling had turned his attention elsewhere as someone else approached the booth.

"So, what has you got?"

"Excuse me?" Andi blinked and cast a quick, apologetic glance at a young girl who stood on tiptoe trying to see over the counter. Although Andi had noticed the child's poor grammar, she was most struck with her lovely mahogany skin and bright, brown-black eyes. "What did you say?" she asked kindly.

"I *said,*" the girl repeated, "what has you Mormons got to give away?"

"We have the restored gospel of Jesus Christ!" Sterling declared as Andi's hand moved toward a stack of pictures of Jesus, at which the girl gazed longingly. Andi tried not to roll her eyes as Sterling expounded Church doctrine to this dirty and clearly skeptical child. But since the child was older than eight and younger than dead, Andi knew her ex-boyfriend would preach until the girl was either converted or frightened off altogether.

Not that Andi didn't admire Sterling's devotion. Elder Channing had been home from his mission only a month now, and, after apparently converting most of South America, he had clearly commenced work on the Northern Hemisphere.

I wonder if Greg will regret not serving a mission, Andi thought as she watched Sterling in action. She knew that Greg had talked earnestly with her bishop, Dan Ferris, about it. But with the year he would have to wait before being eligible to go, and then the twenty-four months he would serve, it would be at least three years before they could marry. Andi was pleased that Greg was willing to do whatever the Lord asked of him, but was even more pleased at the bishop's counsel that at almost twenty-five, Greg was ready to start a family.

"The Lord knows your heart," the bishop had told him, "and has placed you where you are for a reason. You'll have plenty of opportunity to touch others with the gospel."

So, they had "only" a year to wait. And although Bishop Ferris had said he didn't normally encourage such long engagements, he supported their decision to marry right the first time—right here in the Arizona Temple.

Her hand still on the stack of pictures, Andi glanced at Sterling then looked at the fidgeting child. *If he so much as pauses for breath*, she determined, *I'll speak to this beautiful little girl myself.*

"Uh, I don't think I's be needing any articles on faith," the girl told Sterling seriously. "You's got any on basketball?"

Andi suppressed a giggle as Sterling frowned.

"Where are your parents?" he asked, scanning the crowd for a possible match to the dark skin and ebony hair.

"They's around," the girl said evasively, reaching for the picture Sterling had removed from the stack.

He withdrew the poster as the girl's fingers grasped the corner. "We'd like to talk to them," he persisted. "We'll give your father the picture and tell him how you can become a forever family."

The child's big, chocolate-brown eyes narrowed in distaste. "No, thanks, mister. But I'll take the picture of Jesus, since it's free."

Andi extended another picture before Sterling could respond. Her smile widened at the fleeting grin of gratitude she received before the child whirled and darted down the sidewalk, clutching the prized picture of the Savior in one hand and trailing a filthy cotton pillowcase in the other.

Sterling turned toward Andi, perhaps to set his "junior companion" straight on missionary booth protocol, but seeing that her eyes had returned to Greg's billboard, he sighed instead. "So, how's Howland doing?"

"Hmmm?" Andi asked absently, resting her chin in her palm as she stared into the incredible blue eyes on the sign and unconsciously returned the grin beneath the cute little milk mustache. When Sterling ran a hand in front of her face, she blinked. "Oh, Greg? He's fine, thanks. He'll be released from the hospital any day now."

"Then he'll go back to Chicago?" Sterling asked hopefully.

"Um, no," Andi said slowly, trying to gather her thoughts. Maybe Clytie was right. Maybe she *should* tell Sterling that she and Greg were engaged. She certainly didn't want to lead him on by letting him believe there was still a chance for them. "Greg and his mother are leasing a townhouse in Mesa," she began, "at least until—"

Sterling, however, wasn't as interested in listening as he was in lecturing. He crossed his arms and said earnestly, "Andi, about this, er, ballplayer—"

"There you are!" Andi's twelve-year-old sister Darlene exclaimed as though they hadn't been standing in the exact same spot the last time she had rushed by. She hitched up her white robe as she came around to the front of the booth, frowning at the dirt and grass stains that already ringed the hem. "Have you seen my trump?" she asked anxiously. "How am I going to herald the birth of the baby Jesus if I can't find my trump?" She stamped a white-sneakered foot on the sidewalk impatiently. "Andi! Help me!"

"Calm down," Andi said, reaching under the counter for Darlene's prop. "It's still right here where you left it." This was vintage Darlene, she thought as Sterling shook his head at her sister's silliness. As she remembered all the "helpful" information Darlene had cheerfully shared with Greg when they first met, Andi shuddered. She could only imagine what her sister might say when *Entertainment Tonight* called to ask about her famous future brother-in-law. The girl's tendency to inhabit other spheres while appearing firmly entrenched in this one was legendary and had caused more than one misunderstanding. In fact, when Andi had told her family about her engagement, she had deliberately excluded Darlene.

"Oh, thanks!" Darlene said, taking the trump and turning to scan the rows of folding chairs for the Reynolds family. "Where's everybody sitting?" Before Andi could point, Darlene saw her parents, younger brother and sister, and Greg's mother on blankets spread out on the grassy bank. Her hazel eyes narrowed in concern. "Will they be able to see me from all the way back there?"

Smiling, Andi looked up at the tall scaffolding specially erected for the event. "Darlene, they could see you from a mile and a half away."

"You understand, of course, that you are not in the pageant to be seen," Sterling reminded Darlene. "You are in the pageant to help illustrate scenes and parables from the life and teachings of the Living God."

Darlene stared at him for several seconds. Finally she nodded slowly. "Uh huh. That too."

"Have you seen Clytie?" Andi asked. She'd been hoping her sister would come by to take her place in the booth so that she could go to sit with Sadie Howland.

"She's with Brad," Darlene said, waving a hand in the general direction of anywhere. "He wanted to hang out until the pageant started and Clytie tagged along. She hopes that if she flirts enough, one of Brad's gooney senior friends will invite her to prom."

Andi was sorry she'd asked. She should have known better. Darlene was notorious for speaking her mind without pausing first to consult her brain. And poor Clytie. If anyone deserved a date for that dance—and was unlikely to get one—it was Clytie.

"*Everybody* doesn't have a checklist-for-choosing-an-eternal-companion like you do, Andi," Darlene added helpfully with a not so subtle look toward Sterling. "So they *have* to flirt and stuff to get to know each other and see what they think."

Andi's cheeks burned despite the cool night air. It was well-known by all her family and friends that several years before she had carefully compiled, posted, and broadcast a list of prerequisites she would require in a potential husband. It was well-known, too, that of anyone she had ever dated, Sterling Channing was the best match of her list. He was (1) a committed member of the Church, and (2) a returned missionary, with (3) a temple recommend, and (4) a strong LDS family. In other words, he was four-for-four list-wise while Greg Howland had hovered right around a negative two.

Embarrassed, Andi tossed her mane of copper curls over her shoulder while trying to ignore Sterling's smug look. "It was nice talking to you, Darlene," she said insincerely. "But shouldn't you be with the rest of the little angels?"

"Oh yes!" Darlene said, as if suddenly remembering. Securing her trump under one arm like a lance, she turned to charge off into the crowd. "Be sure to look for me!"

Andi watched Darlene dart through the crowd, then looked up to find Sterling regarding her carefully. Clytie was definitely right. She took a deep breath, determined to tell him about her plans to marry Greg, but was halted by a young Hispanic couple with a baby who came up to the booth at just that moment. More relieved than disappointed, Andi wiggled her fingers at their child and cooed to him in universal baby-speak while Sterling engaged the parents in fluent Spanish.

When after a few moments the baby's attention returned to his mother, Andi looked back across the street toward the bus stop billboard. The girl with the pillowcase was seated on the bench, turning a basketball over in her hands. Her bare, knobby ankles swung together and apart as she watched the last stragglers hurry toward the temple grounds for last-minute seats.

Next year at this time, Andi thought wistfully, *Greg and I will be sitting together in the crowd.* And if his baptism could be scheduled as soon as he hoped, perhaps they'd have a stack of wedding invitations beside them to address while they waited.

Greg read along as the nurse wrote the familiar morning message on the white board across from his bed: *Today is Saturday, April 15. You are in Rm. 613. Your nurse is Jill.*

Though the daily updates had been more than a little helpful as he struggled to maintain consciousness during his first few days out of ICU, they were more than a little annoying now. Greg ran long fingers through his thick blond hair as the nurse drew the customary heart to dot the "i" in Jill and wondered how she thought he could forget her name in the first place. After all, she had been in his room almost every day now for the past two weeks.

And in and in and in, he thought. *Doesn't this woman ever take a day off?* As she finished writing and walked over to her cart, he noted the date and commented, "I hope my accountant remembered to file a 1040 form for me." He realized as he spoke that even an offhand allusion to his tax bracket was a mistake. The nurse's smile widened flirtatiously as she turned to offer him a cup of juice.

"Don't they say that nothing's sure but death and taxes?" she teased.

"And I wouldn't be too sure about death," he replied with a lightness that belied the intensity in his face. The look in his eyes discouraged her from asking what he meant. Everyone in the hospital—and most people in the nation—seemed to know that Greg Howland had been knocked unconscious by a baseball during a spring training game, but no one knew what had happened during the time he had lain comatose and near death. Greg held the experience sacred and had shared it only with Bishop Ferris, in hopes of understanding it better himself. One day he would share it all with Andi, but he certainly would never tell anyone like this pesky nurse.

As she moved to his side for a check of his vital signs, Greg looked away from the flirtatious batting of her eyes. It was the way those eyes had assessed him that had caused him to substitute the more familiar—and substantial—sweat pants and T-shirt for the hospital-issued attire.

Jill unrolled a pair of black rubber tubes and wrapped the blood pressure cuff around the top of Greg's arm, the tips of her fingers brushing his bulging biceps as she cooed in admiration, "Are all baseball players as strong as you?"

Before Greg could think of a response, Andi appeared in the open doorway. Dressed in khaki for a day's work at the zoo, the drab color of her uniform heightened the appeal of her tanned skin and burnished copper tresses. As she came into the room, Greg's blood pressure rose quickly.

"Hi!" he said happily. "I didn't expect to see you this early."

"Hi yourself," she responded, pushing aside a blanket to perch on the end of his bed. She had dreamed all night of Greg's embrace but couldn't imagine approaching him with the nurse present. She hoped the color she felt rising to her cheeks wouldn't betray her intentions.

"Guests are not to sit on patient beds," Jill told Andi firmly, then added as Andi stood up, "And you've come before visiting hours. Mornings are reserved for doctors' rounds and therapy."

"Andi's the best therapy going," Greg interjected quickly, wincing as the nurse inserted an electronic thermometer into his ear with a little more zeal than was technically necessary. When she removed it and recorded the results on his chart, he asked, "So, think I'll live another four hours?"

Jill lowered the aluminum clipboard with a look calculated to be devastating. "As far as I can see, you're a *perfect* specimen." Brushing her hand against his chest, she said softly, "And I'll be back much sooner than that." Returning to her cart, the nurse pushed it toward the door. There she turned back to Andi. "You can stay fifteen minutes," she directed on the way out.

"Ignore her," Greg said, rising from the bed to Andi's side.

Her eyes narrowing, Andi watched the nurse's hips as they swayed out the door and down the hall. "I will if you will."

"Easy," he assured her. "I may not remember everything about the day I came to after that ball hit me, but I *do* happen to recall a promise that my 'most eligible man in America' days are thankfully behind me." He smiled as the spots of color deepened around Andi's adorable dimples. Her given name—Ariadne—was Greek for 'divine' and Greg found it apt. He leaned close and whispered, "And I thought we'd clinched that deal the other night."

Andi took a deep breath and looked up into his eyes. "I—" she began before a clatter of mop and pail interrupted her response.

"Mind if I clean up in here, Mr. Howland?" a custodian asked meekly from the doorway.

The floor was spotless and the timing was rotten. "The room's fine, thanks," Greg said, barely looking at him, intent as he was on deciding the exact shade of green that he saw in Andi's eyes.

The young man, though clearly apprehensive, was dogged in his duty. He edged the bucket forward a few inches and mumbled, "I've got to get every room on this floor done before they bring the breakfast trays."

Greg finally looked away from Andi long enough to catch the hopeful look on the worker's face. "It's all yours," he conceded, taking Andi's hand to lead her from the room. As they entered the hallway, he pulled her closer and said, "Let's take a walk."

"A walk?" she asked. "Where do you want to go? I can only stay a few minutes, I have to—"

"I know, I know. You have to go to work," Greg finished for her. "Some people still have a life." He squeezed her hand. "So, take me with you. I can think of a secluded spot or two along the Tropics Trail . . ."

"I'd have to smuggle you out of here first, you know," Andi smiled, "and you're a little large to fit in my fanny pack."

"I'm thinking of tying sheets together to make a rope," he said with little humor. "This place is driving me nuts."

As they turned a corner into a quiet hallway, Andi observed, "Well, it can't be because you feel neglected. Between that self-assigned private nurse of yours and the Cubs' press agent—what's his name?"

"Dawson Geitler."

"Yes, him. Between him and Jill and everyone else who manages to get past Security, your room is busier than the zoo."

"Yeah, and it clues me in on how the animals feel in their exhibits." Greg slowed his pace to look down at her as he asked, "So, what's it like in the real world? Did you and Channing have a good time at the Easter Pageant last night?"

Andi's shrug indicated little interest in the subject and Greg smiled broadly. Little interest was just about as much as he wanted her to take in Sterling Channing. Greg hadn't forgotten that not all that long ago Andi had been planning to marry Elder Tall, Dark, and Devoted. And despite their recent promises to one another, Greg wouldn't feel really secure until he knelt across an altar from Andi in the temple then shook hands with Sterling at the reception immediately following. He doubted for a moment the wisdom of their secret engagement. More than anything, he wanted to slip a ring on Andi's finger. A conspicuous one. One Channing would be sure not to miss. But before he could even shop for the ring, he had to get out of this hospital.

"Sterling is a stake missionary, as you know," Andi said, breaking into his thoughts. "And he takes his callings very seriously."

"You're telling *me* that?" Greg said. "He was up here with Elder Owens earlier this week, remember?"

Andi hooked her arm around Greg's, gazed up into his face, and teased, "Then I'd say you certainly ought to be converted."

Greg pulled her close. "I've been converted since the first day I saw you."

He was the one teasing now, Andi thought, though she dimpled in pleasure. She knew that not only had Greg completed the missionary discussions here in the hospital, he had spent a significant amount of time with her bishop, Dan Ferris, as well. Andi had introduced the two men to each other at a young adult activity; later, the police sergeant/bishop had been the person Greg turned to for help when things with his publicist-turned-extortionist Zeke Martoni were at their worst.

"Of course, I can't do much about my baptism," he added with frustration, "or anything *else* while I'm stuck in here."

"Be patient, Greg," Andi said, the softness of her voice belying the urgency of her concern. "You almost died." As he shook his head impatiently, she glanced up at him from beneath bronze lashes. The bruise on the right side of his head above his temple was still tinged yellow and blue, but the swelling was gone and the scar from the incision to remove fluids from his brain barely evident. Still, Andi wondered if he were completely well now when the injury had been so very serious.

"Bishop Ferris gave me a blessing," Greg reminded her. "I'm doing great. It's time I get off the disabled list and back on the mound. I have to take care of my mother."

Andi was silent, thinking. She knew that even though the doctors hadn't yet promised him a full recovery, Greg still hoped to return to the Cubs. She had read the articles in the paper that debated whether he would ever play professional baseball again. As Greg looked down at her quizzically, Andi managed for a moment to push her worry for his health aside—only to find worries about what his career might mean to their life together rushing in to take their place. She didn't hear Greg's next sentence as her father's words of caution echoed in her head.

Trent had said remarkably little besides warning her that life with Greg would be a package deal—good and bad.

"It's one thing to sit alone in a sacrament meeting because your husband's on the stand," he had said. "It's another if it's because he's out on a ballfield."

At a loss to put her fear and longing into words, Andi forced herself to concentrate on the one part of Greg's complicated life that she thought she understood—his anxiety for the welfare of his family. She couldn't help but share his concern. After years with an alcoholic, abusive husband, Sadie Howland was barely literate, didn't drive, and scarcely spoke to anyone but Andi's mother, Margaret.

"Greg, your mother's doing fine at our house," Andi tried to reassure him. "She doesn't have to move into the townhouse right away."

Greg shook his head. "She can't stay at your house forever."

"Yes, she can," Andi insisted, wanting to reach up to smooth away the small lines of worry that had formed around Greg's beautiful eyes.

"My mother's the Relief Society president. She's used to—" Andi stopped herself before she said "needy people" and diplomatically substituted " . . . 'guests.'"

"Your mother's an angel," Greg said sincerely, laying strong hands gently on Andi's shoulders, and looking down into her eyes. "Like mother, like daughter." He bent to kiss her then, oblivious to a student nurse exiting a nearby room. At the surprise of seeing Greg Howland in person, the young woman dropped her water pitcher. The plastic container hit the floor so hard that the lid popped off, and a quart of icy water arced across the hall, soaking Greg's pant leg from his waist to his ankle.

Shielded from the shower herself, Andi watched sympathetically as the girl shrank against the doorframe in dismay.

"That's okay," Greg told the white-faced young woman. "Don't worry about it. I've had worse things poured on me." He pulled the cold fabric away from his leg as best he could and forced a grin to put her at ease. "Honest. You know, it might even be worth losing a pennant race to get out of the champagne showers in the locker room. That stuff is nasty."

The nurse's knees seemed even weaker now, Andi noted, though she suspected it was more the result of Greg's smile than the recent mishap. That lopsided grin of his affected her the same way.

"Really," he said over his shoulder, as he steered Andi rapidly down the hall, "no harm done."

Patients and employees stuck their heads from the rooms at the sound of Greg's voice. Watching him try to ignore the commotion that inevitably followed in his wake, she smiled as he muttered, "A multi-billion dollar facility here and no place in it for two cents' worth of privacy."

Oblivious to Greg's rapid pace, Andi gazed up at perhaps the highest-profile face in the country on surely the humblest, kindest man. No wonder she loved him. Her thoughts flashed back to her carefully prepared checklist-for-choosing-an-eternal-companion. *No, no, no and no,* she thought with a sigh as she silently matched Greg with the qualifications on her list. He had none of the qualifications her reason suggested, yet all the qualities her heart yearned for.

Distracted by her thoughts, she bumped into Greg when he stopped suddenly in front of a steel door. Although there was a lighted "EXIT" sign overhead, a large contradictory label had been affixed to the door itself. When he pushed the bar, Andi hung back. "It says, 'Not an exit,'" she pointed out.

"It also says 'Exit,'" Greg smiled down at her as he opened the heavy door with one hand and pulled Andi along with the other. The breezy rooftop service area was a bright contrast to the clean, artificially lighted environment they had just left. Greg surveyed it with satisfaction. "See?" he said. "No alarms or guard dogs. And it's just the place we've been looking for . . ." He lifted Andi's chin tenderly and hesitated just a moment to gaze reassuringly into her eyes. He hoped that whatever questions they were asking him now could best be answered by a kiss. "We're finally alone—"

"Aside from myself."

Startled, Greg turned to regard a slight young man who had leaned around a large, green refrigeration unit. He wore rumpled hospital pajamas, a baseball cap and, despite the early morning hour, a pair of dark glasses. Sunglasses and a cap with the bill pulled low over the face had long been Greg's signature disguise. He stared, thinking that in other circumstances this would be a kid after his own heart.

"But I'm blind," the youth continued, "so go ahead and kiss her if you want to. I won't watch." When he received no immediate response, he shrugged. "That's what you two came out here for, isn't it?"

"Well, yeah," Greg said.

Andi felt the color rise in her face. "Greg—"

"Well, it is," Greg said, grinning at her discomfiture, "and since *he* doesn't mind, it still seems like a good idea to me."

"I have to go to work," Andi decided quickly, ducking under Greg's arm. Nothing she wanted to do or say here called for a peanut gallery—even an unseeing one. "You stay on the roof and get some fresh air. We can . . . talk . . . later. I'll be back with Clytie and Enos this afternoon."

"I'll probably be here," Greg replied, his amusement fading to disappointment.

Andi stood on tiptoe to barely touch her lips to his. "Then I'll see you later." As he reluctantly opened the door for her, she added, "And please don't worry about baseball . . . or your mother."

"I guess that doesn't leave me much to worry about." Greg held open the door then stood with his back against it as he watched Andi walk away. *Not much to worry about at all,* he repeated silently. *Unless, of course, I was the type to worry about brain damage or my wacko family or, let's see, putting away Zeke Martoni, who clearly has no morals and a score to settle . . .*

Still, as he watched Andi disappear around the corner, Greg felt the sunshine warm him through the open door and remembered the greater warmth of the light at the end of the tunnel. *Everything happens for a reason,* he thought. *I had a reason to return to earth. Right now I need to get out of this hospital and buy that reason an engagement ring.*

As the steel door closed behind him, Greg caught it on impulse and looked back at the youth scrunched on the concrete rooftop. The kid reminded him of someone. He appeared to be about the same age as Andi's brother, seventeen or so, although he was slighter and several inches shorter than Brad. No hair showed beneath the black Chicago Bulls cap, though it was pushed up on his forehead. His face was ruddy and fair.

He's fine, Greg told the still, small voice that had urged him to pause at the door. *He just wants to be alone.*

Besides, Greg's top priorities were to first get out of these wet sweats, and then to get out of this hospital, neither of which could be accomplished from the rooftop, especially considering that he hadn't brought any sheets for a rope. Nevertheless, as he released the door, he couldn't shake the picture of the scene on the other side. It was the way the boy sat—legs pulled into his chest and chin resting on his knees—which had caught and held Greg's attention. It was a posture subconsciously calculated to shield an aching heart, and it reminded him, Greg realized suddenly, of himself. He pushed the door back open and cleared his throat.

The boy lifted his chin. "Why didn't you leave with your girlfriend?"

"Because the doctors won't let me." Greg took a step onto the rooftop as the door clicked closed behind him. "Besides, I thought maybe you'd like some company."

"You thought wrong."

Greg ignored the rebuff and walked over toward the low wall that ran along the edge of the building. "I could use some fresh air. Do you mind?"

"I don't own the place."

"No loss," Greg said, raising an eyebrow at the stark panorama of building tops and, below, the unattractive back lot of a shopping center. "You don't have much of a view from here."

"I don't have much of a view from anywhere."

"Sorry." Greg rubbed his face in consternation. He had never excelled at small talk but this was a new low, even for him. He tried again. "I guess you'll have to take my word for it." When there was no response, he walked over to where the boy sat. A thick-boarded chess set sat atop the transformer box at the boy's side. The pieces were arranged as if in the midst of a game.

"Are you playing a computer?" Greg asked.

"You're the one with eyes. You see anyone else around?"

Greg watched the youth press a white chess piece onto a pressure-sensitive square. An automated voice responded, "F4 to E3." Without hesitation, the boy moved a black piece diagonally to capture a pawn. Greg looked on with admiration as the procedure was repeated several times. When the computer conceded the game, Greg observed, "You're good."

"It doesn't take much to beat this lame piece of junk," the kid responded.

"I've always wanted to learn to play chess," Greg said, "but . . ."

The sunglasses rose slightly. "Behold the Ultimate Truth."

"Huh?"

"'But' is simply and always an acronym for 'Behold the Ultimate Truth,'" the youth declared. "What's the truth about you not learning chess? Not enough patience? Not enough intelligence?"

"More like no one to teach me," Greg said, lowering himself onto the concrete between the transformer box and the wall, and struggling to find a compact enough arrangement to allow his body to sit and pump blood to his legs simultaneously. "Know anybody competent?" He grinned as the kid turned off the computer and began to move pieces back into starting position, never mixing a light or dark piece in the even alignment. Upon closer inspection, Greg noticed that the white pieces had been scored to make them distinguishable by touch. "By the way," he added, "my name's Greg."

"Thaddeus."

Greg's grin changed to a frown of concentration as Thaddeus began a rapid introductory course on the history of chess, including the piece names and how they could move. By the time the boy was midway into the mile-a-minute dissertation, Greg had begun to suspect that his lacking the intelligence to match this kid might be closer to the ultimate truth, after all.

"That's all you need to know," Thaddeus concluded finally. "White goes first." He pushed a pawn forward into a center square.

"That's it?" Greg asked doubtfully. "Aren't there entire libraries devoted to this game?"

"I thought you wanted to play chess, not discuss it."

Greg fingered a knight, figuring he should start there before he forgot how the piece moved. Lifting it, he moved it two spaces forward and one to the side, set it on the board, and considered how to phrase an explanation for what he had done. "I put the horse, er, I mean knight, that was on the, uh, queen's side—"

"Look," Thaddeus interrupted impatiently, "that rigmarole will take us all day. Square A-1 is in your lower left-hand corner, okay? Using that grid, just tell me what square you moved from and where you went. I'll know what the piece is."

"But won't that be backward for you? And how will you possibly remember where—"

"I'll remember," Thaddeus said shortly. "And don't try to cheat. I'm blind, not stupid."

The kid must have some kind of memory, Greg thought, *if he can keep all thirty-two pieces straight.* He said, "A2 to C3," then asked, "How long have you been playing chess?"

"My father taught me when I was little. I guess it beat having to go outside to toss a football around in the yard." Thaddeus' face turned toward the warmth as a fluffy white cloud moved from in front of the sun. "Turned out to be a good thing," he added sarcastically. "Obviously, I couldn't catch a medicine ball in my current situation."

"How long have you been blind?" Greg asked quietly.

"About a year."

When Thaddeus removed Greg's knight from the board, Greg frowned. "What's the earliest I should worry about losing this game?" he asked.

"Three moves. It's called Fool's Mate."

Since he had already taken two moves, Greg figured he had one left. He pushed a pawn forward and identified its location before asking, "So, you and your dad play a lot of chess?"

"Nah. He's too busy."

"What does he do?"

"Runs things. My father owns a piece of every major project between LA and London."

"Impressive."

"Then you're too easy to impress." Thaddeus quickly claimed Greg's queen with his bishop and added, "Check."

Greg saw a temporary way out and took it. "What does your mother do?"

"Hard to say. She's dead."

"I'm sorry." Greg moved a pawn past one of Thaddeus'. When the kid removed it from the board on his next move, Greg objected.

"I forgot to tell you," Thaddeus explained. "It's called an *en passant.* When your pawn is in the sixth rank, and your opponent's pawn moves forward two spaces, it cheats you of a move, so you can capture the piece the same as if it had moved one space. But you have to do it on the next turn."

"So much for that brilliant evasive tactic," Greg observed dryly as he picked up another piece. "Do you see much of your dad, then?"

"More—now that I'm back in Phoenix."

"Back from where?"

"Chicago."

"Practically my home town. Must be where you got the hat." He watched Thaddeus reach up to finger the embroidered patch. "Souvenir of a Bulls match?"

"Nah, they dragged us to a baseball game."

"Did you see the Cubs or White Sox?"

"I didn't *see* anything," Thaddeus reminded him derisively, "but it was a Cubs game—the most boring afternoon of my life."

"Sorry I asked." Watching Thaddeus purse his lips at the memory, Greg gave a half-hearted attempt to suppress a chuckle, but then gave in to the feeling.

"I missed the joke," Thaddeus said suspiciously.

"I'm sorry, it's just that . . . Honestly, Thaddeus, you're an even worse conversationalist than I am."

"You mean you intended this to be a conversation?" Thaddeus retorted. "With all those questions, I had assumed you work for the FBI." On his next move, Thaddeus switched his king with his rook.

Greg's eyebrow rose. "Is that another kind of *en passant* you 'forgot' to mention?"

"It's called castling to the king's side. There are a few conditions, of course."

"Like someone has to remember to tell you about it?"

Thaddeus almost smiled. "Like, the king and rook can't have made prior moves and they can't cross a square that's under attack. Oh, and the king can't be in check like yours will be again if you move the piece you're thinking about."

The kid had lost his sight, Greg thought, but his other four senses were incredibly sharp and he might have developed a sixth sense as well. He looked the board over again and was pleased to see where he could take a bishop.

"Only rank amateurs concentrate on capturing their opponent's pieces," Thaddeus proclaimed after Greg had announced his move. "The object is to develop a strategy to capture the king. Anyway, file that tip for future reference. You're finished."

"Huh?" Greg studied the board in surprise. He had thought he was doing pretty well.

"The game's over."

"But my king's not in check—"

"You almost never play to checkmate," Thaddeus replied. "When the less able player sees that his cause is hopeless, he tips his king to resign. It's considered good sportsmanship."

"Abner Doubleday must not have had anything to do with chess," Greg said, tipping his king with a shrug. "In baseball, you play until the last out even if you're twenty runs behind."

"Abner Doubleday had very little to do with baseball, as a matter of fact," Thaddeus told Greg as he began to return the playing pieces to the board. "He receives undue credit as its creator. And I'm surprised that anyone would think to compare the intellectual sport of royalty to the base entertainment of rabble." He smiled at his own pun and Greg found the infectious nature of the grin hard to resist. He laughed when Thaddeus added disdainfully, "Don't tell me you're a baseball fan."

"Well, early in the season, at least."

"I still say it's the most boring pastime on earth," Thaddeus declared. "Another match?"

"Why not?" Greg said with a grin. "You can't beat chess for excitement. But are you positive there isn't a thing or two more you could teach me?"

"Maybe a simple strategy," the youth conceded. "For instance, you want to control the four spaces in the center of the board. There are several openings, called ploys, to accomplish it."

Greg listened in awe as Thaddeus outlined plays that made the infield fly rule seem simple by comparison. The boy opened up more as the game progressed and Greg fell silent, lost in concentration. In less time than it would take to play one inning of baseball, he had come to genuinely like chess—and Thaddeus.

"So, what are you in here for?" Thaddeus asked finally, in the midst of the third game.

"Abject stupidity," Greg responded absently. He was trying to visualize a few moves ahead to anticipate his opponent's strategy. "I ignored the first rule of baseball and took my eye off the ball. I got clobbered."

"Baseball?" Thaddeus said with surprise. "Don't tell me you're that pitcher everybody's talking about!"

Greg rubbed his chin, still lost in thought over his next move. "Yeah."

The younger boy leaned back against the refrigeration unit to consider the revelation. Finally, he was ready to pass judgement. "Well, you don't seem like such a hot shot to me."

"Hey, thanks, Thaddeus," Greg said, picking up his chess piece at last. "I didn't know you had a compliment in you." When the boy looked embarrassed, Greg stated his move then added, "Since I figure you weren't in Chicago to see me pitch, what were you doing there?"

"Attending a blind school," Thaddeus responded slowly. "When the doctors found out where the glioma's located, they said I'd never get my sight back. That's when my dad shipped me off to some fancy place in Illinois where I was supposed to learn to get around by myself and generally not embarrass him in public." Thaddeus moved a bishop and waited impatiently for Greg's next play, and possibly his response. When neither was immediately forthcoming, he added caustically, "That sure turned out to be a waste of bucks."

Still, Greg didn't reply. *A glioma?* he thought. *The kid has a brain tumor—*

His mind, now far from chess and even Thaddeus, had traveled across country and across time to recall another hospital and another dying young man. *Dear Father, no,* Greg sent a swift prayer heavenward. *Tell me it's not going to be like Jim.*

Realizing that his companion was waiting for a response, Greg tried to remember what he had said. *Some school . . . . a waste . . .*

"I don't know why you'd say that, Thaddeus," he managed to respond around the lump in his throat. "You must have been the star pupil. You're doing great."

"Yeah, great." For the first time, Thaddeus fumbled with a chess piece and knocked over several others in the process of trying to right it. When Greg reached across the board to help, the youth pushed his hand away angrily. "That's why I'm in here, right? Instead of going away after surgery, the tumor only got bigger. So it's straight from the best blind school to the best neurological hospital. My dad doesn't care what it costs." Greg blinked when Thaddeus banged the final piece back down on the board. "You think a couple of months are worth half a million dollars?"

The ballplayer was silent for a moment, then said levelly, "Depending on how a person uses them, Thaddeus, I think two months could be priceless."

"I think the whole thing stinks."

Unable to see the eyes behind the dark glasses, Greg knew now that they weren't hostile so much as hopeless. He knew, too, that the hat disguised a loss of hair and that the ruddy color in Thaddeus' otherwise pale cheeks wasn't, as he had first thought, a glow of restored health but rather a telling after-effect of radiation.

Greg leaned back against the low wall and drew a deep breath. He knew the most likely end of Thaddeus' story, too. He'd lived it already, not many weeks earlier, at his brother's bedside. It was there Greg had lost—at least for mortality—his only brother and best friend.

"So, you want to play or not?" Thaddeus asked in irritation.

You want to play? Greg repeated to himself, wincing when a still-painful spot in his heart replied in the resounding negative—*Not again. Don't let yourself get close to this kid or you'll just have to watch someone else that you care about go through all that pain.*

On the other hand, Greg reminded himself as a slow half-smile crept onto his face, he *had* learned a great deal since his brother's death. He knew now that charity was the key of admission to the gates of eternity and that Jim's life hadn't ended so much as it had progressed. In many ways—the ways that mattered most—his big brother was still alive and very near.

"Yeah, I'll play," Greg said, putting as much enthusiasm as he could muster into his voice. "I'm past the Fool's Mate stage of the game." As he said it, Greg offered a fervent prayer of hope that it was true.

Chapter 5

"Isn't that amazing?" Enos Reynolds asked Greg eagerly, using the finger he'd just run across the page of his book to push thick-lensed glasses back up the bridge of his freckled nose.

"What?" Greg asked, then remembered that the child had been reading aloud. "Oh, yeah, Enos—amazing."

"But it's *true,*" the nine-year-old emphasized. "That's what the book's called—*Amazing But True Baseball Stories.*"

Greg nodded, but he hadn't really been listening to Enos or even paying much attention to the child's two sisters who shared a padded bench in a nook near the side of his bed. He was thinking about Thaddeus. To avoid the full-scale search that would have likely resulted if he turned up missing too long, Greg had invited the teen back to his room. They'd spent most of the morning and early afternoon playing chess before Thaddeus was finally hustled away by a nurse to be seen by yet another oncologist. Over the course of their visit, Greg had learned that the Bishers were members of the Church but that Thaddeus' father hadn't been inside a stake center since Thaddeus' mother's funeral. Still, he had insisted his son remain semi-active, so Thaddeus had attended a branch in Virginia while at the boys' boarding school that he claimed to prefer over his father's mansion in nearby Scottsdale.

"Well, I don't think your book's very amazing," Clytie declared.

Undaunted, Enos turned a page. "You'll like the next chapter. It's called 'The Midget of St. Louis.'"

"No, Enos!" Greg said quickly, and perhaps too loudly. He glanced at Clytie but the teenager only rolled her aqua eyes at her brother and reached a stubby arm toward him for the paperback. Greg noted with little surprise that Enos' innocent reference to Clytie's dwarfism had—as usual—bothered him a lot more than it did her.

"No more stupid stories," Clytie insisted. She brushed back her long, blonde hair and uncrossed her short legs to keep her balance as she reached toward Enos to claim the book.

When she seemed to freeze in mid-action, her eyes on the door, Greg looked over his shoulder. Thaddeus had arrived, his unusual metal cane in one hand and the familiar chess case in the other. He had changed clothes since Greg saw him last. The rumpled hospital attire was gone, replaced by striped pajamas and an expensive robe. The sunglasses had been left behind as well. Though unfocused because of his blindness, Thaddeus' eyes were remarkable. They were light brown, almost amber, with flecks of russet and gold. What Greg noticed most, however, was his hat. He'd switched from the Bulls to the Diamondbacks. The pitcher smiled. "Hi, Thaddeus. Come in."

Disappointment registered on the youth's face as he took a hesitant step backwards. "You have company."

"Yeah," Greg said, swinging his long legs over the side of the bed to be ready to pull the reluctant young man into the room if necessary, "and I want you to meet them."

"That's okay," Thaddeus said. "See you later."

"Wait a minute." Greg took two long strides across the room to claim the chess set from Thaddeus' hands on a hunch he wouldn't leave without it. "Andi, Clytie, Enos, this is Thaddeus Bisher. Thaddeus, let me introduce you to just under half of the Reynolds family. You kinda met Andi this morning. Clytie is her younger sister and Enos is her little brother." Thaddeus hadn't moved, so Greg put his free hand into the small of the teen's back to urge him forward. "Thaddeus is a fellow inmate," he continued, prodding his now-mute guest into the room. "He spent most of the day teaching me to play chess."

"Can I use your treasure hunter?" Enos asked, his book sliding to the floor in his excitement to examine Thaddeus' cane. "Brad bought one at a garage sale once. He let me use it and I found a whole quarter!" He extended his hands hopefully and looked crestfallen when Thaddeus appeared to ignore him. "I'll be real careful," he added.

"I'm sorry," Andi apologized to the youth, pulling her brother back by a belt loop on his jeans. "He thinks your cane's a metal detector." To Enos she whispered, "Behave yourself. He's blind."

"You don't have to whisper," Thaddeus said sarcastically. "I was bound to find out that I'm blind sooner or later."

Greg cast Andi a sympathetic look as he turned to her little brother. "Thaddeus uses a special cane to get around, Enos."

"But I thought blind people had seeing-eye dogs."

"This is instead of a dog," Greg explained. "It's real high tech. Thaddeus told me earlier today that it works by sonar."

"Really?"

"Yeah," Thaddeus said, "like a seeing-eye bat."

"Cool!" Enos exclaimed. "That's even better than a treasure hunter!"

Greg studied Thaddeus with a mixture of pleasure and surprise. Despite the sarcasm in his words, he was almost smiling at the little boy. And his smile, as Greg had noted earlier, had the capacity to transform his face. When Andi stood to offer her seat, Greg steered Thaddeus to the bench next to her sister and set the chess set between them. "Do you play chess, Clytie?" he asked. The girl's wide aqua eyes were studying Thaddeus' face carefully, determined, it appeared, not to miss his smile or apparently anything else about him. "Clytie?"

"Yes!" she exclaimed quickly. "I love to play chess!"

"You do?" Andi asked.

"You never play with me—" Enos began.

Clytie's frown halted her brother's complaint. "I like a challenge," she said.

"Well, let me tell you," Greg said with a smile, "this guy'll give you one."

"Hey, I'll go easy on her," Thaddeus offered, opening his case, "since she's just a girl."

Greg tried to suppress a grin at the growing storm clouds on Andi's face. He didn't know what they taught at the fancy academies Thaddeus had attended, but it apparently wasn't charm. Or, he amended, perhaps it wasn't tact. The closer he looked at Clytie, the more convinced he became that at least one of the Reynolds sisters was charmed indeed.

CHAPTER 6

"Who is he?" Andi asked as she watched Greg remove a weight from the machine. He was making adjustments to exercise the muscles around his rotator cuff—whatever that was. With Enos growing restless in the small room upstairs, and with Clytie and Thaddeus to entertain one another, Greg had suggested an excursion to the physical therapy center—the only part of the hospital, with the possible exception of the McDonald's on the second floor—which he actually liked.

Andi liked it here herself. Clytie was clearly interested in the rude young man from the rooftop, and this was the perfect opportunity to learn something about him. And there was certainly nothing unpleasant about watching Greg flex those incredible muscles, she thought with a sigh. In fact, if it weren't for the distraction of Enos flitting from place to place, Andi wouldn't have been able to name a thing she would enjoy more right now than sitting near Greg while he trained.

"What do you know about Thaddeus?" she asked.

He pulled the cable toward his ear with his left arm. "You mean name, rank, serial number—that kind of thing?"

"Seriously."

"Seriously, not all that much. He likes chess, hates baseball, and has a mind that won't quit. And he's a member of the Church." Greg grinned. "See? You have a lot in common—especially baseball."

Andi's heart took the funny little flop it always did when Greg smiled at her that way. "You're wrong," she said quickly. "I like baseball. Didn't I sit with you and watch that entire TV broadcast of the Cubs game just this week?"

"Well, you and your textbooks *were* in the room . . . sort of." He let the weight down slowly with a grin. "Tell me who we played."

She thought for a moment, then shrugged and returned the smile. "Okay," she conceded, "maybe you're right. It must be baseball *players* I like so much."

"Anyone in particular?"

Andi widened her eyes as she pretended to consider. "Who's that shortstop on the VISA commercials? He's cute."

"Uh huh," Greg said with a scowl. "So are you. Real cute."

"But you were telling me about Thaddeus," Andi continued. She had already promised to spend the rest of eternity flirting with Greg; right now she wanted to satisfy her curiosity in case Clytie took it into her head to apply one of the lessons from that silly man-catching book she thought was so well hidden under her pillow. "Have you met his parents?"

"No. His mother died when he was Enos' age," Greg responded, "and his dad, he says, is some kind of corporate bigwig."

"What's his last name again?"

"Bisher."

This time the widening of Andi's eyes was genuine. "Cleon Bisher? *That* Bisher?"

Greg completed his tenth curl, seemingly without effort. "Yeah, I guess so. It was an odd name, at least."

"Cleon Bisher owns a quarter of the buildings in town, Greg."

"Then that must be him all right."

It bothered Andi, for some reason, that Greg seemed unimpressed. "I think he owns a part of the Arizona Diamondbacks, too," she added. To her satisfaction, one sandy eyebrow rose.

"Wouldn't you know it?" he said. "I spend all that time talking chess instead of convincing Thaddeus to ask his father to buy him a slightly used pitcher for his next birthday." He turned on the bench to work his other arm.

Andi admired the braided muscles flexing across Greg's back then forced her eyes toward Enos. It accomplished the dual purpose of seeing that her brother was behaving, and also distracted her from gaping at Greg. Walking around to the other side of the bench, she asked, "Do you know anything else about Thaddeus?"

"Well, I think he's blind."

"Yes and I think he's rude. But that doesn't explain what he's doing here in the hospital. Did he have an accident?"

"No." The weight fell back into place with a clang, and Greg leaned forward to speak quietly. "Thaddeus has a brain tumor."

Andi bit her lower lip as she looked into Greg's eyes. With a face as easily read as his, emotions were no secret. She knew that he was thinking of his brother. "Oh, Greg," she said. "I'm so sorry."

"Yeah, me too." Greg grasped the weight stirrup again, but lacked the enthusiasm to pull it. He let it fall as he reached for Andi's hand instead. "I've been thinking about Jim and Thaddeus all afternoon." He brushed his thumb lightly across her knuckles. "How could I have made it through life if I hadn't met you, Andi? It's impossible to understand this kind of thing without the plan of salvation. Do you know that kid's only seventeen?"

The blood that had seemed to rush to Andi's fingers when Greg touched them now drained away just as rapidly. "You mean—he's dying?"

"The doctors told him that without some kind of miracle, he has only a couple of months."

Poor Thaddeus, Andi thought. Then in the next heartbeat her thoughts flew to Clytie. With her compassionate nature and hopelessly romantic viewpoint, Andi feared her sister would be almost certain to be enchanted by this hopeless young man. Clytie, Andi knew, could fall in love faster than most people could make an introduction. And each time it happened Clytie was disappointed that her affection went often unrecognized and always unreturned. But this time, Andi feared, an interest in Thaddeus could be worse than disappointing—it could be devastating. She berated herself for not catching on more quickly. The kid was a patient in a neurological unit, for goodness' sakes. That should have told her something.

Greg relaxed his grip on Andi's fingers and regarded her worried face quizzically. "What's wrong?"

"Did you see the way Clytie looked at Thaddeus?"

Greg swung his right leg over the bench. "Well, I don't know—"

"Greg, you know Clytie," Andi interrupted. "She's all hearts and flowers and happily-ever-after. And now she's been reading this ridiculous book on how to catch a man." She shook her head when one corner of Greg's mouth quirked upward humorously. "What if Clytie falls in love with him?" she pressed. "Thaddeus' story can't have a 'happily ever after ending' if he's going to die."

She was so earnest and so sweet and so concerned. Greg wanted to kiss her. Glancing across the room at Enos, he reached for Andi's hand instead. "People don't fall in love while playing chess for half an hour."

Andi moved nearer, grateful for Greg's reassurance even though she knew for certain that he was wrong. She had fallen hard for him in even less time while lecturing at an alligator swamp. Looking up at him, she saw his face soften and knew that he had realized it as well.

"But they're just kids," he said, caressing her fingers. "And maybe Clytie can help Thaddeus. Maybe we all can."

"How?" Andi asked, lowering her face when his eyes told her that he didn't have the answer. She loved him so much. The pain of almost losing him just two weeks ago welled up in her heart, and Andi determined afresh to do all she could now to protect her little sister from an even worse hurt. When Greg still didn't respond, she extracted her fingers from his carefully and turned slowly away. "Come on, Enos," she called. "We need to go."

Enos slid reluctantly from his perch on a stationary bike. "Aren't you coming, Greg?" he asked when his hero made no move to follow them toward the door.

Greg rose slowly. "Yeah, I guess I am."

"You, of all people, should understand," Andi whispered as he reached her side and Enos bounced happily ahead toward the elevators. "I'm just as worried about how this will affect you. Are you really ready to face what you went through with Jim again?"

Greg regarded Andi thoughtfully. "I must be," he replied finally, "or God wouldn't have given me another chance at it so soon."

Chapter 7

"I thought you were going to go easy on me," Clytie complained good-naturedly after a resounding loss at the chessboard.

"I gave you a dozen moves," Thaddeus said. "That's more than Greg ever gets."

Clytie looked at Thaddeus closely. He appeared to be gazing over her right shoulder as his hands flew across the chessboard, arranging pieces for a rematch. She couldn't quite decide if he was really cute, or if it was just those awesome, amber eyes. "Well," she said with a little shrug as if to concede the point, "I'm impressed."

Thaddeus would never have admitted it, but that *had* been the general idea. The realization surprised him, though. He hadn't had much experience with the fair sex, having spent puberty in a boys' school and without a mother. Nevertheless, he had formed an opinion about women: they were shallow, self-absorbed, and vacuous. Except, he conceded grudgingly, for this one. She was friendly, funny, and not too bad at chess.

"Want another shot at me?" he asked, affixing a hopeful smile to his face in case she was looking.

At the smile, Clytie's decision was instantaneous: Thaddeus was definitely cute. And, if not exactly charming, he was at least more pleasant than he had seemed at first. She was glad too, she thought guiltily, that he was blind. Even without employing a single lesson from the book, Clytie was finding it easy to be herself around a guy who didn't watch her every move. Or maybe, she worried, she was only at ease because Thaddeus didn't know she was a dwarf. For the first time in her life, Clytie was in a young man's presence *and* feeling graceful and pretty—almost like a homecoming queen.

"What do you look like?" Thaddeus asked bluntly as he turned the board to allow her the first move in their second game. When Clytie didn't immediately respond, he added, "I mean, I'd like a mental picture—if you want to tell me."

"I don't mind telling you," Clytie said quickly, but not entirely truthfully, as the romantic notion of the homecoming title popped like a balloon on the royalty float. *That stupid book was useless,* she thought as she desperately searched for a possible response. *Nowhere in it was a single tip for how to tell a blind guy that you're a dwarf.* Finally she said, "It's just that I, um, don't really know how to describe myself."

Clytie gazed across the room into the full-length mirror on Greg's closet door. *Not that I need a full-length mirror to see all three-foot-six-inches of myself,* she thought with a frown. She didn't need a mirror at all. She knew exactly what she looked like—short, stubby arms, thick, bowed legs, and all. "Well, I have long, blonde hair," she began tentatively, looking into the reflection for moral support. "It's almost to my waist. And my eyes are blue."

"I know you have long hair," Thaddeus said. "I felt it brush my hand once when you leaned across the chessboard."

Clytie continued to stare into the mirror. *I'm not embarrassed to be a Little Person,* she reminded herself. *Heavenly Father had a plan to send me to earth this way.* But since she truly wasn't embarrassed, she wondered what she *was* feeling. Wistful, perhaps, to lose the role of romantic heroine so soon? Or sorry to disappoint Thaddeus, who surely hoped for a prettier girl to picture? "I'm wearing blue overalls and a pink T-shirt," she continued evasively, "and—"

"How tall are you?"

Her eyes left her reflection to seek Thaddeus' face in surprise. "I'm kind of short."

Thaddeus leaned against the wall on his side of the nook. "I figured you were, Clytie. Since I haven't heard your feet on the floor as we've been playing chess, I have to assume either they don't reach it or you're paraplegic or something."

"Do you watch a lot of detective shows?" Clytie asked in awe.

"I don't watch a lot of anything," Thaddeus responded automatically, then regretted it. He smiled to soften the sting. "I used to read a lot of Sherlock Holmes."

"Well, you'd make a good detective," Clytie said, vowing silently to choose her words more carefully in the future. "I am a Little Person."

"Uh huh."

"I mean, I'm a dwarf." Clytie watched his face carefully for signs of revulsion or, at least, surprise. She was puzzled when he only nodded and fingered a chess piece. "Did you hear me?" she asked at last.

"Yeah, Clytie," he responded, moving a pawn forward on the chessboard. "I'm blind, not deaf, remember?"

Clytie watched him flinch as he realized how sarcastic his words sounded. When he smiled sheepishly, she realized how hard he was trying to be nice and smiled when he did.

Thaddeus tried again. "So, what's it like?"

"You mean to be so small?"

"Yeah. Do people stare at you?"

"A lot of the time."

"I'd hate that," Thaddeus declared. "The only good thing about being blind is that I don't have to watch people pity me."

"I don't think people stare because they pity me," Clytie said slowly. "I think they're curious, mostly."

"That's just as bad."

"No," Clytie disagreed, rolling a pawn between her fingers as she considered. "I think it's normal to wonder about people who are different. I mean, you asked what it's like to be a dwarf."

"You're right," Thaddeus acceded with a frown. "I'm a jerk."

"No, Thaddeus," Clytie said quickly. "I don't mind. I just wish I knew how to explain it. Can you tell me what it's like to be blind?"

"I can show you." Thaddeus reached across the chessboard toward Clytie's face. When she leaned forward, his fingers spread across her forehead, then joined to cup gently over her eyes. "So, what's it like, Clytie?"

"Dark."

"Now imagine if the darkness never went away."

Clytie was silent for several moments. Finally, she sighed. "I can't."

Thaddeus slowly removed his hands. "I couldn't either, until it happened to me."

"You weren't born blind?"

Thaddeus shook his head. "No, it's a new experience. The whole time I was in the blind school, I kept asking myself if it was better or worse to be able to see for the first sixteen and a half years of my life. At first, it seemed lots worse to be suddenly blind, because this way I know what I'm missing. Lately, though, I'm not so sure I was right about that." He leaned forward conspiratorially. "Okay, here's where I'm preparing to launch into the first semi-flirtatious repartee ever attempted by a socially inept blind guy talking to a dwarf. In a hospital. On the Saturday before Easter. Working without a net." When Clytie giggled, he grinned. "Ready? Here goes: I'm glad now I haven't always been blind since the mental picture I see of a petite girl with long, blonde hair and big blue eyes is very pretty."

"Even if she's built like an Ewok?"

Thaddeus clearly couldn't decide if he should laugh at Clytie's self-deprecating jab. When finally he couldn't resist a chuckle, she beamed. "You're lucky to have the pictures in your head, Thaddeus, if they make you laugh."

"*You* make me laugh," he corrected, "and that's something I haven't done much of in the last few months." He shook his head in admiration. "Are you always so upbeat?"

"I don't know . . ." she began thoughtfully, then stopped.

"Really, Clytie, isn't there something about your life that drives you crazy?"

"Well," she confided, "I don't like to shop. You wouldn't believe how hard it is to find a shoe in my size without Big Bird on it. At the mall, at least, it's pretty lousy being different."

"If being small is what makes you different, Clytie, every girl in the world ought to be just your size."

Clytie drew in her breath and held it. *He means it*, she thought euphorically. *He really means it.* Clytie had never felt this way before and hoped the warmth that had spread from her heart to her cheeks would stay forever. She was still admiring Thaddeus' way with words and wishing she could think of another clever response when her sister appeared in the doorway with Greg and Enos in her wake.

"Hi," Andi said, almost breathless from the racer's walk she had sustained since leaving the physical therapy room. One look at Clytie's radiant face, however, assured her that she had been right to hurry back. "I see that your game's over," she said. "That's good. We, um, need to go."

Clytie looked up at Andi in surprise. "But I thought we were staying until Mom comes with Mrs. Howland."

"I've had a change in plans."

Enos had climbed under the hospital bed to retrieve his book and Greg was clearly a spectator, which told Clytie that this change of plans was Andi's show and didn't have anything to do with either of them. Clytie glanced at Thaddeus and her heart rose with happiness at the look of disappointment on his face. When she turned back to Andi and saw that she was staring at Thaddeus as well, she suddenly knew what had changed her sister's plans, though she couldn't imagine why.

Her defenses rose immediately. Maybe it was true of every big sister, but Andi—to Clytie's way of seeing things—held particularly fast to the annoying belief that she had been divinely appointed to oversee her little sister's life. Still, no matter how well-meaning Andi was, Clytie didn't like it one bit. From now on, she wouldn't let her get away with it, either. She turned appealing aqua eyes on Greg.

"You don't mind if I stay, do you, Greg," she said, "since Andi has to leave early? I'll ride home with Mom."

Greg's gaze moved warily from Clytie to her sister. It appeared that battle lines could be forming, and he was standing uncomfortably near the center of the field. "I, uh—"

"Greg's too busy for guests," Andi said calmly. "He hasn't finished physical therapy."

Enos' red head protruded from under the bed. "That's 'cause you—"

"I said we need to go," Andi interrupted firmly. "Come on, Clytie. We can talk in the car."

"We can talk here," Clytie insisted. "You don't mind, do you, Greg?"

"I, uh—"

Thaddeus rose and reached for his cane. "I think it's about time to exercise this seeing-eye bat of mine."

"Can I come with you?" Enos asked Thaddeus eagerly, scrambling to his feet.

"No," Andi responded. "We're leaving."

Clytie shook her head emphatically. "*I'm* not."

"I'll go with Thaddeus and keep an eye on Enos while you two decide," Greg suggested. "Take as long as you want." He followed Thaddeus to the door with even more eagerness than Enos.

As he reached it, Clytie called, "Greg, please stay. Maybe you—"

"No, Greg, go ahead," Andi said, waving him on. "I want to talk with Clytie alone."

"In chess, your position's called a *zugzwang*," Thaddeus told Greg before starting down the hall with Enos. "That's a German word for 'you lose no matter which move you make.'"

"Yeah," Greg said ruefully, resting the back of his head against the doorway and resisting the urge to smack it against the metal frame. "Thanks a lot." He watched enviously as Thaddeus and Enos started down the hall.

Inside Greg's room, Clytie's voice was firm. "I'm going to stay here with Greg," she repeated.

"You mean with Thaddeus," Andi countered.

Clytie glared mutinously at her older sister. "If I want to."

"Listen Clytie," Andi said patiently, sitting on the bench so she could look right into her sister's face. "Greg told me something I don't think you know about Thaddeus."

Hearing his name, Greg looked back through the doorway. At the suspicious look Clytie cast him, he forwent good judgment and took a hesitant step back into the room. "I told her that Thaddeus has a brain tumor, Clytie," he explained. "He may only have a few weeks to live." Greg watched her blink back sudden tears and wondered if perhaps Andi wasn't right after all.

Clytie crossed her arms across her chest as if to hold in the pain and turned back to her sister. "So?"

Andi smiled at her little sister fondly. "So, I saw the way you looked at him. But you don't know him yet, Clytie, and I don't think you really want to. Think how it would break your heart if you grew to like him then had to watch him die." She reached for her tiny hand. "I know you, Clytie."

"You think you know everything!" Clytie cried, pulling the hand away stubbornly. "You've told me what to do all my life and I'm tired of it. I *already* like Thaddeus and I'll spend every day with him if I want to."

"Clytie, be reasonable—"

"If you ever say that again," Clytie threatened, "I'll scream!" She turned to Greg. "That's all she ever says, 'Clytie, be reasonable.' Falling in love with you is the only wonderful thing that's ever happened to her, and she'll probably mess that up by trying to *reason* her way out of it."

"Clytie!" Andi was on her feet, but Clytie was impervious to her sister's advantage of height or experience.

"For your information, Andi, *life* isn't reasonable," she continued. "If it was, I wouldn't be three feet tall and Thaddeus wouldn't be dying!"

The tears coursed down Clytie's cheeks now, but Greg couldn't tell if they were tears of pain or frustration. When he glanced at Andi, the look she cast him was imploring.

"Greg, you tell her."

It was a moment that called for diplomacy, Greg knew—definitely not his long suit. He settled, as usual, for candor. "I think Clytie's right, Andi. You know . . ." His voice trailed off at the look of hurt and betrayal on Andi's face, and he looked down, seeking something of interest in the vicinity of his shoelaces.

"Thanks for your support," she said quietly. Before Greg could point out that he had signed with the major leagues rather than the diplomatic corps for good reason, Andi had picked up her purse and Enos' book and edged past him. "Good-bye, then."

Greg followed her out the door, testing out various words and phrases in his mind as he went. Unfortunately, all but one still sounded like the wrong ones. "Andi—"

"Come on, Enos," she called to the little boy who stood at the end of the hall examining Thaddeus' cane with fascination.

He looked up. "Can't I stay with—?"

"No." Her voice was curt and Enos knew finality when he heard it. He rushed to meet his big sister at the elevator door.

"Bye, Thaddeus!" he called back with an expansive wave that the youth couldn't possibly see. "Bye, Greg! I'll read you another amazing baseball story later."

"Okay, Enos. See ya." Greg took a deep breath, "Good-bye, Andi." The only response was a slight stiffening of her already straight back. He let out his breath in a low whistle as Thaddeus returned to the doorway, his face questioning. Greg patted him on the shoulder and said quietly, "Clytie hung around for another game of chess."

Thaddeus smiled and nudged Greg on his way into the room. "Then I'd bet this is the second time today that your girlfriend didn't kiss you good-bye."

A ghost of a smile flickered across Greg's face despite himself. "You'd bet right."

"Maybe next time."

Greg watched Andi pull Enos onto the elevator and thought he caught a glimmer of tears in the quick look she cast his way before the doors closed. "I sure hope so, Thaddeus," he said slowly. "In fact, I hope you're right about there being a next time."

Chapter 8

"You think it's going to be okay, then?" Greg asked, looking with concern at the Polaroid glossies of his new townhouse, then into Dan Ferris' rugged face. Clytie and Thaddeus had been in the midst of their fourth or fifth chess game—Greg had lost count about the time he had found a baseball game on TV—when the bishop arrived for a visit. After a quick introduction, Clytie left with Thaddeus for a walk while the bishop and Greg discussed his new property.

Finally, Greg set the pictures aside on the bed with a sigh. He could hardly believe that he had leased this townhouse sight unseen, but the main selling point in his mind was that the gated community was near Andi's neighborhood and in Bishop Dan Ferris' ward.

Nevertheless, Greg had to ask and not for the first time, "You're sure my mother will be safe there?"

The bishop nodded. "Couldn't be safer, Greg."

"It's just that I'll be on the road so much . . ."

His face crinkling into a warm smile, Dan Ferris said, "You're still bound and determined to play out that contract this season, aren't you, son?"

"I've got to fulfil my contract," Greg said with determination, "but Andi and I want a normal family life, which is something we'll never have while I'm playing baseball. Of course, by the time I can take Andi to the temple—" he caught himself with a grin. Bishop Ferris already knew more about his hopes and aspirations than anyone on earth.

Dan Ferris returned the smile. He had come to know Greg well over the last couple of weeks, personally and professionally. He had been impressed first, as a bishop, when Andi had introduced him to the earnest young investigator and later, as a police sergeant, when he watched the ballplayer refuse to buckle under the threat of a greedy and dishonest publicist, Zeke Martoni. Later, in the hospital, Ferris had listened as Greg told him about the abusive past he had survived and the bewildering present he faced. With a maze of professional, personal, and promotional demands facing Greg, Bishop Ferris wished there were more he could do to help.

"Anyway," Greg said, laying the pictures aside, "I just want to make my mother happy."

"You can't *make* your mother happy, Greg," Bishop Ferris reminded him kindly, "any more than you can cure your father of alcoholism or make your sister-in-law into the mother you want her to be to Jim's two boys." He reached forward and clasped the young ballplayer's shoulder. "You have a good heart, Greg—but fixing other people isn't part of your mission statement." He removed the hand to reach into a bag he had brought along and pulled out a heavy, gold foil box. "This is, though."

Greg removed the lid from the gift and, with a surprised glance up at Bishop Ferris, tipped a leather quad into his left hand, gazing at it reverently. He ran a finger across his name, which was embossed on the scriptures' cover, and swallowed before he tried to speak. "I don't know what to say, Bishop. Thank you."

"I was going to give it to you at your baptism," the older man said, "but my wife thought you ought to have it for Easter." He chuckled. "At the rate you read, you'll be able to finish a good chunk of it before your first day at church a week from tomorrow. Still think the doctors will release you by then?"

"I'll be out of here after Monday's tests," Greg said with certainty. He opened the book and turned the thin pages of the Doctrine and Covenants slowly, unable to resist reading a line or two of the intriguing, unfamiliar passages. "How soon can I be baptized?"

"Just as soon as you've attended a sacrament meeting and talked with the mission leader," Ferris assured him. "Have you thought who you'd like to perform the ordinance?"

Greg looked up from the book in surprise. "I assumed that . . . I mean, I only know a few men who hold the priesthood—" he considered for a moment, "—and my future father-in-law . . . well, I'll just say he isn't exactly my biggest fan."

Bishop Ferris pretended to scratch his head thoughtfully. He knew Andi's father had been expecting his oldest daughter to marry Sterling Channing. "No, I wouldn't trust Trent Reynolds not to drown you when he had the chance, although I think he'll come around before too long."

Closing the scripture, Greg leaned forward earnestly, trying to think of words to express the depth of his appreciation and love for this great man, unaware that his face now said it better than he ever could. "I'd be grateful if you would baptize me, Bishop."

"You don't know how happy that'll make me, Greg," Bishop Ferris said gruffly, again clasping the younger man's shoulder in his beefy grip. "I never had a son, you know, but if I had, well, I'd want him to be like you." Not a man of emotion, Ferris rose quickly. "I've got a shift to cover tonight, so I'd better shove off."

At the door, he paused. He still hadn't told Greg the extent of Zeke Martoni's involvement in syndicate gambling and drug running. He started to speak, then gave a little shake of his head. Better let it rest until the kid was at least out of the hospital. He forced a smile. "Quit worrying, will you? Your new place is safe and sound, and you've got a whole ward family now. Your mother will get along fine."

Greg tightened his grip on the scriptures and leaned back against the hard, plastic pillows as Bishop Ferris left his room. *What would I do without him,* he wondered, *or without the Reynolds?*

The youngest son of a violent father and a mother capable of withdrawing into a shell quicker than any box turtle on earth, Greg had been self-sufficient almost as long as he could remember. So, as grateful as he was to have found Andi—and to have already felt the support of the Church—it was still unnerving to be stuck in a hospital bed, reliant on others for practically everything. To make things worse, he'd apparently blown it big-time with Andi this afternoon. As his frustration mounted, Greg pulled a pillow roughly from behind his head and threw it across the room.

"Practicing with pillows since they won't give you baseballs?" a quiet voice asked from the doorway. "Or are tantrums like mine contagious?"

"Andi!" Greg sat up quickly as she scooped the pillow from the floor and returned it to the foot of his bed. When she sat across from him on the bench, he lay the quad aside and moved to join her.

Twin dimples winked into her cheeks with the sheepish smile she offered. "Thank you for acting happy to see me."

"I'm always happy to see you," he assured her quickly.

"I took Enos home, then rode back with our mothers. We met Bishop Ferris in the hall and they stopped to talk about your new house. I'm glad," she added, brushing a spiraled lock of hair back from her face. "I needed a few minutes with you to apologize for the way I left here this afternoon."

"You don't owe me an apology—" Greg began but Andi cut him off.

"Yes, I do. You *and* Clytie." She looked toward the doorway. "Where is she?"

"She went for a walk with Thaddeus," Greg said, leaning forward to search Andi's face. "You're okay with that now?"

"I don't know," she replied with a slight raise of one slender shoulder, "but it doesn't matter. No one seems to care what I think in this particular instance."

Greg put his hands gently on Andi's arms to turn her toward him. "Andi, just because I might not agree doesn't mean I don't care."

Impulsively, Andi lay her cheek against his chest and sighed happily when his strong arm circled her shoulder. "Oh, Greg, I don't know what to think. I was sure I was right about Clytie and Thaddeus. But after I got home, I felt so restless about the way I acted here that I thought I'd better try to concentrate on something positive. So I started to prepare my Relief Society lesson for next Sunday. But by the time I had read the first page, I wanted to crawl under my chair."

Greg loosened the embrace enough to look down into her troubled face. "Why?"

"The lesson is on the council in heaven," she said. "And here's Lucifer offering a plan in which no one has to worry, or suffer, or make a wrong choice. All anyone has to do is listen to him and life will be easy."

"Uh huh," Greg said slowly, remembering a recent discussion with the missionaries on the subject. "But where do *you* come in?"

"I'm just like Lucifer!" Andi exclaimed miserably. "'Listen to me, Clytie,' I say 'and you won't get hurt.' She was right. I *do* think I know everything."

"You may have some pretty strong convictions, Andi," Greg said, trying to suppress a smile, "but you're no Lucifer. As I heard the story, Satan was after absolute control and eternal glory." He brushed a soft, copper curl from her cheek. "You want to protect your sister, not control her, and your only motivation is love."

"But—" she protested and Greg held a finger to her lips.

"Does every single picture in your book have to be in black and white, Andi?" he asked softly, but even as he said the words, Greg knew that it was her inclination to see life as illuminated by the light of the gospel which had drawn him to Andi in the first place. Even that first morning in the alligator swamp—when she had told him that she talked to God—he had somehow believed her. Later, he had come to understand that Ariadne Reynolds knew she was a daughter of God and she would love Him and do her best to position herself in the very center of the straight and narrow path that led back to His presence. Now that Greg had recognized God as his Father as well, he loved and needed Andi more than he had dreamed possible. It *wasn't* good for man to be alone. A man, Greg believed, was ill equipped to make the journey toward exaltation without a woman like this one at his side.

Andi's liquid eyes met Greg's, clearly still considering his original question. "I don't know—" she whispered.

"Do you know that I love you—just the way you are?" Greg said softly.

Her little gasp of joy gave her the hiccups and she raised two fingers to her lips in consternation.

"I know a sure-fire cure for hiccups," he promised, holding her tightly with one arm and raising the other so he could slip his fingers into her curls and tilt her face up towards his own. "Say, 'boo.'"

"Boo?" she questioned, and as her lips puckered into the word, Greg bent to kiss her.

Something in the core of his being seemed to expand as Greg's full lips met Andi's softer, yielding ones, and the spicy, sweet fragrance of her threatened to overwhelm his senses. She was trembling—or he was—as her hands skimmed over his face, up around his neck into his hairline, and locked there.

After a few moments Andi murmured Greg's name. Then she hiccuped.

Greg scarcely heard the soft, shaky sound of her giggle through the blood pounding in his ears, but he drew marginally away with a little half-smile, still holding Andi close, his gaze on her face. Seeing himself there in the sparkling green seas of her eyes, he felt as if he were adrift in them—just as he had that first day at the zoo.

The bronze flecks dancing on the surface brightened mischievously. "I think we got the treatment backwards, Greg," she teased softly. "You're the one who's supposed to say 'boo.'"

The smile widened, then he repeated the word. "Boo."

Andi's fingers trailed down the nape of Greg's neck to tighten on his broad shoulders as she pressed her lips to his again in another sweet, quiet kiss that left her with little breath and no hiccups. She had just laid her cheek against his chest and whispered that she was cured when her mother and Sadie Howland entered the room.

Andi almost toppled over when Greg released her abruptly and jumped to his feet. "Uh, hiccups," he responded to Margaret Reynolds' quizzical look at her pink-cheeked daughter. "Andi's been, uh, holding her breath to try to cure them." He turned gratefully away to peck his mother's thin cheek and pulled forward a chair for her, trying to think of something else to say. "So, Ma," he managed finally, "what do you think of our new house?"

"To tell you the truth, it worries me a mite," she admitted.

"Worries you?" Greg looked at Margaret for translation. After only a few days, she seemed to understand his mother better than he ever would.

"She's afraid it's too expensive," Margaret explained.

Greg turned back to Sadie. "Ma, no, it's not. Really."

"It's mighty fancy, Greg. We could do without all the gewgaws."

Greg wondered which "gewgaws" she meant. Clean running water? Central heating and cooling? A roof without holes? They were all more than she was used to in their house back in Iowa. "If there's something about it you don't like—" he began, but not knowing how he could possibly reassure her, stopped abruptly.

"If it's what you want, it's fine." Sadie leaned back into the chair and Greg wondered if it was just his imagination that she seemed to disappear a little more each day. Her hair, once the color of saffron, had faded to old ivory and seemed to blend in with her sallow complexion. Even her clothing, which she steadfastly refused to replace, was threadbare and dull. The only spots of color about her were her cornflower-blue eyes. Someday, Greg thought, like the Cheshire cat, his mother would disappear completely, leaving only two melancholy eyes to haunt him wherever he went.

"I want you to have what *you* want." Greg perched on the end of the bed across from her chair. "I'm sorry you didn't get to choose much but I thought that leasing the furnished model would be easier under the circumstances." He glanced apologetically at Sister Reynolds. "Of course, I'm sure there's still a lot to get . . ." His voice trailed off. Actually, he couldn't imagine what it took to properly set up housekeeping. The closets and drawers in his Chicago apartment were virtually empty.

"We're looking forward to shopping," Margaret said brightly. She seemed determined to pull Sadie in by the sheer force of her enthusiasm. "We'll go on Monday as soon as Andi gets off work."

"I hope it isn't too much trouble," he said.

"Don't be silly." Margaret smiled as she slipped onto the bench next to her daughter. "Three women going to a mall to spend your money is only trouble for you, Greg."

He returned Sister Reynolds' smile gratefully, but a quick look at his mother told another story. Greg leaned forward. "Get everything you need, Ma. Okay?"

"I don't *need* anything," she said simply.

"Well, anything you like then." Looking helplessly into her face, Greg knew that even in one of the largest shopping malls in the Southwest there would be little, if anything, she liked. "Please," he begged, "get something."

Even as she nodded, her eyes slid down toward her carefully clasped hands, and Greg knew he had lost her attention.

"Well," Margaret said to break the ensuing silence, "where did Clytie wander off to? I had hoped to meet the young man Andi told us about."

Uneasy about his mother and still shy about kissing Margaret's daughter practically in front of her, Greg was grateful for any excuse to move. "I'll see if they're in the hall," he volunteered. To his disappointment, they were just outside the door, which made a lengthy reconnaissance mission unnecessary. He motioned to Clytie. "Your mom's here. She wants to meet Thaddeus." As the young man passed, Greg touched his arm and whispered, "For Pete's sake, try to be nice. At least be polite."

Although it was likely for Clytie's sake, Thaddeus breezed through polite. By the time an hour had passed and they were walking the ladies to the elevator, he was closing in on pleasant.

"I guess they taught charm at that fancy boarding school of yours, after all," Greg said as the elevator doors closed and they turned to go back to his room.

"Yeah," Thaddeus said, "but I'll need correspondence courses to become a lady-killer like you. Here comes your favorite nurse now."

Greg stared at Thaddeus before looking down the hall toward Jill and back. "How did you know it was—" he said under his breath.

"Take a whiff," Thaddeus snickered. "Only Jill—and maybe a Victoria's Secret store—smell like that."

"Well, hello there," Jill said as she took Greg's arm, sparing hardly a glance at Thaddeus. "Did you miss me?"

"I was kinda surprised you had most of the day off," he admitted.

"I traded my day shift for an overnighter." She ran a hand over her sleek hair and smiled sweetly. "I hoped it would give us more time together."

Thaddeus stuck a thin elbow into Greg's arm. "At night she can dole out sleeping pills to get all the rest of us pesky patients out of the way," he said in a dramatic stage whisper.

Thaddeus' blindness spared him Jill's forced smile, but not her authority. "Time to return to your room, Mr. Bisher. You've been up too long today already." She turned back to Greg, automatically adjusting the radiance of her smile as she looked up at the ball player. "I'll go straighten up your bed," she said archly and turned away with a sway of hips calculated to persuade Greg to follow.

"Meet you on the rooftop in ten minutes," Thaddeus whispered.

"Five," Greg said. "You bring the chess set and I'll bring the sheets to tie together. I'm telling you, Thaddeus, if Jill doesn't at least have Sunday off and they don't clear me for discharge on Monday, I'm using that rope."

After completing an extensive battery of neurological fitness tests on Monday afternoon, Greg had only three questions for the assembled specialists: Can I go home? Can I drive? and Can I play baseball? The answers—yes, no, and maybe—went barely a third of the way toward fulfilling his hopes. Still, Greg thought, you do the best you can with the pitch called. He phoned his mother and Andi first, then the Cubs. The former were out shopping.

The latter had a representative in his room in thirty minutes. The representative, of course, was Dawson Geitler.

A maven of the minutiae, Geitler had orchestrated the public relations aspect of Greg's recovery from the day it was determined with some certainty that there would *be* a recovery. He rerouted roomfuls of flowers and gifts to children's charities, catalogued each card and letter, and dutifully acknowledged the senders in Greg's behalf. He also took photos, wrote press releases, answered the media's questions, and in general spent eight to ten hours a day handling Greg's life better than the young celebrity could ever hope to handle it himself. Greg thought Geitler was amazing—if more than a little manic.

Dawson stopped pecking at his laptop computer long enough to run the limber fingers through his thinning brown hair. "Tomorrow's not much notice, Mr. Howland."

Greg had long since given up saying, "Call me Greg." He crossed his legs beneath himself on the bed and settled in. He'd learned by now that public relations always took a while and often seemed more integral to sports than the game itself. "Maybe the hospital will let me stay a few more days while you work out the details of the press conference," he suggested with a grin.

Geitler looked up hopefully. "Wednesday?"

Greg restrained the impulse to roll his eyes. "I was kidding, Dawson."

The thin nose returned to the computerized grindstone. "Tomorrow at nine, then. That'll put us live on morning shows on the West Coast and noon newscasts in the East."

"Now *you're* kidding." Greg was amazed, as always, that there were actually people in the world, apparently thousands of them, who took an interest in his personal life. He let out his breath in a low whistle. His decision to keep his engagement to Andi strictly secret was looking more inspired all the time.

Dawson hit a button to bullet the items that required highest priority for the news conference. "Neurologist. Hospital administrator. Cub Executive." He stopped bulleting to tap the index finger against his pursed lips as he considered. "We oughta humanize this thing somehow. How about bringing in your mother?"

"No," Greg said quickly. "Believe me, Dawson, she's worse in public than I am."

"Hmm."

Greg smiled. Geitler knew him pretty well already.

"Andres!" Dawson exclaimed, hitting keys in earnest. "Good, the Diamondbacks are home." He looked up in triumph. "Like the angle?"

"I don't get it," Greg said slowly. Apparently, Dawson Geitler conserved most of his verbal skills for the printed page. He spoke in bulletins and seemed to consider explanation superfluous. As usual, he'd lost Greg. "Who's Andres?"

"He's the batter that took you out."

"Oh, yeah . . . that catcher out of the Dominican Republic. He came up here to see me." The young man's repeated apologies—sincere and soft-spoken in broken English—had made Greg feel worse for Jorge Andres than for himself in the ICU. Now he felt bad again for forgetting Jorge; he could have at least sent him a letter in care of his team. At the thought, Greg's eyebrow rose. Hadn't Geitler said, "Diamondbacks"?

"You know," he said, looking at Dawson carefully. "Maybe my brain's still damaged, but I could have sworn we were playing the Rockies when I got hit."

"He was traded."

"Yeah? Well, it doesn't seem right to drag an innocent bystander into this media circus." Greg paused thoughtfully. On the other hand, Geitler could invite the Mormon Tabernacle Choir for all he cared. The more people there to draw attention away from him, the better. "You could ask Andres, I guess."

With a quick nod, Dawson hit a button to close the press conference file and tapped a key to open the next. "Parlays: electronic and print. Exclusives?"

Greg stared at the young Cub rep. "Dawson, is there an English translation for what you just said?"

"Interviews."

"Oh." Greg tried to focus his attention and wished he could see Geitler's computer screen. Maybe a visual prompting would help him understand what this guy was talking about.

"Exclusives?" Geitler repeated.

"Great." When he could get away with it, Greg gave exclusive interviews exclusively since they had the monumental appeal of coming in sets of one.

"Who do you like?"

"In the media?" Greg thought for a minute, then shrugged. "No one."

Dawson pulled a bottle of Excedrin from his pocket, flipped off the lid, and popped a couple in his mouth. He had already begun chewing by the time Greg could reach for the pitcher beside the bed, and he declined the proffered cup of water with a frown and emphatic shake of his head. "Germs."

Greg made a face. "You'd rather chew aspirin?"

"It's more efficient." Dawson swallowed and continued. "Walters and *SI,* then? Double duty."

Greg drank the water himself and wished a pain reliever could be enough to get rid of this public relations headache. "Honestly, Dawson," he said finally. "Talking to you is like trying to grasp the news from someone who'll only read you the headlines."

Dawson drew a deep breath. "You've got corporate sponsors who advertise on Walter's show and in *Sports Illustrated.* You could meet your obligation to the Cubs' PR department and make some ad execs happy at the same time."

Greg grinned, impressed and grateful not only for Dawson's essay answer, but for the man's thoroughness in his behalf. He hadn't missed a detail. A sudden idea caused Greg to lean further forward. He might need a good press agent to keep his relationship with Andi under wraps, but he'd surely need a great one like Dawson Geitler if the media heard wedding bells despite his best efforts to muffle them. "Dawson, would you like a job?"

The bald spot shone at the crown of Dawson's head as he bent again over his laptop and muttered, "I'll never finish this one."

"Walters and *SI* are fine," Greg said quickly. "Just tell me when and where to show up." As the man typed rapidly, he added, "I could really use a guy like you."

"For—" Dawson asked, his attention to the keyboard belying his interest.

"To keep doing what you've done the past couple of weeks," Greg said. "If somebody doesn't figure out what all I've signed in the way of endorsement agreements and get me where I'm supposed to be to do them, I'm going to be in big trouble. You already know everything about me. And you're better organized than the Borg. I'll pay you whatever the Cubs do. More."

"Isn't Zeke Martoni your publicist?"

"He, uh, well." Greg cleared his throat then continued honestly, "He went to jail, Dawson."

Geitler didn't know that. "For—"

"Extortion, gambling, drugs, trying to rig games." Greg rubbed a hand across his face. "It sounds even worse when you try to explain it." He didn't notice the veins pulsing beneath the thin skin at Dawson's temples, or he might have been aware of the media specialist's sudden interest.

With difficulty, Geitler kept his eyes focused on the computer screen as he asked casually, "You involved?"

"Indirectly, I guess," Greg admitted, then added quickly, "but what I'm guilty of is not being too bright." Greg wondered with amusement if Dawson's quick nod was one of sympathy or agreement. "Anyway, you interested?"

Before Dawson could answer, the phone at the side of Greg's bed rang. He reached for it with an apologetic motion for time-out. To his dismay, it was the daily call from his sister-in-law, Bobbie Jo Howland. Speaking of not being too bright, he thought, he had yet to figure out how to handle the dysfunctional mother of his brother's two young sons.

"Where are you, Bobbie?" Greg asked, though he had a pretty good idea already. The country western music, loud male voices, and clink of glasses in the background suggested that she was less than truthful when she claimed to be calling from home. The slur in her speech was an even worse sign. "Is Wanda with the kids?"

He listened to Bobbie recite her litany of child-rearing difficulties with increasing dismay. She seemed to lose ground daily. Despite himself, Greg pictured Jim's hopeful, trusting face. He had promised his brother more attention to his boys than the twenty-year-old nanny he currently employed as a stopgap measure. Although Greg had every intention—now that his mother had left Iowa—to walk away from his home and his father without looking back, he couldn't abandon Bobbie Jo. Of course, he couldn't give up Andi either, which had become Bobbie's latest and dearest campaign.

When she paused, likely for another drink, he said, "Bobbie Jo, I've told you a dozen times you're living a fantasy. I could never think of you as anything but my sister-in-law." Though kind, it wasn't entirely true. Increasingly, he thought less of her as a sister than as a lost cause. "Look, Bobbie," he added hastily, speaking a little louder to be heard over her exaggerated sobs, "I get out of here tomorrow. I'll come out there as soon as I can, okay?" As soon as he said it, he knew it was a mistake. The crying had stopped, but now he could almost hear the wheels turning in her head. He sighed. "I'll call you tomorrow with a new phone number. I, uh, I've got someone here now." He glanced uncomfortably at Dawson. "No, it's not Andi. It's a business associate. I'll call you later, Bobbie. Bye."

Greg put down the receiver then pushed the phone away for good measure. "My sister-in-law," he said to Dawson, as though the man hadn't already gathered as much. "Actually, she and my brother were in the process of a divorce, but she *is* the mother of his two sons. My brother died in January and I promised him . . ." Although Geitler had looked up in interest, Greg's words trailed off self-consciously.

"You mentioned a job?" Geitler asked, changing the subject to Greg's enormous relief.

Dawson's enthusiasm must be greater than he had thought at first. "I'll meet whatever deal you have with the Cubs for handling the press," Greg offered eagerly. "Plus pay you the going percentage on all the other stuff. Does that sound okay?"

The press agent's nod was so brief and noncommittal that Greg had no way to know just how much more than okay it sounded. It sounded, in fact, like it could possibly be the break for which Dawson Geitler had waited his whole life.

CHAPTER 10

"I hope we're not *too* late," Andi said as she ushered her little sister, Francie, through a back door of the hospital and toward the large room Dawson had shown her the night before.

Morning traffic had been heavier than she'd anticipated all the way into downtown Phoenix so, in hindsight, the stop she'd made at the Child Crisis Center in Mesa had been a mistake. Of course, she'd planned it to be brief—just in and out to drop off diapers. The donations that she routinely collected from her co-workers had been taking up most of her backseat for the past couple of weeks, and now she needed the room for Greg. But when a pair of children she had tended caught sight of Andi, the stop had lengthened into a hug and then three choruses of "The Wheels on the Bus" before she was finally able to get away. Now she was almost thirty minutes late. At least the handicapped parking spot—on the opposite side of the building from the satellite trucks and news vans—had been kept open by security as Geitler had promised.

"Greg's meeting won't have lasted this long," she told Francie, taking the little girl's hand to hurry her along. "He'll be waiting for us."

Though it really hadn't been purposeful, Andi would have freely admitted her relief at missing the event. A press conference represented in her mind the one part of Greg's world that she didn't wish to share. By now, though, it would surely be over and in a few minutes they'd be uneventfully on their way home. Then Greg would fully recover from his accident, join the Church, take her to the temple, and eventually get that job teaching math that he'd said he always wanted.

There might be some excitement about his celebrity for a little while, she told herself slowly, smiling at a number of hospital staffers lining the halls outside the conference room. *But that will fade quickly enough when we're married and the only baseball Greg throws might be for a church team. And no matter what my father and Sterling say, that's what Greg and I both want—a quiet, normal life together.*

Her spirits as high as her hopes, Andi pushed open the door then froze. She barely noticed when Francie darted around her and into the crowded room.

"Look out, kid," a photographer snapped. He had almost fallen over the six-year-old as he cut across the back of the room to jockey for a better position in the crush of people.

"Stay with me, Francie!" Andi commanded, regaining her wits enough to pull her little sister over to a corner, out of the way of the harried photographer and an overwhelming assemblage of his peers.

"But I can't see Greg!" Francie protested. "You said we were coming to take him home. What's everybody else here for?"

Andi wished she knew. Obviously, this press conference was a bigger deal than anyone had let on and a much bigger deal than she had understood. Though his fame was the part of Greg's life that she purposefully ignored, it was impossible to overlook under the present circumstances. Andi moved aside as a technician readjusted a powerful spot. Somehow, she thought unhappily, today's media light was doing its best to obscure the bright tomorrows with Greg that she had envisioned.

Regardless of how bright his tomorrows looked, Geitler thought, snapping the lid from a new bottle of Excedrin as flashbulbs popped at the front of the room, he'd have to get through today first. He stood off to one side at the press conference and watched his new superstar client muddle through it. Despite everyone Dawson had lined up to participate, all interest was focused on the handsome young pitcher seated at the center of the table. Clearly uncomfortable, Greg rarely looked into the cameras and offered mostly two- and three-word responses to reporters' questions. *And he calls me uncommunicative,* Dawson thought with a shake of his head. With Howland approaching this deal with an enthusiasm generally reserved for root canals, Geitler knew he'd have to handle the press personally from here on out.

And handle them he would—if for no other reason than to assure his own future. Howland's offer, as made yesterday afternoon, had sounded more than okay to Dawson Geitler. And a contract with Greg's signature, without the ironclad non-disclosure clause mandated by the Cubs and every celebrity with any sense, could well be the ticket to his dreams.

Dawson was a talented, ambitious young man who, at thirty-two, was a half dozen years behind a self-imposed schedule for fame and fortune in the literary world. A graduate of the Columbia School of Journalism, he dreamed of writing the Great American Novel. But as he entered the field of public relations and began to rub shoulders with the rich and famous, his ambitions had changed proportionately with his cynicism. Professionally, Geitler had met few people he liked and none that he admired. He stayed in the field only because he was good at it. Dawson knew what sold and how to write it, but he had never caught a break. Until yesterday.

He had been up much of the night then, turning over and over in his mind how a slick tell-all of Greg Howland's sordid secrets would not only make the unauthorized biographer wealthy, but would assure his literary efforts prime window space in every bookstore in the country. Just one book on such a hot topic, Dawson knew, would allow him all the time, royalties, and name-recognition he would need to switch to his first love in writing and someday give John Grisham a run for his money.

In the meantime, he thought, methodically chewing the pain reliever, *there's today.* Geitler's eyes wandered to the back of the room and came to rest on the titian-haired young lady in the corner. *It's about time she got here.*

Howland had introduced Andi as a "special friend"' and Dawson had gathered, from the half dozen times he'd seen them together, that the emphasis was on "special." He paused for a moment to figure how she fit into his book. He had already penciled Greg into the outline in his head as the archetypal hero and had assumed (from what he had read of him in the tabloids) that women were his tragic flaw. But this girl had impressed Dawson as more of a quiet, new breed of feminist than a femme fatale.

Although looking at her more closely, Dawson noted that Andi seemed to lack the apparent self-confidence that had prompted her inclusion into the getaway plans for Greg. Her wide eyes darted from place to place, taking in the television cameras, bright lights, and crush of people. When she finally glanced at Greg, her fingers clutched her sister's shoulders so tightly that the little girl squirmed away. Geitler popped another Excedrin, condemned himself for working with amateurs, and sidled discreetly to Andi's side.

"We okay, here?" he asked anxiously. Although she responded in the affirmative, Dawson detected a waver in her voice. "Why don't you and your sister wait in the back lobby I showed you?" he suggested. "We'll wrap this up and meet you there in ten."

Andi seemed relieved to go, Dawson thought, and relaxed a little himself when no one noticed her departure. This thing could still work out okay. He glanced toward the front and met Howland's eye. Someone *had* seen her leave, Geitler noted. If it were possible, Howland now looked more lost than ever.

Greg wondered if he had ever felt dumber in his life as he lowered his athletic 6'4" frame into a wheelchair, scrunched himself up as much as he could manage, and allowed Dawson to drape a pastel blanket about his shoulders and over his knees. The press conference had been bad enough—after the glare of lights, Greg still saw spots and it would be another hour or so before his mouth lost the aridness of the Sonoran desert—but this bait-and-switch idea of Dawson's was purely harebrained.

It was easy, at least, to avoid Andi's eyes. He imagined she was thinking all this was sillier than he did as she stared out the tinted glass doors at the young man Dawson had hired to impersonate him. Greg took a good look at the actor in the sunglasses, Cubs jersey, and hat and had to admit that his resemblance to the decoy didn't miss the mark by much. It was close enough, at least, to fool the horde of press and other onlookers who flocked after the actor as he walked out the main entrance of the hospital to the waiting limousine

Still, Dawson was taking no chances. He plopped a flowery, pink sleeping-cap over Greg's sandy hair, added cat-eye sunglasses, and stood back to assess the results. "Pull up your knees a little more," he directed. As Greg did so, he shook his head at the less-than-hoped-for results. "Whatever." Turning to Andi, he asked, "Where's the little girl?"

"I'm a medium-sized girl," Francie insisted from just behind his left elbow. "In fact, Daddy says I'm tall for my age."

"Whatever. Stay with your sister and your 'grandma.'"

"Greg doesn't look like Nana," Francie giggled. "My Nana's real pretty. She—"

"Whatever." Geitler snapped as he pulled the blanket a little higher. "Ready?"

Wordlessly, Andi moved quickly to grip the handles of the wheelchair.

"Head down!" Dawson commanded.

Greg was only too happy to comply. Dawson peered out the window. "Okay . . . go."

He had felt dumber on one occasion, Greg decided as the doors swished open and they passed through. A rookie's initiation into the major leagues usually involved a dramatic switch of clothing in his locker before the first out-of-town trip. Greg had been forced to wear a little off-the-shoulder gold lamé number all the way from Chicago to San Francisco. *That* had been worse than this. His teammates had called him Goldie ever since. The press had picked up the golden nickname but applied it, thankfully, to his pitching rather than his wardrobe. Hopefully, no one would notice him this time. He'd hate to spend his last year in baseball known as Granny.

Andi opened the door of her car and Greg slid quickly onto the backseat, followed by Francie.

"Careful Grandma!" Francie sang out, proud of her part in the production.

As Andi pulled out of the parking space, a quick glance told Greg that the limo hadn't moved a quarter of an inch in the press of people. Suddenly, Dawson's efforts in his behalf seemed more heroic than harebrained. Hiring him had probably been the smartest thing he'd done in years. Well, he amended, the second smartest. Nothing he would ever do would be as smart as adopting those reptiles at the zoo.

As soon as they hit the ramp onto the freeway, Greg yanked off the cap and glasses and smiled at the redheaded crocodile keeper's reflection in the rearview mirror. She merely blinked and looked away, leaving him puzzled and unsure.

"You wanna play a game?" Francie asked from his side. "Winner gets to make a wish!"

"Francie," Andi said hastily, "let Greg rest." Although she hoped she was sincere in her concern for Greg, she worried that what she really wanted was quiet in which to think. After all, she reasoned, when she'd had some time to think it through carefully, she knew that what she'd seen at today's press conference wouldn't bother her in the least. For that matter, it shouldn't bother her now—should it?

She glanced over at a pile of textbooks on the seat. A sweatshirt from the zoo was draped carelessly over the top of them and probably smelled like fish. Andi reached for it and tossed it hastily on the floor, her nose wrinkling in distaste—more at herself than at the faint odor. The books made her feel like a schoolgirl. The uniform reminded her that her most notable skill was mucking out an alligator swamp. She sighed involuntarily, wondering what all those people in the pressroom would have made of them as a couple. She could almost see the headline in her mind: *Man of the Year to Wed Girl Next Door?*

"All I've done is rest," Greg was telling Francie. "Besides, I could use a wish." Actually, he thought, he could use a couple. "What's the game, Francie?"

The strawberry-blonde ringlets bobbed as she bounced on the seat in happiness. "It's the ABC game. You hafta find a sign or a license plate with a letter on it and say it out loud before the other person does."

"Any letter?"

"No. It has to be in alphonetical order."

"Alphabetical," Andi supplied automatically.

"Whatever," Francie said, giggling at her own imitation of Dawson Geitler. "Okay, Greg?"

"Sure." Greg was hazy on the rules, but figured he could pick them up as they went along.

"A and B!" Francie cried out as they passed an Albertson's billboard. It wasn't long before she'd added C through F then, steadily, more of the alphabet. Though stalling on X and Y until they entered Mesa and passed a fast-food outlet advertising extra-crispy chicken, she easily won with an AriZona license plate. "You wanna know my wish, Greg?" she asked with wide, hopeful eyes.

"Will it come true if you tell me?"

Her tone was earnest. "If *you* want it to."

"Then it's a sure thing," Greg said, although he had no idea what she was talking about.

Francie crossed the fingers on both hands and squinted her eyes closed. "I wish Greg to come to my class for Show and Tell."

"Francie!" At Andi's voice, the little girl jumped and the color rose in Andi's face. She had seen Francie use that winsome make-a-wish ploy on their father only yesterday. Andi couldn't believe that she'd been so preoccupied thinking about Greg today that she'd let him fall for it. She cast a quick warning glance over her shoulder. "Greg just got out of the hospital," she reminded her little sister, who uncrossed her fingers and looked up at Greg in disappointment.

"Are you still sick, Greg?" she asked.

He smiled at the genuine concern in the pixie features. "No, Francie, I'm fine. And I'd be happy to be shown and told."

"You mean, you'll come?"

"Francie!" Andi's voice rose with her dismay. "It isn't fair to put Greg on the spot like that." *Wonderful,* she thought. *Here's the most eligible man in America, and my sweet adorable baby sister thinks he has nothing better to do than tour kindergarten classes.* "I don't think he can make it to your class, sweetie," she tried to let her sister down gently.

"Why not?" Francie pouted. She turned to Greg to explain, "My best friend, Sally James, thinks she's so great because her father came and brought his fire truck."

"I don't have anything as cool as a fire truck," Greg warned.

Francie pursed her lips into a perfect rosebud. "But you were on TV today—"

"That's because Greg's famous," Andi said, then bit her lip as she realized that the implications of his fame were only just beginning to dawn on her as well.

"What's famous?" Francie asked.

"It means I was on TV," Greg teased.

"And it means that he doesn't have time to go to every kindergarten class that wants him," Andi added, wishing this conversation would end quickly.

"Not *every* class," Francie corrected, "just Ms. Sherwood's. She wants us to bring in people with important jobs. Sally James brought a fireman."

Andi sighed at her sister's tenacity. "Francie, Greg is *much* more important than a fireman."

"Huh?" Greg stared at Andi's profile, bewildered. He wished now that Francie hadn't won the game and the free wish. Forget hoping for world peace or an end to global hunger, he only wished he knew what had gotten into Andi all of a sudden. Since they'd met, she'd teased him a little about his celebrity status, but she'd never been impressed by it. And if there was a profession she thought was less important than playing baseball, he didn't know what it was. He tried to catch her eye in the rearview mirror. "Are you doing okay, Andi?"

Her eyes never left the road. "I'm fine. I'm just trying to explain to Francie why you're too busy to go to her kindergarten class."

"But I'm not."

Francie hugged him happily. "We have Show and Tell every Friday. Can you come this week?"

He smiled at the little girl sharing the back seat with him. "Sure, Francie. I'd love to come to your class." To Greg's relief, Andi let the subject drop.

When he saw the tall, silver light poles at HoHoKam stadium where he had trained with the Cubs, he knew at last where he was and concentrated on committing the route to his new home in The Coves to memory. As they approached the entrance to the gated community, he looked up at the high walls and frowned. "Are they trying to keep people in or out of this place?"

"Out," Francie said with certainty. "It's in our ward, but Mommy won't let me go with her to visit people here. I think it's 'cause they're all rich and snooty and they don't like little kids."

"Francie—" Andi began, then let it go. Probably, Greg thought, because her little sister's observation was pretty astute.

"Well, I like you, Francie," he said quickly. "You can visit me anytime." Andi inserted Greg's security card into a small slot near the gate and punched four numbers onto the electronic keypad. The large gate swung inward slowly. At night, Greg thought, no doubt an armed guard was added to the entrance formula.

Greg gazed out the window as they drove down the quiet, winding avenue. He wondered whose daily job it was to rake the pea-sized gravel into precise geometric patterns in each yard fronting the windowless townhouses. The homes were set well apart to insure privacy and the pristine sidewalks were deserted, making the neighborhood seem more like a vacant movie lot than a community. It was nothing like the open fields Sadie was used to outside of town in Iowa, or even the car-cluttered, child-filled street where Jim had lived in Peosta. His mother would hate it here, Greg realized quickly. What had he done now?

Andi pressed a button on a remote to raise a nearby garage door, and swung her car in next to her mother's. Then she turned to hand Greg the entry card and the garage gadget. "Welcome home."

"Thanks," he said. At least she was smiling at him now. Maybe when they were alone, she would tell him what had upset her earlier.

"Let's go see your new house, Greg!" Francie said excitedly, pulling on his arm before he had even unfastened his seatbelt.

Within a couple of minutes, Greg was walking from room to room with his mother, Margaret Reynolds, and two women who had been introduced to him as Sadie's visiting teachers. At the end of the tour, Greg turned toward the large-boned woman who had hold of his elbow at the moment.

"You like lefse, young man, ya?" she asked, her plump face creasing into a broad smile.

What is lefse? Greg wondered. *For that matter, what is a visiting teacher?*

It had been almost a month now since Greg had asked Andi if her church published a Mormon/English dictionary. But even without such a handy guide for the uninitiated, Greg had picked up quite a bit of needful information on his own. He now knew, for instance, that a stake house wasn't a restaurant, people didn't wear camping clothes to a fireside, and LDS deacons were *nothing* like the ones depicted in Nathaniel Hawthorne stories. He'd cultivated at least a passing familiarity with organization names as well: Beehives, Mia Maids, and Laurels were teenage girls; deacons, teachers, and priests were teenage boys. And adult women attended something called Relief Society because, as Andi's mother had explained with a smile, they liked the society and they needed the relief.

Now, as representatives of this Relief Society, Sister Jorgensen and her younger companion, Laura Newton, had been there all morning and much of the day before to help his mother move in. The cupboards were full, the beds were made, and something on the countertop in the kitchen *(lefse*, perhaps?) smelled wonderful. Whoever these women were, Greg hoped they would visit often and that his mother would learn whatever they came to teach.

"I like everything," he told Sister Jorgensen, extending his grateful smile to include Sister Newton. "Thank you very much."

Sister Jorgensen pumped his hand with enthusiasm. "We go now—you rest." She turned to Sadie and enveloped her in an enthusiastic hug. "You have our telephone numbers. You call us anytime, ya?"

Sadie, to Greg's consternation, pulled away with a barely perceptible nod. He watched Sister Newton move quietly to her side. Laura was petite and pretty, probably in her mid-thirties. Her auburn hair had been pulled back from her face making her brown eyes seem larger yet. Her voice was soft and her words were for Sadie alone. Greg was relieved when his mother's next nod was, thankfully, a little more convincing.

"Come along, Francie," Margaret called to her youngest daughter. The little girl was peering out the large picture window in back, fascinated by the blue, man-made lake that curved up the grassy bank to the patio, lending additional privacy and giving the community its name.

"Can't I stay? I want to swim in Greg's lake."

"It's not for swimming, dear," Margaret said. "It's just to look pretty."

"Then I'll ride home with Andi."

"I have a class in a little while so I need to leave, too," Andi said, with a brief glance toward Greg that seemed to convey both an apology and an appeal. "Greg needs some time to get settled."

He might have objected had it not been plain that something was bothering Andi, despite her efforts to make it appear otherwise. *What is it?* he wondered. *And if we had been alone, would she have told me?*

Though confused, Greg nodded and was rewarded with a grateful smile. They were both under a lot of stress right now, he decided. And Andi was right. He *did* need to spend some time with his mother before he found out what all Dawson Geitler had committed him to. And talking with Jorge Andres before the press conference today had given him an idea. Greg could hardly wait to pick up the phone to contact his agent about a possible Diamondback trade. He'd call Andi as soon as he had something to tell her. She'd probably be herself again by then. He walked the ladies to the door. "There's no way to thank you for all you've done—"

"You're welcome, Greg," Margaret replied with a brief hug of reassurance. "Your home is beautiful. I know that Sadie will be very happy here."

Greg nodded slowly, knowing full well that behind his back, his mother's pale face, staring blankly into the expensively decorated room, told another story.

Chapter 11

Andi stashed a rake along with her hip-high waders in the small food prep area next to the alligator swamp, padlocked the door, and glanced at her watch. Friday's shift at the zoo was over and it was still early enough, if she hurried, to make it to Francie's class in time to see Greg at Show and Tell. It would be the first time she'd seen him since Tuesday, unless she counted video images from the news and/or a series of Barbara Walters promos which seemed to air at quarter hour intervals around the clock. Of course he had called her every day, but the conversations had of necessity been brief, sandwiched as they were between business meetings he had just attended and interviews he was on his way to. More than once she had hung up the phone worrying that "Call Andi" had merely been another item on Greg's long list of "Things to Do."

As she climbed on board her electric cart and started the motor, Andi recalled the TV interview teasers with the beginning of a frown. Clytie had recorded them all, presumably in the few free minutes that she wasn't at school or on the phone with Thaddeus. (Released from the hospital in time to compete in a weekend chess championship, Thaddeus claimed to be fully recovered and was looking forward to the date Clytie had planned for Monday afternoon.)

Andi, however, had no use for Clytie's videos. Her personal, in-head recorder could easily retrieve anything that concerned Greg. And, without the previews or even a premonition, she dreaded the interview. Already, every accidental glimpse she'd caught of him on

TV had made her feel as strangely uncomfortable as had the press conference. How could she reconcile the public whole of celebrity with the private part of the man she loved?

"I keep forgetting who you are," she had told Greg soon after they first met. His response had been: *"Baseball is what I do, Andi. You know who I am."*

When she was with Greg, she knew that those sacred promises made across an altar would be hollow with anyone else. But as Andi found herself thinking about Greg's father, and his impact on his two sons, she wondered if Greg's was a heritage she would wish for her children. As hard as it was to believe that Greg could ever become anything like his father, it was equally hard to believe that Greg could have avoided being damaged by him. This was her father's fear, as well, along with a concern that having suffered such poverty then achieved such incredible fame, the call of the world would ring louder in Greg's ears than the call of the gospel.

You're looking at the world in black and white, Greg had responded the few times she had wondered aloud about the differences in their backgrounds and lives. That, she had to admit, was probably true. Certainly, she had always believed that choosing the right would lead to a seamless pattern of perfection.

But, she reflected, slowing the cart as she approached a group of children on a field trip, "right" had once seemed to define her relationship with Sterling. Compared to what she now felt for Greg, planning for forever with Sterling may have *seemed* inspired but it had always been uninspiring. Maybe monochromatic wasn't everything she'd believed it to be. She knew that what she felt for Greg was no whimsical crush or turn of head because of his wealth or celebrity. She was sure that she'd be infinitely more comfortable without them. Nevertheless, every part of her loved Greg—body and soul.

As she stopped the cart to let the children pass, Andi admired a colorfully quilted vest worn by their leader. There was no apparent design to the jumble of hues and textures of the fabric, but the result was stunning. As she stared, Andi thought about the jumble of emotions—the joy and sorrow, consternation and exhilaration—she had felt since meeting a certain celebrity athlete. The warm thoughts became a warmer tickle, which flowed down the back of her neck and into her heart.

"My Father is making a quilt," she sang softly to herself as she restarted the cart with a smile, *"and sometimes it seems kind of crazy."* Unable to remember the rest of the words, Andi repeated the chorus again and again as she accelerated to make it to Francie's class in time to see Greg.

Almost an hour later, Andi watched the next-to-the-last scheduled Show and Teller carry his jar of pink, pickled pig feet carefully back to his cubby. She could tell by his strut that he was pleased to have just completed the best "P-week" presentation ever given by a kindergartner.

His teacher, Ms. Sherwood, consulted the crayon-shaped hands on the clock above the dry erase board, glanced at Andi, then settled her regretful gaze on little Francie. "I guess Mr. Howland couldn't make it today."

The teacher's disappointment was understandable, Andi thought, considering the lengths she had gone to prepare for Greg's visit. Andi had seen the young woman several times before—when she picked Francie up from school and once when she had come in with her mother to help with a class party—but Andi had never seen her like this. This afternoon, Toni Sherwood could have stepped directly from a Glamour Shots studio. Her hair was poufed, her eyes lined and her lips glossed. Still, from what Andi could tell, her students were clearly unimpressed. Of course, Andi doubted that they were the ones she had set out to impress in the first place. She watched Ms. Sherwood tug the hem of her incredibly short skirt down a quarter of an inch and hoped the woman wouldn't have to reach up for anything today. If she did, likely she'd show even more than she intended and probably wouldn't know *what* to tell the parents leaving messages on her voice mail after receiving shocking dinner-table reports from their six-year-olds.

"Wait another minute, Ms. Sherwood," Francie pleaded. "Greg promised he would come."

The little girl turned her hazel eyes despairingly toward the door, and Andi expected to see them overflow with tears any second. She was sorry that she hadn't thought to warn her sister that this might happen. Although she didn't think Greg would disappoint Francie on purpose, it wasn't surprising that he would forget, given all the interviews and other business that had occupied him since he left the hospital.

"I'm sorry, Francie," Ms. Sherwood said, "but he's already thirty minutes late. We have to move on to . . ." Her voice trailed off as the door opened and Greg appeared, followed by the principal, vice-principal, and Dawson Geitler.

Andi's heart beat faster as Greg's eyes swept the room and met hers with a look of pleased surprise. He wore a sports jacket with blue jeans and a soft denim shirt that made his azure eyes seem deeper yet. The ball cap that he usually wore in public was in his hand and his hair, lit by sunlight from the open door, was platinum-streaked and boyishly tousled. In a word, Andi thought, he was gorgeous. Even if he had lacked incredible fame and fortune, she could see why women would look at him the way Ms. Sherwood did now.

Suddenly, Andi was self-conscious. Why hadn't she thought to put on a little makeup, at least? She nervously pushed some of her own windblown tresses back over her shoulder and tried to return Greg's smile as his eyes lingered upon her.

Francie was already on her feet. "Greg, you comed!"

"I'm sorry I'm late, Francie," he said, his grin shifting to the little girl who wrapped grateful arms around his leg.

"My fault," Mr. Preston, the principal, said quickly. Greg had actually arrived pretty close to on time but had lost a half-hour following the administrator through a gauntlet of fifth and sixth graders on lunch recess. If Mr. Preston hadn't used his two-way radio to summon reinforcements in the persons of the assistant principal, a custodian, and two playground aides, he might never have gotten Greg free of the mob and across the small campus to the kindergarten classrooms.

Francie's teacher finally regained her voice, if not her composure. "I'm Toni Sherwood," she said giddily, extending a freshly manicured hand to Greg, "Francie's teacher. We are so pleased you would come, and we think you're just—just wonderful!"

"Thanks," Greg said, trying to take her hand while Francie tugged on his knee to move him toward the front of the class. "It's great to be here."

The children were talking animatedly, so Ms. Sherwood clapped her hands three times for attention. Still, most of the children turned toward the back of the room. They had never before had *two* principals in their classroom, and they couldn't resist staring at the administrators standing back by the low sinks with their own eyes locked on Greg.

"Ms. Sherwood!" one little girl said excitedly over the noise. "P is for principal!"

"That's right," Ms. Sherwood agreed, "but Francie brought a special guest today, who—"

"And P is for Preston!" a boy added. "Principal Preston! That's two Ps—like pickled pigs."

Mr. Preston gave Greg a sheepish look, obviously embarrassed to be stealing the show. He said, "Please turn around and listen to Mr. Howland."

Most of the little heads turned obediently toward the front.

"I brought Greg Howland for Show and Tell," Francie began slowly, wishing now she'd thought to invite Mr. Preston instead. "He's a baseball player."

"B—baseball doesn't start with P!" Sally James pointed out.

Andi wondered if Sally had brought her fabulous fireman father on F week. Judging by the look of dismay on Francie's face, she probably had.

"I'm a pitcher," Greg offered helpfully.

A few of the children nodded their approval, but one girl raised her hand to ask, "What's a pitcher?"

Greg glanced down at Francie, wanting it to be her Show and Tell, but she obviously didn't have any idea what a pitcher was. He said, "I throw baseballs."

"How come?" the girl asked.

"For batters to hit. Or," he added with a smile, "for them *not* to hit, if I throw them right."

Sally James was unimpressed. "Is that a *real* job?"

Greg shot Andi a quick look of desperation. If she hadn't felt so bad for Francie, she might have giggled. Who would have guessed that there was a place on the planet where thirty people—granted, kindergartners—would have absolutely no idea who Greg Howland was?

Ms. Sherwood came to his rescue. "Mr. Howland is a very good baseball pitcher," she told the children. She picked up a news magazine from the top of the piano. "He's famous. See? His picture is on the cover of my magazine."

Though a couple of the children scooted nearer to examine it, most had turned their attention back to the better-known school celebrity, Principal Preston. Their disinterest in Greg was understandable, Andi realized. They couldn't read *Newsweek,* went to bed long before *20/20* came on TV and, perhaps most importantly, were disappointed that Greg hadn't brought a fire engine or even a bottle of pig feet.

Greg gazed into Francie's upturned face with undisguised alarm. The little girl was near tears again and he clearly felt responsible. Andi offered a silent p-word of her own and suspected Greg of doing the same. She knew their prayers had been answered when he suddenly squatted down beside her sister and raised two fingers to his lips for a quick, but effective, whistle.

"Hey! You guys know what?" he asked as the children turned back to him curiously. He paused for dramatic effect as he looked carefully from face to face, then lowered his voice conspiratorially, "I know Big Bird."

The children's eyes widened in respect and Greg winked at Francie. "Really, I do. I was on his TV show last fall."

"With Mr. Snuffleupagus?" a little girl asked breathlessly.

Andi couldn't contain her smile. These children all knew *Sesame Street.*

"With Mr. Snuffleupagus," Greg agreed with a grin. "I taught him and Big Bird to play baseball."

"Until you hit Oscar's garbage can with a ball and he told you to get lost!" the boy with the pickled pig feet offered in delight. "I remember you now!"

"Me, too!" another child said, clapping her hands. "You wore your baseball suit and the Count counted you throwing balls."

Greg grinned, surprised that he hadn't considered a guest appearance on the Children's Television Workshop the highlight of his career before now.

In the end, Andi turned out to be one of the few people in the room who had missed the show and she was sorry for it. The children asked dozens of questions and Greg, now sitting cross-legged on the floor with Francie in his lap, affably described every detail of his day at the Muppet studio.

It was almost twenty minutes before Ms. Sherwood, with obvious reluctance, intervened. "We are so glad you could come, Mr. Howland." She smiled at the quick chorus of assent from the children. "You're the most interesting visitor we've ever had."

"You're the best class I've ever visited," Greg said, setting Francie on her feet and motioning to Dawson as he rose himself. "I brought you something to thank you for inviting me." He took the blue plastic duffel from his press agent and unzipped it. "The people I work for were nice enough to give me all this." He pulled out a thick stack of his team's *Cub Kid* newsletters with a coloring page featuring his likeness. Each tabloid also had stickers and a pencil inside. He placed them on the piano, then looked back in the bag. "The rest is for Ms. Sherwood, I guess—I'm not sure what it is." He pulled out an eight-by-ten glossy of himself, then stuffed it back in quickly as he handed Francie's teacher the duffel with a self-deprecating shrug.

By the infatuated look he received, Andi had no doubt that Ms. Sherwood would put Greg's picture in a silver frame and sleep with it under her pillow.

A few minutes later, Andi stood by her car in the parking lot and watched Greg shake the principals' hands once again as the playground aides held the children at bay. When he turned to wave goodbye to his young fans, she smiled. His way with children was one of the things she had first admired about him. No matter how good he'd been at baseball, he'd make an even better teacher. Seeing him this afternoon made it easy to forget who he was and where he came from and only remember why she loved him.

When Greg walked over to where she stood—Dawson a single step behind—her smile widened and she reached for his hand. "Thank you for coming, Greg."

He extended both hands to envelop hers, his own smile bright enough to bring a warm glow to Andi's cheeks. "Thank *you* for coming."

"I'm glad I did. I never knew you had friends in such high places."

"You mean Big Bird?"

"Who else?" Andi laughed.

"I thought maybe you meant God." He squeezed her fingers. "Thanks for praying for me. I was sure I was a goner there for a while."

"Heavenly Father inspired your thoughts, Greg," Andi replied, "but the rest of it was you. You're wonderful with children."

Before he could respond, Geitler cleared his throat. Andi watched impatience flicker briefly across Greg's face. "Yeah, Dawson?"

The publicist tapped the crystal on his Seiko.

"What time is it?" Greg asked, tightening his grasp on Andi's hands in order to raise them to consult his own watch. He frowned in dismay. "Just a couple minutes—"

"We don't have two minutes, sir."

"Sure we do." He turned back to Andi and pulled her a little closer. "I never thought I'd miss being in the hospital, but at least then I got to see you every day—"

"It's okay, Greg," she said quickly, secure now in the heady joy of his nearness. "I know you don't have time—"

"For what?" he interrupted. "You mean for you?"

"For anything. You have a lot of things to do—"

"Yes," Dawson interjected. "As a matter of fact—"

"As a matter of fact," Greg interrupted again, "the reason I haven't been over is because I've been working overtime to wrap up old business and swing a deal that will give us more time together. You can help me with it," he added, "if you will."

Andi's heart leapt with happiness. With this old business wrapped up, perhaps they wouldn't need to keep their engagement a secret. After observing Ms. Sherwood, Andi wanted to tell at least half the world—the female half. She looked up into Greg's boyishly anxious face and knew there was nothing she wouldn't do for him.

"I need a date for a charity ball tomorrow night," he continued. "I know it's super-short notice, but I was only invited today myself." He rolled his eyes. "Actually, it was more of an order than an invitation. We wouldn't have to stay long."

A date? Andi thought. *We're finally going on a real date?* Before his accident, she'd been the one to invite Greg to dinner on a handful of occasions. But each time she had called it "fellowshipping." And although the evenings they had spent together in the hospital had been warm and wonderful, not one of them would qualify as an actual date. "A date," she whispered, her dimples deepening. "I think a first date with the man I promised to marry is a wonderful idea. What time?"

Greg swiftly glanced over his shoulder at Dawson.

"Eight o'clock," Geitler said.

"Eight o'clock," Greg echoed.

"Yes!"

"Thanks a lot, Andi," he said, raising his knuckles to lightly brush them across her flushed cheek. "I'll really look forward to it."

Her response was barely above a whisper as he bent his face nearer. "Me, too."

"Mr. Howland," Dawson interrupted insistently, "we *are* late."

Greg straightened and shook his head ruefully. "He says that a lot. I think I may have hired away Alice's White Rabbit." Taking a reluctant step backwards, he said, "See you tomorrow night, Andi."

She watched Greg follow his press agent across the parking lot and climb into the passenger side of the black compact car. As they pulled out of the lot, Andi raised a hand in farewell and wondered just how long it might take Greg to wrap up all his old business.

Dawson's car turned a corner and disappeared, leaving Andi to gaze forlornly down the empty street. *Finish up with the world soon, Greg,* she thought, allowing the hand to fall to her side. *Even the most beautiful quilt in the world isn't very comforting when it's designed for two, and I'm the only one wrapped up in it.*

Who was the masochist that designed the first tuxedo? Greg wondered as he fumbled with the small onyx button covers on the front of his starched white shirt. *And why haven't the men of the world outlawed the stupid things by now?* Finishing with the buttons, he searched the dresser top for cuff links. *For what you have to pay to go to one of these things, you ought to be able to wear sweats and sneakers.*

Still, he was grateful for tonight's invitation. If his appearance at the ball went according to plan and helped push through a trade with the Arizona Diamondbacks, the chance to look after his mother and see his fiancée more than twice in six months would be worth a fortune—not to mention a little discomfort.

His agent had laid the groundwork for the trade and now, no matter what it took in salary concessions, extra effort, and/or courting the big brass, Greg was determined to swing the deal. He'd made an early morning visit to Bank One Ballpark that day for a talent show of sorts before the Diamondbacks' manager, trainers, and pitching coach. After his hour-long workout, the field staff had done everything but genuflect. Greg had to admit that the command he felt on the mound and the triple-digit readings on the radar gun had surprised even him. If he'd ever doubted the significance of Bishop Ferris' ICU blessing, his faith in priesthood power was now certain. There was no earthly explanation for such an astonishing comeback.

Of course, the Cubs didn't know the results of the blessing and wouldn't believe it if he told them, so bartering a trade shouldn't be much of a problem from that standpoint. With a recent World Series pennant fluttering in the breeze above Waveland Avenue, the Cubs owners would be happy to pass a multi-million dollar gamble on to an expansion team. The wild cards who stood between him and a new locker location then were the trio of Arizona businesspeople who owned the Diamondback franchise. He needed to sell himself to Thaddeus' father and his associates tonight—literally as well as figuratively.

Fortunately, he had the best guy in the world on his side, Greg thought as he shrugged into his vest and surveyed the result in the mirror with satisfaction. Dawson Geitler was amazing. Who else could have gotten him to the ballpark, through three conference calls, and even to most of Thaddeus' chess tournament today and still come up with a limo and perfectly fitted tuxedo? If there was anything Dawson couldn't do, it wasn't in Greg's book.

Greg did wish, however, that Dawson had come up with one of those self-tied numbers for the bow tie. As he pulled out the crooked knot in frustration, Greg wondered why there wasn't a remedial Dress for Success Class offered for jocks with thick fingers and little patience. After another aborted attempt, he left the tie dangling around his neck, grabbed the silk jacket from the bed and started down the hall toward the living room. Maybe Sadie could help him with the stupid thing.

His mother was concentrating on the work in her hands as he dropped down into a chair opposite hers. "You look right nice, Greg," she said.

He wondered if she had seen him at all in the brief glance that she'd spared him. Greg's eyes followed hers to the project in her lap. There, nimble fingers worked quickly, unraveling thick yarn from a blue cardigan sweater. She had made the sweater herself, Greg knew, probably before he was born. Throughout his life, he had watched it serve as her only coat, even through the most bitter Iowa winters. It must have been among the few items she stuffed into the battered suitcase in her hurry to leave Peosta before Roy Howland left the local tavern.

Greg watched her pull out row after row of knitting, rolling the worn, kinky yarn into a tight ball. A pair of long, silver knitting needles lay ready on the side table. Though the task was obvious, her objective was unclear, so he asked what she was doing.

"We don't have potholders," Sadie responded matter-of-factly, her eyes never leaving her lap. "But that sweet little Laura Newton loaned me some needles so I could make us some."

"What?" Greg had raised his voice without realizing it and cringed when his mother did.

"I'm real sorry, Greg," she said hastily, a tremor shaking her already soft voice. "I know it's wrong to be beholden. I'll be real careful though and sit up to get these done tonight and the needles right back to Laura. Honest I will, Greg."

"Ma," he said, his voice so low now it was barely audible. "Ma, I'm sorry I yelled. It doesn't matter about the needles." How, he berated himself, could he have been stupid enough to believe himself the only victim of his father's explosive temper? Sadie still flinched every time the phone rang though Roy had yet to make any effort to contact them. Greg leaned forward cautiously, "I was just surprised, is all. You don't have to remake things out of your sweater. I can buy us a truckload of potholders if we want them."

"Reckon you can at that, Greg," Sadie said flatly as her fingers stilled atop the knotted yarn. "Reckon you can buy anything you want nowadays."

If that were true, he thought, looking pensively at his mother's worn, freckled hands, he'd buy her all the happiness she'd missed in life. Any money left over he'd spend on a little empathy and common sense for himself.

Since the day his mother had arrived in Arizona, she had been under the care of strangers. First the hospital staff, then the Reynolds family, had generously tried to anticipate and meet Sadie's every need. Finally, with the best of intentions, he had bought her this spotless, upscale isolation ward and left her alone in it for the most part, with nothing to do but feel like a burden. Only Laura Newton, Greg realized now, silently blessing the inspired visiting teacher, had seen what his mother truly craved: an opportunity to feel useful and needed herself.

He swallowed to clear the thickness from his throat and hoped he'd be able to say the right thing for once. "Ma, I just thought that blue yarn looked nice as your sweater," he began. "I always liked it on you." When Sadie's chin raised a fraction of an inch, he added, "But you know best."

"From what I hear, there's not much use for heavy sweaters here in the desert," she said timidly.

"From what I hear, you're right." Greg reached across her lap to pull a couple of rows from the garment himself and smiled when she slowly resumed the task. "In fact, when you finish with that, maybe you can knit me a pair of swim trunks and I'll try out that fancy lake we're paying so much for."

"I don't think it's for wadin', Greg—" she began, then saw his grin. "Oh you . . ." Her own lips trembled with the faintest hint of a smile.

"But I have been thinking," he continued hopefully, "that we ought to get something for Margaret Reynolds—to thank her for all her help. The trouble is, I haven't been able to come up with anything that would do. I don't want to put you out, but I can't help but think how much she'd love a handmade throw. You know, like that beautiful lacy thing you made for Jim and Bobbie Jo's wedding. If we got you some yarn and your own hooks maybe, do you think you might have the time to crochet something?"

He was rewarded with the first full view of his mother's face he'd seen in a week or more. "Honest, Greg? You reckon she'd like it?"

Greg felt a pang at the faint light in her eyes, realizing that he couldn't remember the last time he had seen it. "I honestly think she'd love it," he said.

"We could go for yarn then, I reckon," she nodded. "When you have the time."

"First thing Monday."

"When you can," Sadie insisted. "I've never seen a man so busy as you."

"Yarn's a top priority, I promise." As she nodded again, Greg looked around the room and wondered if his mother felt more like they were living in a magazine layout than a home. He frowned. As anxious as he was to please the Diamondback owners, and as glad as he was for the chance to finally spend some time with Andi, Greg still hated to press his mother between the pages of *House Beautiful* while he went out yet again. "I'm sorry to leave you all alone tonight—"

"Don't fret about me, Greg," Sadie replied quickly. "You know I couldn't be more tickled that you found yourself a girl like Andi."

Greg smiled gratefully. "Well, why don't you at least watch TV?" he suggested. "With all those channels on the dish, there ought to be something on you'd like."

Sadie worked silently for a minute at straightening the tangled yarn. Finally she admitted, "I don't know how to work the confangled thing."

"Oh," Greg said, rising quickly and looking around the room for the remote control. When he found it, he perched on the arm of her chair. "It's easy, Ma. You just point this at the TV and push the red button to turn it on or off. These arrows change the channels and volume. See?" Trying to demonstrate, Greg managed to tune in a split screen with two different programs and a timer in the upper corner, but no sound. "Uh, just a sec."

As he pressed more buttons, the tint turned green, words for the hearing impaired appeared at the bottom of one screen in Spanish, and the volume came on at a deafening decibel. Greg hit the off button quickly and frowned at the device in his palm. Finally, he tossed it into an empty chair and confessed, "I don't know how to work the confangled thing, either." At an unaccustomed sound, he looked down at his mother in astonishment. When was the last time he had heard her laugh? "I might be able to turn on a radio," he suggested with a grin. "Do we have one?"

"You go on now," Sadie said with a wave of her hand as the doorbell chimed. "Have a good time with your friends."

Greg walked across the room to the door. "Except for Andi, they're not exactly my friends." He pulled open the door expecting a chauffeur and stepped back in surprise. "Dawson? What are you doing here? Did you tell me you were coming?"

"Yes, Mr. Howland."

Maybe he was suffering short-term memory loss from the accident, Greg decided. He scanned Dawson's tuxedo—perfect bow tie and all—and noted that it fit as well as his own. "But you only left here an hour ago—"

"Fifty-two minutes, to be precise."

Greg frowned as he opened the door wider. "What have you got, Dawson, a Batcave somewhere?"

Geitler ignored the question. "I purchased three tickets to the ball in your name. If you would prefer I not accompany you—"

"No," Greg said quickly. "I'm glad you're here. You can tie a bow tie, right?"

"Of course."

"Of course. Hey," Greg said, with more enthusiasm, "I bet you can turn on a TV, too." At Dawson's look of disdain, he added quickly, "It's not as easy as it looks."

"We're—"

"Late," Greg supplied. "We're always late, White Rabbit. You fix the TV for my mother and I'll pay the speeding ticket, deal?" Greg smiled as Geitler stepped into the room with a sigh. He'd set the TV, Greg knew, and tie the tie and even pull some yarn out of a top hat if he had to. Except perhaps for making himself disappear, Dawson Geitler could do anything.

CHAPTER 13

Andi slipped her mother's formal gown over her head and let the shimmery fabric fall into soft folds over her curves. Her hair was already upswept, her makeup done, and the day's work soaked from her skin by a hyacinth-scented bubble bath. She closed her eyes as she turned toward the mirror, fearing to behold the ultimate truth. She'd certainly seen enough tabloid covers at the grocery store to know that Greg Howland was more accustomed to having a model on his arm than a zookeeper. Still, as she opened one eye then the next, she allowed herself a little smile. The antique ivory of the gown perfectly suited her own creamy complexion, and the fabric swirled deliciously as she made a quarter turn to examine herself from the side. *Not too bad,* she decided.

"Andi, you're beautiful!" Darlene proclaimed.

"You look like Cinderella!" Francie added. "'Cept you don't have glass slippers."

"No, sweetie," Andi laughed. "And I don't have a pumpkin carriage, either."

"Oh, Andi," Clytie breathed from atop her stool by the window where she had stationed herself as lookout, "you have something much better! Look!"

Andi joined her little sisters at the glass and drew in her breath at what she saw. A long, pearl-gray limousine gleamed under the street light in front of their house. A nattily uniformed chauffeur had just circled the front of the car to approach the house when the limo's rear door opened and Greg climbed out. Andi let out the breath in a soft sigh of delight when he called the driver back and came up the path to the door himself.

"Now that's a handsome prince," Clytie sighed. She looked up at Andi enviously. "I wish that *I* were Cinderella tonight."

"You're too silly, Clytie," Andi said affectionately, letting the curtain fall back into place. "I'm hardly Cinderella. My three sisters are the sweetest in the world, for one thing." She gave Darlene a quick little hug and planted a coral-colored kiss on Francie's forehead before picking up her beaded evening bag and casting Clytie a final wish-me-luck look.

Still, Andi thought, as she descended the staircase with as much grace as she could muster, considering that Greg stood at the foot with her parents, *I* am *on my way to an honest-to-goodness ball.* When he turned to look up at her with a dazzling, appreciative smile, Andi reached for the banister and felt a newfound empathy for the girl in the fairy tale. *If Cinderella felt anything like I do tonight, it's no wonder she lost her slipper,* she thought giddily. *I can scarcely keep my feet on the ground when Greg looks at me that way. I'd never manage to keep my toes in a slippery glass shoe.*

Greg extended his hand as she reached the bottom stair, and Andi's heart seemed to pause until her hand was safely in his. *Clytie's right,* she mused, gazing up into her love's handsome face. *Cinderella only* thought *she was marrying the real Prince Charming.*

But why does my prince always have to be accompanied by this annoying little henchman? Andi wondered in the limo as Dawson politely interrupted her again to point something out to Greg on the screen of his laptop computer. This time, it was an annotated list of the pros and cons of renewing a shoe contract.

Andi studied the press agent's face carefully. Try as she might, she couldn't bring herself to like Dawson Geitler. There was something insincere about him—sneaky even.

Greg flashed her an apologetic look as the business discussion continued, and Andi turned her attention to the plush interior of the car. *The TV/VCR probably works,* she thought. *Maybe I ought to watch a movie. Or perhaps I could ask to sit up front. The driver might not be too busy to talk to me. At the very least, he might let me change the radio station. This elevator music is driving me nuts.* Just as she was fiddling with the buttons on the door to try to open a window so she could perhaps scream her frustration into the night, Greg leaned back beside her and reached for her hand.

"So, now that I finally got you to agree to a first date with me, have I blown every chance for a second?" The gratitude and warmth in his eyes quickly melted Andi's frustration. "After Tuesday, of course," he added with a grin. To Dawson he explained, "Ordinarily Andi dates only temple-worthy Mormon men. I think she's making an exception with me tonight because she knows that in just three more days I can at least begin to qualify."

"About Tuesday night, sir—"

"Seven o'clock," Greg said.

"But—"

"My baptism's at seven." He held up a hand to halt Dawson's response. "I've already told you—Sunday morning and Tuesday night are non-negotiable." He turned to Andi. "I'm still trying to talk my mother into going to church with me tomorrow."

"About tomorrow—" Dawson interrupted.

"You keep forgetting the good news, Dawson," Greg said. "You have Sunday off. Monday, too."

"Not necessary."

"Off," Greg repeated. "Both days. The Cubs have offered me a car and driver to take us to church tomorrow and to my appointment at the hospital on Monday. Then I'm going to spend at least part of the afternoon messing up the house so my mother will have something to do Tuesday. Besides, after the hours we put in this week, we both deserve a break."

"Mr. Howland—"

"Dawson, look," Greg began, then realized the voice wasn't Dawson's and had come over the intercom from the driver's seat. "Uh, yeah?"

"We've reached our destination, sir."

"Oh. Great. Thanks." Greg reached for the door handle as the car came to a stop then, at the negative movement of Dawson's head, released it with a sigh. "I don't think I'll ever get used to this celebrity thing." He used the hand instead to stroke Andi's cheek. "Are you sure you're ready for this?"

"Yes," she said confidently. She'd been silly to feel the least bit insecure about the press conference and the TV spots. She knew Greg loved her and was as anxious as she was to put all this behind them when they were married.

As the door on her side swung open toward the carpeted curb, Andi glanced back at him with a self-assured smile. "Of course I'm ready."

Of course she was wrong. Nothing in her dreams could have prepared her for the press of people lining the walkway outside or for the glitz, glamour, and grandeur of the Pavilions Ballroom itself. Blinking rapidly, Andi couldn't decide if she was seeing stars or just the flashing after-effects of more than a dozen flashbulbs.

Fortunately, she thought, gripping Greg's arm as if tethered in place, *you were wrong as well.* Except for a very obvious aversion to paparazzi, there was nothing in his demeanor to suggest that Greg Howland was less than adept at what he had called the "celebrity thing."

Their trio quickly became a foursome when Joe McKay, a stocky, middle-aged man with a walrus mustache, stationed himself at Greg's right and ably cleared the way through the crowd toward three people he seemed intent for the young ballplayer to meet. If anyone had mentioned to her who McKay was, Andi had missed it. She caught on quickly however that the triumvirate for whom he worked was a force to be reckoned with. They must be the people Greg hoped to impress.

The tiny, elderly woman in the center might have been eclipsed by the statures of her two male companions if not for her innate strength of presence. Perhaps it was the diamonds glittering at her earlobes and throat and weighing down her wrinkled fingers that first caught one's attention, Andi thought, but it was her stately bearing and haughty look that held it. The way Lillian Dresmont extended her hand like Old World royalty made Andi suspect she had intended for Greg to kiss it. That he had taken the freckled fingers gently with his most charming smile must have sufficed however, since she granted him a benevolent nod in return.

The man introduced as Gerald Brock was tall, dark-skinned, and courtly in manner. Andi liked him instinctively when he greeted them warmly and welcomed Greg to the Valley.

The second man was shorter, probably in his early forties, and oddly familiar. As Andi tried to remember where they might have met, she almost missed McKay's introduction of Cleon Bisher. Recovering quickly from her surprise, Andi extended her hand to Thaddeus' father. "Hello, Brother Bisher."

She watched Cleon's face harden at the curious looks he received from his associates and, too late, Andi realized her mistake. This was no Relief Society social. She looked sheepishly up at Greg. If he had noticed her faux pas, he gave no indication.

Instead, he extended his own hand cordially. "Nice to finally meet you, sir. I had thought I might see you at Thaddeus' chess tournament today."

Cleon Bisher pointedly ignored Greg's hand. "Young man, allow me to congratulate you. You are beyond doubt the smoothest operator I've come across."

Could he mean Greg? Andi wondered.

Clearly, Greg wondered the same. "Excuse me?"

"There is no excuse for someone like you," Bisher said disdainfully. "How low do you have to be to use a sick boy to get what you want?"

Although Andi was so stunned she dropped Greg's arm, he responded calmly, "Thaddeus and I met by coincidence, sir, but now I'd say that we're friends."

"I didn't get where I am by being stupid," Bisher shot back. "You and I both know that even before that accident you were washed up in baseball."

Greg's shoulders squared. "I don't believe that, Mr. Bisher. I intend to fulfill my contract this year."

Before turning his back, Bisher said coldly, "Then see that you do it in Chicago."

Andi and at least a dozen others watched Thaddeus' father stalk away. After a moment's pause, Brock followed. Overtaking Cleon, he grasped the younger man's elbow to pull him to a stop as he spoke earnestly in his ear.

Joe McKay had turned to Greg, his ruddy face dazed and apologetic. He opened his mouth, but no words came out.

"Now Joseph, don't have a stroke," Mrs. Dresmont said severely, waving a heavily jeweled hand in front of the Diamondback manager's face before resting it possessively on Greg's arm. "Cleon is a minority partner. I run this team and I always get what *I* want." She released Greg's elbow to take a step back to assess the merchandise. After looking him over carefully, she nodded. "I rather like the looks of him. Perhaps you'll get that new acquisition you want so badly, Joseph. Mightn't he, Mr. Howland?"

"Uh, yes, ma'am," Greg said. "I hope so."

Mrs. Dresmont nodded again then raised a finger as though motioning to a servant. She said, "Come along with me now, Joseph. We'll let the dust settle then have a little chat with Gerald and Cleon."

"What was that all about?" Andi asked as Lillian Dresmont walked regally away with McKay in attendance.

Greg shook his head. "I'm not sure I understood all of it myself."

"Well," Andi continued, reassured at Greg's apparent confusion and wondering why Greg had wanted to meet these people in the first place. "It's no wonder Thaddeus is politeness-challenged. Cleon Bisher is horrid."

Greg's voice was thoughtful. "I don't agree," he said slowly. "In fact, I'm sorry to have misjudged him. It's clear that he loves his son very much."

"It isn't clear to me," Andi declared, taking Greg's arm again. "Thaddeus is crazy about you, Greg. I'd think his father would be eternally grateful for the interest you've taken in him."

"You don't understand, Andi," Greg explained. "Mr. Bisher thinks that I want to use Thaddeus to get to him."

"Get to him how?" Andi asked. Could Greg possibly mean that he wanted to play ball for the Diamondbacks? She had heard him tell Cleon that he intended to fulfill his contract this year, of course, but she had scarcely believed his words. Why would anyone want to continue to pitch after surviving such a serious and frightening accident? "Isn't it too soon to even talk about baseball, Greg?" she continued reasonably. "The doctors haven't . . ." Her words trailed off at Dawson's approach and she sighed in vexation. *Here that man is back before I even had time to be grateful he was gone.*

Greg was so intent on Andi's words that he hadn't noticed his press agent. "Andi, I have a contract. At least I'd be in Arizona—"

"Excuse us, Mr. Howland."

Not only had Dawson returned, he'd brought along a stunning platinum blonde in a slinky black sheath. At least, Andi was willing to grant the woman the benefit of the doubt she was even wearing a dress; it looked more like some kind of fabric spray paint.

The society reporter extended five dazzling, red-tipped fingers to Greg and gushed, "Elise Etherbridge from *About Town.* How enchanting to finally meet you!"

"Hello," Greg said warily.

From the look on his face, Andi suspected Greg already knew Elise, at least by her reputation. She wondered if this was the gossip columnist who had written about him and Hollywood starlet, Jacy Grayson. Probably so. Elise would almost *have* to make up her stories, Andi surmised. There certainly wasn't anywhere on her person to carry a pencil, let alone a steno pad for accurate notes. Andi gripped Greg's arm tighter.

Apparently, it got his attention. He stammered, "And this is, uh—"

"Ariadne Reynolds," Andi supplied, alarmed that Greg might forget her name in light of all that stunning cleavage.

Elise cocked her head coyly, flicking her eyes at Andi, and back to Greg. "And who is she?"

"Andi Reynolds," Greg repeated with obvious reluctance, looking helplessly at Dawson.

"I heard that, dearheart," Elise said with a smile, "but every woman in the room wants to know who she *is*. When my Monday column hits the streets, every woman in town—if not the country—will be asking."

Unsettled at Greg's sudden lack of confidence—and color—Andi squeezed his elbow again. First it had been Jill, the hospital nurse, then Francie's teacher, and now Elise Etherbridge. The appeal of a secret engagement was dwindling by the second. *Say that I'm the love of your life*, she urged silently. *Or say that I'm your best friend.* Still, he hesitated, his eyes on his press agent. *Say* something!

"Miss Reynolds is a friend of the family," Dawson supplied smoothly. "She graciously agreed to accompany Mr. Howland to the ball tonight to divert gossip from his current romantic entanglement."

Elise clasped her hand together in delight. "Oh! Do tell! Are you still seeing Jacy?"

Andi glanced at Greg then quickly away from the look of gratitude and admiration on his face as he regarded his press agent. She gazed instead over his head into the twinkling crystals of the chandelier as she tried to sort out her jumbled emotions.

While she *didn't* want to be tomorrow's gossip and was grateful that Greg wanted to protect her, she felt strangely discounted. It was one thing to have Dawson give such a glib explanation and another to have it so readily accepted. Clearly, this society columnist didn't consider her Greg Howland's type.

Greg loves me, she reminded herself. *We are going to be married and blissfully happy, and I will never see this woman again, so why should it matter what she thinks?* But although her reason told her one thing, her heart ached at the other—a seemingly effortless dismissal from Greg's life.

"I'm sure Dawson can tell you everything you want to know," Greg said, casting his publicist a get-rid-of-her look as he steered Andi in another direction. "Nice to meet you, Miss Etherbridge."

They hadn't gone two steps when a new group approached, and Andi forced herself to smile through more meaningless introductions. At least, she hoped her lips were turned upward as her heart seemed to sink to the proximity of where her glass slippers were supposed to be. This should have been the most beautifully romantic night of her life, she thought, raising her face back toward the chandelier to keep the few tears from running down her cheeks. But the situation seemed to demand that her Prince Charming treat her more like a business partner than a princess. *So much for my night at the ball.*

"Would you like to dance?" a quiet voice intruded on her thoughts, and Andi lowered her eyes in surprise.

"I'm not great at it," Greg admitted quickly, clearly puzzled at the sparkling of tears apparent in Andi's eyes, "but I did date a dance instructor for a little while."

Yes, you did, Andi thought, remembering again the tabloids, *and an Olympic ice skater and a former Miss America and who-knows-who-else. How did you ever end up with me?*

"Please?"

More people were coming their way now, Andi noted, and there was no way she could manage another smile without first coating her teeth with Vaseline. She nodded briefly and allowed Greg to take her hand to lead her to the dance floor.

The throng didn't part for their first dance as it had in the ballroom scene from Cinderella, but Andi couldn't have felt more conspicuous if they had. Surely, the eyes boring into her back as Greg took her into his arms had counted every stitch in her gown and passed judgment on the heart-shaped mole behind her left ear. She stared steadfastly into his starched shirt, trying to avoid meeting any of the eyes as he moved her smoothly across the floor. (Was it the floor? It seemed they were above it somehow.) And Greg had taken more than one lesson from the dance instructor, Andi observed with a curious mixture of dismay and delight.

"A man invented dancing, you know," he said. "Maybe you've heard the story, with your father's background in Greek mythology and all."

Greg seemed relaxed to her now and more like himself than he had all evening. As he pulled her a little closer, Andi concentrated on breathing and forestalling the collapse of her increasingly weak knees. "No."

"Then I'll tell you about it," he offered, his voice low so that only she could hear. "It happened a long time ago at the foot of Mount Olympus. The mortals were gathered for a party like this one. Don't ask me why," he interrupted himself with a grin. "I guess these things are just one of the trials of mortality. Anyway, there was one guy there who just couldn't take his eyes off a certain young woman on the far side of the Parthenon. No matter who spoke to him or how loud the orchestra played their music of the spheres, all this poor guy could think about was that beautiful girl with red-gold hair and big eyes the color of . . . alligators."

Even if she *had* been able to speak, Andi would never have told Greg that the Parthenon wasn't built for parties and there wasn't an alligator within a thousand miles of Athens. Instead, she lay her cheek against his chest and listened to his warm, husky voice as he continued.

"Well, a man couldn't just walk across a room and take the girl in his arms like this—not without calling down the Furies, at least. Fortunately, he was inspired by . . . Who was the goddess of wisdom, again?"

"Pallas Athena," Andi said. "The party was at her house."

"Really?" Greg said. "I guess I *did* learn something in those college lit classes—and people think jocks don't pay attention." Preparing to conclude his tale with a flourish, he added, "So, Athena inspired the desperate guy with a brilliant idea to get the girl—and he called it dancing."

Andi waited a few moments for her head to clear then asked, "Did the dance teacher tell you that story?"

"Who? Oh, no. I was kinda inspired myself." The orchestra had finished its number, but Greg's arm tightened around Andi's slender waist. "A myth has to start with someone, you know. Dance with me again," he whispered.

Is the world spinning faster, Andi wondered, *or is it only the room?* As the music began and she nestled her head against Greg's chest, she thought again of that silly Cinderella. Right now a hundred clocks could strike midnight, the limo could turn into a pumpkin, and her dress could fall to rags while every person in the room transformed into a scurrying white mouse, and Andi wouldn't take a moment's notice. Cinderella might have been easily enough distracted to run out on *her* prince, but Andi Reynolds was smarter than that. As long as she and Greg could be together this way—if only for a few moments—she wasn't going anywhere.

CHAPTER 14

The noisy hands-on pavilion at the zoo was fifteen miles from the Hilton Pavilions—and it seemed as many light years away. On that starry Saturday night, Andi, dressed in a flowing, ivory gown, had danced with Greg until she felt she was flying. Yesterday, she had worn her best dress and sat blissfully beside him in sacrament meeting. Now, it was a sunny Monday afternoon and Andi was back in khaki, trying to keep her thoughts on the assorted rainforest insects in her charge and the even more numerous school children flocked around them.

But thoughts can be contrary and worry caused her to glance frequently at her watch. Greg had his final check-up today. *He must be at the hospital by now*, she observed. *He won't be here for a couple more hours, at least.* She said a quick prayer—to reinforce the dozens of previous petitions that the doctors would find him well—then added another prayer for Clytie, who was celebrating an early release day from school by exploring the zoo with Thaddeus.

Andi wished the teens had waited until summer to come. Today was a Bluebird Day, dubbed as such by the zoo staff for the Bluebird school buses that snaked in long lines around the parking lot. With school winding down for the year, every elementary class in the state seemed to have chosen this destination for a field trip. As she closed her prayer, Andi knew that God was the only one who could keep Clytie from being hurt by the thoughtless, and sometimes cruel, remarks that were often directed her way.

Despite her concerns, Andi smiled at the approach of a curious child who now stuck one small finger toward the saltshaker-sized creature in her hand. "It's called a hissing cockroach," she said, leaning forward to better display the squirming bug before launching into her well-rehearsed routine about it and the other small tropic-dwellers currently in her care. As familiar as the spiel was, Andi never tired of giving it. This had to the best job on earth, she thought. After all, where else would you be able to spend the day outdoors, marveling at the miraculous creation of animals and the boundless joy and enthusiasm of the children who had come to see them? So, despite her concern for Greg and Clytie, Andi's afternoon teaching the school children about the creatures in her charge would keep her more than adequately distracted.

"There's only one meerkat sitting outside of the tunnels," Clytie reported to Thaddeus, who leaned against one of the tall, concrete "anthills" that fronted this popular exhibit along the African Trail.

"He's the guard," Thaddeus replied. "Meerkats are fascinating creatures. They're one of nature's most social and cooperative animals. They take turns guarding the colony, babysitting the offspring, and gathering food."

Clytie gazed up at him in admiration over everything he knew. When she had wondered aloud why zebras were black and white striped, he had told her that when a zebra herd is under attack the wildly moving lines confuse the predator and protect the zebras. Thaddeus was just so smart. She tried to think now what she might know to interest him.

"I remember when these meerkats first came to the Phoenix Zoo," Clytie said. "They were from Africa and they hadn't seen humans before. They all stuck together and stared back at the crowd."

"But they lost interest in people after a while?"

"Uh huh," she said. "Before very long they stopped worrying about who was looking or pointing and went on with their lives."

"I guess that proves Walt Disney's theory," Thaddeus declared. "Animals *are* smarter than people."

Clytie shot him a quick look of concern. Did Thaddeus somehow perceive the curious stares they'd received since walking in the front gate with Andi? More likely, she realized, with his other senses heightened by blindness, he'd probably overheard pointed comments that she, thankfully, had missed. Her pretty face set determinedly as she reached up to take the hand without the cane. She didn't care what people thought or said about either of them. She was who she was—a Little Person—and Thaddeus was who he was—a smart and perceptive, if blind, young man. She liked him more than she had ever liked a boy. More important even, he was quickly becoming her best friend. Spending time with him was worth any possible threat to her pride.

Thaddeus squeezed her hand. "You and me, Clytie—a couple of human meerkats, right?"

"Yes!" Clytie agreed happily, leading the way down the asphalt path. If those little animals could ignore the inquisitive crowds, certainly she could as well. After all, this *was* her first date. "The Baboon Kingdom is next," she told Thaddeus, reading aloud from the sign.

"Baboon Kingdom? Who's the king?"

"Umm, probably that big guy sitting in the middle of the grass. All the females are gathered around grooming him."

"What a life," Thaddeus said wryly. "Remind me to tell Greg we ran into his simian counterpart this afternoon."

Although unable to stifle a giggle, Clytie said, "Why do you always give Greg such a hard time?"

Thaddeus shrugged. "Somebody has to keep his head in the same zip code as the rest of him."

"Well, I don't think Greg's conceited—" Clytie began, hoping not to have to choose between her fierce loyalty to Greg and her blossoming love for Thaddeus, over such an offhand remark.

"Hey, I know," Thaddeus agreed quickly. "I told you that he and that goon who follows him around came to my chess tournament on Saturday afternoon. That's a lot more than my father managed. *He* sent his executive secretary along with me so he could get ready for some big shindig that night."

"It was a ball!" Clytie offered eagerly. "Andi and Greg met your father there." She paused, having now told Thaddeus as much as she knew herself. Andi had been surprisingly unwilling to share any details about meeting Cleon Bisher. "Didn't your dad tell you?"

"No," Thaddeus replied, "but behold the ultimate truth: he isn't interested enough to remember my friends' names in the first place. And that dance was a business deal for him, like everything else."

"Oh, but it must have been so beautiful!" Clytie declared rapturously. "Like some kind of wonderful dream, and Andi was simply breathtaking. Francie said that she looked like Cinderella and she did! Oh, I wish it could have been me, Thaddeus!" She stopped self-consciously, then added quickly, "Of course, I'd never look like Cinderella—or be invited to a ball, either. I haven't even been asked to prom." She turned her head away, though Thaddeus couldn't possibly see the pink spots of regret that stained her cheeks.

Thaddeus was quiet for a long moment, then let the strap tether his cane to his wrist as he put both hands firmly on Clytie's shoulders and pointed his earnest face in the direction of hers. "You know, Clytie," he said finally, "Thumbelina was every bit as pretty as Cinderella, and there was a prince waiting for her, too."

Clytie's lower lip trembled as she blinked back happy tears. She had read every fairy tale ever written and, more recently, dozens and dozens of romances, before finally buying *How to Catch a Man,* in the hopes of bringing at least one of her fantasies to life—a date for the prom. If she had learned anything from these varied sources, it was that virtually every successful romantic heroine was willowy, graceful, and witty, and that their gallant heroes were . . . well . . . they were like Greg. But as she looked up now into Thaddeus' pale, thin face, Clytie thought that no book had been written with a hero that could make a girl's heart beat faster than hers did now.

Greg let out a long sigh as he drummed on the seat cushion between his legs. Hating the pretension of the limo the Cubs had sent for his short shopping excursion with his mother and then the longer ride to the hospital, he had elected to take a taxi to meet Andi at the zoo. Now seated in a small, smelly cab, he felt cooped up like some kind of livestock being driven to market. When he considered it, he admired the apt analogy. Released by the doctors as of Friday to return to baseball, he now had less than a week to get himself sold into the Arizona bullpen or he was on his way back to Chicago, the former livestock capital of the world.

Greg leaned forward to peer out the front windshield at the desert sky. It was as clear and blue as a picture from *Arizona Highways*. More than ever he missed his leased convertible and the sense of freedom it had given him. Unconsciously, he increased the drumbeat.

"You want I should stop somewhere?" the driver asked with a long look in the rearview mirror.

Greg looked out the side window. The Phoenix neighborhood they were passing through was likely one of the least picturesque in town. He strongly suspected that the only motorists who stopped on this street drove patrol cars. "Uh, no, thanks."

"You want I should drive faster?"

The graffiti-marked palm trees lining the avenue seemed to whiz by as it was and had already prompted Greg to offer a prayer for protection for themselves and any errant pedestrian they might encounter. "No," he said quickly, "no faster."

"You're that baseball player, aren't ya?" the driver asked. "The guy with brain damage."

Greg caught the man's suspicious look in the mirror. "Which would account for me pounding on your seat like a madman, right?" He quit drumming. "Sorry." He almost had to sit on his hands, though, to keep them still as his claustrophobia grew. Maybe he could amuse himself with Francie's alphabet game.

Looking for an A, he thought. *There's one—Honest Abel's Used Autos.* A sudden inspiration caused Greg to examine the run-down lot more closely. A split-rail fence lined the inside perimeter, just inside a ten-foot chain-link fence topped by rolls of razor wire. The sales office was a beat-up trailer with a ridiculous faux-log exterior. *They've got to be kidding.* Imprudently, Greg unclicked his seatbelt as they passed and turned around hoping to get a glimpse of Honest Abel, himself—perhaps in a long, black coat and stovepipe hat. "Hey!" he said suddenly, "Stop here, okay?"

The driver took him at his word, causing Greg's still-turned head to impact first with the headrest, then the back windshield. Greg pulled the bill of his cap from over his eyes. *If I didn't have brain damage before, this should cinch it.* "Thanks," he said a little shakily. "What do I owe you?"

"You sure I should let ya out here?" the driver asked. Greg was already opening the door. "Want me to wait for you?"

"No, that's okay." Greg pulled a bill from his wallet and extended it through the open window. "Will this cover it?" As the driver pulled away, Greg jogged the block back to Honest Abel's.

On the lot, he strolled between the rows of cars deliberating if it would be most fitting to kick a tire, lift a hood, or give up this stupid idea and call another taxi. What did he know about buying a car anyway? Though his brother had taught him to drive on the back roads in Iowa, he hadn't applied for a license until his college years when he was working enough hours to perhaps afford insurance in the not-too-distant future. Still, his first and only cars had come after signing with the Cubs—leased or offered gratis so that they could be sold a few months later with his name attached.

You don't know anything about buying a car, he told himself again. On the other hand, he reasoned, these machines barely qualified for the name. Most likely they were berthed here at Honest Abel's en route to the salvage yard. Greg's confidence rose. He had plenty of experience with wrecks; he was the son of Iowa's least prosperous auto mechanic, after all.

By the time a salesman approached (who was neither the image of Abe nor of honesty), Greg had found an open-air vehicle that looked like it belonged in the Arizona desert and suited him perfectly. He doubted, however, that anyone at this place would have ever heard of him *or* American Express and wondered if they would take a personal check. As he surveyed the wreck of choice again, he grinned. Likely, he had enough cash in his pocket to complete the transaction.

Chapter 15

Two hours and two hundred children later, Andi gave a tired smile and a wave to the last group of first graders, who had reluctantly left the fuzzy black-and-orange bird-eating spider only at the insistence of a harried mother-helper. The spider, Andi observed, was busy burying itself in the bark of its exhibit, probably as relieved as she was that their workday was over.

Andi shifted the cockroach to her right hand to consult her watch. Where were Clytie and Thaddeus? They were supposed to meet her and Greg here at two. She stood for a better view and was surprised to note the approach of a familiar, dark-haired young man. He was about the last person in the world she'd expect to see at a zoo.

"Sterling!" she called. "What are you doing here?"

He glanced over his shoulder as he approached the kiosk, obviously pleased that no one else was around. "We need to talk, Andi."

"Here?" she asked. "I'm working." She held up the hissing cockroach for proof and suppressed a smile when Sterling took a quick step back.

"Don't you get off at two?"

"Yes, but I have plans."

Sterling grimaced. "Howland?"

"And Clytie and her friend."

"Well, Howland is what we need to talk about." He moved marginally closer. "Andi, you have to appreciate my patience about this whole—"

"I do," she said quickly, willing to grant Sterling patience as a virtue. Truly, one of many virtues. He was also intelligent, reliable and, despite a tendency to be a little overzealous, unequivocally committed to the gospel. In fact, Andi thought, the only thing she had against Sterling as far as marriage material went was that he wasn't Greg.

"I think I've been very patient," Sterling repeated, "through this whole girlhood infatuation of yours. I mean," he amended quickly as Andi's green eyes narrowed, "what *woman* wouldn't be flattered by Howland's attention?" Pausing for a moment to better gather his thoughts, he pressed on, "You *know* what I mean, Andi. Why do you think he even came to church yesterday?"

"Because he believes in the gospel," she said firmly, "and wants to be baptized."

Greg had come to sacrament meeting for the right reasons, Andi reflected, and had received what was perhaps the warmest reception ever accorded an investigator. He hadn't actually autographed Sunday programs, of course, but he did shake almost every hand in the congregation at the end of the block. He might be standing in the foyer yet if Bishop Ferris hadn't ushered them into his office and turned on the "Do Not Disturb" light until his second counselor reported that the building had finally cleared out.

During that office visit, they had discussed the gospel and Andi had been amazed—as she had been when he read the Book of Mormon in a weekend—at Greg's thirst for knowledge. He and the bishop spoke mostly about temple work, and while Andi knew that much of the ardent light that had come into Greg's eyes was in anticipation of their eternal marriage, a bit more had to do with his near-death experience. He had told her little about it yet, but she would not be surprised to learn that she wasn't the only one counting on his conversion.

Sterling was still clearly skeptical. "But surely you don't believe Howland's serious—"

"Serious? Well, nobody's as serious as you are Sterling, but—" Andi caught herself in mid-sentence. She wasn't a tease by nature and this was as opportune time as any to tell him about their engagement. She'd get right to the point. "You see—"

"I see all too well," Sterling interrupted. "In fact, I may be the *only* one who sees how Howland's using the Church." Misinterpreting the shocked look on Andi's face, he hastened to explain. "Don't feel bad, Andi. It's easy enough to be deceived, especially when you want to believe that people are doing things for the right reason. You have to remember that lots of celebrities join off-beat religions just to get their names in the paper."

Andi couldn't suppress a giggle. "Does Bishop Ferris know that you consider the gospel of Jesus Christ an off-beat religion?"

Sterling frowned in irritation. "You know perfectly well what I mean. At best, Howland's so-called conversion will be a flash-in-the-pan kind of thing—like his romancing a naive young girl like you."

"Well, thank you, Sterling," Andi said coolly. Suddenly, she didn't feel nearly as much like confiding in her former boyfriend.

Sterling's face softened. "Andi, you're misconstruing my words on purpose. I'm trying to point out that leopards don't change their spots. You're too trusting and I don't want to see you be hurt."

Andi stroked the cockroach. "Thanks for your concern, Sterling, but—"

"Will you please put that disgusting thing away," he interrupted. "How can you even stand to touch it?"

Instead of putting it back, Andi allowed the bug a little leeway to crawl over the top of her hand before capturing it again and smiling innocently at Sterling. "Didn't you see bugs as big as him in South America?"

Sterling rolled his eyes. "Yes, and we squashed them."

"I hope you didn't hear that," Andi told the cockroach. To Sterling, she said with mock accusation, "You could have been talking about some of his Peruvian cousins."

"Andi," Sterling said, barely containing his exasperation, "you know I hate your tendency toward anthropomorphism."

"Her what?" Clytie asked Thaddeus as they rounded the corner from the back of the pavilion.

"'Tendency toward anthropomorphism,'" Thaddeus repeated. "In this case, it means talking to bugs like they were people. Usually, it's used as a big word for dissing Disney movies."

Andi wondered how long they had been on the other side of the exhibit and how much they had heard. She felt the color rise to her cheeks at Clytie's pointed look. Why hadn't she just come right out and told Sterling when she had the chance?

"Sterling Channing," she said quickly to cover the awkward silence, "this is Thaddeus Bisher. He's a friend of Clytie's."

"And Greg's," the young man added.

Though it was difficult to be sure from Thaddeus' lack of expression, Andi perceived his words as directed toward her and colored more deeply.

"Anyway, Sterling—" Thaddeus continued, "—you don't mind if I call you Sterling, do you? I hope you're not disparaging Greg with the insects today in an effort to court Andi yourself. I mean, I'd hate to see a person waste his time on something that's just not meant to be. Surely, a bright young man like you can recognize the hand of Providence."

Sterling, Andi noted, looked politely bored, but Clytie hung on Thaddeus' every word.

"How long have you known the Reynolds?" the boy continued.

"All my life," Sterling announced as if defending his right to Andi.

Thaddeus nodded. "Then you've certainly had time to catch on."

Sterling was obviously irritated at this interruption. "Catch on to what?" he said, with a peevish note in his voice.

"Come on, Sterling," Thaddeus smiled, "say the Reynolds kids' names with me: Andi, Brad, Clytie, Darlene," he recited, emphasizing the first letter of each name. "You notice a pattern developing there? Let me finish it up for you: Enos, Francie—*Greg*. It's kismet."

Sterling was nonplussed, but Clytie was dazzled and delighted. "Then Brad marries a Hilary—"

"Yes," Thaddeus agreed, then affected a deep sigh as he melodramatically clasped a hand to his heart, "but poor you, Clytie! That sticks you with–uh—Ignatius. Do you happen to know any Iggys?" Andi couldn't help but smile as her sister giggled at Thaddeus' antics. They all turned as someone approached the kiosk. "Is that you, Iggy?" Thaddeus called out.

"Sorry, no," Greg said, pulling up the brim of his Phoenix Suns cap for better light. It was difficult to tell what he might be thinking behind the mirrored lenses of his sunglasses, but he appeared to be looking at Sterling. "Who's Iggy?"

"Allow me to explain," Thaddeus offered enthusiastically.

"No!" Andi and Sterling said in unison.

Greg looked from one to the other with the beginning of a frown. "Obviously, I've missed something here."

In her happiness to see Greg, Andi had loosened her grasp on her six-legged charge. Sensing its chance, the cockroach scurried between her fingers and up her arm. Unnerved, Andi couldn't suppress a cry of dismay.

Greg grabbed the bug in less than a second. Holding it gingerly, he raised it to eye level for a better view. One sandy eyebrow rose. "Are you hissing at me, little guy?"

Clytie and Andi giggled—mostly at the look on Sterling's face.

"I can see that I didn't choose a good time to talk, Andi," Sterling said. It was hard to tell if the look of disdain he cast Greg was directed at him or at the bug. "But you think about what I said and we'll get together soon."

As Channing walked away, Greg said to the cockroach, "That guy would have a tough time choosing which of the two of us he likes best."

"Well, I like you best," Andi assured him.

"Better than him?" Greg asked hopefully, motioning with his chin after Sterling. "Or better than the bug?"

"Both."

Greg grinned. "Are you sure?"

"Well, I'm not absolutely certain," Andi admitted, reclaiming the cockroach. "The bug *is* kinda cute." She opened the door to its habitat. "And he's certainly easier to keep track of than you are."

"Yeah, but can he take you out to lunch in his new car?" Greg said.

"New car?" Andi asked, her heart beating faster as she realized that her prayers for him had apparently been answered, "Does that mean—?"

"Yep," Greg nodded, "the doctors gave me a clean bill of health. I can work. I can play. I can stand on my head if I want to. Can your bug do any of that?"

Andi grasped Greg's arm euphorically. "Not at all," she teased, "but Sterling Channing can do it all and more, Howland, so until that day you take me to the temple, you'd still better watch your step."

Chapter 10

"What do you think of my new Jeep?" Greg asked as Andi, Thaddeus and Clytie gathered around the auto.

"It's new?" Clytie asked doubtfully.

"It wasn't new in 1980," Andi declared, taking her eyes off the car only long enough to cast Greg a bewildered look. Had he bought it as a joke? It certainly looked like one. Smiling uncertainly, she added, "And a better question, Clytie, is if there were any survivors of its last wreck."

"Don't listen to her, Thaddeus," Greg said, with an obvious effort to suppress a grin of his own. He ran a hand fondly across the hood. "It's a classic."

"What color is it?" Thaddeus asked.

"Red."

"That's rust," Andi pointed out sweetly.

Greg tried to affect a look of wounded honor. "No, it's not." But he looked away as he ran his hand down the side of his jean leg, hoping to remove the Jeep's oxidation from his palm. Then, turning deliberately toward his most dependable ally, he asked, "Clytie, what do *you* think?"

"I think it's, well, it's . . . it's—awesome!" In Clytie's eyes, anything Greg said, did or had *must* be awesome. Although, as she remembered her ride in the dreamy white convertible he used to drive, she honestly couldn't imagine what he saw in this thing.

"See?" Greg told Andi as he gave Clytie an affectionate, conspiratorial wink. "Your sister's with me. You're not recognizing its potential."

Andi pushed her hair back over her shoulder, her green eyes dancing. "You mean the potential it gives you to kill yourself, or the potential you'll have to spend all your time at the side of the road waiting for a mechanic?"

"That's one of the best things about it!" Greg defended his car. "I can fix it myself."

"Didn't some optimist say the same thing about Humpty Dumpty?" Thaddeus asked.

"Hey!" Greg objected, "Really, I can. My father's a mechanic, you know."

Andi certainly would never mention the acre of inoperative, abandoned autos that she knew surrounded Greg's childhood home. Instead, she eyed the Jeep's chipped and dented roll bar and pointed out, "It doesn't even have a top, Greg."

"That's another of the best things about it."

Thaddeus let out a little hoot. "Never been to Phoenix in July, have you?"

"No, but—"

"Don't worry," Thaddeus smiled. "The mercury rarely tops a hundred and twenty-two. And it sometimes gets as cool as a hundred and three in the shade."

"You're talking *degrees*?" Greg asked incredulously.

"Yeah, but it's a dry heat."

"Meaning?"

Thaddeus shrugged. "Meaning you'll be able to fry an egg on the driver's seat."

"Well, it's nice out today," Clytie interjected quickly. "Why don't we all ride in it to the restaurant?" She almost wiggled in pleasure at Greg's grateful smile. Sure, he was taking their ribbing good-naturedly, but still she worried that his feelings might be hurt. Her eyes left Greg for the Jeep only when her reasonable sister asked if it had seatbelts.

"Well, the lap belts in front are almost decent," Greg responded, "but the back ones are kinda chewed up. I'm going to replace them—"

"Chewed by animals?" Clytie asked with wide aqua eyes.

"Well, that's what it looks like, but—"

"Don't worry, Clytie," Andi interjected with a giggle. "Those animals are probably extinct by now." She turned back to Greg and marveled at the odd relationship between men and their cars. What had Greg been thinking to *buy* such a piece of junk? Couldn't he have satisfied the craving with a visit to Rent-a-Wreck?

"Hey," Greg said. "A little respect would be appreciated. Wait 'til you ride in it."

"I can hardly wait," Andi said, "but I, um, I have my car here." She smiled meaningfully at Greg. "Unfortunately."

"Yeah, I can see just how bad you feel about it." He turned to Clytie. "But you're riding with me?"

"Well, it *is* kinda high for me to get in," she replied evasively, still pondering what kind of animals might have been hauled around in the thing. "Maybe I'd better go with Andi."

"Hey, I'll ride with you, Greg," Thaddeus volunteered. "After all," he explained to Clytie, "it's not as terrifying if you can't see what you're getting in to."

Though Greg gave Thaddeus a gentle shove, he finally recognized defeat. After making sure the youth was settled, Greg climbed in on his own side and leaned down toward Andi. "Well, okay," he said, "but you girls really don't know what you're missing."

"Maybe not," Andi responded with affection, "but we can see what *you're* missing, Greg: a roof, two seatbelts, three hubcaps, a knob on your gear shift, most of the upholstery—" she reached up to tap two fingers gently in the center of his forehead "—and apparently more of your brain cells than the doctors suspect."

Windy City was a squat stucco building wedged between a tire shop and a filling station not far from the Phoenix Zoo. It boasted the best BBQ west of Chicago and was, Andi noted with dismay, exactly the wrong place to have brought Greg. The walls were covered with Cubs pictures—several of Greg—and other memorabilia of the team's near-century in baseball. She had come here often with friends from the zoo. How had she missed taking in the decor?

She looked now at the young pitcher who, even with sunglasses and hat firmly in place, didn't dare to raise his face high enough to look at the order board. "Are you sure we shouldn't go someplace else?" she whispered.

"Are you kidding?" he said, tipping his ear toward Clytie to better hear her read aloud from the posted menu. "The food smells great."

"But can you imagine what will happen if someone here recognizes you?" Andi asked with a shudder. "They'll call a taxidermist to have you stuffed and hung on a wall."

"So, keep a low profile," he advised with a grin.

Andi couldn't suppress a giggle at the ridiculousness of the directive. Here she was in the Cubs' capitol of the Southwest accompanied by their reigning demigod, a bald blind boy with a big mouth, and a pretty blonde dwarf—and Greg wanted her to keep a low profile. She might as well have brought along the hissing cockroach to let loose on the countertop.

But she managed to order and collect their food without incident and led the way to a far corner, ignoring the eyes that popped over the top of newspapers to follow Clytie's progress. She expected Greg to sit with his back to the room and was surprised when he slid into a chair facing the bar. A quick glance over her shoulder, however, showed that WGN was broadcasting a Cubs game, and the television over the long counter had been tuned to it. She looked around nervously. It was probably okay, she decided, since the few mid-afternoon patrons were watching the game as well, with their backs to Greg.

Clytie chatted happily with Thaddeus as they ate but Andi chewed in silence, watching as Greg's glasses crept steadily down his nose with his growing involvement in the game.

"Did you see the morning paper?" she asked him finally. It was a commercial break and Greg had turned his attention momentarily back to his food.

"Yeah," he said, dunking a French fry in ketchup. "We lost again yesterday, but I don't think the Mets are gonna get the sweep."

"Excuse me?"

"Well, we're up here in the seventh, and Wilson can hold 'em—" Greg's brows knit at the startled look on Andi's face. He pushed the dark glasses back up the bridge of his nose as if in self-defense. "I'll bet you weren't talking about the sports page, huh?"

She shook her head. "Is that the only section you read?"

"I look at the comics if I have time." At Andi's look of alarm, he added quickly, "I read a couple sections of the Doctrine and Covenants this morning. Can we talk about that?"

The twin dimples winked into her cheeks. "Yes, we can talk about anything that isn't baseball-related."

"So, tell me what I missed in the paper," Greg asked, then immediately regretted the question. More likely than not, Andi had brought it up because she'd seen something there about him.

"Your picture!" Clytie said quickly, confirming his fear.

"I ought to be old news by now," he muttered.

But Clytie continued happily, "This wasn't old; it was from the dance on Saturday night. You looked really handsome in the tuxedo, Greg."

He reached for another fry to buy a little time to think. Clytie's apparent enthusiasm over the picture was probably a good sign that Andi wasn't terribly upset to be the latest and probably hottest gossip. Still, when he had come clean after the evening and told Dawson that he and Andi were engaged, he had believed his new press agent's assurance that he could keep that particular piece of news out of the headlines. Greg dreaded to see Andi dragged into the fishbowl of scrutiny so soon. She—and her father—would hate every word printed about her, fact or fiction. Well, it was apparently too late now for anything but damage control.

"Your sister was certainly as pretty as a picture," he began carefully.

"I wasn't in the photo," Andi told him. She'd felt grateful to have been excluded from the gossip column until Greg's quick smile brought back that confusing little pang of uneasiness. Dismissing it as quickly as she could, she said, "The picture was of you and your new best friend."

Startled, Greg asked, "Who?"

"You know, the White Rabbit."

"Dawson?" So he *had* managed Elise Whatshername, Greg thought with relief. With lightning reflexes Geitler had had fed the society reporter a false story with choirboy sincerity. It didn't occur to Greg now that the gift for deception he admired in Geitler was a trait he had despised in his scurrilous former publicist, Zeke Martoni. His only thought was that Dawson was amazing. "That's great!"

"Yes," Andi repeated slowly, still struggling with her conflicting emotions. "Great."

Clytie's wide eyes slid from Andi's face to Greg's and back again. "Who's ready for frozen yogurt?" she asked.

Andi looked at the almost full plate Clytie had pushed away and wondered if she had been watching her weight—a constant struggle considering the size of her tiny legs—or too enamored with Thaddeus to eat. Both explanations tugged at her heart, so the smile she gave her sister was especially tender. "I'll get it," she offered, as though she weren't the only possible candidate to do so. "Vanilla, chocolate, or swirl?"

"Swirl," Clytie decided.

"Swirl," Thaddeus echoed.

Andi turned to Greg with a little sigh as she realized she had lost him once more to the Cubs game. Well, all right, she thought, but he'd get vanilla.

She had delivered the first two desserts and was back across the room at the soft-serve machine when she heard Clytie's anxious cry. Whirling, Andi saw Thaddeus' face pale as he pressed two long fingers to a spot above his right eye and grimaced in pain. Rushing back to the table, Andi put a comforting hand on her sister's shoulder.

Greg stood and bent over Thaddeus, his right hand massaging the back of the youth's neck as he leaned close and spoke quietly into his ear. Andi could see two images of the boy's distress, one in person and another equally frightening reflection in Greg's lenses

"Should I call the paramedics?" she asked.

"No," Thaddeus said quickly. "I'm okay now."

"Are you sure?" Greg asked, his voice low.

"Yeah, I'm sure."

Indeed, Thaddeus seemed to recover quickly, Andi thought gratefully a minute or two later when he raised his head with a wan smile. Her pulse began to slow until a quick glance at Greg sent it pounding. His jaw was set and fine lines creased his forehead and crinkled from the corners of his eyes. It was how he had looked whenever he talked about Jim or his father. Clearly, he wasn't convinced that Thaddeus was fine at all.

"A textbook case of 'brain freeze,'" Thaddeus assured Clytie as she reached for his hand and asked again if he was okay. "It happens when the icy cold from the ice cream hits the back palate. That activates a nerve center that controls the blood flow to your head. The nerves then make the blood vessels swell, and that gives you the sudden, severe headache."

"Really?" Clytie asked, impressed as always and now reassured.

"Absolutely," Thaddeus said. "It only lasts a few seconds."

"You're so smart."

As Andi continued to study Greg's worried face, she wished she possessed Clytie's innate willingness to accept a person's word at face value. If only she were as naive as Sterling had charged, perhaps she could believe that Thaddeus would recover, the world would fall out of love with Greg as quickly and completely as she had fallen into love with him, and everyone would live happily ever after, just like in one of Clytie's romance novels. Unfortunately, Andi's sensible nature had a difficult time ignoring those signs to the contrary.

"Then you'll still come over to the house this afternoon?" Clytie asked Thaddeus.

"You bet," the youth replied.

Clytie turned happy, hopeful eyes toward Greg.

"Count me in," he said. "I haven't beat Thaddeus at chess in a long time."

"You've never beat me at chess," Thaddeus protested. "What's more, you never *will* beat me at chess." He groped for Greg's arm and, when he found it, patted it in mock sympathy. "Sorry, old man, but to be a champion you need aggression . . . fire . . . the killer instinct—"

"Yeah, yeah," Greg interrupted good-naturedly, "you got that line from my pitching coach, didn't you?" At that moment, a thin, digitized whine emanated from the vicinity of his wallet, and Greg reached into his pocket for his cell phone.

Andi watched him open it with a shrug. "Must be Ma," he mouthed, but after a brief greeting, Greg sat up straighter, his face alert and his full attention now focused on the person on the line.

"Mrs. Dresmont!" he said, surprise and delight mixing on his face. "No, you're not interrupting anything. I'm glad you called."

Mrs. Dresmont? Andi wondered, searching her memory. *Where have I—*

"Diamond Dresmont?" Thaddeus asked no one in particular. "How does Greg know Tiger Lily?"

Diamonds! Andi thought. *Mrs. Dresmont was the woman Greg was so anxious to impress at the ball.* She watched him pull an autograph pen from his pocket and search the table for a clean napkin.

"An early dinner would be great," he said quickly. Andi's eyes widened at the tall stack of rib bones and empty cartons of beans and potato salad on his plate. "The Compass Room?" he repeated, jotting it on the napkin. "That's fine. I'll be there in—" he looked down at his jeans. "Can you give me a couple of hours to change clothes?" There was a pause and then, "Thank you, Mrs. Dresmont. I'm looking forward to seeing you, too."

Greg flipped the phone closed jubilantly. "Can you believe it? That sweet woman called me."

"I've heard Lillian Dresmont called a lot of things, Greg," Thaddeus said dryly, "but 'sweet' has never been one of them. And—news flash—I don't know how you got involved with her in the first place, but you'd better run for your life before she chops your legs off at the knees."

"Really?" Clytie asked, her eyes glowing with excitement at the bit of intrigue. "Who is she?"

"She's a hybrid," Thaddeus replied. "A one-of-a-kind cross between a rich old lady and a man-eating tiger."

"Knock it off, Thaddeus," Greg said. "She only invited me to dinner."

Thaddeus leaned forward. "*To* dinner or *for* dinner?"

Greg rolled his eyes. "If you really want to be helpful, you'll tell me where the Compass Room is so I can get changed and over there before six."

"It's your picnic," Thaddeus shrugged, "but don't say I didn't warn you." He gave directions then offered, "I can call my driver to take you."

"Thanks, but I have my Jeep now."

"The Compass Room is on the top of the Hyatt Regency building, remember?" Thaddeus replied. "When you pull up to valet parking in that—uh—Jeep of yours, they're going to show you to the delivery door—if you're lucky."

"Then I'll go up the back stairs." Greg stuck the napkin and pen in his pocket as he pushed his chair out from the table and stood over Andi. "I'm sorry to run off on you this way, but this is what I've been hoping for. I'll call you tonight."

"Or not," Thaddeus interjected. "I've heard of braver men than you who went to dine at Tiger Lily's and never came back."

Greg bent to kiss Andi then reached over to pull down the brim of Thaddeus' cap before heading toward the exit. "Thanks for the warning, Thaddeus, but I promise you, this is important enough to take my chances with fierce little old ladies."

A light seemed to click on for Thaddeus as he raised the bill of his hat with a thumb and readjusted it over his smooth forehead. "So *that's* what my dad was fuming about all morning," he said with a slow smile.

Andi flashed a glance at Clytie, but the younger girl was clearly as puzzled as she was.

"Very interesting," Thaddeus continued to himself. "Lillian Dresmont *and* Cleon Bisher. I'd say that without intercession, Greg's chances of coming out of *that* dinner intact are roughly on par with his winning the Indy 500 in his 'new' Jeep." His forehead wrinkled and he seemed to make up his mind. "Clytie, could I have a rain check on the rest of this afternoon? You know what they say—a friend in need is a friend indeed—and Greg's gonna need one before too long. We'll get together again tomorrow night at Greg's baptism, okay?"

When Clytie reluctantly agreed—it was for Greg, after all—Andi watched Thaddeus fumble in his pocket for the cell phone to call his driver. *What is going on?* she wondered. *And when is Greg going to get around to clueing me in?*

Though Greg had called on Monday night to tell her that his meeting with Mrs. Dresmont had gone well, Andi was still clueless twenty-four hours later about what it had entailed. That she was, was nobody's fault but her own. She hadn't even remembered to ask Greg about it. And when that realization had dawned on her after hanging up the phone, it hadn't surprised her. She was only curious about Greg's business, after all, but she was delirious about his baptism. That had been what they had discussed at length then and all she had been able to think about since.

And this moment, Andi thought euphorically, using the back of one hand to wipe thankful tears from her cheeks as Greg came up out of the waters of baptism, *has finally come.* She yearned to throw herself into his arms as he stood in the font; or to kiss him as he came up the steps—pure and delighted and dripping. If her father hadn't been standing so near, Andi might truly have defied convention in her desire to be close to Greg. As it was, she had to settle for crossing her arms demurely and hugging herself for joy.

There are no two ways about it—Greg Howland is a strange duck, Dawson mused as he shifted uncomfortably in his seat in the back row of the Relief Society room. He wished he dared pull his laptop computer from beneath the chair. He'd like nothing better right now than to get the proceedings of this peculiar evening into a memory more reliable than his own.

What a chapter he could write after tonight about Howland's initiation into Mormonism. Everything from a vivid description of the young woman who spoke about a "holy" ghost to the young pitcher's imminent ordination to some kind of priesthood would be lapped up by an avid public. Dawson had expected to have to fabricate here and there to produce a bestseller, but the truth he'd discovered about Greg Howland, if not stranger than fiction, was certainly as sellable.

And while the religious stuff might be good, what he'd dug up on his two days off had been priceless. Geitler had found Zeke Martoni.

From his cell at the Madison Street Jail in downtown Phoenix, Zeke had provided Dawson with an earful and then some. Studying the tall young celebrity now taking a seat at the front of the room, Dawson could well understand Howland's aversion to the press. No one in their right mind would want to risk an interview that focused on his drunken, abusive father or drug-addicted brother. Howland had done a good job of keeping them out of the papers so far, and Dawson resolved to do everything he could to maintain the status quo. After all, he wanted to be the one to break the news on the morning talk show circuit himself—he'd sell a heck of a lot more books that way.

Dawson was certainly smart enough to realize at once that Zeke wasn't above embellishing the details of his dealings with Greg and Jim Howland. In fact, despite the man's suave demeanor, well-groomed appearance, and glib story—or perhaps because of them—Martoni had given him a real case of the creeps. Dawson had realized with a start his own opinion of his source when he found himself backing out of the jail cell, then walking quickly down the hall as though he couldn't get away fast enough. Once he was away, he had had to remind himself repeatedly that it is the job of a good biographer to seek out and accurately quote sources, then let the chips fall where they may. Ultimately, it would be Zeke who was accountable for his words. Dawson would be nothing more than an instrument of expression.

And such expression, Dawson thought. *He came right out and accused Howland of experimenting with drugs and agreeing to rig games.*

Dawson smiled to himself. Across the room, Greg caught his eye and smiled in return, causing the publicist to glance quickly away.

Howland liked him, Dawson knew for a fact, and trusted him. When occasionally Dawson felt a twinge of conscience at the misplacement of that trust, he attributed it to heartburn and popped a Tums. He didn't want to be liked, any more than he wanted to admit that it was his growing admiration for Greg that made dishing the dirt on him so much harder than digging it up.

He'd freely admit, however, that he was looking forward to having Howland out on the road playing baseball by the end of this week. Maybe then all the biography writing that had faltered would finally flow. There was something about Greg that Dawson simply didn't understand and spent altogether too much time pondering. Howland, he'd observed, wasn't just someone who'd stop to smell the roses, he was more the type to plant rosebushes of his own in case a stranger should happen along later needing rose hips.

Dawson desperately hoped that this oddball behavior was rooted in Greg's freak accident and that it was a near-death experience that had changed Greg's life. Eventually, the candid young man would get around to sharing it, then Dawson would have his potentially most crucial chapter. He figured that some people might actually believe Howland while others would ridicule him, but either way, millions of people would buy the book to read about a celebrity's take on the hereafter.

Dawson leaned back in his chair as a small group of men gathered around Greg and placed their hands on the top of his bowed head. *A strange duck*, Dawson thought again, but the thought caused him to smile. It was this very strangeness that was going to make his press agent a rich and famous man.

Dawson Geitler is definitely odd, Andi thought, casting him a quick glance out the corner of her eye. *And I don't like the way he looks at Greg.* He reminded her of the reptiles in the zoo swamp. For hours on end they lay quietly on the banks of the lagoon, seeming to soak up the sun and smile benevolently. Then, when your back was turned, they slipped beneath the slimy surface of the water and reemerged with their prey clasped between long, toothy jaws—their sharp smiles wider than ever as they shed crocodile tears. Andi liked alligators, mostly because she understood them, but she didn't understand Dawson Geitler and she couldn't make herself like him very well, either.

On the other hand, she thought with a sigh, shifting her attention back to the front of the room, not withstanding the fact that she didn't understand Greg, she loved him. She had thought her heart would burst when she first came into the room tonight and saw him standing near the baptismal font with Bishop Ferris, barefoot and dressed in white. The place where Greg stood at that moment was brighter in Andi's eyes than the rest of the room and was surely the brightest spot in the world. As she stood staring, Greg had smiled and crossed the room to her side. She hadn't been able to hear his whispered words over the pulse of emotion in her ears, but she could still feel the clasp of his strong hands as they engulfed her own, and she savored the lingering prickles of joy where his lips had brushed hers.

Greg had wanted his baptism to be private, and Bishop Ferris had done his best to comply; still, their group filled the small room to overflowing. Andi couldn't help but wonder how many people had come to be supportive of a new convert and how many had used their callings to satisfy their curiosity. Feeling vaguely guilty to have had such a thought, Andi turned her attention to Thaddeus and Clytie. Seeing them holding hands between their seats, she smiled. She'd seen that silly man-catching manual again this morning, but this time it was in the wastebasket.

Perhaps Clytie considers herself a graduate of the course, Andi mused. *Hopefully she's finally admitted that a book touting "Dress for Sexcess" is the last thing in the world she, or any girl, needs.*

Her eyes strayed next to Sadie Howland, who was seated between Margaret Reynolds and Laura Newton. Greg was pleased, Andi knew, that his mother had come tonight and was grateful to everyone who had gone out of his or her way to make her feel welcome and accepted.

Laura leaned toward Sadie to whisper a few words of explanation, and Andi thought, *It's no coincidence that while sacred ordinances such as baptism are the keys to the kingdom of heaven, membership in the Lord's kingdom on earth offers the surest way to temporal happiness as well.* Here was Sadie, a perfect example of what could be accomplished by applying the Relief Society motto: Charity Never Faileth. This timid, unhappy woman who had probably never had a friend in her adult life now knew women who genuinely cared for her. Sister Newton particularly, a widow of several years and lonely herself, had clearly sought to become less of a visiting teacher and more of the sister for whom Sadie had longed.

Andi watched Greg's mother watching him, and smiled to see the love and pride Sadie felt for her son so transparent on her face. Wanting her father to see it as well, Andi tried to catch his eye as he joined the priesthood circling Greg's chair. Surely this night when the Spirit had been so strong would convince Trent of the purity of Greg's intentions and the possibilities that lay ahead for his family. If her dad would only stop harping on Greg's past and overlook the headlines that followed the star ballplayer everywhere he went, Trent Reynolds would come to love Greg as she did. Andi was sure of it. And wasn't this sacred covenant a major indication that Greg meant to leave all that behind?

The eyes Andi finally raised at the end of an incredible blessing glistened with tears of awe and gratitude. She blinked them back, knowing that when the mission leader concluded the meeting, she would need to rise to lead the closing hymn.

Though Andi couldn't find her voice to sing, she could keep time for the pianist with little effort. At least she could until Greg raised his eyes from the hymnal to meet hers and held the look long after he had lost his place in the hymn and stopped singing. Then Andi lost her place in the music—and seemingly in time and eternity as well. She felt her cheeks grow hot as her hand dropped, for several counts, to her side.

The meeting ended and Andi watched others gather quickly around Greg. Her heart in her throat, she hung back, wanting the moment she went to him to be private. Then, with her nervous energy too great to allow her to stand idle, she turned to pass the long minutes gathering and stacking hymnals, then turned to remove the plants and pictures from the table and piano tops. She had just whisked her mother's snowy cloth from the table and was struggling to fold it without dragging it on the floor when Greg came to her.

"Here, let me help you with that."

Andi froze in mid-action, her eyes seeking his. With all that truly mattered to be said, she found that she could say nothing.

Greg's hands covered hers as he took the lace covering and folded it easily before returning it to her with a smile. "Sorry I threw you off during that last song," he said, although the light of gratification in his eyes told a different truth.

With difficulty, Andi looked away from the fathomless sapphire of those eyes, knowing it was the only chance to recover her voice. "It was a beautiful baptism," she managed finally. There was so much to talk about and so many plans to make, but with Dawson Geitler hovering in the background, this wasn't the place. She continued, "I know that you didn't want refreshments served here, but we have strawberries from the garden at home and Clytie baked an angel food cake . . ." Her words trailed away in her confusion at the look of regret and guilt on Greg's face.

"There's nothing I'd like more, Andi," he said truthfully. "You know that. But I can't. I . . . I'll have to leave from here as it is."

"Leave?" Andi echoed blankly.

"I'm eligible to come off the disabled list," Greg hastily explained. "Dawson's booked us on a flight to Chicago in about an hour."

Andi's thoughts flew too fast for her reason to keep up. *Disabled list? Chicago?* Nonplussed, she almost dropped the tablecloth, but when Greg reached for it, she recovered and clutched it tightly to her chest as she took a step backward toward the table for support. When she felt the edge against her thigh, Andi sat back and waited for Greg to explain.

"I didn't know what I was doing myself," he said, hoping to reassure her that she hadn't simply been left out of his plans. "At least, I didn't know for sure until I got a call on my way to the stake center. I'll say one thing for her, Mrs. Dresmont doesn't waste any time when she makes up her mind. And it sure didn't hurt to have Thaddeus show up at the restaurant. I think Cleon Bisher would do anything to make his son happy—even take a risk on a pitcher dumb enough to get himself taken out by a bean ball."

"But you said you were going to Chicago," Andi pointed out as her bewilderment grew. *What* is *he saying?* she wondered as she shook her head slowly and looked up into Greg's eager face. *That he's going back to baseball? That couldn't be it. Him pitching so soon after that horrible accident just couldn't be a good idea.*

Greg pulled up a chair from the first row so he could sit and look directly into Andi's troubled face. He explained gently, "The Cubs hold my contract, Andi. They expect me in Chicago before ten tomorrow."

"It's not like the Cubs *own* you," Andi protested.

Greg's lopsided grin was bemused. "Actually, it's a lot more like that than you might think. I'm under contract for another season, Andi. Since the doctors have released me to play, I have to go."

Andi tried to swallow the baseball-sized lump that was forming in her throat and wished she had bothered to learn more about the sport—or at least realized earlier what it meant to be under contract to it. It meant that Greg would be occupied with baseball almost every single day, she knew for sure, and playing on the Sabbath. And it probably meant that he would gain more of the fame and money and all the rest of the things that she often wished he didn't have now.

And what will people—especially my father and Sterling—think about Greg running off on the night of his baptism? Andi wondered unhappily. *If it were anyone but Greg, what would I think myself?*

With effort, she raised her chin. "So you're leaving tonight," she said quietly, "because, I guess, you have to. May I ask when you expect your life be your own again?"

"Well, the season's over in September," Greg said, trying to keep his voice light and suggesting with his lopsided grin that Andi should take it as a jest. "Or October, if we make the playoffs."

But Andi clearly wasn't amused. At the sight of a single tear sparkling in the corner of her eye, Greg leaned forward to run a knuckle tenderly along the set of her jaw. "Andi, I'm sorry to spring it on you like this . . ." Suddenly, he brightened. "And I haven't had a chance to tell you the good news." Trying to ignore her skeptical expression, he said, "The Cubs have been terrific about everything. I'll have a day and a half to clean out my apartment and get down to Peosta to see Jim's boys." He glanced over his shoulder to make sure no one was in the room but them and Dawson and added, "Then first thing Friday, I'll be traded to Arizona. Then I can fly to Milwaukee to meet my new team before that day's game with the Brewers."

"That's the good news?"

"Well, yeah," Greg said. "I thought you'd be glad that I can be here with you at least half the season."

"Here—with me?" Andi repeated. Her bitter disappointment caused her to speak before she thought. "You mean you'll be in Phoenix—with your team."

"You're marrying a baseball player," Greg said evenly. "Remember?"

No, I'm marrying you, *Greg!* But instead of speaking the words aloud, Andi looked down at the white cloth in her hands. She couldn't bear to see the disappointment that had replaced the earlier joy on Greg's face and feel her part in it. But had he actually expected her to be *pleased* that he was risking his health—and perhaps their future—for the sake of that silly game? Besides, she simply dreaded the thought of having to face her father every time the Sabbath rolled around and Greg was now conspicuous at church only in his absence. "I remember," she said miserably.

"Then what did you expect me to do?"

"Whatever happened to selling shoes?" she asked impulsively, her voice a little louder than she had intended in her frustration at being trapped in unpleasant circumstances neither one of them could control. Her eyes, darkened now to shades of jade, were imploring. "Or teaching math? Or retiring to that Little League field you like to talk about?"

"Greg?" Clytie called from the hallway. "Andi?" She appeared at the door a moment later with Thaddeus trailing behind. "Thaddeus says we can all ride back to our house in his limo," she said excitedly. "Are you ready to go?"

"Greg is," Andi said, relieved at the interruption. "But you'll have to detour by the airport. He's on his way to Chicago."

"Chicago?" Clytie asked incredulously. "Why is he going to Chicago?"

"The Windy City is a popular tourist venue," Thaddeus suggested. "It's known for a variety of landmarks. For instance, Chicago is on the banks of Lake Michigan and downtown there's the Sears Tower and Lincoln Park which boasts, I might add, a fabulous chess pavilion." He paused with a wry smile, "But, since this is Greg and we all know how well he plays chess, my bet is that Wrigley Field is his destination."

"Thanks for the travelogue, Thaddeus," Greg said, massaging a newly developed sore spot between his eyebrows. "Now would you all excuse Andi and me for a minute, please?"

"Mr. Howland," Dawson interjected, "if this takes more than a minute, we're going to be late for our flight."

Andi scarcely glanced at Dawson as she rose and moved toward the closet to return the tablecloth. "Go," she said softly to Greg. "Have a nice trip."

He stood up quickly, nearly upsetting his chair. "Andi, I love you."

"I know," she managed to say as she closed and locked the closet door, almost wishing that she were on the inside. "And I love you." *Unfortunately,* she thought, *the poets are wrong. Love doesn't conquer all—sometimes it just complicates everything.*

But Andi didn't want to think about that now. She'd have all the days ahead while Greg was away playing baseball to sort out how she felt about it—and him. Right now all she wanted to do was escape that room with what was left of her composure. She didn't want to hurt Greg any more, or alarm Clytie, and she certainly didn't want to give Dawson Geitler the satisfaction of seeing her cry.

"We have to talk about this," Greg persisted as she reached the door.

"We will," Andi said, escaping into the hall before the first sob. "Call me in October."

Chapter 18

"Do you understand women, Dawson?" Greg asked, turning the wheel of his rented convertible onto beautiful Lakeshore Drive. They were returning to Greg's apartment in Chicago's exclusive North Side just before sunset Wednesday.

After catching a red-eye flight from Phoenix the night before and a few hours of sleep this morning, they had embarked upon a whirlwind day of meetings that finally concluded with a stop at Wrigley Field. The length of time Greg had stood in the Cubs' dugout gazing out at the historic, ivy-covered brick walls and watching his former teammates take batting practice had almost convinced Dawson his employer regretted his decision to move to Arizona. Now the ball player seemed almost back to normal. Except, of course, for this thing with the girl.

"I don't understand them, either," Greg continued, as if Dawson had responded in the negative. "Like, all those letters I get, you know?"

Dawson nodded, though he thought Greg's train of thought had derailed somewhere up the line.

"Half of them—more than half—are from women," Greg said. "They send pictures and house keys and even marriage proposals when they don't know anything about me. They only want to marry me because I'm a baseball player." Arriving in the terrace district, Greg turned into the basement-parking garage of his building and removed his sunglasses in the dim light. "And then there's the one girl in the world I *want* to want to marry me, and you know what she said?"

"She said to call her in October, Mr. Howland."

"Yeah." Greg braked to a stop at the security checkpoint and turned his eyes toward his companion incredulously. Did Dawson remember every word spoken in his presence? "I don't think she meant it," he continued, "but the point is, if Andi doesn't want to marry me, it's *because* I'm a baseball player. Does that make sense to you, Dawson? Before the other man could respond, Greg turned away to enter his security code. "It doesn't make sense to me, either."

Geitler wondered what it would take for Howland to come to his senses about this girl. Andi Reynolds, frankly, didn't do anything for him. Her looks hovered in the average-to-pretty range but she certainly wasn't in the league of women with whom Greg had been photographed in the past. Besides which, she wasn't wealthy or able to further Howland's career in any way Geitler could discern. Yet, even Dawson couldn't deny that something almost tangible passed between the two of them with every look exchanged.

As they stepped inside Greg's twelfth-floor apartment, Dawson was impressed again by the spacious, ultramodern accommodations. Greg had offered him the master bedroom—insisted he take it, in fact—and Dawson had thought then that when his exposé was published and he "arrived" himself, he might move to Chicago and lease this very suite. He couldn't decide which view he most admired, the breathtaking cityscape framed by a large picture window in the front room or the more tranquil setting offered from a tiled bedroom terrace overlooking Lincoln Park and the lake.

Dawson glanced at Greg who had dropped his duffel on the thick carpet near the couch and was now at the phone calling his service for messages. He couldn't help but eye him disdainfully as he thought, *All this luxury, all those people fawning wherever you go, all those women and you want to throw it away for one ordinary girl, a house in the suburbs, and 1.6 children. Or maybe,* he amended with a little smirk, *it'll be 6.1 children now that you're a Mormon.*

He set his laptop carefully on the glass tabletop with a shake of his head over Howland's idiotic waste of opportunities that some men would kill for. *It's a good thing I'm not writing my novel about this guy,* he reflected. *I'd never be able to nail a motivation for Howland's character.*

"Bobbie Jo called again," Greg said, returning the phone to the cradle. "She's expecting me at noon."

Dawson noted the resignation in his employer's voice without comment. This sister-in-law of his was still one of the relatively unknown factors in Dawson's info file.

"Peosta's about three hours from here," Greg continued, "but I think I'll leave early." He walked into the kitchen and pulled open one cupboard, then another. "You'll be able to find something to do around here, right?"

Dawson quickly joined him in the kitchen. "I thought I'd go to Iowa with you, Mr. Howland."

Greg paused with his hand on the refrigerator door. "Not a good idea, Dawson."

"Because—" Even though he knew the answer, Geitler was still interested in the response.

"Well, because it's, uh, family stuff." Greg opened the door and peered inside the nearly empty fridge. "You'd be bored."

Howland was a lousy liar, his publicist thought with satisfaction. Plus, he had another flaw that could always be worked to advantage—a "responsible streak" a mile wide.

"Regretfully, we have a tremendous amount of work to do before Friday morning," Dawson reminded him. "I know how you feel about facing press conferences unprepared . . ." His satisfaction deepened at the ballplayer's reaction: a subtle bracing of the muscles across his broad shoulders. "I had planned to put our travel time to good use tomorrow," Dawson continued, pressing his advantage. "And you needn't worry about me interfering with your family time. I always bring personal work along in my notebook."

He waited anxiously for Greg's response as he watched the young man survey a jar of fossilized peanut butter, a hockey puck of cheese, and a half-gallon plastic jug with contents that had passed from milk to sour cream to toxic waste sometime during Greg's absence.

Greg caught Dawson's concerned expression but misinterpreted the cause. "Don't worry," he said quickly, nudging shut the refrigerator door as he reached toward a nearby drawer. "The kitchen's always been Plan Z for dinner. I keep Plans A through Y in here." He pulled out a thick stack of papers containing the menus of virtually every restaurant in Chicago that had a reliable delivery service. Fanning them out like a card dealer, he offered, "Pick a meal, Dawson. Any meal."

"About tomorrow—"

"I don't know—I'll think about it. Let's settle dinner first." When Dawson hesitated, Greg said, "Pizza then. After all, it's your first visit to Chicago—we ought to do it right."

By the time the food was delivered, it was time for the news. The men consumed dinner and data, washed it down with root beer, and were ready to call it a day. Dawson went into Greg's bedroom to work on his manuscript while Greg propped himself up on the bed he had made on the couch and pulled the lamp nearer for better light. Dawson could see the back of Greg's sandy head from where he sat and wondered what it was he read that held his interest so completely. After a fruitless hour of effort at the keyboard, he turned off the laptop and attributed tonight's lack of enthusiasm for writing Howland's biography to the excitement of tomorrow's promise of new inspiration. With Geitler's gentle, expert prodding, Greg had finally—if reluctantly—agreed to let him tag along to Peosta.

Entering the bathroom, Dawson frowned at the glass on the sink top. He could barely stomach the thought of using what passed for tap water here in Illinois to brush his teeth. You'd think with all his money, Howland could afford bottled water to replace this stuff that tasted like it had been pumped directly from Lake Michigan. Well, it couldn't be helped, but at least he needn't take it from a dirty glass. He gingerly picked up the one he had used last night. At the rate germs multiplied, Dawson was surprised everyone didn't use paper cups.

Greg looked up with a smile as Geitler passed the couch on his way to the kitchen. "Hey, Dawson, listen to this." He raised the black leather-bound volume and read: "'And now remember that whosoever perisheth, perisheth unto himself; and whosoever doeth iniquity, doeth it unto himself; for behold, ye are free; ye are permitted to act for yourselves; for behold, God hath given unto you a knowledge and he hath made you free.'" His blue eyes shone in the soft, golden light. "That's it, isn't it?"

"It?" Dawson asked, sorry now he had come into the living room and found out what Howland was reading. There was little in the world worse than a religious convert.

"The whole thing in a nutshell," Greg continued excitedly. "Life. Don't you see? Psychologists are always telling us that we're products of our environments—that we can't help it if we're dysfunctional. But Samuel is saying just the opposite here. He says it doesn't matter who our parents are or where we come from. Our Heavenly Father gave each of us free agency to act for ourselves." He lifted the volume. "Listen to the rest: 'He hath given unto you that ye might know good from evil, and he hath given unto you that ye might choose life or death; and ye can do good and be restored unto that which is good, or have that which is good restored unto you; or ye can do evil and have that which is evil restored unto you.'" Greg closed the book triumphantly. "So, God gives us the freedom and knowledge to determine what we receive in this life and the next, no matter who we are or where we come from. Right?"

"Um, yes," Dawson agreed in hopes of ending the conversation. "I think I've heard it called the law of the harvest." He took two steps toward the kitchen before being forced to pause when Greg spoke again.

"Yeah. And I think that's why Jim—my brother—was . . . well, where he was." Recognizing how cryptic the remark was, Greg added quickly, "He made a big mistake by trusting Zeke Martoni, but even without the gospel in his life, Jim was the most genuinely nice person you'd ever want to meet. I guess it was the light of Christ. Let's see, how did Moroni put it?"

Dawson eyed the dirty glass in his hand as Greg reopened the scriptures, pondering the benefits of sanitation over the relief of an escape back to the bedroom. Before he could advance or retreat, Greg began to read: "'The Spirit of Christ is given to every man that he may know good from evil; wherefore, I show unto you the way to judge; for every thing which inviteth to do good, and to persuade to believe in Christ, is sent forth by the power and gift of Christ; wherefore ye may know with a perfect knowledge it is of God.'" He looked back up at Dawson. "I guess that's why you can't do something wrong and feel okay about it. Don't you think?"

Dawson glanced uncomfortably over his shoulder toward the laptop in the bedroom. Was all this rigmarole just Howland's way of hinting that he knew what his press agent was up to? He returned his eyes warily to Greg's face and relaxed. His employer's expression reflected only interest in Dawson's opinion, security in his own beliefs, and—something. At first Dawson didn't know what the something was, then it occurred to him that it might be joy. Geitler regarded the young man now in genuine astonishment. This was apparently much more than the posturing of a neophyte Christian disciple. These words of scripture had clearly spoken to Greg on a personal level and brought him peace.

Dawson took a tentative step closer. "What are you reading?"

Greg extended the volume. "The Book of Mormon. Sorry I only have the one copy here in Chicago. Want to borrow it?"

"No!" Dawson said, surprised at his own momentary lapse of common sense. "Uh, no thanks. I'm turning in for the night."

Greg nodded, noticed for the first time the glass in Dawson's hand, and swung his long legs over the side of the couch to dig into his duffel. "I almost forgot. I picked something up for you in the clubhouse today." He extended a couple of plastic liter bottles with a grin. "I couldn't help but notice you don't much like Lake Michigan water."

Dawson accepted the gift wordlessly. He didn't know what he might learn about the rest of this man's family tomorrow, but tonight he had discovered that if what Howland had said about his brother's kindness—and tendency to misplace trust—was true, then Greg must be very like him.

Chapter 10

"Perhaps we've arrived too early," Dawson suggested as they walked back around to the front of Howland's Automotive Shop before nine on Thursday morning.

Under other circumstances, Greg might have been struck by the irony of these particular words coming from Dawson Geitler. As it was, he barely heard them. "There aren't any cars in the bay," he said, kicking aside a crate he had used for the extra foot-and-a-half needed to see in the high garage window. "And the grease spots are old. Nobody's worked here for a couple of weeks, at least. Maybe longer."

Although Dawson suspected Howland of talking to himself, he nodded as he watched his gaze shift in resignation from the barbershop to the west of the garage and back toward the liquor store to the east. When Greg finally moved toward the latter, Geitler had to jog to keep up.

The young pitcher paused at the entrance as if to reconsider, then pushed open the fingerprint-smeared glass door and blinked as his eyes adjusted to the dim, smoky interior. "Stan?"

A pale, flaccid man looked up from a magazine. "Greg Howland! Well, I'll be danged." He slapped the tabloid closed, stowed it guiltily behind the counter, and came quickly around to greet his unexpected guest. "Haven't seen you in a month of Sundays, not since Jim's—Well! And then to hear tell that you were almost a goner yourself. Jeez, life's just full of—"

"Have you seen my dad lately?" Greg interrupted him to ask.

Dawson looked on from behind Greg's shoulder at the man whose small eyes lit up with interest, met Greg's for an instant, then darted past the beer display down toward the dirty linoleum floor. "Can't say that I have, Greg."

"Since when?"

"Not since your Ma left. We all wondered," he added quickly at Greg's start of incredulity. "Matt took the patrol car out to the house, even. Weren't no sign of him or his truck anywheres. We all figured he'd lit out for Arizona."

"Matt hasn't called us," Greg began, "and Bobbie Jo hasn't said—"

Dawson watched the young celebrity swallow his words at the eager smirk on the face of the liquor store owner. He knew how much Greg must have hated to give this man the satisfaction of asking after his father in the first place. Clearly, he was now dreading the mean-spirited gossip that would follow today's visit—as it had likely followed him every day of his life in this small town.

"Bobbie Jo's been real distracted-like," Stan offered enticingly. The glint in his eye and a quick dart of pink tongue to wet his lips showed how anxious he was to share this salacious tidbit of Howland family news. "You know she's got herself a new boyfriend and—"

Dawson had leaned unconsciously forward, but then fell back as he saw any words Stan might have said next freeze in Greg's icy stare.

"Thanks for your help, Stan," Howland said, turning away to grip the door handle with white knuckles.

"What's gonna happen to your dad's shop?" the man called after them.

Greg pulled open the door and stepped through it, pausing on the threshold. "I guess you'll have to ask him that yourself the next time he comes in."

"Did I understand the proprietor to say that your father's missing?" Dawson asked as he ran to keep up with the long strides Greg was taking toward the car. "And that the local constable is unable or unwilling to assist in the matter?"

"Huh?" It had taken Geitler's questions to remind Greg that he was there. He slowed his steps and waited for him to catch up, wondering what had possessed him to bring the man to Peosta in the first place. Something like that scene in the liquor store was almost bound to happen. And now he'd have to take Dawson out to the house with him.

My stupidity hasn't been terminal so far, Greg thought, pausing for a minute at the driver's side of the convertible, *but it doesn't seem to be curable, either.* Finally he shrugged and said tiredly, "Missing's a relative term when it comes to my dad, Dawson. Get in the car and I'll explain it to you on the way out to the house."

Despite his offer, Greg drove silently across a landscape of fertile farmland and endless blue sky. It was less unwillingness on his part to explain his feelings to Dawson than it was an inability. As a child, he had feared his father; as an adult, he had hated him. With both these emotions in the past, for the most part, Greg could only wonder what it was he felt for Roy Howland today.

As they drove past fields of oat, soybeans, and alfalfa, Greg considered the verdant promise of harvest stretching as far as a man could see and remembered the scripture he had read to Dawson the night before.

You are free to choose, he paraphrased silently, *to do good and have good restored to you.* He had chosen a new birth, he thought with the beginning of a smile, and a relationship with a newly discovered Eternal Father. Hopefully by next April or May, he and Andi would have begun a new forever family. Surely, these blessings would be enough to heal scars that remained from his childhood, no matter how painful or deep.

To his credit, Dawson had remained quiet and unquestioning. As they reached the dirt road that led to the house, Greg glanced over at him and finally began to share a little information about his life. Within a few minutes, he found that he welcomed the opportunity to verbalize his feelings to someone so obviously interested. *Everyone,* he thought with gratitude, *should have a friend like Dawson.*

"So, by the time I was thirteen," Greg said, concluding his narration some minutes later, "I had decided that I'd keep throwing rocks ten or twelve hours a day if that's what it took to become the best. Then I'd play baseball in school and sacrifice whatever I had to to become so rich and so famous that no one—not even my dad—could ever touch me again."

"And you did it," Dawson observed with keen admiration. "You made it all the way to the top."

Greg closed his eyes for a moment before returning them to the washboard road. "I don't know about that, Dawson," he said quietly. "I think instead I found out that the top I was aiming for is a lot lower than most people think."

The farm access route soon narrowed, circling behind the fields into flat, uncultivated acreage. Dawson watched Greg frown, then followed his line of vision. Surely that run-down shack in the distance wasn't his childhood home.

Greg caught his eye and nodded. "It's pathetic, isn't it? But the whole of my family's life is sad, Dawson. I've been trying to imagine on the way out here how it must have been for my father, especially after my mother finally left him. Somehow, he must have come to a place in life where he believed he could just disappear, and no one in the world would know or care."

Not no one, Dawson mused, looking from Greg's profile back toward the ramshackle farmhouse. It had taken a great deal of effort—actual and emotional—for Roy Howland's son to come home today. *Obviously,* someone *cares.*

Greg pulled to a stop in the dirt yard and rested his chin against the top of the steering wheel. Deliberately, almost affectionately, he surveyed the house he had barely looked at for the last twenty years. *The crack in the front window must have finally given way*, he thought, noting the rough-cut square of plyboard that replaced a pane of glass. White paint hung in curls from weathered wood or had disappeared altogether, leaving bare board to face the alternating seasons of rain, sun, and snow.

It was several minutes before Greg finally left the car, with Dawson trailing behind, to climb the few stairs to the long, wrap-around porch. The rotting steps bowed beneath his feet and almost gave way, making Greg wonder how much longer the house could stand before giving way itself to the wild morning glory vines that twined up onto the railings and seemed to tug the rock foundation deeper into the earth.

Trying the brass knob, Greg wasn't particularly surprised to find the door unlocked, considering what little of value was inside. He started to lead the way into the cramped front room, stumbled over something on the bare wood floor, and grasped the doorframe for support as his mind tried to grasp the implications of the shambles.

At first, Greg thought local farm boys must have ransacked the house in his father's absence. Then, eyeing the mess more closely, he saw a numbing common denominator to the vandalism. The dozens of baseball trophies that had once lined a cup shelf along the wall comprised the vast majority of the clutter. A National League Rookie of the Year award—likely used to knock down the other trophies—had been broken itself and flung into a far corner. Moving his foot cautiously, Greg saw that he had stepped on his first Cy Young award as he came into the room. The second protruded from within the bowels of the black and white television screen where it had probably been swung into a video image of its owner.

As Greg's head sunk onto his chest, he saw the remnants of the pathetically thin Howland family scrapbook. It had been opened, perused, and mostly demolished. Childhood pictures of him and Jim were strewn across the room. An eight-by-ten Cubs publicity picture that his mother had placed in a dime store frame also lay face up on a colorless, frayed rug. The glass spiraled out from the center in whorls from the impact of a heel. Greg used the toe of his shoe to push the picture out of sight beneath the threadbare couch, then, finding it increasingly difficult to withstand the sickening sensations spreading out from his own center, sank onto the sagging springs.

From the open front door, Dawson's eyes darted around the room, carefully cataloguing every detail for future reference and finally coming to rest on Greg. His young employer's hands were clasped between his knees and his head was almost low enough to rest on top of them. He didn't stir when Dawson picked his way carefully through the debris to peek into the adjoining room.

The kitchen, Dawson noted, had been left orderly and had remained unvisited, except by flies that had come through the torn screen of an open window. Powdery silt had also sifted through the screen and covered every exposed surface. Geitler walked over to close the window, then, wrinkling his nose in disgust at the odor of bananas rotting in a bowl on the chipped, linoleum table, reconsidered and left it open. On his way back to the living room, he paused before a doorless cupboard of Blue Willow dishes. Though the bone china set was obviously long-used and had many pieces missing and others chipped or cracked, Dawson let out a low whistle at their probable value. He knew his own mother, an avid collector of antique porcelain, would likely have swooned.

Geitler walked back through the living room and, with a quick look toward his still motionless employer, down the narrow hall. He tried a light switch only to find that the bare bulb had burnt out or, more likely, the electricity had been disconnected.

The first room he came to was furnished with twin beds whose matching quilts were hand-tied affairs of cheap cotton fabric and old blankets. The dresser was a long, mirrorless antique, the value of which had also been overlooked by its owners; the pair of boys who shared this room had carelessly allowed the impact of rocks and sticks and one another to mar the bureau's finely crafted workmanship. A faded maroon and gold Fairmont High banner stretched across the cracked, plaster wall. Beyond this, the room was bare.

Despite his desire to see the rest of the house before Greg cut short their visit, Dawson lingered at the door. He told himself that it was his instinct as a writer that gave him pause and made him want to reconstruct Greg's youth for himself from the clues he had received in the car and here in this shabby home. But instead of forming eloquent paragraphs about abuse and vivid impressions of poverty for inclusion in Howland's biography, his mind stubbornly replayed the words the man had read last night and the light in his face when he had read them: *Ye are permitted to act for yourselves; for behold, God hath given unto you a knowledge and he hath made you free.*

Irrelevant, Dawson told himself, moving quickly away from the door as he pushed away the words which seemed to have been whispered into his ear. *Life is decided by fate—occasionally impacted by brilliant or stupid choices. Howland was dealt a bad hand at birth but still managed to draw to an inside straight. If he's as free as he thinks he is, he'll cut his losses and walk away from this place without a backwards glance.*

Dawson peeked into the narrow, gloomy bathroom before approaching the last unexplored room of the Howlands' tiny house. Dust motes danced in the beam of light slanting through a crack between ancient chintz curtains. This furniture was antiquated as well, but carefully maintained. Though now covered, like the rest of the rooms, in a filmy patina of Iowa farmland, these pieces had been obviously well oiled and well loved for generations.

The armoire was open, its cedar-lined insides half empty. Only masculine clothes remained on the thin, wire hangers. One drawer had been pulled out and depleted as well and now hung balanced between the chest and the worn, bare wood floor.

"It doesn't look like he took anything with him, does it?" Able to see easily over the shorter man's head, Greg had paused in the hall, several feet back, to lean against the faded, rose-patterned wallpaper. Dawson turned guiltily, but Greg waved off any forthcoming apologies with a single gesture. Finally, he sighed and stepped around his friend to enter the room.

"My dad must have had a fit to find Ma gone. I don't think he'd ever been alone. He probably couldn't stand it." Greg lowered himself onto the bed and sat pensively for a few minutes. "You know, Dawson, I guess in his way he really loves her."

"You think he's alive?" Dawson had blurted the words out without thinking and now berated himself for the impetuosity.

"Yeah, I do," Greg responded slowly. "Despite how it looks around here, I've given him all the money he would need to disappear. And if something bad had happened, they could have traced him to me through the truck registration." He smiled ruefully. "As you know, Dawson, I'm not exactly hard to find. My dad's gone 'cause he wants to be. He'll show up again—when he's ready." Greg stood and took another melancholy look around the room and, before Dawson felt he had accurately labeled the young man's conflicted emotions, walked out. In the hall, he paused as if halted by an unseen hand.

"Dawson, help me look around for a sec," Greg said suddenly. "My mother had a family Bible from the nineteenth century. I need to find it."

"In fact," Geitler responded helpfully, "it appears that your family has several valuable antiques. Perhaps we should call to make arrangements to have them secured before we depart."

Greg hesitated, then walked back into his parents' room. "Nobody comes out this way much," he said over his shoulder, "but we can lock up before we go, I guess." He said something else as he knelt beside the bed, but the words were muffled in the worn counterpane as he leaned forward, then finally stretched face down on the floor to hook an arm under the low four-poster bedstead.

Dawson watched him rise a few seconds later, dusty but triumphant, a linen bundle in his strong hands.

"Look at this," he said, laying the package on the bed to unwrap carefully. As the old ivory-colored fabric fell away, Dawson moved forward to inspect the ancient book it had protected. About the size of a modern dictionary, it had a leather binding of tooled acorns, now tattered and worn almost smooth by generations of handling. "My mother kept it wrapped up and out of the light and dust," Greg explained as he carefully lifted the brittle cover. "But every once in a while, she got it out to show us."

Dawson watched Greg's eyes soften as he turned the yellowed pages, pausing at a picture of the biblical Samuel as a youth, lost for a moment in poignant memories. Then he came to the place he had sought.

When Greg spoke again, his voice was almost a whisper. "'Paulser Jacoby born 5 May 1791. Married Elizabeth Lange 1 April 1815. Elizabeth born 12 April 1796.' Ma's parents gave them this Bible as a wedding gift, Dawson. Look, here are the birth dates of their eleven children written in Elizabeth's own hand."

Despite himself, Geitler couldn't help but marvel at the scrunched, spidery scrawl—faded and smeared in places—but still mostly legible after almost two hundred years. "Your mother's family?" he asked. Greg nodded and, seemingly with effort, skipped several pages to the last of the handwritten section. Dawson looked to where he pointed at his own name painstakingly printed in black ink under his brother's and just ahead of his two nephews. "That's remarkable," Geitler said finally.

"More remarkable than you might imagine," Greg responded. He was tenderly rewrapping the tome, but his mind was on what Bishop Ferris had told him about temple work, and then on the many family members who he knew waited for that work. Suddenly, he bent again. "There was something else under there." A minute later he pulled out a sepia-toned photo in a frame that might have been silver or pewter or a combination of the two.

Looking over Greg's shoulder as he knelt beside the bed, Dawson examined the assembled group. There was an elderly couple seated on the porch of this very clapboard house—probably at the turn of the century—surrounded by more than a dozen of their grandchildren, babies to young teens. Dawson noted with particular interest the weathered patriarch in his Sunday-go-to-meeting suit. He had one strong arm around a laughing baby, the other gently encouraging a shy granddaughter to step forward. Certainly uncharacteristic for the period, the old farmer had smiled into the camera—a boyish grin that was lopsided and warm and reminiscent of Greg's.

Geitler took a step away to turn his attention back to the old man's youthful descendent. Greg still studied the faces intently, and Dawson wondered if the soft shine in the corners of his blue eyes was a glint from new moisture.

"I know these people, Dawson," Greg said in an undertone. "They're a lot of the reason I chose to live."

Geitler's heart beat more rapidly at the confirmation of his suspicions. Hoping to hear more, he stood perfectly still, scarcely daring to breathe. His hopes dropped, however, at Greg's next words.

"Come on," Howland said, securing the linen around the Bible and cradling it with the photograph as he rose to his feet. "Let's get out of here."

Dawson followed Greg back down the hall and through the trophy-strewn front room. As the young pitcher pulled open the front door, Geitler hesitated. "Your awards, Mr. Howland—"

"Leave them," Greg said, already crossing the sagging porch.

"Shall I at least lock the front door?"

"If you want to, Dawson, but I already have everything from there that matters."

Geitler set the lock and began to pull the door closed behind him, then remembered the open kitchen window. Moving through the rooms, he closed and latched the window quickly. As he returned to the living room, he could see Greg in the car through the open front door, his blond head bowed again over his family picture. Dawson bent hastily to scoop up a handful of childhood pictures for inclusion in his book and slipped them carefully into a back pocket before hurrying out to the convertible. He'd already decided to send a photographer out later to take pictures of the house. Still, Dawson couldn't resist a last look over his shoulder as they pulled out onto the narrow lane.

“It’s something to see all right,” Greg observed dryly, glancing in the rearview mirror in response to his publicist’s craned neck. His next words were delivered in a tone of voice somewhere between amusement and apprehension. “But if you think that branch of the family tree is something, Dawson, wait until you meet Bobbie Jo.”

CHAPTER 20

Andi's eyes strayed to the clock for the second time in six minutes before they settled on the screen at the front of the classroom. *Myth is a past with a future, exercising itself in the present,* she read before copying the quote in her notes. After a minute or two, the professor switched overheads and began to relate Fuentes' words to some of an early twentieth century existentialist.

Fortunately, there were only ten minutes left in class, Andi sighed. If she were lucky. When he happened upon a subject he found as intriguing as this, Dr. Trent Reynolds was infamous for an ability to lecture not only past the end of the period but—and his daughter shuddered now at the thought—oftentimes on in to his family's dinner hour as well.

Having dutifully copied Berdyayev's name beneath Fuentes', Andi underlined it for good measure as her father searched his notes for another particularly apt citation. When he found it and began to read, Andi thought that the quote might as well be in the philosopher's native Russian for all the sense it made to her.

She propped an elbow on the desk and sank her chin into an open palm, her eyes moving away from her careful notes to the cover of the text on parallel mythology. Capering among the metaphorical drawings of planets and trees of life were mythological creatures. She recognized Pegasus, of course, among the griffins and gargoyles, serpents, unicorns, and flying dragons. And there was the Minotaur—half man, half bull—the legendary inhabitant of the Labyrinth.

The world's first bullpen? Greg's wry words came back to her with a mental picture of his shy grin and she smiled at the memory. Andi hadn't understood the baseball pun that first night they had sat and talked for hours under the stars—anymore than she understood the young athlete with the cerulean eyes and the tender heart of a poet.

It was that same night, she recalled, that she had told him the Hellenic myth from which her father had taken her name. Greg had remembered and had later given her a bracelet with a spool charm, signifying the story of Ariadne, daughter of the king of Crete, who had offered the visiting Greek hero Theseus his life in exchange for his love.

But Theseus abandoned Ariadne in the end, Andi recalled as the sentimental smile faded. *He went off in search of the Golden Fleece—no, that was Jason. Maybe Theseus was the one who fought the Nemean lion—no, it was Hercules. Well, he went somewhere*, Andi concluded. *To play* baseball, *for all I know—*

Feeling vaguely injured for her namesake and annoyed at herself for forgetting the details of a fable she had heard all her life, Andi consulted the index of her mythology book then turned to the ancient love story. "Theseus agreed to take Ariadne to Greece," it said, "where they would marry. But on the way, she became ill and Theseus dropped her off on the island of Naxos . . ." Andi frowned. *What a creep,* she thought. *The poor girl was probably only lovesick.* Noting an asterisk at the end of the paragraph, her eyes sank to the footnote. "Another version of the story is that Ariadne became tiresome and nagging during the voyage and was simply left there."

Now it was her heart that sank. *Call me in October*, she heard herself say and saw afresh in her mind the injured look on Greg's face. *I was worse than tiresome,* Andi thought in alarm. *I was immature and selfish. And I haven't done anything to correct it, either. I wouldn't blame Greg if he never wants to come back for me.*

Several people had brushed past Andi's seat before she recognized that sometime during her reverie the class had been dismissed. *Thank goodness,* she thought in relief. *I can call Greg right now. I probably can't catch him, but I can at least leave a message.* A shadow fell across her desk. Andi looked up at her father and forced a thin smile through her impatience. "Um, bye, Daddy."

"I'm glad you're still here, Ariadne," he said, ignoring the farewell. "I'd like your input on an idea I've been turning over in my mind."

"Could we talk about it later?" she asked imploringly. "I have another class and I—"

"It'll only take a minute. You heard that the speaker I lined up for the next lecture in the Humanities Symposium series had to cancel?"

"Um, yes," Andi fibbed, hoping to save herself a lengthy explanation. She couldn't believe her father wanted to talk with her about this in the first place. Always scheduled for a Saturday night because they were Trent's notion of an ideal date, the meetings were generally well attended only because they provided easy extra credit to offset a rotten score on one of Dr. Reynolds' notoriously wicked exams. With finals coming up, this last lecture was virtually guaranteed to be packed to the rafters and deathly dull. On the spot, Andi vowed to redouble her study efforts—if only to avoid the symposium.

"I thought Sterling Channing might fill the bill," Trent continued. "He had an opportunity to take an impressive number of photographs while serving as an assistant to his mission president, you know."

"Yes," Andi said slowly, "I saw them at a fireside, but—"

Trent plowed forward, like a used car salesman listing the attributes of his finest deal. "And his grasp of Peruvian culture is truly impressive."

"I'm sure it is, but—"

"I'm glad you agree with me, Andi," he said. "Sterling is having the photos converted to slides in the AV department. I told him that you would help organize his presentation when he gets them back in the next week or so."

So much for wanting my input, Andi thought. As usual, "turning over an idea in my mind" had meant to her father something between deciding it in advance and carving it in stone.

"Not only do I appreciate your help," Trent said, offering Andi her textbook for inclusion in her backpack, "but I knew you would appreciate the impact this project can have on your grade. Really, Ariadne," he continued, now in a professorial tone, "I do suspect your attention of being less than focused since you met Greg. To have a student with your capacity in the low C range—"

"I'd love to help!" Andi said quickly, zipping her backpack and retreating toward the door. "I'll call Greg." She flushed at the slip of tongue. "I mean I'll call Sterling—sometime this week." Feeling her father's sharp eyes looking deeper into her than was comfortable, she paused at the door and stammered, "I mean, I'll call him tomorrow." Her father raised one eyebrow. "Today? Good idea! If I hurry I can call him right now. Bye, Dad!"

Andi pushed open the door and slipped into the bright Arizona sunshine. As she walked quickly toward the Student Union in search of a phone, her good intentions of calling Sterling were eclipsed by thoughts of Greg. *If myth really is a past with a future, exercising itself in the present,* she thought, *and if that means what I hope it means, then this Phoenician Ariadne is going to hold on to her hero yet.*

CHAPTER 21

Bobbie Jo Howland always got her man. Breathing into her cupped palm to assure herself that a recent swig of Scope would obscure the lingering odor of the wine she had swallowed throughout the morning to bolster her confidence, she cast a final warning look at the two tow-headed boys posed on the couch. Nodding in satisfaction at their silent, wide-eyed compliance, Bobbie Jo ran lacquered nails through her freshly bleached hair then down the side of her sleek, leopard print mini and slowly opened the door.

The sultry smile widened in appreciation. This man looked even better than she had remembered—if that were possible. Bobbie Jo's stomach fluttered at the thought of the time and effort she'd wasted first on his loser of a brother and recently on a semi-wealthy local redneck when she should have been patient enough to hold out for Greg Howland. If the stupid doctors in Arizona hadn't said he would die, none of this mess would have happened in the first place. She tossed her head to clear it and show to advantage the dangling gold earrings she'd bought yesterday with Greg's money. What was past, was past. She'd have Greg now, Andi Reynolds or no Andi Reynolds.

When he didn't move, Bobbie Jo stepped out the door and threw thin, freckled arms around her brother-in-law's neck. "Greg!" she whispered breathily into his ear. "You don't know how much I've missed you!"

"Uh, hi, Bobbie Jo," he responded, disentangling himself from the embrace and turning his head away as he sneezed at the overpowering scent of Narcisse perfume. Taking a step back, he gratefully pulled Dawson forward. "This my new press agent, Dawson Geitler. Dawson, meet my sister-in-law, Bobbie Jo Howland."

This time it was Bobbie who stepped back, her heavily lined eyes narrowing in surprise and disappointment that Greg hadn't come alone. "What happened to Zeke?"

Greg ignored the question as he gazed over his sister-in-law's head into the room. "And these are my nephews, Dawson," he said. "At least, they *look* like my nephews. They're kinda quiet for the boys I remember, though. Maybe their mom traded them in for statutes, or had them stuffed, or—"

When Greg stepped around their mother with outstretched arms, the boys forgot every threat about their new clothes, carefully combed hair, and company manners. They bounced up in unison and yelled, "Uncle Greg!"

He met them halfway, grabbing one under each arm before whirling them around and collapsing with them into a wrestling match on the floor. "Okay, okay!" Greg laughed after several hectic minutes. "I give, already! When did you guys get to be so strong? Have you been sneaking carrots again after I told you to eat cookies?"

"Lookit my muscles!" the six-year-old cried, making a fist and pressing it into his shoulder while still stretched across Greg's broad chest. "Ain't I strong?"

"I'm stronger!" the eight-year-old insisted, trying to push his resistant brother off their uncle as a demonstration.

Greg separated them, one boy to each side, as he sat up. "Who's strong enough to open the trunk of the car to see what I brought you?"

"Me!" they yelled together.

"Tell you what. Justin, since you're the oldest, you open the trunk and then after you each get your bag out, Jason, you close it. Okay? But you've got to play with the stuff in the yard. You bring those super-soakers inside and your mom will skin us all alive." Grabbing the keys, the boys were out the door in a flash. Greg's grin faded quickly at the look of undisguised contempt on their mother's face as they stampeded past.

"Those are new clothes, Greg," she whined, allowing the screen door to bang closed behind them with Dawson just barely inside. "I bought them special for your visit and now they'll be ruinated."

"I'm sorry, Bobbie," he said slowly, conscious now of the heavy makeup that did little to enhance her sallow, pinched face. At twenty-six, Bobbie Jo was only a couple years his senior but looked much older. Sadie, who had assumed the chore of taking Bobbie's daily calls since they'd moved into the townhouse, had told him she'd been complaining of ill health. Greg had largely discounted it as another ploy for attention, but now he realized it might be true.

"I got the boys' hair cut, too," she added, "not that you noticed."

"They look real nice, Bobbie."

"I took them to the barber shop myself."

That took you, what—thirty minutes? Before Greg could berate himself for his cynicism, Bobbie Jo ran a trembling hand through her straight, stringy hair and continued. "Kids are so much *work*, Greg. You have no idea."

"What about Wanda?"

"Oh, *Wanda!*" Bobbie Jo sank onto the plush loveseat, striking what she thought was a provocative pose and patting the cushion beside her. "Come sit by me so we can talk about it."

Instead, Greg leaned back against the oak entertainment center. "I'm fine here on the floor, thanks. But you ought to offer Dawson a seat."

She raised a bony shoulder to her chin in a careless shrug. "Oh, sure. He can sit wherever he wants."

Greg watched Dawson choose an uncomfortable chair as far away from Bobbie Jo as possible. His obvious effort to blend into the background struck Greg as thoughtful, and he smiled sheepishly before turning back to his sister-in-law. "About Wanda—" Each day over the past few months, he had been grateful for the remarkable young au pair with the heart of Dorcas and patience of Job.

"She's leaving."

"Leaving? Why?" *As if it isn't obvious,* he thought in consternation. *I wouldn't last ten minutes around here myself.*

"She said something about going back to school," Bobbie Jo began vaguely. "It don't matter anyway, Greg. Now that you're back in Chicago—"

"Listen, Bobbie Jo, that's what I came to tell you." Greg leaned forward marginally and hoped for the best. "I'm not going back to Chicago. I've been traded—will be traded tomorrow—to the Arizona Diamondbacks." Since he'd worried about a possible explosive reaction, his brows came together at her apparent lack of interest. To make sure she understood, he added, "So, I'll be living in Mesa."

"Well, don't expect me to move in with your mother."

Greg's eyes widened with sudden understanding. Apparently, all the chemicals Bobbie Jo poured on her head had sunk through to affect her brain. As it was, two thousand miles was barely enough distance to maintain between his ex-sister-in-law and himself. But what about Justin and Jason? He couldn't leave them here alone with a woman who seemed to be a mother in name only. He owed his nephews more than that. And he had promised Jim.

Gently, Greg suggested, "When Wanda leaves, why don't I take the boys out to stay with Ma for a while?"

If Bobbie Jo had known how ugly the distortion made her features, she might have at least attempted to conceal her contempt. "Your ma, Greg?" she sneered. "She can't look after herself, let alone a couple of rowdy boys."

Greg looked up at the motionless ceiling fan. The sad thing was, Bobbie Jo was probably right. He thought for a moment about standing to turn on the fan then realized that the stifling feel of the room had little to do with the temperature. He said, "I'll hire a nanny to help her."

"Where does that leave *me*?"

"I'm trying to, uh, give you a break, Bobbie," Greg said kindly and mostly truthfully. "You'll stay here and, uh—" He paused and pursed his lips at the sudden threat of her large, crocodile tears.

"I couldn't live without my babies!"

Greg remembered the look she had given those "babies" on their way out the door and couldn't forget either that they had lived solely with their father prior to his death a few months before. *If those teardrops spill over,* Greg thought now with much of his sympathy for Bobbie Jo fading, *they'd be blacker than beetles from all that mascara.*

"What do you want from me, Bobbie Jo?" he asked tiredly. "A bigger house? More money? What?"

"I only want you, Greg!"

The candor in her expression brought the blood quickly to the surface of Greg's fair skin. He was careful to avoid her eyes—and Dawson's. "Bobbie Jo—"

"It's always been you, Greg!" she continued passionately. "Even before Jimmy died, I—"

"No!" Greg's hasty rise to his feet lent unnecessary emphasis to the word since the raw aversion crossing his face was clearly not lost on either onlooker. "You don't know what you're talking about!" He turned toward the wall and rubbed his forehead as if to forestall thought long enough to regain control of emotion. Finally he motioned to Dawson who rose immediately. Looking past Bobbie Jo's shoulder, he said, "We're going to take the boys in to Dubuque for the rest of the day. Make sure that Wanda's here when we get back. I want to talk to her." Hoping that his tone of voice left no room for argument, Greg waited for Dawson to step out the door before adding, "And lay off the booze, Bobbie Jo. Maybe that'll help you think clearer."

Bobbie Jo Howland put a palm unconsciously over her churning stomach as she stood at the window to watch Greg drive away with Jim's boys buckled happily in the back seat. The twin tracks of mascara that streaked her cheeks as the car turned the corner were black indeed. But they were no indication of a lady lost in love. They were tears of outrage from a woman rejected but resolute.

Her lips compressed into a thin fuschia line as the raccoon-rimmed eyes narrowed. She didn't know how she'd do it yet—or even when—but Bobbie Jo was sure that she knew somebody who *would* help her find a way to make Mr. High and Mighty Greg Howland sorry for rejecting her. If he thought he could just push people like her and Zeke Martoni aside now that he was famous, well, as her daddy used to say, he had another think coming.

CHAPTER 22

Was she ever going to get through to Greg? Andi wondered as yet another operator took yet another of her calls.

"Mr. Howland hasn't rung in for his messages," the woman reported. As soon as the words were out, she winced. It was her first night on the job and a training supervisor might be monitoring the call. Likely, she wasn't supposed to give out any information. Well, she could justify the slip, at least. This Andi Reynolds must be *somebody*. She had Howland's personal number, after all, and her name had been logged almost a dozen times on the computer screen since afternoon. The operator affected her most professional tone in case Andi was important. "May I take a message, please?"

Andi hesitated and glanced toward Clytie who lay on the next bed waiting her turn for the phone. Her sister had recently added a third part to her nightly ritual. Now, it consisted of reading a page of scripture, saying her prayers, then calling Thaddeus to talk and giggle for thirty minutes before going to sleep. Andi knew she was disrupting the routine. "Yes," she said finally, "please ask him to call me. He has the number." She lay the receiver on the cradle and pushed it across the table toward her sister.

"Greg hasn't received my messages," she told Clytie as the younger girl hesitated in concern. "And it's almost midnight in Chicago. He'll call me in the morning."

As Clytie nodded happily and began to dial, Andi lay back on the bed and thought about her last conversation with Greg. What if the operator was mistaken—or had been instructed to say that Greg didn't receive messages from people he didn't want to talk to?

She pulled a pillow out from under her head and, hugging it to her chest, curled herself around it. She'd be sleeping—or at least pretending to be—by the time Clytie hung up. She could barely *think* about Greg tonight; talking about him would be too painful. *He'll call tomorrow,* she promised herself, squeezing her eyes closed to offer a prayer to make it so. *But if he doesn't—* She heard Clytie greet Thaddeus and thought involuntarily of the boy's pet axiom: behold the ultimate truth. *The truth is,* she thought miserably, *if Greg doesn't return my calls, I'll know exactly where we stand.*

Bright pinpoints of stars glowed in the black background of sky as the car sped past the outskirts of Freeport on its way west to Chicago. After exhausting his supply of bubble gum over the course of one of the longest days he could remember, Greg had resorted to chewing on his lower lip. It was raw now and tasted of blood, which reminded him, not of how far he had come, literally and figuratively, from Iowa but of how far he had yet to go.

There had been a time, he thought, and there had in fact been many times, when his father could have dropped off the face of the earth and Greg would have felt only relief. But now that it seemed to have happened, his feelings confused him. For the last few weeks he had assumed that Roy Howland was merely too drunk or too indifferent to call looking for his wife and son. But from what he had seen at the house today, although Roy had almost certainly been drunk when he returned home to find Sadie gone, he clearly had not been indifferent to her departure.

And what of his mother? Since she'd been in Arizona, Greg had never heard her speak her husband's name. Yet they had been married for more than thirty years. She couldn't have forgotten him or put that life behind herself so quickly. Could she?

Greg tried to put his parents out of his mind and concentrate on the road ahead under a growing weight of mental and physical fatigue. Unfortunately, thoughts of Jim's boys came quickly to fill the void. What would he do when Wanda left Peosta in early August? Bobbie Jo was in a worse state than he had realized. According to the nanny, in the time since his accident, Bobbie had been away frequently, occasionally disappearing for days at a time. That she was home now was most likely due to a lingering case of the flu. Her illness had done nothing to improve her disposition or make her more tolerant of the two rambunctious little boys who would soon be out of school and under foot full-time.

Greg's teeth sunk into sore flesh as he thought about the little boys who had recently lost the father they adored. Now all they had left was an indifferent mother, "missing" grandparents, and a famous uncle they saw mostly on TV. What they needed was a family. But even if he was prepared to take on the full-time responsibility of their care, Greg suspected that his legal chances of getting them away from Bobbie Jo were slim to none. The only option then was to hire another au pair—as soon as he made sure Wanda had everything she needed in the way of money for school.

Anyway, Greg decided finally, if he stewed anymore tonight, he'd not only make himself crazy but a swollen lower lip would make him look more like a lousy prizefighter than an ace pitcher at his press conference tomorrow morning. Then wouldn't Mrs. Dresmont—who had hired him mainly, she had said, for his clean-cut, All-American look—have a fit?

He glanced over at Dawson pecking away on his laptop. The man had worked steadily since crossing the Mississippi River. Greg raised one eyebrow and asked, "Do I pay you enough, Dawson?"

With the laptop turned sideways, it was impossible for Greg to see the screen. Still, Dawson slapped it down quickly. "What? I mean, yes, sir." His eyes darted from Greg to the computer and back. "Of course you do."

"Well, I sure couldn't afford to pay you by the hour," Greg continued. "What do you work on average—five a.m. to midnight?"

"Oh!" Dawson said, visibly relaxing as he caught the drift. "Actually, I wasn't working for you just now, Mr. Howland. I was, um, writing. A—a—novel."

"Really?" Greg asked. "That's great. Sorry I bothered you. Go ahead and write. I'll be quiet." Stifling a yawn, he watched Dawson raise the screen again. He was silent for the better part of five minutes before curiosity got the best of him. "A mystery?"

"Uh, no," Dawson replied, his fingers slowing over the keyboard.

"An adventure?"

Dawson shook his head.

"Horror? Science Fiction?"

"No, sir."

"Well, don't tell me you're writing a romance."

"It's a—a—" Having stupidly eliminated most genres, Dawson wondered what was left. "It's historical fiction," he said finally.

"Really? That's great. Michener's one of my favorites. What's your book about?" From the corner of his eye, Greg saw Dawson reach in his pocket for the roll of Tums and quickly apologized again. "You work. I'll keep quiet and drive." He turned up the volume on the radio and tried to concentrate on the long, unchallenging road ahead. When he spoke again, it was to himself. "That's really great. I like to think that someday I'll do something important like that."

Dawson stopped typing to regard his employer in astonishment. "Mr. Howland, you pitched a no-hit game in the last World Series."

"So?"

"So?" Dawson echoed. "How many men have done that?"

"A couple, that I know of," Greg replied.

"My point, exactly."

"My point," Greg said with the beginning of the lopsided grin, "is who cares?" He removed one hand from the wheel for a moment to wave off Dawson's objections and continued. "I bet you couldn't find one person on earth tonight besides me who cares." Greg reflected on the event for a minute then added, "Including me. But look at you. You're writing a book. Books can change lives." Greg's brows knit as Geitler's eyes remained downcast. He seemed to be examining his fingernails in the green glow of the LCD screen. "Look, Dawson," Greg tried to explain, "I feel different about baseball—and other things—now."

"Because?"

"Well, you know how they say that when you die—almost die—your life flashes in front of you? Yeah? Well, something like that happened to me when I was hit by that ball in spring training. But I didn't see my life experiences so much as I *felt* them. The best I can explain, it was kinda like living things all over again, but this time I was blessed with sense enough to recognize what was really important. And you know what I felt in that World Series game, Dawson? Pride. Not gratitude to my teammates for some great back-up plays, or even gratitude to God for giving me a one-in-a-million gift and the opportunity to use it. Just *pride*." He shuddered. "I don't ever want to feel anything that negative again."

"Then," Dawson began carefully, since this was the closest Greg had come to sharing his near-death experience, and the press agent wanted to get everything from it he could, "what do you think is important now?"

Greg glanced at his companion. "Mostly little things," he said. "Like the way you reached out to take Jason's germy little hand when we crossed a busy street this afternoon. It was okay," he added quickly with a smile at Dawson's evident embarrassment, "to rinse off later with that antibacterial stuff you pull out when you think no one's looking." Greg stifled another yawn and hunched his shoulders a couple of times to stay awake. "And some not-so-little things are important, too—like your Great American Novel, for instance. So, get to work, Dawson. We're still almost an hour outside of Chicago."

Dawson nodded and turned back to the screen where he had begun to list Greg's accomplishments for an appendix. He drummed his fingers lightly on the side of the keyboard for a few seconds then turned off the computer and lowered the top.

"Why don't I drive instead?" he offered. "You ought to get some rest. You've got that press conference to look forward to tomorrow, then a flight to Milwaukee and a ballgame. Besides," he added when Greg hesitated, "you do the writing that supports me at present—signing my monthly paycheck."

Greg grinned gratefully and slowed the car. As he pulled to a stop on the shoulder of the highway, he reached over to clasp Geitler's shoulder. "Thanks for everything, Dawson," he said. "You always seem to be around at the right time."

Geitler had been leaning over the seat to stash his computer in back, which hid the startled, guilty look on his face. Howland's sentimentality had a way of rubbing off on you if you weren't careful, and for a moment Dawson wondered uncomfortably how it would make him feel to have Greg learn the motive for all this togetherness. Then, with a shrug, he tried to inject a healthy shot of reason into the remorse.

Sure, Greg read Michener and Stone and probably even Tolstoy, he thought as he circled the car to the driver's seat. But over the years the rest of the world had moved on from an appreciation of historical fiction to a hysterical fixation with celebrity. And for sheer volume of material, if nothing else, today had been beyond belief. Thanks to whatever patron saint looked after sleazy biographers, Dawson not only had fact that was stranger than fiction, he had a couple of weeks to work on it safely away from Howland's little sermons and good turns and—especially—his overtures of friendship.

As he slid behind the wheel, Dawson almost smiled at the thought that the Diamondback's two-week road trip would keep Greg occupied with baseball and out of his hair for a little while at least. Without this virtuous young man around to make him feel uncomfortable, Dawson could finish his book and clear out long before the World Series.

Greg settled into the passenger seat as Dawson pulled onto the highway. Opening his cell phone, he glanced at his watch. Even with the time change, it was a little late to call Arizona. Instead, he punched in enough security code numbers to reach the president and greeted his own operator. "Any messages?" he asked, then repeated himself after several moments of dead air.

The operator struggled to recover her senses. First she'd drawn Greg Howland's account on her very first night and now she had actually heard his voice. She was going to love this job.

"Hello?" he repeated.

"Hi!" she said quickly. "I mean, good morning. No, I mean—good evening! Thank you for calling Mr. Howland's—No, that isn't right!" She hit a button to advance the screen from the greeting she was supposed to give callers, to the messages she was supposed to give Greg. But something was wrong with her computer. The screen where the list had been a few minutes ago was white. She hit another button, then another. What had she done with the messages?

"Are you still there?" Greg asked after a few more seconds.

"I'm here," she managed to squeak.

"Great. Any messages?"

"I, uh—" Really, she decided, she hadn't liked this operator's job much, anyway. She'd rather work in a department store when it came right down to it; they gave you an employee discount. "Well," she said honestly, "your message screen is blank."

"Okay," Greg responded with a sigh. "Thanks." He dropped the phone between the seats, looked up at the numberless stars, and chose the brightest to wish that when October finally came and he was able to reclaim that part of his life, Andi would be waiting.

Chapter 23

"And the vinyl top snaps off so you can see the sky," Greg told Thaddeus to conclude the narration of a long list of upgrades he had arranged to have made on his Jeep. Although Greg couldn't say as much for his time on the road with his new team, his car's days in a local dealership had been well spent. Greg wasn't sure there were any original parts left on it, but it was air-conditioned now—in anticipation of July—and certainly respectable enough to chauffeur Sadie, Thaddeus and, hopefully, Andi. Yet, it was still a classic, as Greg assured the youth, still carmine red, and still bore at least a passable resemblance to the wreck he had liked at first sight on the used-car lot.

And that's what was important, after all—the principle of the thing.

"And how much did all these little renovations cost you?" Thaddeus asked, running his left hand along the new leather seat while his right confirmed that the cracked passenger window had also been replaced.

"Oh, not much more than a new Corvette." Greg cast his friend a sideways glance when he chortled, then looked down at his watch as he turned onto the Reynolds' street in Mesa. "Four o'clock on the nose. Perfect timing."

"Thanks again for the ride," Thaddeus said.

"It was my pleasure," Greg responded. "I'm happy to finally have a day off to see you."

"And looking forward to seeing Andi while you're at it?"

"Well, yeah," Greg admitted as he braked to a stop in front of her home and noted with disappointment that her car wasn't in the driveway. "I guess. You know, Thaddeus, when Andi didn't call me, I kind of chickened out on calling her. It's been eight days since I've talked to her."

"How many hours?"

Hundreds of hours, Greg thought, *but it seems like thousands.*

The front door opened immediately and Clytie appeared on the porch at about the same time her brother Brad came through a side fence, trying to tote a rake, tree trimmer, and weed whacker while also pulling a heavy mower. When he dropped the sharp trimmer, narrowly missing his sandaled right foot, Greg swung open his car door.

"Do you need an extra hand there, Brad?" he asked, covering the distance between them in a few long strides.

"I need more hands all right," Brad muttered, too disgusted at the moment to remember to be awed by the pitcher's presence, "but no one's around when they're supposed to be."

Greg picked up the trimmer then took the weed whacker and rake away as well. Scanning the already manicured front yard, he asked, "So, what're you doing?"

"Cleaning up at Sister Anderson's," Brad replied dourly. "It's *supposed* to be a quorum project, but I called every priest in the ward and they all have something better to do."

"You didn't call me."

Looking up at Greg, Brad suddenly remembered he was talking to an American icon. He reached quickly for his landscaping tools. "Gosh, no. I'd never call you."

Greg held the utensils out of reach. *"I'm* a priest and I'll have you know," he said with a smile, "that I spent more than my share of days clearing cow pastures to earn money for my first glove and cleats. I'll bet I still have what it takes help out with the little patches of grass that pass for yards here in the desert." He returned to the Jeep and tossed the utensils behind the back seat. "Where to?"

"Sister Anderson lives just around the corner—" Brad said hesitantly.

"Bring the mower, let's go."

By this time, Clytie had finished a quick consultation with Thaddeus and climbed into the back seat of the Jeep. "We'll help, too," she offered brightly.

"But I'll have you know, Brad," Thaddeus said, imitating Greg, "that unlike Horatio Alger here, I've *always* been a rich kid—never pulled a weed in my life."

"Yeah, but he's a bright boy," Greg grinned, restarting the car. "He'll learn fast enough." As Brad carefully balanced the mower and climbed in afterwards, Greg added, "I don't think you'd better trust Thaddeus with a weed whacker, though. I've seen how he swings a cane. You get him started and there won't be a plant left between here and Cleveland."

Sister Anderson's front yard was not only a fraction of the size of a cow pasture, Greg noted with satisfaction a few minutes later, it lacked the territorial bulls he had especially hated in his previous line of work. "Okay, Brad," he said cheerfully, "you're the foreman of this project. Tell us what to do."

More than an hour later, after being nipped by Sister Anderson's dog—an arthritic dachshund with more attitude than any bull on earth—and surviving what he had at first feared might be a losing battle with an overgrown bougainvillea bush, Greg's only recollection of Iowa cow pastures were nostalgic ones. He removed one work glove to suck the fleshy part of an impaled finger and muttered under his breath, "What's with this stupid plant?"

Thaddeus, who crouched nearby carefully placing ice plants into the holes Clytie had dug for them, responded, "If you're referring to the shrub you've been trimming, Greg, bougainvillea are a South American import distinctive for their long, needle-sharp thorns."

"No kidding," Greg said, placing the trimmed branches gingerly into the yard waste recycle barrel and wondering if Thaddeus had ever heard of a rhetorical question. He stood back to survey the job. "Is this okay, Brad? Brad?" Greg glanced around the yard and finally spotted Andi's brother at the edge of the lawn, leaning on his mower as he gazed down the street.

"Brittanie Paisner—" Clytie told Greg, following her brother's line of vision, "—the blonde. She's head cheerleader at our high school and the love of Brad's life."

"Really?" Greg took a step away from the house for a better view. The girl stood on the sidewalk, half a dozen houses away, talking animatedly with a friend. Greg took in the short shorts and halter-top with a slight raise of one eyebrow. "Brad's dating her?"

"Dating Brittanie?" Clytie responded with a roll of big eyes. "Only in his dreams. She *may* have stepped on his adoring face on her way to a pep rally once—but he would have been grateful and she wouldn't have noticed."

Oh, Greg said to himself as he walked toward Andi's brother, *one of those*. When his approach failed to break into Brad's daydream, Greg extended a hand to nudge the young man's shoulder. "How's it look?" he asked.

"Really great," Brad murmured towards Brittanie.

"I'm talking about the bouga—whatever you call that porcupine of a plant."

"Huh?" Brad turned in embarrassment. "Oh, the bush. It's fine. Thanks."

"Yeah," Greg said, surveying his work with satisfaction. "I'll expect a letter from the mayor. I probably saved the city from that monster." Noting that Brad's eyes were again locked on the young woman down the street, Greg added, "Would you like some free, unsolicited advice about Brittanie?"

Brad looked at him in surprise. "You don't know Brittanie."

"Do you?"

"No," Brad conceded. "Girls like her only go out with—well, you know—guys like you."

Greg smiled. "Brad, when I was your age I was a poor, gangly math nerd who happened to throw a baseball. Girls like Brittanie thought they were too good to spit on me, let alone date me." He tightened his grip on the young man's shoulder. "This is my point, Brad. It's been a few years, a few hundred baseball games, and a few million dollars since then, but who do you think has really changed—the girls or me?"

"You," Brad responded without hesitation.

Greg reconsidered his thesis with a wry shake of his head. "Let me put this another way. I've dated women like Brittanie since college and, believe me, you want to stick with taking out girls like your sisters." At Brad's dubious expression, he added, "Would you really want to go—I don't know, say to the prom—with a girl who cared more about the impression she made on the crowd than the impression she made on you?"

Greg sighed at the besotted look Brad cast Brittanie. He was getting nowhere fast. Maybe, he concluded, there was only one way to learn this lesson—in the legendary school of hard knocks. "Do you have a date to the prom?" he asked impulsively. At the negative movement of Brad's head, he added, "Does Brittanie?"

"I doubt it," Brad said slowly. "I heard she broke up with the captain of the basketball team this week."

"Then go ask her," Greg urged.

Brad regarding him incredulously. "I can't just *ask* Brittanie Paisner to Prom."

"Why not?"

"That isn't how it's done, Greg," Clytie said. Although she'd tried her best to remain silent, she was constitutionally unable to mind her own business when romance was involved. "Brad would have to come up with something to impress Brittanie. Like—" she searched her mind for ideas she had admired. "Like a mime with a bouquet of balloons or a singing gorilla."

"A singing gorilla would be especially impressive," Thaddeus observed from behind her shoulder, "since gorillas have severely limited vocal capabilities."

"A costumed gorilla," Clytie giggled, "not a real one. Or a costumed *something*. Guys get other guys to go to the door dressed as clowns and butlers and—all kinds of things. It's so fun."

"What have people come to your door dressed as?" Thaddeus inquired.

"Nothing," Clytie admitted regretfully. "I've never been asked to a dance and Andi always went with Sterling." She frowned. "He thought the costume thing was silly."

Greg couldn't disagree with Channing on that count. Still, looking at Brad, he could see that the young man hadn't taken his eyes off of Brittanie. "How about some guy who looks sorta like a celebrity baseball player? Think that could work?" Before Brad could respond, Greg had picked up his trimmer and headed for the rose bushes. "I don't think Sister Anderson will mind sacrificing a few prize blossoms for such a good cause." He snipped three perfect red buds with a boyish grin and added a couple of white vincas and a spray of asparagus fern for good measure. "Wish your brother luck, Clytie!" he called as he stepped over her newly planted ground cover onto the sidewalk. "We'll see how well I measure up for him against a singing gorilla."

Clytie stood next to an open-mouthed Brad as they watched Greg jog down the street. Though she had never imagined seeing Brittanie Paisner disconcerted over anything, Clytie thought now that the homecoming queen couldn't have been more astonished if a little green Martian had appeared to revoke her crown. She smiled to see Greg wave a flat palm back and forth before Brittanie's mesmerized face as he spoke. Then he pressed the makeshift bouquet into her hand and turned to point toward where Brad stood. Brittanie's eyes never left Greg's face, but she nodded numbly and, at his urging, raised a feeble hand toward Brad in acknowledgment. Greg said something else then turned to jog back up the street while Brittanie's friend grabbed her excitedly and escorted her, shaking and squealing, into her house.

"She said yes," Greg reported upon his arrival back in Sister Anderson's yard, "and I didn't even have to sing." He watched the look of astonishment on Brad's face change to exhilaration and added quickly, "But don't thank me, Brad, because I, for one, doubt that I've done you a favor."

"Hello, Bishop!" Andi called as she reached back into her car to pull out her backpack before walking up the driveway toward her house. "Does anyone know you're here?"

Dan Ferris, a brave man by anyone's standards, stood a couple paces back from the Reynolds' front door, trying to decide if he should advance on the Lord's errand or retreat in order to live to serve another day. He turned now to Andi in relief. "No one except for this attack duck of yours."

"Icarus!" Andi called, running lightly up the stairs.

Instead of retreating from its self-appointed guard post, the green and brown mallard puffed up its feathers and elongated an already impressive wingspan. Andi dropped her backpack on the porch with a sigh.

"Come on, you big faker," she smiled, scooping the fowl up from underneath and causing a quick refolding of wings. "Get out of the way. We have company." When the mallard opened his strong beak to quack a final warning to the intruder, Andi walked over to the railing and dumped Icarus unceremoniously over the side. Watching in satisfaction as the duck glided to the ground then waddled off toward the side of the house, Andi called, "Go in the backyard, please!" Then she turned to the bishop and reached for the door handle to finally allow him inside. "I'm sorry—"

"No problem," Bishop Ferris said, following her into the entryway. "I brought these food order forms over for your mother, but I'm glad to have a chance to see you."

"Oh?" A slight stiffening in Andi's back was barely perceptible.

"I hear you haven't talked to Greg since he left."

"No," Andi said, glad that her face was turned away to hide the glow that must be creeping into her cheeks. "But I've been by to see Mrs. Howland every day. She says that Greg's had a great trip."

"That, of course, is what he told *her*."

"What has he told you?" Andi asked, turning quickly, heedless now of her burning cheeks and Dan Ferris' slow smile. "I mean, is there something I should know about Greg?"

"That depends on how much you care for him, Andi."

Andi began to respond, then pursed her lips and looked away from her bishop's probing eyes. She cared more about Greg than anything, but when he hadn't returned her calls, what else could she do but try to push him out of her mind the way his return to baseball had apparently crowded out thoughts of her in his mind? She had even, after almost eight impossibly long days, had some success. She could now *not* think about Greg for as long as fifteen seconds at a stretch. "I love Greg," she said finally.

"Does he know that?"

"Well, I called *him*—" she began.

"Now I'm *sure* he doesn't know that. I wonder what happened." Ferris leaned his stocky frame against the door jam and continued reflectively, "You wonder sometimes just how many trials have to come before those blessings. I'd hoped that after everything Greg's been through in life, and everything he's committed to, he'd finally find a little joy and reassurance." He shook his head and looked back at Andi. "I guess, then, you didn't know that he's been back to Iowa."

Andi had only barely been listening to the bishop as she berated herself for not calling Greg again after that first day. At Ferris' last words, however, her thoughts shifted gear rapidly. "He went to see his father?" she asked, distaste flitting candidly across her face.

"Yes, but Roy hadn't been there for some time."

"Then where—"

"No one knows," the bishop answered. "I ran all the standard checks down at the station, but nothing turned up."

"Mrs. Howland hasn't heard from her husband?"

"No, and according to Greg, she hasn't asked about him." The bishop nodded as if in agreement with Andi's thoughts. "But it may not be as strange as it seems when you consider the circumstances, Andi. They must have lived a hellish life." Ferris looked down at the forms in his hand as he seemed to consider. Finally he said, "I think Greg might pursue a search for his father more aggressively if he weren't so concerned at the moment about his mother. Trying to look after her and make arrangements to take care of his nephews back in Iowa is about all he can handle at the moment."

"What exactly is wrong with Bobbie Jo?" Andi asked.

"Well, I don't know if it's a mental or physical breakdown, but I do know she's got Greg's attention. Plus, the nanny he hired is leaving them in a month or two, and he has to find a replacement. Of course," Ferris added, "he has to do it all long-distance while worrying about fitting in with his new team and getting ready to pitch here for the first time tomorrow night. And it took a lot of effort and a lot of nerve to leave the team he came up with for the Diamondbacks, you know."

"And Greg does want to be good at baseball," Andi murmured sympathetically.

Bishop Ferris reached forward to grasp Andi's arm. When her eyes rose to meet his, he said, "What Greg wants is to play out his contract this year—and do it as close as possible to the people he loves." When he was sure Andi understood his meaning, he added with a smile,

"And now that he's back in town, he's *really* up to his neck in thorns. When I went by Sister Anderson's a little while ago, I saw him there with Brad, taking on that two-story bougainvillea bush of hers."

"Greg's out doing yard work?" Andi asked incredulously. "This is the only day he'll have off for a month and he's spending it—"

"Serving a widow," Bishop Ferris finished for her. "Does that surprise you?"

Andi shook her head slowly then looked longingly out the still-open door. "My mother's around here somewhere—" she began.

Dan Ferris ushered Andi onto the porch with a smile. "You run see Greg," he instructed. "I'll stand here and ring the doorbell and hope your mother answers before Clytie's attack duck returns to his post."

Chapter 24

Greg lugged the heavy recycle bin back to its berth at the side of Sister Anderson's home, grabbed the rake he had left leaning against the wall, and returned to the front yard. Rounding the corner, he stopped short. Was it the unaccustomed spring heat, he wondered, that had made him delusional enough to start seeing mirages?

Andi was kneeling on the grass next to Clytie and Thaddeus, admiring their newly planted flowerbed. The late afternoon sun caressed her shoulders, brightening her curls to an ethereal halo of copper and gold. Recovering from his surprise, Greg quickened his steps, remembering the first prayer he had offered at the zoo and thanking God again for sending him this angel in response. Then Andi looked up and in an instant he remembered her last words at his baptism. He hesitated, doubt crossing his face before Andi had had the slightest chance to see his initial delight.

"Hello, Greg," she said almost shyly as she rose gracefully and took a step forward to meet him. "How was your trip?"

"It had its ups and downs," he replied slowly.

Ups? a sarcastic little voice in his brain taunted. *Name one single up.*

"I thought about you all the time," she said, knowing by the look in his eyes that he had no idea how true it was. "But when you never returned my calls, I . . ."

Greg wondered if he had misheard Andi's quiet words under the rumble of a passing jet plane. He ran a couple of fingers across the mingled sweat and dirt on his forehead and took a tentative step nearer. "You called me?"

"The day after you left. When you didn't call me back I thought you were angry because I had behaved so badly after your baptism." Andi's eyes were luminous. "I'm sorry, Greg."

Greg glanced around for a spot to lean the rake then dropped it instead to keep anything from standing between himself and Andi. With mirages like this to offer, he vowed never to leave Arizona. As he moved close to her, he said, "No, I'm sorry. Sorry I didn't get your message. Sorry I was too dumb to call you. Sorry I missed eight days of hearing your voice." Ignoring the dirt on his hands and everyone else in the yard, Greg took Andi's fingers in his own and pulled her close.

"Well, this place looks good to me!" Thaddeus announced loudly. "I say we wash up and all take in dinner and a movie."

It took a minute for Thaddeus' words—and his good intentions–to sink in. When they did, Greg turned with an affectionate grin. "*Looks* good to you, huh? Maybe that's why Brad's the foreman of this project."

"It looks good to me, too!" Clytie added, sticking a pudgy elbow into her big brother's thigh.

"Yeah," Brad chimed in at the nudge. "It's great. Thanks for all your help."

Greg glanced around the yard and noted that it would look pretty good by anybody's standards. He considered the blind youth for a moment, wondering how much his friend would enjoy a movie. Finally, Greg decided that if Thaddeus was game, he'd be ready, willing, and grateful himself for a couple of hours of sitting in a dark theater next to Andi.

"Well," he said, turning back to her hopefully, "I think that's Thaddeus' version of an invitation. Shall we double date this evening?"

"Yes!" she said, then her face fell as she remembered Sterling's symposium on Saturday night and the fact that she had already put off her promised help until virtually the last day. She could kick herself now for her procrastination. If she had met with Sterling immediately, as her father had wanted, it would be done now and she would be free to go with Greg tonight. It was just that when Greg hadn't returned her calls, Andi had felt she simply couldn't face an evening listening to Sterling expound on Greg's unsuitability as marriage material. Especially since it would undoubtedly be a double billed lecture with her father elucidating Sterling's utter suitability.

Her thoughts whirling, Andi bit her lower lip in consternation. "No."

"If it's a multiple choice answer," Greg replied, "I choose A."

"It's just that I—"

"I'll go home and wash Sister Anderson's yard off me first," he offered, though he knew it was to forestall Andi's refusal more than to convince her otherwise.

"I wish I could—"

"You can even choose the movie," Greg offered quickly. "Nothing about baseball, I promise. We won't even go to anything with Kevin Costner *in* it."

"Greg," Andi said, rushing the next words before he could interrupt again, "I can't go. Sterling's coming over this evening." As Greg's eyes darkened to indigo, she added, "Only because we have to—um—do a class project. Sort of." Above all, she didn't want Greg to misunderstand what she was doing. The look on his face, however, suggested that he already had. She hurried to explain, "You see, I told him—Sterling—that I'd help to organize his mission slides. He has a presentation to make at ASU this weekend. The Humanities Department invited him to speak on modern Peruvian culture and—"

The Humanities Department, Greg repeated to himself as Andi rattled on, *meaning your father, the department chairman.*

"—and, well, it's a good missionary opportunity," Andi concluded helplessly.

"Oh, yeah," Greg muttered. "Education, entertainment, and eternal enlightenment. Leave it to Sterling Channing to pull all that off in one sitting."

Andi's look was pleading. "I'm sorry I can't go with you, Greg—"

"No, hey, it's fine," he interrupted with a wave of his bougainvillea-scarred hand. "I could use a free evening anyway. I need to catch up on my—uh—my—"

"Philanthropic work with disabled Serbian refugee orphans," Thaddeus supplied enthusiastically. "And their homeless pets."

Greg stared at his young blind friend. "Huh?"

"Play along," Thaddeus suggested in a mock stage whisper. "I'm trying to make you look good for your fiancée, Howland, but—ultimate truth time here—getting a mere mortal like you to compare favorably to Sterling Channing calls for a little creativity."

The ultimate truth, Greg suspected as he carried his dinner from the microwave to the table, was that it *would* take more than a little creativity to make him look good in comparison to Sterling—especially in Trent Reynolds' eyes. It might well take an Act of Congress. More likely, it would take an act of God.

He slid the TV dinner onto the place mat and reached for the daily paper, grateful to at least have the luxury of sulking in private. He'd tactfully refused an invitation to hang out with Thaddeus and Clytie and, although his mother had carefully taped his game schedule to the refrigerator door, she apparently hadn't understood it. Thinking Greg would be gone tonight as usual, she had agreed to accompany Laura Newton to a quilting night at Homecraft, a charitable center run by the Church. Greg, glad of Sadie's willingness to serve and grateful for the strong friendship she had developed with her visiting teacher, had insisted she go through with her plans.

Unfolding the *Republic*, Greg glanced at the headlines then rubbed a hand over his eyes to blot out the unwelcome sight of his name and picture. Try as he might, he couldn't understand why his first pitch was front-page news twenty-four hours before he picked up a ball.

"Give me a break," he muttered, but even as he said it, he knew the press never would. His dinner was cold again before he had finished reading—and rereading—the feature columnist's clever remarks, but it didn't matter. He had lost his appetite midway through the piece—probably in the paragraph where the writer pointed out that Greg's salary for one game averaged more than twenty times what many American families scraped by on for a whole year.

They pay me four thousand dollars a pitch? he marveled, laying aside the newspaper. *Could that possibly be right?*

Sadie's grocery list lay on the table. Pushing his plate away, Greg reached for the note card, flipped it over, and grabbed a nearby pencil for calculations of his own. *Do I throw a hundred and ten pitches in the average game?* he wondered. *A hundred and twenty sometimes?* He decided to go with the latter. *Now, what do I make?*

Quickly multiplying the number of games he was likely to pitch by the number of balls he was likely to throw, he used the sum as a divisor for the figure most likely to appear on this year's W-2.

The columnist did *exaggerate*, he thought ruefully, dropping the pencil. According to his estimation—and Greg trusted his math more than he did his curve ball—he made a mere $3,894.69 every time he threw a fastball. That, of course, didn't take into consideration money he made from endorsements because he *could* throw a fastball.

Greg crumpled the grocery list and dropped it on his still full plate as he slid back his chair. *No wonder that writer thinks I play in the same league as Ebenezer Scrooge.*

He walked restlessly into the living room and paused to run his hand across the afghan his mother had nearly completed for Margaret Reynolds, admiring her beautiful, skilled work. Then he looked around the room, hoping for something constructive to do himself. His eyes came to rest on what appeared to be a framed document. He was almost sure that it hadn't been there when he left. Curious, Greg walked over to examine the print.

"The Family," he read aloud. "A Proclamation to the World." Tiny invisible fingers seemed to run up and down the back of Greg's neck as he read the nine brief paragraphs through quickly at first, then again more slowly. The third paragraph he read yet again.

"In the premortal realm, spirit sons and daughters knew and worshiped God as their Eternal Father," the First Presidency had proclaimed. "Sacred ordinances and covenants available in holy temples make it possible for individuals to return to the presence of God and for families to be united eternally."

I'm looking for something constructive to do and I guess you can't get any more constructive than that, Greg thought with a smile, heading at once down the hall to retrieve the family Bible that lay safely tucked away in his luggage. He paused in dismay at the door to the bedroom. His suitcase lay open, and empty, on the bed. His mother must have undertaken the chore of unpacking for him this afternoon when he went to pick up Thaddeus. Greg's eyes swept the room and found what he had sought. Sadie had placed the linen-wrapped scripture and old photograph prominently on top of his bureau.

Greg drew in a deep breath and held it as he considered the implications. *She knows, then, that I've been out to the house in Iowa*, he thought. It took less than two heartbeats for his emotions to slide up the scale from curiosity toward trepidation. *Then why hasn't she asked about Dad?*

One thing Greg knew for certain was that pacing around this house all evening would drive him nuts. He strode across the room and picked up the Bible, intent on carrying out the plan suggested by the Spirit when he read the Proclamation. (When he had told Bishop Ferris over the phone about finding the Bible, the older man had suggested a visit to the Church's Family History Center across the street from the temple.) There was no time like the present, Greg thought. He'd see what he could do about a crash course in genealogy, then pick his mother up from her meeting. That way, he'd hopefully come home with some answers about what he should do about *all* his family—living and dead. And if nothing else, he'd at least kill enough time for Sterling to clear out so he could finally call Andi.

As Greg turned from the dresser, the picture caught his eye and he lifted it to grin back at his great-great-great grandfather.

"I'm pretty good at feeling sorry for myself over the stupidest things, aren't I, Grandpa?" he asked softly. "What did *you* ever have in life to be thankful for but your small farm and large family?" He set the picture back carefully and grasped the Bible more firmly. If he did nothing else in life, Greg was determined to give that old farmer a future with his grandchildren worth smiling about.

Chapter 25

A small group of young women in Sunday dress walked happily together up the flower-lined sidewalk toward the east entrance of the Arizona Temple. Across the street in the Family History Center parking lot, Greg felt his heart beat a little faster when the baptistry doors swung open in welcome.

"Else what shall they do which are baptized for the dead, if the dead rise not at all?" he recited quietly as he reached back into his car to gently remove his ancient tome of scripture and family history.

The last few days on the road with unfamiliar teammates had afforded ample time alone to read 1 Corinthians—and every other scripture in the topical guide that made reference to baptism and/or death. The solitude had given Greg time, too, to ponder the lives of the people whose names had been preserved—some for almost two hundred years—for this time. *And,* Greg thought, his eyes moving back across the street, *for this place.*

Greg looked from the temple toward the door of the genealogical center. *First things first,* he thought with a little trepidation over embarking onto uncharted territory. After all, he had no idea what he was doing. *You didn't know what you were doing when you first opened that Book of Mormon, either,* he told himself as he gripped the door handle, *and look how far it's taken you . . .*

"Fam-lies can be to-ge-ther for-ever!" Francie's enthusiastic, off-key solo carried through the French doors and onto the patio where Clytie was seated by a low wicker table enjoying a few of her favorite things: fresh-squeezed lemonade, still-hot snickerdoodles, and Thaddeus.

"Is that song a threat or a promise?" Thaddeus asked as he reached for another cookie while deliberating his next move at the chessboard.

Clytie frowned at the seriousness of his expression. It had been so nice to have him come for dinner with her family. And it had gone so well. Even her father seemed to like Thaddeus. But of course, she thought, a college professor would *have* to be impressed by someone as smart as Thaddeus.

After dinner, they'd baked cookies with Andi and Francie until Sterling came, then she'd brought Thaddeus out to the patio to play chess and introduce him to Icarus. Of course, he knew something about ducks—Thaddeus knew something about everything—and Clytie was usually happy to talk with him for hours about any subject under the sun. But now, his driver would soon be here and she hated to risk ending a perfect evening with the wrong topic now.

Why can't I ever think of a clever comeback? Clytie wondered when Thaddeus repeated the wry question at Francie's third or fourth chorus. "Well, *I* think it's a promise," she said finally, unaware that what she might lack in wit she more than made up in warmth and honesty. Relieved when Thaddeus didn't offer another sarcastic one-liner and curious to know more about his family, a subject they had seldom broached, she asked, "Were your parents sealed?"

"Yep. I was born in the covenant. For all the good it does me," he added cynically.

Clytie couldn't suppress a gasp. The way she felt about her family, Thaddeus' words were almost sacrilegious. "What do you mean?"

"I don't know, Clytie," he sighed. "I guess I mean that it's been hard to figure out what good forever does you when you're so lonely for now."

"Do you mean your father?" she asked quietly. "Or you?"

"Yes," he replied.

Clytie paused to brush the long, blonde tresses back from her eyes as she leaned forward. "Do you remember your mother?"

Thaddeus nodded and it seemed to Clytie that the gold-flecked highlights in his liquid-bronze eyes assumed a deeper glow. "Very well, in fact. I've been able to almost see her again since I've been blind."

"What was she like?"

A smile flickered across his face. "She was pretty, Clytie. And—noisy."

"Noisy?"

"Noisy," Thaddeus affirmed. "That's how I always think of her. If my mother wasn't talking, she was singing or laughing. The stupidest things made her laugh." He leaned forward suddenly, almost overturning his lemonade, and asked, "How do you shoot a purple elephant?"

"What?"

"With a purple elephant gun," Thaddeus supplied the answer with a grin. "How do you shoot a white elephant?"

"With a white elephant gun?"

"No, you squeeze its trunk until it turns purple and shoot it with a purple elephant gun!" He chuckled and Clytie smiled with him, even though she knew that his laughter was more from the pleasant memory of his mother than from the dumb joke. Then he asked, "What time is it when an elephant sits on a fence?"

"Time to get a new fence!" Clytie giggled.

"Okay," Thaddeus admitted, "that's a *real* old one. But my mother knew every elephant joke ever told. Hundreds of them. She called it her claim to fame."

Clytie's eyes widened as she considered her own mother, who had a master's degree in family management, was a talented musician, and could sew like a professional. Still, Margaret Reynolds probably didn't know a single elephant joke and Clytie somehow regretted it. She hadn't responded when Thaddeus continued, "But you know what I remember best?"

Clytie shook her head, then remembered to say "no."

"I remember how excited she was about everything. How captivated she was by—" he paused, searching for the right word, then shrugged, "—*life,* I guess. Once a day, at least, no matter where she was or what she was doing, she'd stop in the middle of it and come to find me. Then she'd hold out her hand and say, 'Hey Thaddeus, come look at this!' Even when I was older and had started school, there'd be a cloud to watch or a stray kitten to play with or maybe even some kind of puzzle that had caught her attention. She'd stop whatever she was doing to include me." His thoughts now were far away as he repeated, "'Hey Thaddeus, come look at this.'" Finally, remembering Clytie, he added, "Everything in the world was new and exciting to my mother."

"No wonder your dad never found anyone else," Clytie murmured.

The comment drew Thaddeus back from his memories with a start. "My father never took his face out of a stock portfolio long enough to look."

"Do you ever wish he would?"

Thaddeus started to reply in the negative, then reconsidered. "For his own good, maybe." He reached up to adjust the ball cap, and Clytie wondered if he were thinking now that because of his tumor, his father was going to end up truly alone. The idea made her heart sink. "Yeah, I guess I do wish he'd find someone," he repeated.

"We could pray for him!" Clytie suggested impetuously. Her face clouded at Thaddeus' derisive snort. "Really," she insisted. "When boring old Sterling Channing was about to come home from his mission and Andi was all set to marry him, I prayed that she'd meet someone else perfectly wonderful. And God sent Greg."

"So why is Andi inside entertaining Channing now while Greg is home sulking?"

Clytie's face puckered without the stimulus of lemonade. "Well, sometimes the righter something is, the harder Satan tries to mess it up."

"Diabolical interference?" Thaddeus chortled. "So *that's* why the course of true love never runs smooth! Leave it to you, Clytie, to solve the mystery of the ages."

Clytie ignored his continuing jests as her mind launched automatically into phase XVI of her pet project: getting Andi and Greg safely to the altar. Although the thing that seemed *most* eternal about their relationship right now was the length of time it was taking Greg to give Andi a ring, Clytie was still most concerned with bringing her father around. Trent had been almost insufferable, especially the first

Sunday Greg was gone. And, come to think of it, he was the one who had coerced Andi into spending this evening with Sterling.

"You know," Clytie said finally, "tonight is actually my dad's fault. I wish there was something I could think of to—"

"Smooth out Greg and Andi's romantic course with a little road construction of our own?"

"Yes!" Clytie said, happily picking up on his use of the plural. With Thaddeus' brilliant mind to help her plan, she figured Andi and Greg were as good as sealed with Trent beaming in satisfaction over the match.

"Well, we could at least see to it that your father sees Greg doing the one thing Sterling can't," Thaddeus suggested.

"You mean pitch?"

"Well, yeah. Besides being able to write with his left hand and not take himself too seriously, I figure that's the only thing he's got going over Channing."

Clytie smiled back at the infectious grin, then reached across the table to squeeze Thaddeus' hand to show her pleasure. At least he was trying. "But I don't think my father will go to a ballgame, Thaddeus."

"He probably would if we all went," Thaddeus said. "You know—a family excursion. And we'll do it tomorrow night for Greg's first home game. We'll take Greg's mother, too. It's about time she saw him play."

"That's a lot of money for tickets," Clytie worried aloud.

"My father has a suite. There's plenty of room for everyone."

"He won't mind?"

"No," Thaddeus said. "He'll probably be too busy to come himself, but he certainly won't mind."

"Oh, I'd love to go to Greg's game!" Clytie cried, then checked her enthusiasm guiltily. "Of course, I know you're doing it for Andi—"

"Or for her little sister."

Clytie was glad, for once, that Thaddeus couldn't see. A deep flush had tinted her cheeks the color of an Arizona sunset and made them feel warmer than the desert sand as well. "You mean Francie?" she teased.

"Yeah," he agreed good-naturedly. "I mean Francie. I'm hoping, Clytie, that if someone teaches your little sister to sing 'Take Me Out to the Ballgame,' she'll give that 'Families Can Be Together Forever' thing a rest."

Clytie giggled. Thaddeus was so wonderful to help her with her father, she decided she would help him with his. God always answered her prayers and Clytie knew just where to reach Him.

Chapter 26

If the middle-aged missionary who met Greg at the door with an offer of assistance had known who he was, apart from a patron, she hadn't cared. Instead, she admired his Bible with awe, applauded his interest in reuniting his eternal family, and led him to a secluded area with a computer where he could begin to accomplish it. After a brief lesson, she left him to begin electronically filling in blanks on a pedigree chart.

When Greg paused some time later in consternation, unable to decipher a name written in an impossibly spidery script, the missionary appeared as if by magic—or inspiration—at his shoulder with a slim text on paleography. In just over an hour, Greg managed to compile half an eight-generation pedigree chart and more than a dozen temple-ready family group sheets on a computer disc.

As he looked over his first effort at genealogy, laid carefully on the Jeep's passenger seat beside the ancient scripture, one corner of his mouth twitched upwards. That little disc was the most definite "up" since his baptism. And it was enough, at least for now, to make him willing to face whatever might come as long as at the end of the enduring, he would qualify to take Andi and his family with him into eventual exaltation.

Minutes later, Greg swung into the lot at the Homecraft building, glad to note that several cars remained and that Sister Newton's was among them. It was dusk, the time of day Greg loved best, when the sun's initial setting pulled behind the mountains the pastels from the sky and left behind an ethereal, cerulean blue, black-fringed by the towering palms. He had parked and climbed out of the car for a better look toward the west when he noticed the girl.

Mahogany-skinned and maybe ten-years-old, she played alone just outside the pool of streetlight, bouncing an ancient basketball against the brick wall of the building. Each time she moved, a multitude of colorful yarn ties bounced up and down at the tips of her short, inky braids. Though dirty enough to have spent the day playing in a construction site instead of a parking lot, she was modestly dressed and possessed a natural grace that would have been the envy of a prima ballerina.

She was so enticing in her energy and seemed to be having such a good time entertaining herself that Greg found himself walking toward her.

"Don't you touch me or I'll hit you where it hurts!" the girl threatened, turning quickly on the balls of her feet and extending the basketball as a weapon.

Greg stopped immediately, several feet away, and held up a hand apologetically. "I'm sorry. I didn't think. You shouldn't talk to strangers."

"I *ain't* talking to you!" the girl declared. But her dark velvet eyes seemed to be looking at him—or through him—intently.

Instinctively, Greg glanced over his shoulder. Except for themselves, the lot was deserted. "Well, sorry I bothered you," he said, retreating toward the front door of Homecraft. "Have fun with your game."

He had taken only a couple of steps when she called, "It ain't a game! It's *practice*. I's gonna be a basketball player an' make a million-trillion dollars an' be on the TV." With the ball tucked securely under one thin arm, she placed the other fist firmly on her narrow hip as if daring Greg to suggest otherwise.

"That's great," he said tentatively, still sorry that he had thoughtlessly approached her in the first place and wondering what she was doing out here by herself at this time of day. "Good luck."

"You wanna shoot some hoops?" she asked as he turned away.

"You were right to be careful around a stranger—"

"I don't figure you's a stranger since I see you most every day."

"But I've never—" Greg began, then turned to follow her thin finger. She hadn't been looking through him, he realized with a grin, but over his shoulder at the lighted billboard across the street. Unconsciously, he ran a finger across his upper lip to remove the nonexistent milk-mustache as he turned back to the girl.

"It's kinda weird," the girl said. "Seeing you up there."

Greg smiled. "Yeah, for me, too."

Considering the billboard and the implications it suggested, she asked suddenly, "Do you know Michael Jordan?"

"Sorry, no."

"You don't gotta apologize," she said magnanimously. "Lots of people don't know him, neither."

"That's true," Greg said, suppressing another smile.

"I'm gonna marry him," the girl confided.

"Does his wife know?"

His question received less than a second's consideration as she bounced the ball and looked back up at him. "Hoops?"

Greg glanced around the lot. "There's no net—"

"It's right there!" she corrected, pointing to a discolored spot about three quarters of the way up the wall. "You hit it right on, you make the shot." She tossed him the ball. "Mama says I gotta respect my elders—so you take out first."

Greg had played some one-on-one with guys from the Cubs, but none of them were as dedicated to the game—or physically able to slip so effortlessly around and under him—as this little girl. "Do the Phoenix Mercury know about you?" he asked finally, collapsing onto the sidewalk after a thorough trouncing.

"They're gonna!" she proclaimed with a wide grin, balancing one foot on the ball. She'd barely broken a sweat, Greg noticed, running his fingers through his own damp hair. "So," she asked suddenly, "you gotta name or you want me to call you Billboard Boy?"

"That's kinda catchy," he said, "but how about calling me Greg?"

"I's Ique."

Greg resisted the urge to stick a finger in his ear to clear out any wax that might be obstructing his hearing. "Eek?"

"Not like 'eek a bug,'" she said disdainfully. "My real name's Martinique—it's French, after my dad." Her face clouded. "But when we run off, we didn't want no part of him goin' along with us. My mama always says that she left the Martin, but she kept the Ique." A hint of a twinkle played in the corners of her chocolate-colored eyes. "I kept his basketball myself."

Greg smiled. "It's nice to meet you Ique. You live around here?"

"Nah. I come around, though, whenever they's here." She motioned toward the door with a pointy chin. "They's awful nice. One lady gave us a real pretty quilt and another one brung me some almost-new clothes and gave me the yarn pieces for my hair."

Fine lines appeared around Greg's eyes as he pieced together bits of what he saw with what he'd just heard and was beginning to suspect. "Where *do* you live, Ique?" he asked finally.

"Around."

"Around—where?"

"Anywheres." She raised the chin defiantly. "We's got a nice place—better than a house with *him*. And nobody say we can't live like we please."

"But where do you go to school?"

"I's home-schooled. My mama—she tries real hard."

"I'm sure she does," Greg nodded. "Is it just you and your mother?"

"An' my little brother."

"How about I give you a ride home?" Greg asked suddenly. "I'd like to meet your mom."

Ique's eyes narrowed suspiciously. "Is you a cop?"

"No," Greg said, motioning back over his shoulder in the hope of putting her at ease. "I'm a billboard boy who doesn't know Michael Jordan, remember?"

"I'll take you to see my mom," she offered, deliberately bouncing the ball up and down on the sidewalk and daring him with deep velvet eyes, "*if* you can beat me at a game of one-on. Ten points."

Greg dragged himself back to his feet with an expression hovering between a grin and a grimace, determined to help this little girl or die trying.

By the time his advantages of height, athleticism, and sheer determination paid off and gave him a victory at the improvised hoop, his mother was walking out of the building with Laura Newton.

Realizing that his success at the family history center and interest in Ique had caused him to forget entirely the second part of his original mission, he felt some dismay at the thought of bringing Sadie along on his next one. Still, he thought as he opened the car door and watched her climb into the back as Ique grabbed a grimy pillowcase from the sidewalk and scrambled up front, his mother could always be counted on to be silent and patient.

To his surprise, Sadie *was* patient with Ique, but Greg was the one who was silent as he listened in amazement to his mother, in her quiet, almost whispery voice, draw the child out. His amazement turned to incredulity at the girl's story.

It had taken Ique little time to learn to get around the city, walking and begging quarters for bus fare as she canvassed churches, office complexes, and restaurants for contributions to the thin, cotton pillowcase that was the sole support of her small family. That her mother couldn't control her and had fallen between the cracks of the social system was apparent. The only question in Greg's mind was if it was by default or design.

At Ique's direction, he turned off the main street just behind a bus stop and before a bar and drove to the end of a service road used mostly by the gravel companies that excavated this perennially dry portion of the Salt River bed. It was dark except for the moon and stars and a hazy glow at the horizon of a nearby bank.

"This is as far as you can go," Ique announced, grabbing her pillowcase in one hand and scooping up the basketball in the other. "Thanks for the ride, Billboard Boy!"

"Wait a minute!" Greg said, reaching for her elbow, but failing to take into account her speed. She was out of the jeep and most of the way up a sandy bank before he could finish protesting, "You said if I won, I could meet your mother."

"I lied!" she called back cheerfully as her brightly tipped braids bounced out of sight.

Glancing at his mother, Greg hesitated and would have gone home—at least for the night—but Sadie pushed forward the front seat so she could get out. Despite his better judgment, Greg followed.

"Leave the headlights on," she suggested, "so we can see where we're going."

Where they went was another world.

The transients' makeshift camp stretched from one edge of the riverbed toward the other. Shallow caves scooped from the high riverbank sheltered a few; others crouched near weathered cardboard boxes and lean-tos of corrugated tin. The most affluent, Greg saw, possessed makeshift awnings and battered tents. The glow he and Sadie had seen from the road had come from a few small cook fires and kerosene lanterns.

This couldn't possibly be more than five or ten miles from his own expensive neighborhood, Greg thought in disbelief. But, sandwiched between the northern rim of Mesa and the southern boundary of the Salt River Pima Indian Reservation, this rocky, littered, no-man's land was apparently all the home that Ique and a handful of other indigent children knew.

The columnist's mocking words came unbidden to Greg's mind, sank to his stomach, and knotted there, cold and sickening. He stood transfixed, feeling as if he was on a bank of the Colorado River, looking out over the rapids where life rafts had somehow upended, sending dozens of people overboard in shock to battle cold, churning waters as they grasped at limbs and one another in a desperate effort to stay afloat. Appalled by the misery before them, Greg still had no idea where to approach or how to reach out a hand to help.

He might never have moved at all if his mother's thin fingers hadn't wrapped around his wrist. "Laura gave me a book about that Mother Teresa from India," she said softly. "I read where this reporter went up to her once and asked how she kept herself going, knowing she couldn't save all those people who were ailing. You know what she told that fellow?"

Greg shook his head slowly, his eyes still on the image of the transient campground, now beginning to blur from the tears that pricked at his eyes.

"She said, 'God didn't command me to do everything. He commanded me to do *something*.'" Her fingers moved down to curl as trustingly as a child's into her son's strong hand as her pale blue eyes rose imploringly. "We can do *something* here, can't we, Greg?"

His vision cleared as he looked down into his mother's face. Could this be the same frightened, hopeless woman who had first come to Arizona? Closing his eyes for a moment, Greg thanked Heavenly Father for causing miracles to happen behind his back even as he had been wondering if God had forgotten him. "Yeah, Ma. We can do something."

Hours later, after bidding his mother good night and going into his own room to stretch his tired body gratefully out on the bed, Greg still couldn't rest his thoughts. They'd found Martinique, and the rapport Sadie had established with the child's mother, Mahala, had been amazing. Of course, he thought, they had a lot in common. Mahala had left her husband the night he broke their daughter's arm and had never stopped to count the cost in physical comfort. That she didn't know where Martin was now—or care—was revelatory in itself, and Greg reflected with gratification that he had fulfilled his evening's mission after all—and then some.

But if he had been surprised at Sadie's empathy, he was amazed at her resolve. This woman who had barely managed to purchase a toothbrush for herself almost bought out a local Circle K while "Billboard Boy" sat in the getaway car with a *Pennysaver* over his famous face. Returning to the campground, Sadie, Mahala, and Ique ably dispersed canned goods, candy bars, and compassion. Indeed, they'd done *something* and, if he could figure out how to swing it, Greg intended to do more.

All in all, he thought, staring at the ceiling, *tonight's experience wasn't much different from falling down a rabbit hole with Alice*. Grinning at the analogy, Greg quickly rolled over onto his side to reach for the telephone. *No one but God could have touched my mother,* he thought, *but when you need a manmade miracle, you call the White Rabbit.*

"Hi, Dawson!" he said happily, failing to catch the curt, thanks-a-lot-for-interrupting-me-at-the-worst-possible-moment tone in the publicist's greeting. "Are you writing?"

"I *was.*"

"Good for you! Hey, listen, have you got a couple hours you could spare me tomorrow?"

"I *do* work for you, Mr. Howland," Dawson replied with a sigh.

"Then could you come over around, say, ten? I've got to be at the ballpark by two and I don't know how long this might take us."

"How long *what* might take us?" Dawson asked. His lack of interest was more than evident in his voice, but Greg was too euphoric to give it more than passing notice.

In fact, Greg was finding it impossible to keep a straight face with the joy he felt over being in a position to make a difference and having his mother as a partner and Dawson to swing it. His press agent, Greg knew, could have a safe house for battered women and children established and staffed in less time than most people would take to form a committee to study the problem.

"I met the most incredible girl tonight," Greg began, his enthusiasm evident—even to Dawson—in his voice. "And I want to buy her a house. The biggest, most beautiful house we can find."

"You—met a—and—you what?"

Greg held the phone away from his ear as his agent's question dissolved into a sputter and series of coughs. "I've told you and told you to drink water when you take those pills, Dawson," he joked. "So, is ten okay?"

Scarcely able to recover his faculty of speech, Dawson managed, "I can be there by nine, Mr. Howland."

"Even better! And bring your computer, will you?"

"Yes, sir," Dawson responded eagerly. "I wouldn't think of leaving it."

Chapter 27

Andi had planned to apply her lipstick while she waited at one of the stoplights between her home in Mesa and the Phoenix Zoo. At the last red arrow, however, she once again had to forego lip-gloss for a yawn. It didn't matter, she thought, readjusting the rearview mirror toward traffic as she pulled forward onto the parkway, the zoo animals didn't care what she *looked* like as long as the large pails she toted *smelled* like breakfast. And as for the yawns, she'd have happily traded a week's worth of sleep for the couple hours she had spent on the phone last night with Greg.

She turned off the radio and happily pushed the mental start button on the audiotape in her head to recall Greg's deep, warm voice. He had told her about his visit to the Family History Center, and they had eagerly set a date for his next day off to go to the temple to do baptisms for the dead. By the time they had finally, reluctantly, hung up sometime after midnight, they'd talked of everything and nothing, as much like old friends as new loves.

And that certainly proved her father—and his arch-ally Sterling Channing—wrong. Last night, she suspected, Sterling had come over to politic against her involvement with Greg more than he had to polish his presentation. His theme, of course, had been the same as ever: *You only* think *you know Howland. Watch him at the game tomorrow night and you'll see the real man, Andi. Leopards don't change their spots, only their tactics.*

As Andi approached the entrance to the zoo, she smiled. If there was one thing Sterling knew less about than leopards, it was Greg.

And she certainly *would* watch him at the game tonight. In fact, she couldn't wait.

Dawson Geitler was already standing in the outside entryway when Greg, yawning and stretching out muscles used more routinely by landscapers and basketball players than pitchers, opened the front door. Dawson extended the *Tribune* with a smile. "Front page article on your move to Mesa today, Mr. Howland."

"Don't tell me you have a paper route, too—"

"And yet another good write-up in the *Republic,*" Dawson added, putting the competing daily atop the one already in Greg's hand.

"Define good," Greg said skeptically, glancing at his bare wrist, then turning to look around the room for a clock. "What time is it, anyway?"

"Any publicity is good publicity," Dawson said, following Greg inside, "and it's 8:28."

"Didn't we say nine?"

"Yes, sir. But your call last night was so—intriguing—that I didn't want to waste valuable time today getting on it."

"You're really something, Dawson." While Geitler set up his laptop on the low table in front of the couch, Greg went into the adjoining kitchen and pulled open the refrigerator door. "Want me to make you an egg? How do you want it?"

What Dawson wanted was information about the mystery woman, over easy. He'd settled for sunny-side up, or even scrambled, as long as he got it. He tried to keep the impatience out of his voice as he said, "Nothing, thank you. I've had breakfast. I'm ready to work."

"You don't mind if I eat while we work, do you?" Greg asked from within the fridge.

"Certainly not."

When Greg returned to the living room, he eased into a chair across from Dawson and set his large tumbler of orange juice on the table so he could better balance the serving bowl of cold spaghetti and marinara sauce on his lap. "Carbs," he responded to his agent's surprised look. Wrapping several long strands of pasta around the fork, Greg raised it toward his mouth. "I pitch tonight."

"Whatever." Dawson flicked on his computer and leaned forward. "About this, um, young woman you mentioned last night—"

Greg nodded eagerly as he swallowed the first mouthful. "Yeah. She's great, Dawson! I saw her playing basketball. Her name's Martinique and—"

"A basketball player," Dawson repeated. "Is that how you met?"

"Well, I'd gone to Homecraft to pick up my mother—" Puzzled that Geitler's fingers were busy at the keyboard, Greg paused, then added, "but you don't need to—"

"Where did you meet?"

"Homecraft. It's a charitable center—run by the Church—and we met in the parking lot, but—" Anxious to get to the point, Greg sighed when Dawson interrupted again.

"Then this lady is a Mormon?"

"No," Greg said. "And she isn't exactly a lady, either."

"Oh—" Dawson said, barely able to contain his glee over catching another break so soon after Iowa, "I see."

Studying Dawson's face, it suddenly dawned on Greg just how much information he had given and what, exactly, Geitler had "seen" in it. He put a fist over his mouth to secure the spaghetti as he laughed. Finally he recovered enough to say, "No, I don't think you do, Dawson. We've been talking about a *real* girl. A little girl. A homeless, little girl."

As usual with Howland, Dawson found the yolk on his own face. "And you want to buy her a house," Dawson concluded, fighting the urge to drop his forehead against his computer screen. For *this* shocking revelation, he had gotten up before the sparrows.

"Yeah. But not just a house," Greg said eagerly. "I want to establish Ique's Place—a women's and children's shelter in her name."

Dawson massaged the bridge of his nose with a thumb and finger as he fought to shift his brain from overdrive into cruise control, determined to take what he could get. This wasn't as good as he had expected, obviously, but it was still might be usable on another front. He said, "That's a good idea, Mr. Howland. Children's charities are hot right now—works for lots of guys. Now, do you want a press conference or—"

"No!" Greg interrupted emphatically.

"Of course, not a press conference," Dawson said, surprised at his own slip. Howland didn't seem to know any four-letter words, but found the five-letter "P word" obscene. "I was thinking out loud about how best to get this out—"

"I don't want any publicity. In fact, I've been thinking we can run this through my investment group so that nobody knows I'm behind it." His blue eyes were hopeful. "You can help me do that, right?"

"Mr. Howland," Dawson responded patiently, "as your press agent—"

"I don't need a press agent for this, Dawson. I need a friend. A skilled one, like you. "

"Still," Dawson persevered, ignoring the familiar pang he felt every single time Greg used the word "friend," "the public relations ramifications of your good works are too significant to pass up without careful consideration."

"You want to hear the real ramifications of good works, Dawson?" Greg interrupted, setting aside his bowl to reach for his scriptures.

Not really, Dawson thought, leaning back into the couch, *but knowing you, I'm going to anyway.*

"This is Jacob talking to the Nephites about their love of riches," Greg said, looking up at Dawson to make sure he was listening.

> Let not the pride of your hearts destroy your souls! Think of your brethren like unto yourselves, and be familiar with all and free with your substance, that they may be rich like unto you. But before ye seek for riches, seek ye for the kingdom of God. And after ye have obtained a hope in Christ ye shall obtain riches, if ye seek them; and ye will seek them for the intent to do good—to clothe the naked, and to feed the hungry and to liberate the captive, and administer relief to the sick and the afflicted.

"Advice from a man who probably lived thousands of years ago," Dawson commented under his breath, "and thought riches were six sheep."

"Or a commandment from the living God." Greg lay down the book as if everything was settled and reached again for his spaghetti.

"Someday you'll know for sure which it is. Are you willing to take your chances in the meantime?" Greg watched as Dawson's eyes returned slowly to his computer screen. "So, you can do it?"

"Yes," Dawson said resignedly, "I can do it. If you'll let me plug into your phone line, I'll see what's already available. That'll give us a baseline for what we're looking at in the way of startup." Annoyed at the look of admiration Greg cast him, Dawson connected his modem and ran his fingernail across the touch pad.

Greg took a last bite, set the bowl on the table, and moved to join Dawson on the couch. "I ought to join the computer age, I guess," he said. "There's a pitcher on my new team who lists every ball he throws on a laptop like yours."

"Easily enough done."

Greg watched the screen change from site to site quicker than he could blink and asked, "What all can you do on that thing?"

"There's little I can't do," Dawson replied. He tapped a key. "I can tell you the latest news, for instance." Returning his finger to the touch pad, he continued, "Weather, sports." Glancing at Greg, he moved to Search. "You mean you've never seen any of this?" Typing in his employer's name, he pulled up more than two thousand web sites with links to Greg Howland. "Nothing official—except, of course, the Cubs and Diamondbacks. Groupies, mostly, having fun. I could design a page for you if—" he paused at Greg's gaping stare.

"Who looks at all this stuff?" the young pitcher asked incredulously.

Dawson's shrug implied that it was everyone in the world except Greg. On his way back to the home page to get down to business, Dawson accidentally hit a bookmark and was instantly inside *amazon.com.* Glancing at the prominently displayed cover of this week's bestseller, Dawson thought, *Six months—maybe eight—and you and I will be the #1 feature, Mr. Howland.* Before he could exit, he felt Greg's hand on his arm.

"Books?" he asked. "You can buy books on the computer?"

"Buy them, read them, whatever," Dawson replied casually. "Not only books but clothes, gifts, groceries—anything and everything delivered to your door in two days or less. I do everything online."

"You don't have to go in to a store?"

"No."

"And you can buy anything?"

"Well, maybe not anything," Dawson said slowly as he recognized that these last questions were leading somewhere. "What do you have in mind?"

"Can you buy jewelry?" Greg asked. "I've thought every single day about buying Andi a ring, but I haven't been able to figure out how to walk into a jewelry store to buy an engagement set without making the front page of some newspaper."

Dawson's eyebrows arched almost up to his receding hairline. "I assume then that Miss Reynolds has agreed to speak with you again prior to Halloween."

"Yeah," Greg grinned. "She and her family are even coming to my game tonight."

"Will wonders never cease?"

"I hope not," Greg said sincerely, remembering the change in his mother's life he had seen in just a few weeks. And come to think of it, he was still waiting for that act of God to bring Trent Reynolds around. "I really hope not, Dawson."

Chapter 28

Clytie ran stubby fingers through her silky blonde hair and dropped back on the bed among her stuffed toys with a sigh. "I wish I had curls like you, Andi."

Across the room, her sister pushed a hanger aside in the closet and laughed. "For just four hours at a beauty shop and a small fortune you can." Andi sobered quickly when she saw the look on Clytie's face.

During their call last night, Thaddeus had reported that a miracle had occurred right at his own uptown address. His father had cleared his schedule and would be at the game tonight. Although not surprised—she *had* been praying her heart out for Thaddeus and his father, after all—Clytie was so anxious about meeting Cleon Bisher that she'd slept only fitfully and been a nervous wreck all day.

Andi could feel the knot of apprehension in her own stomach, as well. Despite what Greg had said about the man's apparent change of heart during lunch with him and Thaddeus, she still remembered the look of disdain Cleon had cast her at the ball. Imagine the look he might give her diminutive sister. With an effort, she affixed one of her brightest, most encouraging smiles before turning from the closet. "Your hair is beautiful, Clytie," she said. "Everything about you is beautiful—especially your heart."

Clytie swung her short legs from the bed onto a low stepstool, paused a moment for balance, then stepped down to the floor. "I'm sick of hearing how pretty I am on the inside. I wish that just once I could be pretty on the outside, too."

"You *are*," Andi said, berating herself for tacking on that "heart" clause. Even though it was true, it was probably the last thing Clytie wanted to hear. After a year's work on the prom committee, she was the only girl among her group of friends without a date. "You're very pretty."

"You mean, for a dwarf."

The words, said in a tone of regret and despair Andi had seldom heard from Clytie, hung in the air until Andi dispelled them with a sweep of her hand. "I don't mean that at all. You don't understand—"

"*You* don't understand," Clytie insisted. "You can't. You're tall and slender and beautiful, and you don't have any idea what it's like to have people stare at you because you're a freak."

"Clytie!" Andi cried in dismay. "Don't say that!"

"It's true."

"It isn't," Andi insisted, even though she had to admit to herself that it probably was. She well remembered the difficult teen years when she was convinced that everyone in the world was looking her way—and had found her lacking. But she recognized now that, in her case, it hadn't been true. Clytie was right. She was the only one of the two of them who knew what it was like to have people point and stare and confirm your worst fears. Andi's eyes filled with tears of sympathy and frustration.

Seeing this, Clytie approached quickly and said, "Don't pay any attention to me, Andi. I'm just nervous about tonight."

Andi nodded silently, touched as always by Clytie's quick empathy. Her sister might not want to hear it again and again, but it was true: Clytie's heart was very beautiful and very rare. Andi wished that the entire world could see beyond the tiny stature into a heart larger than any. When the doorbell rang a minute later, Andi said, "You finish getting ready. I'll answer it."

Descending the stairs, she could hear Francie already at the door.

"It isn't Halloween," the little girl told someone through the crack she had opened, "and Mommy and Andi and Clytie are all on diets, so we don't have candy, anyway."

"Who is it, Francie?" Andi asked, stepping into the foyer just as her little sister closed the door.

"Trick-or-treaters."

"Who?" When the doorbell rang again, Andi moved Francie gently aside to answer it herself. She blinked twice as her emerald eyes swept from the wide, velvet hats adorned with ostrich feathers, down the gold brocade tunics and pantaloons and quickly past the knobby knees clad in deep maroon tights. Apparently, Andi thought, trying to suppress a smile at the ridiculousness of it all, either Francie was right or these guys were a couple of latter-day escapees from the court of King Louis XIV. "Can I help you?" she asked finally.

"We're here to see a Miss Catherine Reynolds," the taller of the two announced.

"Clytie!" Francie called from the foot of the stairs before Andi could stop her, the eager voice rising with excitement. "There's some trick-or-treaters here to see you!"

"What is this about?" Andi asked the pair suspiciously. With everything Clytie was going through, if these two were jesters instead of musketeers, Andi would have them *wishing* they were in King Louis' court.

The shorter man raised a scroll tied with velvet ribbon. "We have been dispatched with a message for Miss Catherine Reynolds."

"What message?" Andi persisted. Managing a glimpse between them, she was relieved to see that at least they had arrived via modern transportation. The sedan sported the name of a local talent agency on the driver's door. Andi relaxed a little as she realized the men were actors. Maybe Clytie had won one of those silly radio contests she was always entering.

Whoever the pair was, Andi noted, they didn't seem surprised to see that Clytie was little. When she arrived at the door, the men bowed deeply, and then one pulled forward a three-legged stool with a flourish. "Miss Catherine, if you please."

With a bewildered look at Andi, Clytie seated herself on the bench. It was the perfect height. Whoever planned this, Andi thought in growing astonishment, must have considered the details. She watched the tall man kneel before Clytie and reach for her tennis shoe. "If I may?"

Clytie's eyes were as large and bright as aquamarines. She nodded uncertainly and seemed grateful to have Francie move close to her side for a better view. The man removed her shoe and sock, carefully set them aside, and reached into the front of his tunic.

"I've seen this!" Francie announced suddenly. "It's Cinderella!"

It is *Cinderella,* Andi thought with a quick intake of air as the man removed a slipper that was probably acrylic, but looked for all the world like glass. Unconsciously, Andi leaned forward and expelled the air only when the shoe fit Clytie's foot perfectly.

Francie's strawberry blonde ringlets bobbed as she clapped her hands

With a smile, the shorter man proffered the scroll. "You, Miss, must be the one. His Highness, son of King Cleon, asked that we give you this. He will await your reply."

Andi's eyes widened as Clytie accepted the scroll and the men turned to walk back to their car. *King Cleon?*

"What does it say?" Francie asked eagerly as her sister tugged at the velvet ribbon. "Is it really from a prince?"

Clytie unrolled the faux parchment and read quickly. Then she clutched it to her chest. When she looked up, the luster in her eyes had increased to diamond-brightness. "Thaddeus asked me to Prom!" She held up the foot with the glass slipper. "Do you think I could wear this?"

"Only if he gives you the other one," Andi said slowly, recovering from her surprise only to worry that, despite the charm of the invitation, this might not be a very good idea. She could already picture Thaddeus and Clytie at the event. Either one would have a difficult enough time fitting in at a high school dance. Together? Andi bit her lip as her mind formed cautionary advice. But when she looked down at her sister, tempted to deliver it, and saw the rapturous upturned face, the words disappeared and she knelt to hug Clytie fiercely. "You'd better worry more about what else you're going to wear," she teased. "Isn't your prom next weekend?"

"Maybe a fairy godmother will come next!" Francie suggested hopefully.

"I'll bet our own mother will come through just fine," Andi said. She could already envision the long hours Margaret would spend making first a pattern, then a dress that would suit Clytie to perfection. "Besides, when you've landed a prince, everything else is extra."

As her sister's arms tightened around her neck, a small band of fear constricted around Andi's heart. She still believed that this prom date might be a disappointment. And, worse, if Thaddeus were really as sick as Greg still believed, then a ball, a glass slipper, and even a fairy godmother couldn't add up to happily ever after for him and Clytie.

CHAPTER 20

"Take me out to the ballgame. Take me out to the crowd . . ."

Andi stood between Clytie and Darlene at the railing just outside Cleon Bisher's luxury suite at the Bank One Ballpark and watched the sell-out crowd of exhilarated fans sway and sing to the organ music during the Seventh Inning Stretch. Across the field, the three-story Jumbotron flashed replays of Greg's seventeen strikeouts.

"Just four more," an announcer on the small color TV monitor mounted on the side of the skybox repeated exultantly, "and Howland will break the major league record. What a night!"

Gripping the rail for support, Andi felt herself sway between her sisters and suspected that her mouth was open, though she wasn't singing. In the first place, she didn't know the words. In the second place, it had been some time since she had felt capable of making a sound.

There are almost fifty thousand people here tonight, Andi thought, looking out across the mammoth, three-tiered stadium. *More people than I've seen together in my whole life. More people than attend ASU. More people than come to the zoo in a year. Fifty thousand people. And 49,500 of them, at least, came to see Greg.*

She had come to see him as well and had sighed with admiration at the confidence and efficiency of motion he demonstrated on the mound. With his well-built legs firmly planted and his handsome face focused on the small plate sixty feet away, Greg's throws seemed effortless. This was a side of Greg that Andi had never seen and the flow of the young pitcher's muscles was masculine on such a basic level that it took her breath away. She had smiled to think that, surely, this was not what Sterling had meant when he'd so seriously advised her to look for the "real man" at the game tonight.

Unfortunately, when she'd finally pried her eyes off Greg long enough to look around the stadium, she began to realize what Sterling *had* meant. And the realization left her reeling

"For it's one, two, three strikes, you're out, in the ol' ballgame!"

As the crowd cheered and the Phillies took the field, Andi glanced back toward the glass-protected reception area where her parents sat with Sadie Howland, Laura Newton, and Cleon Bisher. Comfortably seated on the plush furnishings, they chatted as they watched the game on a large screen television. Brad and Enos, thanks to Greg's intervention, had been invited to sit in the dugout. Andi could scarcely believe how thrilled they were, but she had also seen enough baseball by now to know that if they came out of there with their shoes covered with spit and sunflower seeds, they had no one to blame but themselves.

As she watched, Cleon Bisher offered Laura a soda then took the seat beside her on the sofa. Andi had been forced to admit that Thaddeus' father wasn't really "horrid" after all. He had been friendly tonight not only to Greg's mother and her friend, but to Clytie and her family as well. Andi might have stayed inside with the other adults, in fact, if she hadn't thought that sitting out with Thaddeus and her sisters would give her a better view and more opportunity to think. Not that she had been able to decide yet *what* to think about the proceedings.

Thaddeus had been invited to the dugout too, of course, but had chosen to stay up here with Clytie. "One legend is that Howard Taft was attending a ballgame in 1910 and got up to stretch during the seventh inning," Andi heard him explain now as the top of the Diamondbacks' order came to the plate, ahead 4-0, "—and the crowd, of course, stood with him. But, actually, the custom of the stretch goes back to the 1860s, and the song is a ditty about a girl named Nelly Kelly who . . ."

Andi shook her head in a mixture of annoyance and admiration. Since meeting Greg, Thaddeus had become an expert on anything having to do with baseball. He had already listed all the baseball trivia he thought would interest Clytie—from the earliest literary mention of the game in Jane Austen's 1816 romance novel, *Northanger Abbey*, down through the latest inductees into the Cooperstown Hall of Fame. Clytie hung on his every word. Of course, her feet hadn't touched the ground since slipping into the glass shoe, so Thaddeus could recite the major league playbook and she would no doubt find it fascinating.

Andi held out her arms automatically as Francie came over to climb into her lap. The game had started at seven and extended well past the little girl's bedtime. Andi was ambivalent about seeing Greg break any kind of record in front of this rabid crowd, but striking batters out seemed like the fastest way to get through an inning, so she wished him well for Francie's sake.

"How come you aren't sitting over there?" her little sister asked sleepily, raising a finger toward an upper deck over the outfield. Andi didn't have to look where she pointed to know that a hand-glittered "Greg's Girls" banner hung over a railing in front of a good-sized contingent of female fans. If Andi hadn't been able to see it for herself through binoculars provided by the suite attendants, she surely wouldn't have missed it on TV. The cameras had panned that section at least two dozen times. "Aren't *you* Greg's girl, Andi?" her little sister persisted.

"I think so, Francie," Andi whispered, pulling her sister close.

"I want to go home," Francie declared, curling up to nestle her curls in the hollow of Andi's neck. "I only like baseball a little."

And I only like a baseball player, Andi thought with a sigh, *a lot.* "Go to sleep, sweetheart," she suggested, resting her chin on top of her little sister's head as she looked back toward the field. "It'll be over soon."

When Greg fielded a well-hit grounder then struck out the next two batters to send the side down in order in the eighth, Andi thought the crowd's reaction might raise the ballpark's famous retractable top. But, mercifully in Andi's view, the Diamondbacks went down quickly as well, bringing up the middle of the Phillies' lineup.

"Only three more outs," Trent Reynolds said from the now-open door as he led the others out onto the balcony. If she hadn't known better, Andi would have sworn that tonight's baseball fever had infected even her father. While Margaret and Sadie sat together on the folding chairs, Trent stood at the balcony rail to watch Greg pitch. "A hundred and two miles an hour!" he exclaimed as the Jumbotron flashed the radar gun reading in red lights and with a digitized "Wow!" "Is that a record?"

Cleon Bisher shrugged, but he was smiling as he offered a chair to Laura Newton. Then he sat beside her, next to his son, and addressed Thaddeus. "I only know that your new friend, my boy, is one remarkable young man," he said genially.

"So, signing Greg wasn't the worst business decision you ever made?" Thaddeus asked wryly.

"It might have been," Cleon responded, patting his arm affectionately, "since he'll be eligible for salary arbitration after this season. If Greg keeps pitching like this, we might have to mortgage the stadium to pay his next year's salary."

Andi glanced at the television monitor. There, close up, she could watch as Greg pulled off his cap, wiped his brow with the back of his arm, then slapped the hat back on and yanked the brim almost over his eyes. Palming the ball, he leaned forward to check signs with Jorge Andres, his catcher. Between the low bill of his cap and the narrow squint of his eyes, Andi wondered that Greg could see the plate at all. She found herself leaning forward with the rest of the crowd in anticipation of his pitch. One more strike, the announcer offered breathlessly, would tie the all-time strikeouts and put Howland's name in the record book once again.

The ball crossed the plate at 97 miles per hour and sailed back toward the swimming pool behind the right field fence even faster. The instant replay showed Greg look quickly over his shoulder to follow the ball's flight, then lower his face and turn away before its splashdown.

Andi shifted the dozing Francie in her lap and gazed from the TV down toward the field. From this perspective, with the triumphant Philly just crossing home plate to bump forearms with his teammates as the stadium grew suddenly quiet, the dirt mound in the middle of the grassy field looked like an island—and one of the lonelier places on earth.

The luck of the island's sole inhabitant didn't improve, Andi noted, nor did his pitching. A lucky, "excuse-me swing" resulted in a blooper to left field and a third batter wrangled a walk before Joe McKay, the manager, finally came out of the dugout and signaled to a closing pitcher warming up in the bull pen. McKay's trot across the field was punctuated by boos and catcalls from still-hopeful fans that changed to cheers only when Greg sheepishly relinquished the ball to jog toward the bench. Before he reached the foul line, a standing ovation had capped his reception to Arizona. Next to an air-conditioned baseball stadium, Greg Howland was, in the hearts and minds of this huge crowd, clearly the best thing ever to come to the Valley of the Sun.

The rest of the short half-inning was anticlimactic in everyone's book. A roving reporter was eliciting declarations of undying love from Greg's Girls, and the Jumbotron was replaying his strikeouts when the third baseman caught the tapper for the last actual out.

Thaddeus asked for someone to turn up the volume on the TV when the post-game interview came on, and both his father and Laura leaned forward to comply. When their fingers touched on the knob, Laura blushed. Andi barely noticed, but caught a glimpse of Clytie whispering conspiratorially about it in Thaddeus' ear before turning her own attention to the TV screen.

Now wearing a headset instead of a ball cap and gingerly holding a microphone in the hand that had so recently gripped a ball with confidence, Greg was back on the field, looking unhappier than he had at giving up the long ball and fielding a string of mostly stupid questions.

How did he feel about missing the record book by one strike? *Pretty bad.* How did he feel about his performance overall? *Pretty good.* What did he like about his new ball club? *Great manager. Great guys. Great fans.* How did he like the new ballpark? *It's great.* What did he like best about playing here in Phoenix? *The great fans, great guys, great ballpark* and, Greg added as an afterthought, *great weather.*

Great interview, Andi thought, wondering for half a moment if Sterling was right about Greg possibly having more jock in him than she had suspected.

Synthesized music was blaring and the Jumbotron had switched to a picture of the moon as seen through a crack in the just-opening roof of the BOB when Brad and Enos were escorted back to the box, wide-eyed and full of information. But it was almost another twenty minutes before the new Diamondback ace arrived in street clothes.

Andi worried that she was using the excuse of Francie in her lap to avoid walking into the suite with the others to meet him. Even her father pumped Greg's arm and congratulated him. Andi caught only a word or two of their conversation, but she heard Brad clearly as he and Darlene followed Greg through the open balcony door.

"And did you see all those *girls*, Greg?" he asked excitedly. "There wasn't one who wouldn't die for a date with you."

Andi felt the warmth begin in her own face as she saw it reflected in Greg's bemused expression. Searching for something to say to break the uncomfortable silence, she blurted out the first thing that came to mind, "Great game," then bit her lower lip in consternation.

"What impressed you the most?" he asked with a rueful smile. "My grand finale on the mound or that eloquent interview afterwards?"

The lopsided grin that had always been endearing was suddenly disconcerting as Andi tried to reconcile the reality of the man who stood before her with the remembrance of the man she and fifty thousand strangers had admired on the field. "It was all just—overwhelming," Andi said finally. "I had no idea."

Clearly, she thought, Greg was puzzled, if not offended, by her lack of enthusiasm. And no wonder. As Brad had pointed out, he was certainly used to female adoration. She had known that, of course. She had seen the nurse in the hospital, the society reporter, and even Francie's teacher, Ms. Sherwood, fawn on Greg. Watching them compete for her fiancé's attention, though distasteful, was at least tolerable. But enduring entire hopeful harems of "Greg's Girls"? Well, wasn't that simply ridiculous?

"I'll drive you home," he said, breaking into her thoughts. "You haven't had a chance to ride in my new-and-improved Jeep."

"What about your mother?" Andi asked.

"What about me?" Darlene asked from the background.

Turning, Greg noticed the twelve-year-old for the first time that night. "Oh, hi, Darlene. Did you like the game?"

"Uh huh," she said happily. "I especially like the Diamondbacks' right fielder. Do you know him?"

"Yeah, kinda," Greg said, trying to fix the rookie in his mind. "He seems like a nice guy."

"He's dreamy," Darlene proclaimed. "And how come you like all the Reynolds kids except me?"

Greg knew from experience that following the twelve-year-old's flitting thoughts in a conversation was like chasing fireflies so he waited for her to continue.

"You invited Enos and Brad to sit in the dugout tonight," she pointed out, "and you went to Francie's class and you had all those pictures taken with Clytie and you gave Andi flowers and a bracelet and you won't even drive me home."

Greg opened his mouth to respond, then closed it. Finally he said, "I'd love to drive you home tonight, Darlene—you and your sister." Before Andi could ask about Sadie again, he added, "And my mother."

It wasn't exactly what he'd had in mind, but then neither was almost blowing the game in the ninth inning. Still, he thought to cheer himself up, he'd forced more than a hundred decent throws out of an arm that had wrestled bougainvillea and basketballs the day before. At $4,000 dollars a pitch, it added up to a sizable chunk of capital to put toward Ique's House. So the game wasn't exactly a washout and the rest of the night would be better yet.

He'd drop his mother off first, Greg decided with a smile and then at the Reynolds', with a little luck, Darlene would go inside and give him some time alone with her sister. He'd first kissed Andi under the flowering citrus trees in front of her home, and he couldn't think of a better spot to kiss her tonight.

CHAPTER 30

"-and-then-Joanie-said that-I didn't-know-what-I-was-talking-about-but-I-did-and-I-told-her-that-if-she-didn't-believe-me-she-ought-to-talk-to-Karen-and-"

Greg cast a sideways glance at Andi to see if she was processing any more of the steady stream of words coming from Darlene in the back seat than he was, but she looked straight ahead, clearly not listening to her sister at all. She and Sadie had been mostly silent in fact, not that Darlene had given anyone much of an opportunity to wedge so much as an "uh huh" into the so-called conversation.

As an arching Mesa streetlight illuminated Andi's pretty, pensive face, Greg's look turned to one of concern. He seriously doubted that Andi's melancholy had anything to do with his blowing the chance to be listed in a record book next to Roger Clemens.

Trying to ignore Darlene, Greg wondered what it meant to wrack your brain. Was it to line up bits and pieces of information logically, like wooden tiles on the racks in a Scrabble game? Or did it mean to stretch your mind out on one of those medieval torture devices to try to wrench a little logic from it? He'd have to ask Thaddeus. In any case, as brain-wracking applied to Andi, he'd tried the first method thus far on the twenty-minute trip home from the ballpark with so little success that he was now moving on to the latter.

Andi had acted a little odd after the hospital press conference as he recalled. Tossing everything he remembered about the two dissimilar events on his imaginary rack, Greg couldn't seem to come up with a common denominator besides himself. He frowned. *I must be doing* something *wrong,* he thought, *but I sure don't know what it is.*

Or, for that matter, *when* he was doing it. She'd been this way since he first walked onto the balcony tonight, but he hadn't even talked to her since the night before. He'd been too busy working with Dawson on Ique's House and finding Andi the perfect ring—an Edwardian antique that would be on her finger tomorrow before he left for the next road trip. *Was* not *calling her today the problem?* he wondered. *Maybe my sins in this relationship are ones of omission.*

Greg shook his head in frustration. If a guy didn't know what he was doing wrong with a girl, how in the heck would he ever figure out what he merely wasn't doing right? *Women ought to come with an instruction sheet*, he decided. *Or at least a warning label.*

Tired of brain wracking, Greg braked suddenly to turn into a strip mall. If the only advantage to throwing nineteen strikeouts in a game was to get it over with fast enough to make it to Cold Stone Creamery before closing, that was reason enough for him.

The sudden change of course startled Darlene into a moment of silence. Greg took quick advantage. "I thought we'd get some ice cream. Okay?"

Only Darlene showed much enthusiasm as he parked the car. Her door was open before he had reached for his handle. He turned in the seat. "Want to come in, Ma?"

"No, and don't bring me anything, Greg. It's too late for sweets."

"I'll wait in the car with your mother," Andi offered kindly.

So much for this brilliant idea, Greg thought, swinging open his own door. "What can I bring you, Andi?"

"Anything is fine with me."

I doubt that, Greg thought, following Darlene up onto the sidewalk.

The two teenage boys behind the counter nudged one another as Greg held open the door for Darlene. A semi-regular patron on nights he was in town and found the shop empty, Greg had already been through the awkward autograph stage with these guys and was now only the highlight of their day.

They'll earn their minimum wages tonight, he thought while Darlene walked up and down the glass case as if invited to select from the crown jewels. He had delivered a small cup of strawberry yogurt to Andi and eaten half of his own blueberry cream before Darlene selected the final ingredient—gummy bears—and the boy began to mix them into her chocolate ice cream with a Snickers bar, cookie dough, and handful of raspberries.

Darlene turned to Greg happily as he paid the bill. "Thanks," she said. "I love this place, but Dad only brings me here after an orchestra concert. Did you know that I play the violin?" Greg shook his head, but didn't have time to respond before she continued. "I'm first chair—that means I'm really good. I'll play for you sometime." She took the proffered waffle cone from the worker and promptly spooned through the ice cream for a bit of chewy candy. "Yummy. This is sooo good. Gee, it's too bad that Andi can't marry you."

"Huh?" Greg fumbled with his ice cream as the last words registered and his fingers went suddenly lax. He set the carton on the countertop and looked down at Andi's sister earnestly. "Why do you say that, Darlene?"

"'Cause you're pretty cool."

"What?"

"It's not polite to fish for compliments," Darlene proclaimed as she reached for a napkin. "But you *are* nice."

Wracking, Greg realized now, had done his brain no good whatsoever. He forgot his ice cream as he followed Darlene toward the door. "I mean, why can't your sister marry me?"

"You haven't seen Andi's checklist-for-choosing-an-eternal-companion?"

"Well, no," he said slowly. *But if she passes out copies, shouldn't I have been eligible for one before now?*

Darlene shrugged. "Well, that's why she can't marry you." Arriving at the glass door, she waited patiently for him to open it.

Instead, Greg stepped between her and the door. He knew Andi had already promised to marry him—and common sense told him that this was Darlene and he should just leave it alone—but still he said, "Help me out here, Darlene. I don't know what, uh, qualifications are on the list. What am I missing?"

"Almost everything."

Greg's eyebrow rose. "Like, for instance?"

Taking a large bite of her frozen treat, Darlene considered. "Well, first you have to be a member of the Church."

Greg nodded, grateful to at least be in the ballpark.

"—from a strong LDS family." If Darlene noticed Greg's sudden blanching, she didn't comment on it. "And you have to be a returned missionary like Sterling Channing—and committed to the gospel." When Greg still didn't say anything, she added helpfully, "People who are *committed* to the gospel don't even *watch* sports on Sunday."

Greg leaned back against the door and stumbled when it swung open at his weight. He recovered his balance, if not his equilibrium, and looked toward the only woman he would ever love. She was turned in the seat, chatting with his mother.

Is that why she's lost in her thoughts? he wondered. *Is she worried about the kind of husband and father I'll be—and about the grandparents I'll bring into our children's lives?*

No wonder you're distant, he thought morosely, walking slowly back to the car to climb up into the seat next to hers. *You know full well that by the time I manage to meet all of the requirements on your list for an eternal companion, that ring I just bought you won't be the only antique.*

Chapter 31

Greg had been in town for only nine of the last thirty days, and Andi had seen him only a handful of times. Twice he sat between her and his mother in a sacrament meeting before leaving church early for an afternoon ball game. Once he dropped by the house to deliver Thaddeus and see her. And, yesterday evening, she had been startled to look up from a game of Chutes and Ladders at the Child Crisis Center to see him and Dawson on tour with the director. She and Greg had barely had an opportunity to speak, but Andi was grateful for the chance to at least *see* him. Though they talked almost every day while he was away, she couldn't help but feel that the distance separating them was more than the hundreds of miles of telephone cable.

Andi rolled over to her stomach on the soft grass of Riverview Park to avoid the glare from the orange, early evening sun. Curling a few fingers toward Enos in response to an enthusiastic wave from atop his five-pound block of ice, she watched halfheartedly as he and Darlene raced down the grassy slope. Then she pulled aside her mane of curls and draped it over one shoulder to allow the breeze to cool her neck. It was only the first of June and already southern Arizona evenings were too warm to comfortably spend outdoors.

But it was a week that called for a celebration, so the Reynolds had invited Sadie Howland and Laura Newton as well as Thaddeus and his father to a Family Home Evening picnic in honor of Brad's graduation, the end of school, and Andi's upcoming birthday.

Everyone celebrated in his or her way. The younger kids ice blocked while the grad stood on the sidewalk not far distant and exchanged measuring looks with a young woman who had just made her third pass by him on rollerblades. Andi, who was in no mood to celebrate at all, envied her brother's heart, which seemed to be constructed of the same stuff as Silly Putty. Although stretched out of shape—if not snapped in two parts—when Brittanie Paisner dumped him midway through the prom, Brad's heart seemed to fuse quickly enough the very next day at a flirtatious overture made by a new Laurel in the ward. And tonight, when this girl stopped in front of him to refasten her skate, Andi saw by the look on her brother's face that his uniquely constructed cardiac organ had clearly regained all its pre-prom bounce.

Andi turned her attention toward Laura and Sadie, who stood together at the bottom of the grassy slope. The women were talking and laughing with almost as much delight as the children sitting on top of the slick blocks of ice. Perhaps, she pondered, *all* human hearts were endowed with elasticity. If they weren't, how could Laura have ever smiled again after losing her husband and young daughter in a rafting accident just a couple of years before?

I'm glad she's found a friend, Andi thought now. Her eyes traveled the short distance toward Cleon Bisher and she smiled. *And perhaps a beau. And then there's Sadie . . .* As Andi watched her laugh in response to something Laura said, she knew that Greg's mother's transformation after years of abuse and despair had been nothing short of miraculous. Andi had accompanied the sister missionaries to one of their discussions with Sadie and had shared in their awe at this woman's simple, childlike faith. After the lesson, Andi had finally agreed with Greg that if Bobbie Jo's need became very great, Sadie would likely be willing and able to care for her grandchildren.

But if I were in either of their places, Andi asked herself, *would I have found the resiliency of spirit to act as they do now?* The natural coral coloring in Andi's cheeks deepened with her thoughts, and she felt ashamed at how she was sulking over missing something as inconsequential as the lunch date she might have had today with Greg.

Yet even as she berated herself and gathered her legs up to sit cross-legged on the soft grass, Andi knew that she had missed much more than lunch. With Greg on the road more than half the time and then spending so much time in Phoenix playing baseball and conferring with Dawson Geitler—securing even more product endorsements or whatever it was the two of them did—there was simply no time left for her. Surely her father hadn't been right about Greg being drawn away by the world; Andi was sure she knew him too well to believe that. But there was no denying that Greg *had* acted at least a little differently toward her since that night at Bank One Ballpark when he'd become the undisputed hero of the Valley. He hadn't called as often for one thing, and when they did talk he seemed unsure of what to say. If it wasn't the world, then what was it?

In spite of her fears—or perhaps because of them—Andi had been overjoyed when Greg had asked her to meet him today after she got off work. Though he had only a couple of hours, he wanted to spend that time alone with her to give her a birthday gift before leaving for tonight's game, and from there back on the road. Clytie had promised—and Andi had hoped against hope—that the gift would be a ring.

Her anticipation overwhelming, she had managed to switch days with a co-worker to give herself the morning free to have her hair done. On the day Greg gave her an engagement ring, Andi was determined to look as if she had come from a salon rather than a swamp.

She arrived early at the upscale Mexican restaurant on the banks of what had once been Lee's Ferry in Tempe and asked for a corner table. The spot she requested was near the kitchen and almost behind a potted palm. Andi congratulated herself on finding a place guaranteed to keep distractions at a minimum. If she had only a few minutes alone with Greg, she intended to guard each one jealously.

Unfortunately, Greg never even made it to the table. With his picture still appearing in almost every paper almost every day, the sunglasses and hat he wore were an ineffectual disguise—especially here in the trendy Mill Avenue district where star-spotting was a sport at least as popular as baseball. Andi heard his arrival heralded by the crowd just before she managed to meet his regretful eyes. With admiring strangers three-deep around him, Andi had little choice but to sit unobserved behind the tropical plant and watch while he signed autographs. Neither of them, of course, had eaten. If not for the eventual intervention of the Tempe police, he might be there yet, she thought. Instead, he was at the ballpark with his bags packed to go on to the next game in Detroit—or Denver—or— Andi sighed. Wherever it was, it was *away* and there were still four months of baseball season yet to endure—five if Arizona made the playoffs.

She had replayed the apologetic message Greg left on their answering machine a dozen times when she got home, wondering what he might have said if they had had a chance to even speak—let alone really talk. As she listened to his deep voice, a little muffled by the car's engine as he spoke from his cell phone, tears coursed down her cheeks. Greg Howland was the only thing she'd ever want for this or any other birthday, but he wouldn't be in town—no matter how hard she wished when she blew out her candles.

Though the crying jag had passed, the hurt had remained through the afternoon and left her the sole person in tonight's group with a melancholy countenance. Even Cleon Bisher—ridiculously overdressed for a picnic in pin-striped suit slacks and a tailored Oscar de la Renta shirt—smiled when Francie did a belly flop on her block of ice and sailed down the grassy bank as smoothly as any Himalayan bobsledder.

As a matter of fact, Andi thought, Cleon Bisher did a lot of smiling when Laura Newton was around. Maybe there *was* a chance, as Clytie had predicted after their first meeting, that they would become an item. (Thaddeus had reported that his father took Laura to the symphony the week after the game and had invited her to dinner at their estate on at least two occasions since.) Andi smiled. Quiet, calm little Laura Newton attracting the attention of self-assured, if not overbearing, Cleon Bisher. Only Clytie—or Cupid—could have thought up that match.

What is it about the human heart that makes people fall so indiscriminately in love? Andi wondered, her eyes sweeping from Cleon and Laura past her happily married parents and toward Brad and his new acquaintance. Finally, she settled her gaze on the lake bank where Clytie sat with Thaddeus. *Everywhere you look people are in one stage or another of romantic involvement, heedless of any heartache ahead.*

And look at me, she thought with a sigh, *and how hopelessly I love Greg. If I were even half as sensible as I used to think I was, I'd be with Sterling tonight.* He was the man, after all, who was constant, reasonable, and reliable—important qualities that Andi both possessed and appreciated. Greg, on the other hand, seemed to make every decision based on the prompting of his heart and could be counted on only to be unpredictable.

Like that Friday almost a month ago, she thought, pulling up her legs to rest her chin on her knees. *Just when I thought he'd forgotten all about Mesa during that week he spent in Montreal, those gorgeous American Beauty roses arrived for Clytie, right on the morning of her prom.* It was just in case, the card had said, that Thaddeus forgot to bring flowers.

But Thaddeus certainly hadn't forgotten anything. Although Andi would have been mortified to ride *anywhere* in a horse-drawn carriage, let alone to a downtown hotel, her romantic little sister had cried so at the charm of it, she'd had to reapply her makeup before leaving the bedroom. Thaddeus had had dinner served at the hotel with candlelight and flowers and then escorted Clytie to a dance that had apparently been divine as well. If anyone so much as looked askance at them the whole evening, Andi knew, well, Thaddeus didn't see and Clytie didn't care.

Andi watched her sister toss bits of leftover bread to the ducks as Thaddeus expounded on who-knew-what-this-time. Clytie never tired of listening—which was fortunate since Thaddeus never tired of talking. His cap lay beside him on the ground and the setting sun lent an amber glow to the back and top of his head. Andi allowed herself a slow smile at the thought of how wrong the doctors apparently had been. Radiation completed, Thaddeus seemed stronger and happier than ever. His hair had even begun to grow back in—baby fine and almost white.

The peaceful tableau they presented contrasted with the rambunctious good time of her younger siblings and, touched by the Spirit, Andi was grateful for the blessing of being a part of it all.

Truly, she thought, *tonight would be perfect—life would be perfect—if only Greg were here with all of us instead of at the ballpark.* She could see him in her mind's eye playing with Enos and Francie—a bigger kid sometimes than either of them. She could see him with his mother and Clytie, too—kind and encouraging—and joking with Thaddeus, his wit one of few fast enough to match the sharp young man.

Greg's constant absence left a gap in the fabric of each of their lives, but none bigger than the hole in hers. Andi gazed up wistfully at the sunset-stained, cotton-candy clouds, then closed her eyes to imagine Greg here. He would sit next to her on the grass, his eyes bluer than the deepening evening sky, and she would lean her head against his brawny shoulder and smell the clean, heady mix of grass and soap and leather gloves that seemed to cling to him even on the Sabbath. Then he would turn toward her and, speaking so low that only she could hear, say—

"Andi!"

Her eyelids flew open but it was a few seconds before she could focus.

"Andi!" Darlene repeated from the top of the ice blocking bank. "The ice is melting and you and Brad and Clytie are missing all the fun." She scanned the park and put one hand on her hip in resignation. "Well, Brad is talking to a girl, so I guess *he* won't be back for a while. And Clytie is being nice to Thaddeus since he can't see to ice block. But you're just sitting there making faces. What are you *doing*? Can't you at least come push?"

Tired at last of her private, pre-birthday pity party, Andi rose and brushed the loose grass and dirt from the back of her jeans. "Yes," she told Darlene. "I can at least push."

She'd taken only a couple of steps, however, when she saw the patrol car pull into the parking area, followed closely by a silver Nissan. When the door of the police cruiser opened, she saw that Bishop Ferris was Sergeant Ferris tonight. She watched him wait while a burly man climbed from the other car, then walked with him over toward Sadie Howland and her parents. Andi quickened her steps and cut down the bank to arrive at the small group at the same time her bishop did.

After a brief greeting, Sergeant Ferris introduced the man to Sadie. "Greg's hired him to stay with you for a few days, Mrs. Howland—at least until he gets back into town himself."

Sadie's blue eyes moved from the police sergeant to the stranger and back again in confusion. "But we already have that silly security system. I can't imagine why—"

"It's not a bad idea," Ferris explained. "I called Greg myself a couple of hours ago to tell him that some hot-shot attorney got Zeke

Martoni out of jail this afternoon." He nodded unhappily at the startled expression on Andi's face. "It just goes to show that our justice system is not only blind—sometimes it's just plain deaf and dumb."

Chapter 32

Greg sat alone in front of his open locker in a corner of the visitors' clubhouse at Dodger Stadium on Saturday, a study in concentration. Since he would take the mound in the first game of today's double-header, his teammates kept their distance, almost tiptoeing if they had to pass behind him at all. The taut muscles in his back and neck as he bent over his knees showed even the veteran players how focused the phenom fastballer was on preparing for the upcoming pitchers' duel.

What nobody noticed was the small card in his hands. Greg had opened it to read the invitation so many times in the past week that the paper had lost much of its stiffness and threatened to tear along the crease. Today was Andi's twenty-first birthday and Sterling Channing was giving her a surprise party.

It doesn't mean anything, Greg told himself, closing the card again. *Why shouldn't he give a party for her?* Nobody knew Andi was engaged, after all, and Sterling and Andi had been childhood friends. *And high school sweethearts,* a nagging little voice reminded him.

They weren't sweethearts, exactly, Greg argued. *Andi only dated Sterling because he was convenient and familiar and—everything she ever wanted in an eternal companion.* This time, when he pulled the card open, it ripped cleanly in half. He tossed both parts into the locker, slammed the door, and kicked it with the bottom of his cleted shoe.

Across the room, a couple of his teammates glanced up from a hotly contested game of cards to look at him curiously. But Joe

McKay, passing by on his way from his office to the field, was the only one with the courage to venture close.

"Doesn't surprise me to see a high-strung pitcher tear up a locker room when he loses a game," the manager commented dryly, coming up behind Greg to assess the damage to Dodger property. "I guess when a guy doesn't lose many games, he's gotta destroy something before the fact. That right, Howland?"

"No," Greg said, studying his offending foot in embarrassment. "There's no excuse."

"Then what's the problem?"

"There's no problem."

"Repairing the door that took the brunt of that 'no problem' is gonna cost you, you know."

Greg nodded.

"So, what's her name again?"

The young pitcher remained silent until he was sure the manager wouldn't leave without an answer. Finally, he sighed. "Andi."

"The redhead at the ball?" When Greg looked up in surprise, McKay continued, "I don't get paid to miss anything, Howland. Now, I'll ask you again—what's the problem with her?"

"Today's her birthday," Greg said unhappily, "and a guy she's known since nursery school is giving her a party. We're in LA, of course, so I'll miss it, like I've missed her brother's graduation and her sister's prom and Mother's Day and everything else that doesn't revolve around baseball. But this, especially, is one more reason for her to think I'm hopeless. She doesn't like what I do in the first place, and in the second place there's this other guy th—" *Great,* he thought, catching himself in mid-word. *As if things weren't bad enough, now I'm starting to talk like Darlene.* He rubbed a hand across his jaw to keep his mouth closed before he removed the last shred of doubt from McKay's mind that his newest ace was actually an idiot.

"Can you give me eight solid innings today?" McKay asked, hooking a thumb toward the field.

Relieved that the manager had obviously worried only about the upcoming game and wouldn't actually give a nickel to hear about his love life, Greg nodded.

The manager raised his voice. "Then I'm sorry to hear about your grandmother."

"Huh?"

"Listen," McKay said, leaning so close that Greg could feel the walrus mustache tickle his ear, "every man on this team's got a wife or a girlfriend and they've all got birthdays. I can't let you run off for something stupid like that." He stood back up and spoke loudly enough for the card players to hear. "Your grandmother's wake—that's important. You can leave after those eight solid innings this afternoon, Howland. But I expect you back in this clubhouse before noon tomorrow. Got it?"

"Uh, yes, sir," Greg said incredulously. "Thank you."

McKay took a step away, then turned and leaned close once again. "You give her a ring yet?"

"Well, no, but—"

"Give it to her," the manager interrupted. "For her birthday. That's an order."

Greg looked at the bent locker door as McKay walked away. Andi's ring was behind it, still safely tucked away in his duffel. Just before the burly manager turned a corner on his way to the field, Greg turned to watch him pull a clipboard out from under his arm to reconsider the starting lineup. A veteran of the National League, Joe McKay had put together one of the winningest records in baseball. *And who am I,* Greg wondered with the beginning of a grin, *to argue with success like that?*

"This room smells like a flower shop," Enos said, wrinkling his nose as he threw his ball glove on the couch and charged past his sister toward the television set. "You wanna watch Greg's game with me? I'm late, so it's already started."

Andi looked up from *Northanger Abbey*, the novel Clytie and Thaddeus had given her as a gift, toward the beautiful bouquet that had arrived that morning. The twenty-one red roses, nestled amid baby's breath and lacy fern, filled the air with a scent worthy of a flower shop—or a funeral. Andi's mood tended toward the latter, even though the roses proved that Greg hadn't forgotten her birthday.

She'd much rather have him—or at least a ring—but he was five hundred miles away in Los Angeles playing baseball and, weeks after his proposal, her finger was still conspicuously bare.

Andi tried to engross herself in her book. Catherine, the heroine in Austen's romance spoof, loved sports. She even liked baseball. Andi wished for a fraction of Catherine's enthusiasm to rub off on her.

"No thanks," she told Enos, but peeked above the cover of the book when the game came on the screen. If she wanted to see Greg much at all anymore, it would apparently have to be on television.

He looks good, she thought, *at least what I see of him under the hat.* As usual when he pitched, the bill was pulled low and his face was focused and intense. As hard as Andi tried to return to Catherine's misadventures in the abbey, her eyes simply would not leave the ballfield while the camera was on Greg.

When he struck out the last batter in the inning and walked toward the bench, Andi closed her book and rose from the chair to leave the room. But at a last, fleeting glance toward the TV, she froze. The camera angle had shifted too soon for her to be certain, and she had seen nothing more than the mug shots provided by Sergeant Ferris in the first place, but a man seated in the crowd behind the Diamondback dugout had looked an awful lot like Zeke Martoni.

What did we do with that picture? Andi wondered, glancing around the room, then walking over to her mother's antique desk. *You're being silly,* she told herself as she pulled open a drawer. *It's been almost a week and nobody's heard or seen anything of Martoni. He's through with Greg and back in Chicago like Bishop Ferris hoped.*

Still, she continued to look for the picture, halting her search only long enough to speak sharply to Enos as he began to sing along with a jingle for a local casino. *Really,* she thought rifling through the next drawer, *these sports franchises ought to know that children are their biggest fans and choose sponsors based on*—her mind went blank. Moral outrage suddenly forgotten, Andi stared at the enlarged mug shot in her hand as her heart seemed to leap into her throat.

Even while being booked into jail, haughtiness was the defining characteristic of Martoni's features. He was undeniably handsome, despite the swollen jaw line Greg had given him before his arrest. But there was something about him, Andi thought, that even if she hadn't known what kind of man Martoni was, would have given her the creeps. Tucking the picture carefully between the pages of her book, she joined Enos on the couch.

"The Diamondbacks are up to bat," he explained.

Andi nodded and leaned forward, only half-listening to her excited little brother's running commentary as she hoped for the camera's return to the crowd. *Please let me be wrong—*

When the next batter fouled out, the camera followed him back toward the visitors' dugout and Andi left the couch to kneel close to the screen.

"I can't see!" Enos protested.

But Andi could see very well. She opened the book for a quick peek then closed it as her heart thudded in her ears. Zeke Martoni was front and center, three rows back. Even though he wore sunglasses, there was no mistaking the thin lips, angular features, and well-oiled hair that glistened with blue/black highlights in the afternoon sun.

Greg hasn't seen him, Andi realized suddenly. *And he might never notice him at all when he's so focused on throwing that baseball.* Fear for Greg caused a momentary indecision. *I'll call Bishop Ferris,* she decided at last. *He'll know how to best warn Greg.*

"Andi!"

Moving away from the set, Andi stood to leave.

"Aren't you gonna stay to see Greg pitch?" Enos asked.

"No," she replied. "I have to make a phone call."

Enos pushed his thick-lensed glasses up his nose in concern. "Are you mad at Greg 'cause he can't come to your party?"

"I'm not having a party, Enos," Andi began impatiently, then paused as her little brother clasped both hands over his mouth in alarm. She sighed. "I wish Clytie hadn't—"

"It isn't Clytie's party," Enos volunteered. "In fact, she's mad 'cause she and Thaddeus weren't invited. Sterling told her it was for *adults*."

"Sterling?" Andi bit her lower lip in resignation. It figured. The only birthdays she *hadn't* spent with Sterling were two when he was in Peru and one, years earlier, when she had had the chicken pox.

"I'm sorry I ruined your surprise," Enos said. "Are you mad?"

"No," Andi said quickly, ruffling his rusty hair before moving again toward the phone to call Sergeant Ferris. "I'm glad you told me. I've already had all the surprises I can stand for one day."

Chapter 33

Greg hesitated for just a moment at the front door of the Channings' large home. Ringing the doorbell, he hoped that Andi would be as pleased at his surprise appearance at her party as he was.

He glanced down at the box in his hand and tried to stop fiddling with it. The clerk in the shop at LAX had done a good job of wrapping it, though it wasn't as apparent now as it had been when he'd left the counter. Greg had handled Andi's present so much on the short flight to Phoenix and the taxi ride from Sky Harbor that the foil paper had become smudged in some places and creased in others. He glanced down at it and nervously straightened the velveteen bow.

Since he hadn't wanted to show up without a gift—and he certainly didn't want to give her an engagement ring in front of an audience—Greg had ducked into a jewelry store at the busy airport. And, he thought, he'd gotten lucky. What he'd come out with was a musical Fabergé egg with a garden design and butterfly key that caused the egg to open like a tulip, revealing within a fountain of crystal and silver. The fountain held a brooch which, when the clerk wasn't looking, Greg had replaced with the ring. He would give Andi the egg at the party tonight and show her how it opened in private afterwards. *If*, he thought impatiently, *anyone ever comes to answer the door.*

As he raised his hand to knock, one side of the double doors swung open. A well-dressed woman looked him over curiously, as if trying to place his face within the carefully organized scrapbook in her mind. Finally she said, "Why, my goodness! You're Greg Howland, aren't you? I'm not sure we were expecting you, especially this late, but won't you come in?"

"Yes," Greg said, following her into the foyer. "Thank you."

"Shall I take your gift?"

"No," Greg said quickly. "I mean, I'd like to give it to Andi myself."

"Well, you've missed our nice dinner," she told him regretfully. "But perhaps I could heat something up for you?"

"No, thanks. I'm fine." *That's a lie*, he thought sheepishly as his stomach rumbled and his eyes scanned the spacious room for a glimpse of Andi. *I'm as nervous as heck.*

Sister Channing lifted her glasses from the gold chain around her neck to help Greg look. "I don't see Andi," she said slowly. "She must be outside by the pool." Leading the way around the group of young adults playing Pictionary in the living room, she stopped at an arcadia door and slid it open. "You go tell her you're here. I'll fix you something to eat."

Before Greg could protest, Sister Channing had turned back toward her kitchen. He stepped through the doors and onto the darkened patio, looking up as he felt a fine spray of moisture touch his cheek. A misting system ringed the deck, lowering the temperature ten or fifteen degrees and giving people as tall as Greg the impression they were standing with their head in the clouds.

He took a single step forward to gaze out at the yard. Bright, flower-shaped candles floated on the surface of a pool that was surrounded by tropical fruit-laden tables, tiki torches, and fishnets, carefully positioned to create an inland luau. Greg was struck not only by the effort that had gone into this party, but also by the expertise and the fact that Sterling had undertaken it for Andi. But neither the host nor the guest of honor was anywhere in sight, so Greg turned to go back into the house. Then he heard Andi's voice.

"Everything has been simply beautiful, Sterling," she said. "Your mother must have worked on this all week."

From where he stood in the shadows, Greg could just see them now through the mist, standing near a tiki light beneath an expansive grape arbor. Andi looked beautiful in a melon-colored shift that had been patterned after a sarong, her auburn hair upswept save for a few, stubborn tendrils. She'd worn her hair in a similar style, Greg recalled, the first night he'd kissed her. He'd taken another step forward when Sterling spoke.

"You know my mother thinks of you as a daughter, Andi."

Greg watched Sterling move nearer and touch Andi's cheek. Torn between conflicting desires to advance and withdraw, he stood still.

"Remember your sixteenth birthday?" Sterling asked.

Andi nodded and laughed softly at the memory. "It was a luau, too—but at that wave pool over in Phoenix. You got so sunburned you could have passed for a lobster."

"I remember your eighteenth birthday even better," he said seriously. "It was the night we first kissed and said that after my mission—"

"I remember," Andi interrupted.

"It's after my mission."

Andi looked up into his brown eyes and almost smiled at the sobriety she saw there. Sterling Channing was assuredly the personification of security and stability, she thought fondly, and she didn't regret the years she'd spent dating him almost exclusively. So what if Clytie had called their relationship boring? At least she had been able to rely on boring not to twist her heart and absorb her every waking hour in longing for the infrequent touch of an unattainable man's hand. For the sound of his voice. For a few moments to lose herself in the celestial blueness of his eyes . . .

"Ariadne? Are you listening to me?" Sterling said, a bit sharply.

"Yes," she said quickly. "You said that it's after your mission."

"Yes, and I still want to marry you." He held up a hand to halt her quick reply. "I know all about Howland, but he isn't here, is he? Are you absolutely certain, Andi, that you're willing to risk your eternal life for that man?"

Am I sure? Andi asked herself, allowing her brain to plead Sterling's case before her heart chose Greg and had the jury sequestered.

Greg isn't *here,* the prosecutor within her pointed out. *He's almost never here. And even when he does happen to be in town, a relationship with him is so—complicated.* She shuddered, remembering how she had felt seeing Zeke at the game this afternoon. Exhibit A. Now to Exhibit B, the empty space on the pew beside her most Sundays; Exhibit C, Greg's father; and D, his sister-in-law Bobbie Jo. Before she could stop them, pictures of Exhibits E through X rushed into her mind in the form of those horrible sections of "Greg's Girls" that seemed to spring up at ballparks around the country.

As Sterling leaned nearer, Andi looked up at him thoughtfully. *Ariadne Reynolds*, she asked herself, *what* do *you want?*

"Remember your checklist-for-choosing-an-eternal-companion?" Sterling asked calmly. Then, interpreting the inclination of her head as a nod, he bent forward slightly and kissed her.

Just in case Sterling's kiss caused the stars to fall and chills to race down and weaken her knees, Andi hesitated. But after a couple of seconds, her knees felt like adobe, her eyelids had shut out everything but darkness, and the only emotion she felt was—euphoria. She opened her eyes and saw that Sterling's had opened already.

"I love Greg!" she whispered joyfully, the jury in and the verdict unanimous.

Sterling shook his head ruefully. "Andi—" he began but stopped at the glow on her face, finally seeing that she had never looked like that for him. Andi searched his face anxiously for signs of heartbreak or at least disappointment, but neither was apparent.

"You *do* have to admit that we've always seemed perfect for each other," he said, "and marriage for us seemed like the most sensible course of action. But . . . still friends?" he asked. She nodded gratefully and allowed him to take her hand in a brotherly gesture to lead her inside.

They are perfect for each other, whispered the little voice that seemed to have taken up residence in Greg's head to replace the Spirit, at least for the time being. *You were stupid to think—*

Shut up, Greg interrupted. *I don't need you right now.* What he needed was to get out of Channing's living room. When Andi had raised her lips to meet Sterling's, Greg had suddenly felt like a Peeping Tom. He had retreated quickly into the house and would have made it straight through to the front door if he hadn't been outmaneuvered by a side flank led by Andi's best friend, Justine Fletcher. Now, she and a group of cohorts had him pretty much surrounded.

"How sweet of you to come for Andi's party!" Justine said to a general murmur of agreement.

"Hey, I saw your game on TV today," one of the young men offered. "I thought that ump was way out of line. No way did you balk—"

I balked, Greg thought as the guy went on to explain a controversial call to the group. Greg's mistake on the mound allowed a Dodger run to score—the only opposing run to score as it turned out—and McKay had taken offense to the ump's catching it. But Greg knew that he had been distracted, plain and simple. "I balked," he said before the fan could finish a dissertation in his defense. "It was my error."

"What's a balk?" Justine asked.

"It's any illegal action on the mound," Greg began to explain. Looking down at her clueless face, he added, "It's making the other side think that you're going to do one thing, then turning around and doing another. It isn't fair."

It isn't fair, the voice repeated and Greg thought of Andi kissing Sterling when she was supposedly engaged to him. He was about to excuse himself from the group—by pleading a sudden onset of malaria if that was what it took—when Andi came in the back door.

"Greg!" She could scarcely believe her eyes. Andi had wished on birthday candles for as long as she could remember, and only once now had her wish been granted. But there he was, standing in the midst of her friends looking handsome and strong and . . . unhappier than she had ever seen him. Her heart, which seconds before had threatened to burst, almost did. Couldn't he at least *pretend* to fit into her unglamorous world for just one night? "Hello," she managed finally.

"Hi," he said, looking past her toward Sterling. "Happy birthday." To the host he added, "Great party."

"Glad you could make it," Sterling responded. "Though I'm surprised."

Andi's next breath caught in her throat as she too remembered that Greg should be in LA. Why *was* he in Mesa? Had Bishop Ferris contacted him about Zeke? She moved near enough to speak quietly, "Why aren't you with your team?"

"He came for your party, silly!" Justine said gaily, taking the package from Greg's hands before he knew what she was doing and pressing it into Andi's. "Open your present. I'm sure it's gorgeous."

Andi glanced up at Greg. *Could the look on his face be alarm?* "Should I?"

Greg's eyes widened. Everyone in the room was now looking at the box in Andi's hand. "Uh, sure," he said finally, his back against the wall and the firing squad assembled. *But please, please don't open it all the way,* he pled silently, as her slender fingers fumbled with the ribbon and paper.

Andi removed the precious egg from the foam protector with a gasp of delight. It was the most beautiful thing she had seen in her life. The cloisonné was exquisite and it was apparent, as she held it up for a better view, that it matched the color of her eyes. Silver tears glittered in her eyes, reflecting the platinum trim as she touched the delicate mechanism at the bottom and it played, "After the Ball."

"Oh!" was all Andi could say for more than a minute as she felt herself swept back to the night when Greg had held her in his arms, moved her across the dance floor, and spoken huskily in her ear. She could hear the music again and the beat of his heart and . . . Finally conscious that they were not alone in the world, or even the room, Andi swallowed and managed to whisper, "Thank you, Greg."

Looking down at Ariadne, the moment was as magical as he had imagined and Greg reached forward, thinking to remove the silver butterfly that was the key. Then Sterling leaned over Andi's shoulder to examine the gift closely. Seeing their casual familiarity, Greg felt a pang. How could he have ever been dumb enough to believe he could really have won her heart when Sterling had been there all along—and was everything she admired and wanted in a man?

"You're welcome," Greg said quickly, desperate now to get away before someone accidentally opened the stupid thing. "Glad I could stop by for a minute. Happy birthday, Andi."

Glad you could stop by for minute? Andi repeated to herself incredulously, excusing herself from her friends to follow Greg to the front of the house. *You don't seem glad.* The light from the foyer spilled out into the entryway as Andi stood beside him at the open door. "Is something wrong, Greg?" she asked before he could turn to leave.

Only everything, he thought.

"Did you come home tonight because I saw Zeke Martoni?"

The shock and fear were plain on his face as Greg stepped forward and grasped her shoulders. "You saw Zeke? Andi, if he—"

"I saw him on television today when you were in Los Angeles," she explained quickly, her eyes growing large at his concern. "I called Bishop Ferris. I thought maybe he called you."

"No, I had probably already left the stadium. McKay let me go after the game so I could . . ." Relief battled with continuing dismay as Greg slowly lowered his arms then crossed them over his chest. "I didn't know about Zeke," he said finally. "Are you sure it was him?"

Andi nodded and bit her lip, her own fear growing at the look of desolation on his face.

"Okay," he said. "Thanks for telling me. I'll take care of it."

"Take care of what, Greg?" she asked earnestly.

Yeah, what? the voice taunted. *What's to take care of? And what do you care, anyway?*

"I don't know," Greg said honestly, trying to ignore both the voice and the void in his heart from whence it came. Zeke had been out of jail without a trace for a week, and Greg had hoped that he'd already endured to the end of that painful episode of his life. He looked down at Andi. Of course, he'd also hoped to spend the rest of his life and all of eternity with this beautiful young woman. No matter how he looked at it now, he'd been off base on both counts. "I'll just—take care of it." He turned and took a few steps down the walkway before turning back for a moment to add, "Happy birthday, Andi. I hope all your wishes come true."

Hopelessly confused, Andi clutched the egg to her heart and watched him walk away. "I wished for *you,* Greg," she whispered into the darkness he left behind. "You'll always be my every hope and prayer."

Chapter 34

The Fabergé egg sat on top of the piano in the Reynolds' living room, just in front of the roses Greg had sent for Andi's birthday the day before. Dressed for church, except for a pair of fuzzy bunny slippers she always wore to choir practice, Clytie paused to admire it once again.

"Please don't play the music," her older sister begged from the chintz-covered armchair. Like Clytie, Andi was dressed for the day's meetings, but would have preferred to go back to bed. It wasn't yet 8 a.m., but Andi felt as though the sun must have had time to rise and set a dozen times since she'd seen Greg last night. She leaned her head against one of the chair wings with a sigh. *It could probably rise a hundred thousand times before I'll ever understand him.*

"We know that Greg called Thaddeus last night to tell him he was in town," Clytie said slowly, demonstrating again not only the uncanny ability she possessed to read minds but her tenacity in seeing a project (in this case what Thaddeus called the "Ever-Evolving-Yet-Eternally-Evanescent-Andi/Greg-Engagement") through to completion. Her forehead wrinkled as she considered. "But he didn't mention your party to him."

"He wasn't there long enough to—" Andi began, then caught herself. They'd been through this and through this already.

"But his gift is the prettiest thing in the world!" Clytie pointed out quickly, as she reached for the egg, determined to help Andi see things differently now that the long night had passed and it was newly light. To Clytie, every day really was a new beginning. So Greg *hadn't* given her sister a ring for her birthday as they had hoped. Maybe he was waiting for Tuesday when they went to the temple to do baptisms. That would be wonderful and romantic. "And there's no way Greg would come all the way to Phoenix to bring you this if he didn't still love you!"

"He barely *spoke* to me," Andi repeated. "And he acted so out of place with my friends. You didn't see his face, Clytie, he—"

When the door chime interrupted her sister's words, Clytie peeked out the window. "It's Sister Channing. Mom said she was coming by to pick her up so they could go visiting teaching after choir practice."

"Ask her to wait just a minute!" Margaret called as if on cue from the next room. "I'll be right there."

Still carefully cradling the egg, Clytie went to open the door. As Sterling's mother came into the room, Andi straightened herself in the chair. "Thank you again for the lovely party," she said.

"My pleasure," Sister Channing responded. "There's nothing I like more than a party." She smoothed her already immaculate hair. "And it *was* nice, wasn't it? I particularly liked the poi recipe. Most people don't care for it, you know, but I thought it turned out well." She plucked a nonexistent piece of lint from her skirt. "I only wish I'd had more of a chance to visit with your celebrity friend. He left rather quickly, though, didn't he? By the time I had a plate prepared, Sterling told me he was gone."

"I'm sorry you went to the trouble," Andi said, surprised that Sister Channing had seen Greg in the first place. "He had to . . . he . . . he's very busy, I guess."

"I'm sure he is," Sister Channing agreed graciously. Her eyes lit on the music box in Clytie's hand and she cooed in admiration. "Is that what he brought you, Andi? Oh, my! I never got a chance to see it. May I?" She took the egg and held it up to the light, humming softly to the clear notes of music. "It's exquisite! One of the finest Fabergé pieces I've seen. No wonder he held on to it so tightly."

"I'm finally ready," Margaret announced, coming into the room in a whirl of perfume, balancing her purse, planner, scriptures, study guide, and hymnal.

The Sabbath might be restful for most of the world, Andi thought, regarding her harried mother fondly, *but for Relief Society presidents it's the busiest day of the week.*

"Isn't this lovely, Margaret?" Sister Channing asked, running the tip of her finger over the platinum filigree vines entwined with enameled flowers and silver butterflies.

"It certainly is," Andi's mother responded, returning her eldest daughter's wan smile with a warm one of her own.

"Simply lovely," Sister Channing repeated distractedly, looking at one side, then the other. "How does it open?"

"Open?" Clytie asked excitedly. She turned to Andi. "Does it open?"

"Of course it does," Sister Channing answered for her. "They all do. What's inside it, Andi?"

"I—don't know," Andi responded. "I thought it was a music box."

Sister Channing ran a nail along the silver base. "See? Here are the hinges. And this," she said, pointing to the smallest of openings at the top, "is where you insert the key. Now where—" Her fingers explored the trinket expertly and, as the Reynolds women held their breath, removed one of the delicate silver butterflies from the side. "The key!" she said triumphantly, passing it to Andi with the egg.

Andi held Greg's gift in her left hand and willed her fingers to stop shaking. When she hesitated too long, Clytie draped herself over the arm of her sister's chair and commanded impatiently, "Open it, Andi!"

"It's odd that Greg didn't show her how to open it," Sister Channing commented to Margaret as Andi finally inserted the key. "There's almost certainly a piece of jewelry inside. A brooch or a locket or perhaps a—oh my!" Sister Channing's fingers fluttered to her throat in surprise. "Well! I've never seen anything like *that* in a Fabergé egg before!"

Catching a ray of sun through the east window, the marquise-cut diamond reflected the light into dozens of rainbow prisms along the wall. A perfect stone surrounded by tiny emeralds in a simple setting of old gold, the ring was classic, understated and heart stopping.

"Well," Sister Channing repeated softly, "that young man certainly can *shop*—"

"Andi?" Margaret tried to meet her daughter's eyes, but though they were wide, they looked as though they might never leave the ring.

"Andi!" Clytie cried, her eyes even wider than her sister's. "Oh my gosh!" Using the chair's arm as a launch pad, she wrapped her arms around Andi's neck joyfully. "I told you!" she bubbled. "I just *knew* that Greg was going to—" Loosening her grip suddenly, Clytie sank back to the floor beside the chair, her pretty face a study in bafflement. "But why didn't he open the egg?" she asked suspiciously.

"I don't know!" Andi said, tears of frustration forming at the number of times she had said those words since last night.

"He was certainly anxious to see you," Sister Channing reported. "He didn't stop to speak to anyone else in the room."

"He talked to Justine," Andi contradicted her. "In fact, he was talking to a whole group of people when I came in."

"When you came in, dear?" Sister Channing asked. "You mean he didn't find you by the pool? I showed him to the patio myself then went to prepare him a plate of food, since he'd missed the dinner." She turned toward Andi's mother in an aside. "It was such a nice buffet, Margaret. I outdid myself, even if I am the one to say so. And I just assumed, Andi, that your friend—" Sister Channing paused to look on curiously as the color drained slowly from Andi's face, leaving only a pale palette of scattered freckles and hastily applied coral blush. "Are you all right, dear?"

"No," Andi whispered, looking from the ring to Clytie and back. When her mother touched her shoulder in concern, she blinked. "Yes!" she amended quickly. "I'm fine. I'm just a little—um—dizzy. I, uh, skipped breakfast. Go on to choir. I'll stay home and, um, eat a piece of toast."

"I'll stay too and, um, make the toast," Clytie said. "So Andi doesn't have to get up."

Margaret wasn't sure whether she should laugh or cry. She looked at the ring still attached to the silver fountain in the egg and let out a little sigh. The last few months since Greg Howland's appearance had been like living on a teeter-totter. Apparently, things were down again between the two of them just now, but if anyone could lift them back up, it was Clytie. For her part, Margaret would be glad when Andi finally settled down with that young man and gave her grandchildren. She patted her eldest daughter's shoulder and cast Clytie a meaningful look. "Good luck," she said. "I'll see you at church."

"Andi," Clytie insisted as soon as the front door had closed, "tell me right this very *second* why Greg didn't give you that ring himself last night."

Andi's mouth opened, then closed, as new dismay brought color back to her face in a sudden rush. She shook her head at the realization of what Greg must have seen—and thought. No wonder he looked so unhappy when she unwrapped his gift and left so soon afterwards. She squeezed her eyes closed at the thought of how she must have hurt him, feeling the pain herself now magnified a dozen times.

"Andi!"

"I think—he must have " Andi opened her eyes to look at her sister and took a deep breath. "Oh, Clytie! He must have seen me kiss Sterling."

"What?" Absolutely certain she had misunderstood, Clytie repeated slowly, "What did you say?"

"He must have seen me kiss Sterling."

Clytie plopped down on the floor, her little bunny slippers sticking straight out in front, looking as pink and surprised as she did herself.

When more than a minute passed and Clytie still hadn't spoken, Andi's jumbled thoughts came out in a rush of words. "What do I do, Clytie?" she asked. "Should I try to call Greg before he leaves for the airport or wait to call until he gets to Los Angeles so we can talk longer? Or should I maybe wait until he comes back to Mesa on Tuesday? Wouldn't it be better to explain in person when we go to the temple to do baptisms for the dead? Or—"

"You *kissed* Sterling?" Clytie said yet again, betrayed and angry in Greg's behalf.

"I—well—I'm almost glad I did," Andi said, trying to put it in the best possible perspective. "After I kissed him I knew I didn't love him and—"

"Even the heroines in those romances you make fun of," Clytie interrupted, "don't have to kiss every man around just to find out they *don't* love them!"

"I've always loved Greg!" Andi said, her eyes sinking slowly back toward the ring in her lap. "Oh, Clytie, you can't even *imagine* how bad I feel . . ."

Her sister was back on her feet and at her side in a moment. "Then call him right now," she urged.

Nodding through her tears, Andi reached for the phone on the table and quickly pressed the numbers. "He's already gone," she reported a few minutes later. "His mother said I only missed him by a few minutes but he forgot his cellular and she doesn't know what flight he's on."

Clytie considered Andi's crestfallen face for a moment, then brightened at a sudden inspiration. "Thaddeus says that Dawson Geitler always knows where Greg is!"

"I don't know, Clytie," Andi hesitated, her distaste for Greg's press agent apparent. At the demanding look on her sister's face, she reached for the phone book. "Well, I could call him, I guess."

Clytie crossed her fingers as Andi dialed the number. Maybe Geitler could even help Andi get to the airport before Greg's plane left. Didn't Greg always say that Dawson Geitler could do anything? Then her eyes rested on an *Ensign* lying on the table, and Clytie remembered Who *really* could be counted on in a crisis. She uncrossed her fingers in order to better cross her arms to pray.

CHAPTER 35

"Thanks a lot," Greg said, pulling his duffel from the backseat of the taxi and shaking his head to refuse help from an approaching skycap. Then he hoisted the bag over his shoulder, adjusted his sunglasses and pulled down the brim of his cap. Though he'd left almost an hour early, just in case, the last thing in the world he wanted right now was to be recognized on his way into the VIP lounge and have to stop to sign autographs. Well, the next to the last thing. Even worse would be to meet up with a photographer of some sort with these dark circles under his eyes and end up on the cover of the *Enquirer* looking like the latest celebrity with a disease-of-the-month.

He winced as that thought led naturally to one of Thaddeus. The youth had insisted that he wanted to stop the treatments that might extend his life by some weeks but were certainly making the days he had left miserable. Although he talked to Thaddeus every day, Greg had only hinted about his own experience with death, wanting the revelation to be in person, in private, and sacred. *I'll have to tell him this week when we do baptisms at the temple*, he decided with a heavy heart. *There won't be many weeks left after this one.*

He wondered now, for perhaps the hundredth time, if he shouldn't tell Clytie the truth about Thaddeus. He'd respected his young friend's wishes in the matter thus far, but he couldn't forget Andi's initial fear over how crushed her little sister would be if Thaddeus died. Greg loved Clytie like a sister himself and felt guilty now for ignoring Andi's warning. Thaddeus would almost surely die and it, even more surely, would break Clytie's heart.

And you'll be responsible for that heartbreak, he told himself as he walked quickly through the terminal, *but at least you didn't completely ruin Andi's life. She still has that perfect eternal companion candidate in Sterling.* Before he could muster any gratitude at all for that one small "blessing," he'd almost arrived without incident at his destination. As Greg turned down the short hall, he heard his name, recognized the smooth voice, and froze.

"Hey, Grego," Zeke Martoni said, leaning one silk-shirted shoulder casually against the wall as he winked at the female security guard who stood waiting to open the door to the VIP lounge. "Long time, no see."

Greg glanced at the guard, dropped his bag, and reluctantly turned to walk back toward Zeke, hoping they'd be out of the woman's earshot.

How Zeke managed to turn up when he did—often at the worst possible moments—had always baffled Greg. This morning, however, he couldn't have cared less if the man had beamed down from an orbiting starship. "What do you want, Martoni?"

One black eyebrow arched slowly upward. "Only what you owe me, kid."

"Owe you? What I owe you is a one-way trip to prison," Greg said. "And believe me, I'm still working on it."

Zeke smiled, showing a row of perfect teeth and no humor. "I guess you and me never did see eye to eye."

"I guess not." Greg's nails dug into the palms of his hands as he wondered where this was going and how he could get it there the quickest.

"How's the redhead?"

"Stay away from her, Zeke," Greg warned. His eyes narrowed above the rim of the sunglasses and his tone was ominous.

"I never had you pegged as the threatening type, kid," Zeke taunted. He ran long, tapered fingers along the facial bone Greg had nearly fractured and shrugged languidly. "But I could have been wrong. Maybe you've got your father in you, after all." He smiled again as the young pitcher's face registered his sudden uncertainty.

"There's not much to do in jail, Grego," Zeke continued, pressing his advantage. "I had a lot of time to think. And you know what I thought about?"

Greg shook his head, his eyes never leaving the floor.

"I thought about where I could hit you back to make it hurt the worst."

Greg's face rose slowly, but he still didn't, or couldn't, reply.

"And that God Almighty of yours was apparently in my corner this time around, kid," he continued quietly, "'cause I'm getting a hand from a couple of the most unexpected places." He stroked a perfectly groomed sideburn as his black eyes narrowed. "Any minute now, Grego, that Mr. Clean image of yours is gonna blow apart like a shotgun blast to a blessed St. Francis statue." Before Greg could respond or even react, Zeke took a step away, then turned with a final sly smile. "I only wanted to make real sure, Howland, that when it does, you know just who pulled the trigger."

Having refused all offers of coffee, tea, and various and other sundry services, Greg sat alone in the lounge pretending to look at the morning newspaper. Since it was Sunday, and still early for the flight to LA, the other first-class passengers had yet to arrive.

What did he mean? Greg asked himself again, turning the brief, mostly one-sided conversation with Martoni over in his mind. Zeke had planted drugs in his locker and hotel room once, Greg recalled, but he'd already looked through his duffel, just in case. And the man had also previously hired a private detective to take photos of him and Clytie. But surely, with the extortion charges still pending, Martoni wouldn't dare go that route again. It was the part about getting a hand from the most unexpected places that worried him. That could mean almost anything. *At least,* Greg thought grimly, *Zeke promised it would be any minute now, so I won't have much longer to wait for the next shoe to drop.*

Before he had even finished the thought, the lounge door opened and Andi came in followed by Dawson Geitler. Greg was on his feet in a split second. *Please, Father,* he prayed, *don't let Martoni hurt Andi to get to me.*

Although she'd rehearsed every word of an explanation on the way to meet Dawson in front of the terminal, even the power of speech left Andi now that she was face to face with Greg. If it was possible, she thought with quick concern, he looked even worse than he had the night before. She tried to smile. "You were right, Greg," she said around the lump in her throat. "Dawson *can* do anything. He found out what flight you were on this morning and then managed to talk our way in here."

Greg looked over her head at his publicist. "Thank you," he said tentatively. His worried eyes returned to Andi's face. "And you're here because—"

Clasping her bag nervously, Andi could feel the outline of the egg under her fingers. If she could just get this out right, the ring would be off the silver fountain inside it and on her finger before she left the airport and Greg left Phoenix. The hope cleared her head enough that she remembered a few of the words she'd rehearsed. "I'm here because . . . because I think you may have gotten the wrong impression about—something. Last night."

Greg remained silent and perfectly still, so it was Andi who turned to Dawson. "Would you please excuse us for a minute?"

"Yes," Dawson replied without enthusiasm. "I'll wait outside the door."

Laying her purse aside, Andi approached Greg shyly. When they were close enough to touch, she said, "I think you might have seen me kiss Sterling last night." The guilty, unhappy look that crossed his face was all the answer Andi needed. With the carefully rehearsed explanations again forgotten, she put both palms on his broad chest and raised herself to her tiptoes. "I kissed him like this," she said, pressing her lips to Greg's for a moment, then moving away.

At the slight rise of one sandy eyebrow, she smiled. "I kiss *you* like this." This time, her slender arms slid up and around Greg's neck as her face rose to meet his. His response was immediate; tender, yet full of need. Andi clung to him to keep from teetering off the edge of the world as within her trembling body, the chills weakened her knees and the bright stars fell, rose, and fell again. "Can you tell the difference?" she asked softly as, at length, they parted.

"I'm not sure," Greg said, his voice low and achingly gentle. "You'd better show me again."

As his arm encircled her narrow waist, the door flew open and Greg looked over Andi's head in surprise. "Mrs. Dresmont."

Lillian Dresmont marched in, flanked by Dawson and a man in an ultra-conservative, three-piece suit. Turning, Andi thought she might understand at last why Thaddeus called her Tiger Lily. The acrylic nail on the wrinkled, bejeweled finger she thrust toward Greg was not unlike like a claw and she didn't speak now so much as she spat.

"Mr. Howland, did I or did I not tell you that our organization was family-centered and concerned, above all, with image?"

"Yes, ma'am," Greg said, releasing Andi and positioning himself without thinking between her and the Diamondbacks' owner. "You did."

"And did you or did you not tell me that there was no truth to the rather scurrilous things previously printed about you in some tabloids?"

"I did."

"You lied."

"No, I—"

"And in the midst of this crisis," she continued as if Greg hadn't begun to speak, "you are *not* where you should be, with your team. Instead you convinced McKay to allow you to return to the Valley for a—a tryst! Don't deny it, Mr. Howland. I have eyes."

From behind his back, Andi could see Greg's ears redden.

"Mrs. Dresmont, I—" Greg's chest expanded as he took a deep breath to regroup. With as much calm as he could muster, he asked, "Crisis?"

"Edwards!" At the flick of her wrist, the man in black stepped forward with a thin sheaf of papers.

"This was delivered today," he said.

Andi stepped around Greg to watch him scan the top paper in the man's hand. He blinked, looked at it again, then took it away to hold closer as he read it a third time. "I don't—" Greg began, dropping the hand that held the documents to his side as he looked at Mrs. Dresmont. "I mean, I can't—" Shaking his head, he sank onto a nearby chair and looked helplessly up at Dawson. "Did they tell you?"

"Yes, sir," Geitler said. "Just now. I don't know what to make of it, either."

Andi couldn't be sure, but she thought there was a gleam in Dawson's eye.

So this is what Zeke was talking about, Greg thought, running his free hand over his face. *Or part of it, at least. "Help from a couple of places," he said. He got to Bobbie Jo—and who else?* Finally, he looked up at Mrs. Dresmont. "It isn't true," he said flatly.

"But you can't *prove* it, Gregory!" Lillian insisted, her small, bird-like eyes flashing. "Not for weeks and weeks, at least. Not until the baby is older, and the tests can be run. By then the damage to your reputation and ours is already done."

Baby? Andi thought, taking an involuntary step back. "Did she say 'baby'?"

At the sound of Andi's voice, Greg turned. "Bobbie Jo is pregnant," he explained. "She plans to sell a tabloid the story that I'm the father."

"We will file suit, of course," the man Mrs. Dresmont had called Edwards declared. "I've already spoken with a top-flight attorney who will meet us in Los Angeles after today's game. He will call in experts and—" he paused in light of the Tiger Lily's fierce look and finished meekly, "—it will take time, of course."

"You have thirty-six hours," Mrs. Dresmont decided. "Gregory, you may take this legal eagle of mine to Los Angeles with you, and I suggest you take that press agent of yours, as well." The claw extended again. "If you don't have this public relations fiasco under control by Monday night, don't bother getting on the team plane. I'll personally see to it that you're released, traded to the Mexican League, or fed to the sharks off the West Coast." The gold bracelets on her thin wrist jangled as she waved her hand to show that it was all the same to her as long as she was rid of him. "Do you understand me?"

Greg nodded, but his eyes had shifted to Andi as the lawyer scrambled to open the door for the team owner. "I don't know what to say."

"You don't have to say anything," Andi responded quickly. Grateful, Greg extended his hand, but Andi didn't see it. She'd closed her eyes momentarily, imagining what the press would write and, worse, what her father would say about the resultant uproar. As her lids raised, the hand was already dropping in resignation and Andi's heart fell with it. She hadn't meant to hesitate, but it appeared that she had. And now, she thought, starting at the loneliness on Greg's face, it was too late. "You know I believe in you, Greg," she said quickly, moving over to put her own hand reassuringly on his shoulder. "And I want to help you, but—"

Behold the Ultimate Truth, Greg thought. *Your father's going to be livid, Sterling's going to say "I told you so," and everyone else you know is going to gossip about me and be embarrassed for you.*

"I understand," he said sincerely, reaching up to take the hand and kiss it quickly before he rose, "and, for what it's worth Andi, I'm really sorry about all this."

CHAPTER 30

"You're late, Mr. Howland," Dawson reported as he ran down the hotel corridor to keep pace with Greg on Sunday night.

Thank you, White Rabbit, Greg thought. "I'm walking as fast as I can, Dawson," he said. "And I'll tell you again, it's not my fault that the game had a rain delay. You'll have to take that up with a higher source."

Personally, Greg had considered the deluge a blessing. The extra half hour his teammates had spent in the locker room had given him time alone to slip out to the visitors' bullpen and watch the large drops plunk onto the canvas that had been rolled out to protect the field. It was the only time he had had to himself since leaving Phoenix that morning. He'd finally had a chance to talk—not to an attorney and a press agent who had plenty of grand notions but no solutions—but to his Heavenly Father, the only source of real help in times of need. And Greg had received an answer, though not the one he had hoped for.

These things will give you experience, the Spirit whispered, *and will be for your good.* With the words had come the assurance that they were true, and even though Greg couldn't see any good in the experience himself, he nevertheless believed that when faith is all you have to go on, well then, all you can do is *go on.*

Dawson had met him in the lobby when he'd returned to his hotel after the game, seeming to think that his presence would speed Greg toward the meeting upstairs. "I'm only concerned because Mr. Lawrence is a busy man," Geitler panted.

"Mr. Lawrence is getting paid more to wait inside my hotel room for an hour than most people make in a month," Greg pointed out, coming to a stop in front of the door and inserting the lock card. "It's like being a major league pitcher, Dawson—not bad work if you can get it."

Within minutes of meeting Mr. Jerome Lawrence, by his own admission the best attorney on the West Coast, and sitting down with him, Mr. Edwards, and the White Rabbit, Greg felt like the Titmouse at the Mad Hatter's tea party. Only, when he thought about it, Lewis Carroll's mathematics-inspired prose had made more sense. It wasn't long before Greg had rested his elbows on the table and his forehead in his open palms. *The best suggestion I've heard so far,* he thought, *is Mrs. Dresmont's that I take a long walk off a short pier.*

"I say we *can* force a DNA test in utcrine," Lawrence insisted.

"But, sir," Edwards pointed out, "before ten weeks, we're talking embryonic."

"You're making my point right there!" Lawrence said, banging his fist on the table. "The benefit to my client, a well-known and respected man, far outweighs any possible harm to a mere fetus."

Greg's head rose immediately and, failing to find a jury present for the histrionics, he looked in disbelief at his new, supposedly LDS, counsel. "You're not suggesting something that could hurt the baby?"

"Mr. Howland," Edwards inserted patronizingly, "there *is* no baby at this point. We're discussing a thing smaller than a guppy. The best course of action may simply be—"

"Out of the question," Greg concluded. "Look, if I could just talk to Bobbie Jo—"

"We can't locate her, sir," Dawson reminded him.

Zeke saw to that, Greg thought bitterly. Even Wanda, who was staying with the boys, didn't know where she'd disappeared to. "Then I'll—" his voice trailed off as he realized he didn't have any idea what he'd do. "—I'll tell you what I *won't* do," he continued finally. "I won't do anything—" he looked Edwards in the eye, then turned to Lawrence and repeated, "*—anything* that might harm that unborn child. Understand?" He leaned back in his chair and his jaw set. "And I'm not going to let some sleazy tabloid writer get away with character assassination, either." Greg glanced at Geitler for confirmation, but Dawson wouldn't meet his eye.

"We only want to help you, Mr. Howland," Lawrence said patiently.

Especially if you can make a buck and look good doing it, Greg thought. Still, there wasn't a better man around to take on the behemoth of the media, so Greg nodded. "I appreciate that. But we'll keep the help on my terms."

"Time is of the essence," Lawrence reminded him. "By tomorrow night, the AP will have broken the news about the upcoming article."

"And that only gives me a week before it appears on the newsstands," Dawson mused aloud, as though he personally should be doing something else this very moment to prepare.

Greg shook his head again, knowing that even Dawson and his amazing Technicolor computer couldn't get him out of this one unscathed. He said to Lawrence, "Didn't you tell me you could stop the publication with the threat of a lawsuit? Or get a restraining order to keep them from printing what they couldn't prove was true?"

"I believe either might work for us, Mr. Howland, but—"

Great, Greg thought, *more Ultimate Truth.*

"It was Brigham Young who said that rumor runs in ten-mile strides while truth is still getting out of bed."

Greg returned an elbow to the table to rest his cheek on his closed fist.

"And that," Lawrence concluded, "is your problem in a nutshell."

Greg nodded but had not replied when the telephone rang.

Dawson pushed back his chair and walked across the room to answer it. "No," he said into the receiver, "this is Mr. Howland's press agent." As he listened, his mouth dropped slowly open. "Uh, yes," he said finally, "he's here. Just a minute, please."

Greg looked from Dawson's face to the receiver he extended. *He looks like he's holding a snake,* Greg thought, fighting a feeling of trepidation as he pushed his own chair out from the table and went over to the phone.

"It's your father, sir," Dawson said, after Greg had taken the handset and was holding it to his chest questioningly.

Greg could feel the blood leave his fingers as he gripped the phone too tightly and drew a deep, cleansing breath. "Thanks, Dawson," he said at last. When his publicist didn't move, he added,

"This might take a couple of minutes. Keep a short leash on those lawyers for me, will you?"

When Dawson returned reluctantly to the table, Greg pulled up a chair and positioned it so that his back was to the three men. Then he slowly raised the receiver to his ear and mouth. *I haven't said anything particularly civil to my father in a decade at least,* he realized without satisfaction. *What can I possibly say to him now?*

"Greg?"

"Uh, yeah. It's me."

There was a long moment of silence before Roy began. "Your ma's the one gave me your number," he said. "A counselor-feller here in Chicago helped me call her. He had to get ahold of the Mesa police to get the number." The next line seemed to be delivered as an apology or a plea: "Your ma said you'd talk to me, Greg."

Is this my father? Greg wondered. The voice itself was familiar but the words, though slow, were clear and delivered without the liquor-induced slur to which he was accustomed. *But what is he doing in Chicago? And did he say "counselor"?*

"Sure," Greg said at last. "I'll talk to you. How, uh—how are you?"

"I'm sober, son."

It took seconds for the words to sink in, and still Greg wasn't sure he believed them. He waited, not saying anything.

"I'm in a halfway house in Chicago," Roy continued. "AA helps to run it. My sponsor got me in after I finished rehab. I been workin' some and goin' to meetings and readin' the books and talkin' to my sponsor every day. That's how I got to the ninth step, Greg. An' that's why I called."

"I don't understand—"

"I joined Alcoholics Anonymous, and we got Twelve Steps that help get us old drunks sober and keep us that way. Number one was to admit that I ain't got no power over booze. I guess I don't gotta tell you or your ma that."

No, Greg thought as he waited for his father to continue.

"But it was number four that liked to kill me. It's what they call a 'fearless moral inventory.' And when I thought of the hell I put you through, I—I wished I was dead—and not for the first time, Greg."

His father struggled for enough composure to go on, and Greg cleared his own throat. "I—"

"Let me just get it all out afore you say anything," Roy interrupted, "will you, son? That day the doctor called and told us you were gonna die, I—I just left out on your ma to be with my bottle. Lost both my boys, I thought, and it weren't no more than what I deserved, a worthless cuss like me. When I finally did go on back home and saw that your ma had up and left me, too, well, it was more than a man could take. I knew she was well rid of me," he added hastily. "I knew it, but her leavin' was the last drop from a dry well. I took the money you give us and just lit out, you know? Weren't nothing left that my boozin' hadn't ruinated."

Greg thought of their home in Iowa and closed his eyes.

"I was just a gonna run my truck into the river and be done with it," Roy continued, "but someways I made it on into Chicago and bought me another bottle. I think I might a bought another after that, truth be told. Anyways, I passed out on the street sometime in the middle of the night. That's when somethin' really happened."

There was a longer pause, as Roy seemed to mull the experience over again in his mind. Finally he said, "'Cept for maybe your ma, Greg, we weren't none of us believing people, were we?"

Remembering his own crisis of faith at Jim's death, Greg said softly, "No, I guess we weren't."

"An' that's what makes expectin' you to believe any o' this all the tougher. Do you think you could—" Roy hesitated, "—could you maybe understan' me now if I told you I've come to reckon there's a Higher Power?"

Greg felt an incredible warmth begin at the top of his head and spread throughout his body. "Yes," he whispered. "I could understand."

Greg's words seemed to give Roy confidence, and he began to speak again. "In AA the second step's to say that only a Power greater than ourselves can get us to sanity. We gotta believe in God and tell Him all the mistakes we've made on the road and ask Him real meek like to take the failin's away. He can do it, Greg," Roy added fervently. His voice was low and earnest and seemed to beg for his son's agreement. "He can do it for us if we'll let Him."

Greg leaned his head on the back of the chair to keep the tears from running down his cheeks. "Yes, Dad. He can do it if we'll let Him."

"But we gotta admit we're wrong," Roy continued, "and believe it and tell the people we've hurt that we're sorry." Greg's father began now to sob in earnest and his words were barely audible. "I—oh, son—I—I don't blame you for hatin' me and I know you can't never forgive me, neither. But you just gotta know if there were any way—any kind of chance on earth that I could do it all over again—"

"Dad," Greg interrupted gently. "Dad, I forgive you." As the sobbing only increased, Greg cleared his own throat again. "Listen, Dad, we can't any of us undo what's already done. But we can rely on Christ's Atonement—that Higher Power you were talking about—to get us past our failings and make us whole."

As his father regained his voice, Greg listened to him tell about the unknown man in a bright white shirt who had taken him to an alcohol rehabilitation center and helped him sign in when he was too drunk to even know his name. He told Greg, too, about the horrible days in detox made bearable only by extensive counseling and a kind AA sponsor who had taken Roy under his wing to help him through the Steps.

That his father had called expecting skepticism and rejection was evident. Roy's voice was low and incredulous when he asked, "And you believe me, Greg? Honest you do?"

"I believe you, Dad," Greg assured him again. "I believe *in* you. And I also believe that that Higher Power has a plan. There are a couple of little boys who need you—and their grandma—very much right now."

As he said it, Greg again felt the pinpricks of the Spirit caper down his arms. Being abandoned by their mother would likely prove to be the greatest good fortune in his nephews' lives. Sadie had grown so much in such a short time. With her baptism scheduled for Tuesday night, Greg's first day off, she already had two of the three things a prophet said are necessary in every life: the nourishment of faith and the blessing of a friend. Now she needed a responsibility. Her grandsons would prove as great a godsend to her life as she would be to theirs.

Greg smiled as he listened to his father speak more freely of what he called his "journey back to sanity." Who could say? he thought. With a little more time, a little more therapy, and, of course, more than a little prayer, perhaps Roy could one day claim his rightful place in their family circle.

Turning in the chair a few minutes later, after finally telling his father good night, Greg looked at the lawyers and Dawson, still plotting a course of action. He set the receiver down with a smile as he remembered Roy's second step: *I have to believe that only a Power greater than myself can restore me to sanity.*

Truer words, Greg thought, rising from the chair to reluctantly rejoin the men at the conference table, *were never spoken.*

Chapter 37

Andi shook out the freshly laundered sheet then let it fall into place over Enos' bed as she gazed out the window across the Lehi Valley. It was midmorning on Tuesday, but to the east it was dark, as though someone had pulled a dusky brown curtain over the sun and the Superstition Mountains below.

She slipped the pillow into its case and listened to the birds excitedly discuss the weather even as they soared to take cover from it. Within moments, a dust devil skittered down the street, a harbinger of the coming storm.

As Andi watched, the wind itself arrived, plucking tissue-thin petals from the jacaranda tree and sprinkling them artlessly across the yard. Within minutes, Andi knew, the swimming pool below would bear more resemblance to a pond, with palm fronds and bits of lightweight debris floating on top while silt and sand settled in layers to the bottom.

Andi had never liked these hot summer storms with lightning that started brush fires and the harsh winds that fanned them. Inevitably, they blew more sand than you would think could still exist on a desert floor upon which a city had been built up, paved, and carefully landscaped. And though they obscured vision and left a gritty feel upon their passing, they brought little or no rain and afforded only a marginal drop in temperature. *"Sound and fury,"* Andi thought at the first peal of thunder, *"signifying nothing."*

Within minutes, Andi watched the summer sky shift from blue to green to gray as the storm arrived with a vengeance. The tall palm trees lining the street behind the house bowed in the wind but stood their ground. Andi took an involuntary step back as grit skittered across the windowpane, all but obscuring her view of the trees and the pool and the rest of the world.

Grateful to be inside, sheltered and secure, Andi turned from the window and reached for a switch to turn on the light beside Enos' bed. Then, almost reflexively, she began to straighten the mess on the bedside table. Her hand froze over a tabloid with Greg's picture on the cover and she forced herself to pick it up. Sinking onto the bed, Andi pulled the pillow into her lap and rested the magazine across it. One nail traced the outline of his face then smoothed the fine lines around his beautiful blue eyes. His lips were pulled back into a smile that brought sudden tears to Andi's eyes for its lack of joy.

She hadn't been able to talk to Greg since Sunday morning but knew that he was still in LA and, according to the news reports, not talking to anyone before the press conference that was scheduled to take place in about an hour. But since yesterday's evening newscast, it seemed that all the world was talking *about* him. Even Andi's father was home today—though her mother was out of town with the younger kids—and planned to watch the event on TV. Afterward, Andi suspected, he'd be ready to pass final judgment on Greg.

But what will Greg do after the conference? Andi wondered. She hoped and prayed that he'd make it back to Mesa in time to do baptisms at the temple as they had planned. She knew it would never occur to Greg to cancel their plans; he felt too deeply the importance of beginning the temple work for his family, work that would open the gate to exaltation and eternal life. Once she and Greg were at the temple together, Andi had thought of a way, she hoped, to assure Greg that she would never again seem falter in her devotion to him—even for a moment.

She looked up at a sudden sharp sound. A frond had come loose from one of the palms and smacked hard against the window. As though it was a slap to her own face, Andi realized all at once that Greg was caught in a storm. It was a storm of even greater malevolence and fury than the one outside, whipped by forces she could neither identify nor understand. It, too, was sound and fury, but the significance could have eternal consequences and Greg was trapped out in the very midst of it.

Laying the pillow and magazine quickly aside, Andi dropped to her knees at the side of the bed to pray for Greg. She asked God to let him have the strength of the palm trees in the raging winds of controversy and deceit, that when the storm passed over he would be safe and strong and standing tall.

Down the hall, the phone began to ring but Andi barely heard it as, prompted by the Spirit, her prayers increased in fervency. The storm, she feared now, had only just begun and was drawing closer.

Chapter 38

Tinker to Evers to Chance, Greg thought, looking from Dawson to Edwards to Lawrence as the three men passed conference notes and legal papers from one to another. *Except they've tinkered with everything and left nothing to chance—or to me.*

Not that he wasn't grateful. Greg would gladly face a line-up of .350 hitters with a World Series at stake before he'd agree to speak to the press representatives eagerly filling the conference room next door. It would be bad enough, he thought, to have to stand mutely to the side in this uncomfortable business suit to be photographed while his lawyer threatened lawsuits and his press agent recited carefully scripted sound bites.

All in all, it had been a miserable two days and, despite everything being done by a phalanx of experts on his behalf, it would probably only get worse. Greg had been all for sticking with the tersely worded statement they had released yesterday and laying low until the storm blew over. But the media, apparently, lived by the motto, "You have the right to remain silent, but everything you *don't* say will be misconstrued, misquoted, and used against you." Finally, he had agreed to a live conference as long as Dawson and Jerome Lawrence did the talking.

I need an aspirin, Greg thought, as the din in the next room increased and his head began to pound. *That and a one-way ticket to some far corner of the earth.* He massaged the back of his neck as he realized that not only was the earth without corners, there was only one place on it he truly longed to be—at the Mesa temple with Thaddeus and Andi and her sisters this afternoon. Greg looked at his watch and knew he would cut it very close for the baptisms, if he made it at all. He thought of the old family picture at home in his room and sighed. His grandfather had waited too long already for this ordinance. Greg couldn't help but wonder what the old farmer would make of all this hullabaloo that threatened to keep his grandson from doing today some of the only work on earth that really mattered.

Maybe I could charter a flight, Greg thought, glancing around the room for a phone and seeing instead Dawson's laptop computer connected in the far corner. *Better yet. He keeps telling me you can do anything on-line.* Greg took a couple of steps toward his publicist before stopping himself. Geitler was already practically living on Tums, he knew, and was now popping painkillers too while deeply engrossed in conversation with Lawrence and Edwards. *Dawson's the one bearing the brunt of this conference*, Greg told himself. *The least you can do is not bother him for one thing you can do yourself.*

He walked over to the laptop and considered the barely familiar keyboard for a moment, wondering which key he should press to activate the screen. Choosing one at random, he was gratified when half a dozen icons appeared.

It's that net navigator, I think. Moving his finger across the touch pad toward the ship's wheel, Greg hit an open file folder by mistake. As he was trying to close it and get back to the menu, his eyes strayed to the screen.

Reading Dawson's notes on his biography was, to Greg, like falling into an icy pond. Shocked and scarcely able to breathe, he scanned the intro quickly then scrolled down to read the section headings. There was "Early Home Life," "Jim's Drug Addiction," "Bobbie Jo," and "Near-death Experience" with a question mark after it. Near the bottom of the list was "Zeke Martoni Interview."

So Dawson is Zeke's other ally, Greg thought, looking across the room at the flushed young publicist who was intently addressing the two lawyers. He thought about the trip to Iowa and everything he'd shared with Dawson since about Andi and Clytie and Ique, and he shuddered as the chill in his veins increased.

Good gosh, Howland, he berated himself, *how could one man be as stupid as you are?* No doubt Andi would be in Geitler's book, he thought with increasing dismay—and Clytie. Greg rubbed a hand across his face. *And just when my parents showed signs that they might make it, this will come along and blow them right out of the water.*

Shaking his head as if to recover from the drowning sensation, Greg picked up the lightweight computer with the thought of flinging it across the room. Reconsidering, he set it deliberately down on the table and closed the file before walking away. There was no way around it; not only did he need Dawson to get him through the press conference today, the last thing he could afford was for the man to go on national TV tomorrow to tell the world everything he knew. Geitler, apparently, was biding his time with the exposé, and Greg would need every minute of that time to prepare the people he loved.

"Are you all right, Mr. Howland?" Dawson asked in concern as Greg approached. "You don't look well."

"I'm great," Greg said curtly. "When are we gonna do this thing and get it over with?"

Dawson glanced at the wall clock, then at his watch for confirmation. "About fifteen minutes. Really, why don't you sit down?"

If he ever gives up writing, Greg thought, as the man he had once considered a friend turned toward a nearby cooler to get him a cup of water, *he could take up acting.* Still, Dawson's concern seemed genuine enough, even to him. He accepted the water and a pain reliever with a brief acknowledgment. Admittedly, he needed it, since even the whine of Edwards' cell phone set him on edge.

The attorney answered then moved toward Greg. "Mr. Bisher's on the phone, Mr. Howland. For you."

Mrs. Dresmont is probably too furious to speak, Greg thought, extending his hand in resignation. *She had to get Cleon to fire me.* "Yes, sir."

"Greg," Cleon said, the strain in his voice obvious. "It's Thaddeus."

"Thaddeus?" Greg repeated, knowing all too well what Mr. Bisher meant.

"I brought him in to Barrows this morning. The doctors say the tumor—" Thaddeus' father paused, unable for a moment to speak.

"—they say it's pressing on the brain stem. His respiratory system—he—"

"How long?" Greg asked.

"Hours—maybe."

"Have you called Clytie?"

"I will next. Thaddeus wants to see you, Greg. I've got a car on the way to your hotel and a plane will be waiting at the airport after you finish—"

"I'll leave now," Greg interrupted.

"No," Cleon said. "We're in a room and Thaddeus is comfortable. He says he'll be watching to see how you get yourself out of this—what's the word, Thaddeus?—*Zugzwang?*"

"Tell him he's the one who's always known all the brilliant maneuvers," Greg managed to respond through a growing thickness in his throat. "And tell him I'll be in Phoenix before he knows it. I still have that—what did he call it?—'eschatology seminar' to conduct."

As he handed the phone back to Edwards, Greg straightened his shoulders and yanked up the knot on his tie. "All right, gentlemen, we do this press conference now or never."

"But—" Geitler began.

"So we're early for a change, Dawson," Greg said grimly, barely sparing him a glance on his way toward the door to the meeting room. "I thought you'd be pleasantly surprised. Besides, I have more important things to do today. Coming?"

"Should I turn this off?" Andi asked, reaching for the knob on the car radio as she glanced at Clytie's ashen face. Greg's press conference had come on just as they pulled out of the driveway to head for the hospital.

Why did my mother have to be gone today? Andi asked God silently. *You know I'm not the nurturing type that she is. Maybe I* should *have let Dad drive Clytie. I don't know what to say to Thaddeus—or to her. Please, Father, help them both. Help Greg. Help me!*

"Leave it on," Clytie said, reaching forward herself to turn up the volume. "I want to hear Greg."

"What can he say—?" Andi began, then was quiet herself to listen to Jerome Lawrence threaten in sonorous tones a satchel full of legal actions against the tabloid that had bought Bobbie Jo's story. Despite her keen interest in the proceedings, Andi couldn't keep her mind from flitting ahead to their destination or her eyes from flitting to her sister's face. *Poor Clytie,* she thought, dragging her eyes back to the road and fearing that it wouldn't be long before she wouldn't be able to see through the tears to drive. *And Greg! He loves that kid. How will he cope with this on top of everything else?*

Andi's attention came back to the broadcast when she heard Dawson Geitler begin to speak. His glib platitudes sounded good, she had to admit, though she didn't understand what point, if any, he was trying to make. She glanced at Clytie when the publicist's words were garbled by an odd sound. "It's on the right channel," she told her sister after fiddling with the knob. "I wonder what's going on."

The sudden reaction of the press, whispering and moving in their seats, disconcerted Dawson, and he hastily scanned his paper to see what he had just read to elicit such a reaction. He jumped when a firm hand clasped him on the shoulder and moved him to one side of the podium.

"I have something to say after all," Greg told him and the packed conference room. "My press agent is great with words but, in this case, he's mistaken."

Dawson watched Greg speak deliberately into the microphones, though his face and eyes were lowered toward the speaker's stand to avoid the bank of cameras.

"There is no 'new morality,'" Greg continued firmly, referring to a statement Dawson had just made. "I have a . . . a friend . . . whom I've accused of seeing things in black and white when the world is mostly gray. But I think I finally understand what she's known all along: that the world is mostly gray only because we've made it that way." He took a deep breath and concluded, "There is morality and decency and there is immorality and wrongdoing. Granted, the filth is everywhere. But no matter how much we popularize and glamorize garbage, it will still be garbage."

Not a single pencil moved, Dawson noted with a pounding heart as, for the first time that he had ever seen, Greg looked directly into the cameras.

"I'm not sure what my lawyer and my publicist were trying to tell you," the celebrity ballplayer stated flatly, "but I'm saying myself that it's enough for you to know that I'm a virgin." To the general murmur in the audience, he gave a wry half-grin. "It's not that I've lacked opportunity," he admitted, "or even desire, but I chose a long time ago to wait until marriage and I've stood by that choice."

Dawson watched as several of the reporters now scribbled away as if in unbelief. He was pretty incredulous himself, come to think of it.

"If that's interesting enough for your papers and news programs, great," Greg said, the grin fading. "It's probably the only true or worthwhile thing you'll ever say about me."

When he turned away from the podium, a female TV reporter popped up in the first row. "Greg, are you saying then that you blame the media for fueling your sister's story?"

The young pitcher, Geitler saw in an instant, hadn't considered fielding questions when he'd come impulsively to the podium and was clearly unprepared. Dawson stepped forward when his client hesitated. "Mr. Howland holds his *sister-in-law* solely at fault in this matter," he answered for Greg.

"No, I don't," Greg said quietly, as much to Dawson as to the reporters. "Bobbie Jo's had it rough, especially since my brother died. She was—lonely—and trusted people she shouldn't have." His eyes met Dawson's. "Anyone could make that mistake."

Dawson felt the blood rush up, hot under his skin, and lowered his eyes to the carpet as Greg turned to address the reporter.

"And I can't blame you, either," he said, "since your bottom line cuts straight through the middle of a dollar sign. You people get paid for selling the most papers and bringing in the highest television ratings. What are you gonna do when the people you're writing for are more interested in scandal and gossip than in the unexciting truth?" Greg paused for a moment to consider, then added, "*That's* where the fault is in all this, and it scares me. God can't just sit back and watch our society go on like this forever."

Another reporter rose excitedly. "Are you predicting the end of the world?"

"Huh?" Greg glanced at Dawson and rolled his eyes.

"You joined the Mormon religion lately, didn't you, Mr. Howland?" the man pressed. "It was your prophet that sent out that so-called proclamation warning of future calamities if we don't straighten up. Did he mean—"

"Excuse me—" Greg held up a hand to halt the question,"—but President Hinckley isn't *my* prophet." Raising his voice to be heard over the resultant buzz, he continued calmly, "He's *our* prophet—*the* prophet—and I won't even begin to speak for him, or even about him, to you. But I think you're talking about the First Presidency's proclamation about families, and you're right on the mark. I suggest you all get a copy. It says everything I've been trying to say much better than I ever could. In fact, *publish* that proclamation in place of whatever gossip you came for today and you just might save our planet." Greg looked at the startled reporter and smiled genuinely for the first time in a couple of days. "Good question, guy. Thanks."

Dawson stared, with Lawrence and Edwards and the media, at Greg as he ignored the rest of the questions being called out and strode from the room. Then the press agent turned back to the crowd at a loss, for once, for words. "Uh, thank you for coming," he said quickly before anyone could address a query to him. "That concludes our press conference."

Chapter 30

Andi stood just inside the door to Thaddeus' room, grateful for Laura Newton's arm around her shoulder as she prayed even more fervently for him and Clytie. The sixteen-year-old girl was perched on a chair in order to be tall enough to lean over the railing of the high bed. Andi's heart constricted as she watched her little sister swallow, blink, and hastily brush the salty signs of sorrow from her face. The doctor had given them only ten minutes with Thaddeus and, through most of them, Clytie had been simply too overcome to speak.

When one of the tears escaped her tiny fingers and fell onto Thaddeus' face, he said softly, "Please don't cry, Clytie. I want all the pictures I have of you to be when you're smiling." With his elbow still on the bed, he raised his forearm, and Clytie lay her cheek against his palm.

Though, thankfully, Thaddeus seemed to be in little pain, talking was increasingly difficult. He lay very still between sentences as if each cost a little of the strength he had left, and words, for the first time in his life, were to be weighed carefully. Still, after a couple of moments he asked Clytie, "What's big and gray—and wears glass slippers?"

Her golden hair brushed softly over his bare arm as, silently, she shook her head.

"Cinderelephant." His long fingers moved now toward her lips, and Clytie, despite the heartbreak so evident on her pretty face, tried valiantly to curve the corners upwards. Thaddeus smiled. "I've been saving that joke—for a special occasion." He turned his head toward the other side of the bed. "Dad?"

Any effort Cleon might have made to fight back tears of his own had long since been abandoned. "It's right here, son," he said, reaching into the breast pocket of his suit coat and pulling out a small, velvet-covered box that he pressed into Thaddeus' free hand.

"I've been saving this, too," Thaddeus said. "Open it, Clytie."

Clytie took the box and slowly lifted the hinged lid. "Oh, Thaddeus!" she choked out at the sight of an Austrian crystal-encrusted shoe on a silver chain.

"It's that—other glass slipper I owe you," he said with increasing effort. "But Clytie—" the sightless amber eyes, so large in Thaddeus' pale face, seemed now to be able to look into her soul, "—don't forget what I told you—about Thumbelina. You're going to meet that Prince Iggy someday—and—well, he's one lucky guy."

"I love you, Thaddeus," Clytie whispered, clinging to his fingers as she clutched the jewel case to her heart.

"I know." Thaddeus wiped a tear from her cheek with one hand and reached toward his father with the other. Cleon took his son's hand and enveloped it in both of his own. "Some dumb jock told me—" Thaddeus said slowly, "—that my last couple of months could—be priceless. He was right." The youth raised his head hopefully at the sound of a door opening, then lowered it with a soft sigh when he realized it was the doctor.

"Greg will be here any minute," Clytie assured him.

Thaddeus nodded. "Yeah—he owes me—for all the help with the—engagement project. Hope it—works out."

"I'll have to ask you to leave now," the doctor told Andi and Clytie. "Thaddeus needs to rest."

"He doesn't want me to be—too tired to die." The youth managed a weary grin as he gave Clytie's hand a final squeeze.

Unable to suppress a sob, Andi approached the bed and bent to kiss Thaddeus' forehead. "I love you, too," she said. Looking over to Cleon, she took Clytie's hand gently from Thaddeus' and added quietly, "We'll wait in the lobby."

"No, Andi," Thaddeus said quickly. "Take Clytie—to the temple—like we planned." When she hesitated, he struggled to sit up. "Please."

"She will," Cleon assured him quickly, urging his son to lay still.

"I want—"

"Shhh, Thaddeus," his father said. "Andi will take care of Clytie. Rest for a few minutes so you can talk to Greg."

Greg! Andi thought longingly as she helped her sister down from the chair and shepherded her gently toward the door while Laura moved back to Cleon's side. *Oh, Greg, please hurry. We all need you so very much.*

If Greg could have offered time from his own life to move the plane faster or extend Thaddeus' life even by minutes, he would have given it gladly. But all he could do was sit next to Dawson and stare helplessly from the window as the Colorado River marked a long, silvery boundary between states.

They had just crossed into Arizona. It would be another twenty minutes before they landed in Phoenix, then it would take at least that long again to make it from Sky Harbor airport to the hospital. *Not enough time,* Greg worried—and the Spirit confirmed, *No, not enough time.*

Greg glanced over at Dawson. The notebook computer, as usual, was open on his lap, but the screen was blank; his press agent wore earphones and appeared to be asleep. Whether he was or not, Greg pulled the phone from the holder at his side. *What's another chapter more or less?* Though sickened by the thought of having something so sacred held up for public ridicule, he determined to keep his promise to Thaddeus to share his own experience about death, no matter what the personal cost now.

Dawson's eyes flicked open as Greg asked for a connection to the hospital where the boy lay dying. His earphones were turned off and he'd been feigning sleep so he could think. Though the other man had turned away toward the window, every word he said was clear. Dawson heard exactly when Thaddeus came on the line.

It was time—right this very moment—to decide about his book. He'd done nothing but struggle with it from the inception. But the problem wasn't in his manuscript, Dawson knew, or even in his head, but in his heart. Over the last couple of weeks, he'd carefully reviewed every word he'd written—and then edited and embellished it for a more stunning effect. Now, carefully filed within the computer in his lap, was the well-crafted and perfectly timed biography of Greg Howland. That it could make Dawson rich and famous was certain. Whether the money and fame would also make him happy was less so.

I ought to be immune to Howland's sentimentality by now, Dawson thought impatiently, remembering the dozens of times Greg had said or done something to cause him to waver in his resolve to publish the exposé. But nothing had compared to the look in his eyes at the press conference today; that one brief look, which suggested that Greg knew of his betrayal, had seemed to penetrate his soul. And, worse, something inside that soul had believed every word the earnest young celebrity had said.

So what do I do now? Dawson asked the universe at large. As if in rapid reply, he remembered the words Greg had read to him in Chicago—*"God hath given unto you a knowledge and he hath made you free"*—and the fire in the convert's eyes when he had read them. And what was the rest? *"Ye can choose good and have good restored to you—or ye can choose evil."*

But doesn't it seem like destiny? a shrill voice argued at once. *Only once in a lifetime—if you're lucky—will a break like this fall into your lap. And how much would it hurt Howland really? If* you *don't do it, somebody else is bound to.*

Geitler's fingers clenched the side of the computer as Greg began to tell Thaddeus of his journey through the tunnel and toward the Light.

Choose now! Dawson commanded himself.

Leaning forward quickly, he depressed a single button then settled back into the seat and closed his eyes as a loud musical coda filled his ears and thoughts and heart.

"Thanks—for—everything, Greg," Thaddeus murmured into the phone that his father held to his ear. "If—you're—telling me the truth—I guess I'll—be seeing you." He listened to the deep voice for another minute and a smile creased his face. He struggled for the breath to say, "Improve your—chess game—before you die then—will you?"

Greg said a few more words, but Thaddeus didn't hear them. He was looking toward the window where a beautiful young woman with honey-colored hair and wide, amber eyes stood as if bathed in noonday light, her hand extended.

"Hey, Thaddeus," she said happily, her smile the brightest part of a glowing countenance, "Come look at this."

Thaddeus moved his hand across the sheet to find Sister Newton's fingers and draw them toward Cleon's. With his new vision still full of the radiant being at the window, Thaddeus whispered, "Stay—with my dad, Laura. I want to go now—my mom's waiting."

CHAPTER 40

From the corner of his eye, Dawson saw Greg hang up the phone and push his seat into a reclining position. Removing the earphones, Geitler started to speak then closed his mouth as he watched his companion massage his eyes with a middle finger and thumb. When he drew them away, Dawson noted, the balls of both fingers were wet.

Sitting silently, Dawson offered Greg his first gift—the privacy to grieve. When the pilot at last announced the final approach into Phoenix and Howland obediently raised his seat upright, he spoke. "Greg?"

At first, there was no response, then Greg slowly rolled his head toward Geitler with a deep sigh. "Yeah, Dawson?"

"I quit." At the rise of one sandy eyebrow, Dawson snapped down the top of his computer and placed it on Greg's knees.

Greg put a hand on the laptop to steady it. "Mind if I ask why?"

"Because I only took the job to use you," Dawson said quickly, before he lost his nerve. "And I lied about writing the Great American Novel. I was writing the great American tell-all." He looked disdainfully at the notebook. "That isn't all I lied about, but it's all there, Greg, I swear—every note, every picture—everything." When Howland didn't respond, he lowered his eyes and added, "And I'm sorry about your friend. He seemed like a good kid."

"Yeah," Greg agreed thickly, "he was." He turned away for a moment to stare out the window while he composed his face and his thoughts. Then he handed Geitler back his computer. "Why don't you write about Thaddeus, Dawson? Him and Clytie."

"What?"

"Clytie told me that in Greek Thaddeus' name means 'courageous.' Hers means 'loyal.' People like them are the real heroes in the world." He tapped the computer with a knuckle. "But you'll have to do it in your spare time. You have a full-time job already, just keeping me behind schedule."

Dawson looked down at the computer in his lap for a long moment. After a quick glance at Greg, he flipped open the lid and pulled up a planner. He was almost himself again as he consulted the screen. "As a matter of fact, Greg, you're going to be late for your appointment at the temple—"

Greg shook his head at the miraculous, welcome return of the White Rabbit. Then, at a sudden realization, his eyes widened. "Did I hear right, Dawson? Are you actually calling me Greg now?"

Dawson Geitler's lips twitched slightly as he admitted, "Well, yes. I believe I am."

Greg leaned back and gazed again out at the fluffy white clouds above Phoenix. "Will wonders never cease?" he said softly. Then, remembering a certain place where wonders never did, he smiled.

Mourning doves, Greg thought as he listened to the birds' sorrowful calls from the tops of the palms lining the Arizona Temple walkway. *But they have no idea how it feels.* It had seemed unreal to him today, as it had the night Jim died, that the entire world could proceed as usual when, to him, nothing would ever seem the same. He had been eternally grateful to get off the plane and come straight to the temple—the only place on earth where death seemed to lose its sting.

Scoured clean by the morning gusts of sand, the sky was perfectly blue and wavering in the early summer heat. Greg glanced up at it as he hastened his steps toward the east entrance to the baptistry, even though he suspected he was too late to meet Andi and Clytie. Brad had confirmed by phone that Andi and her sisters had come late to the temple themselves, but surely they wouldn't have waited this long. Greg had almost decided to turn back when he saw a familiar figure huddled in a small spot of shade on a middle stair. He covered the last few yards quickly and slid beside her onto the hot granite step.

Clytie sat with her head bent, a long, blonde veil of hair covering her cheeks. Greg moved a golden sheet back gently and tucked it behind her ear as he bent close to see her face. Surprisingly, her enormous aqua eyes were dry. He saw that they were focused on a shining silver chain that she had entwined around and through the fingers clasped together in her lap.

"Did you get back in time to see him?" she asked after a second or two.

"No," Greg said. "My plane was delayed in LA. I spoke to Thaddeus somewhere over the desert."

"He loved you."

"Yeah. He loves you, too, Clytie." With her shock and grief so great, Greg felt at a loss to help. He said a prayer as he slipped a strong arm around Clytie and gathered her close. "You know," he continued gently, "a few months ago, a very special young woman brought me here to see this temple. At the time, I was hurting so much I didn't think I could stand it. I'll never forget the things she told me that night. Do you remember?"

Clytie shrugged, but her eyes were growing moist.

"Well," he said, "she told me that everybody has to die and that that's the reason God gave us temples." A single tear coursed down Clytie's cheek and Greg touched it tenderly, willing his own spirit of understanding into her. "I've only told Thaddeus this, Clytie, but I've been to where he is now. Part of the way, at least."

The girl's chin raised just a little as she looked up at him from beneath dewy lashes.

"It's beautiful, Clytie," Greg said, the truth of his words shining from his eyes. "It's indescribable."

"You weren't angry to die? Or sad—or afraid?"

"No," Greg assured her, "and Thaddeus wasn't, either. I told him everything, Clytie. And I heard him speak to his mother—at the end. He knew what was waiting and he wanted to go." Greg stroked the silky hair and fought back his own tears. "I promise you that right this minute Thaddeus is happy and busy and probably explaining the laws of thermodynamics to people who love him as much as we do."

Clytie turned to bury her head in Greg's chest as she wept softly. "But it hurts so much!"

"I know, Clytie, I know." He held her quietly, waiting for the hot tears to wash out some of the cold, bitter grief, then he said, "I read in the New Testament that Jesus wept when told of the death of his friend. It didn't make any sense to me at the time. He knew the plan perfectly. He knew that He had the power to raise Lazarus to life, not just on earth, but for eternity. Why would He cry?" Greg leaned back a little so he could look down into Clytie's face. "I understand it better now."

"But Greg," Clytie asked, her countenance searching, "*was* Andi right? She didn't want me to be friends with Thaddeus at first because he was—"

"No," a soft voice interrupted. "I was wrong."

Engrossed in their grief, neither Greg nor Clytie had noticed Andi exit the temple and slip quietly down the stairs behind them. Now she leaned forward, trying to encircle them both in her slender arms. "I was so wrong," she repeated. "You two made Thaddeus' last months priceless—like you promised him, Greg. And even though we didn't know him very long, our hearts have forever to remember."

As Greg reached to take the hand Andi had laid upon his chest, the gem on her ring finger caught the bright June sun and cast a rainbow on the stair at his feet. He captured the fingers quickly in his palm and held them as he turned toward her. Only when they were face to face, close enough to kiss, did Greg lower his head and look at the hand he was holding.

Andi caught her lower lip between her teeth and her breath in her throat as his blue eyes finally rose. "I got this ring for my birthday," she whispered into the celestial depths of his eyes. "It's the only thing I ever wanted."

"Andi—" Greg began.

"Andi!" Darlene called impatiently from the door. "Are we going to do baptisms, or not? The temple lady wants to know. I *told* her that Clytie's sad, but she said that the temple's the right place to be when you're sad. Oh! Hi, Greg! I'm glad you're finally here. Dad and I watched you on TV today and—" unsteady in the heels she had borrowed from her mother's closet, Darlene clomped down the stairs until she was at their side, "—I've figured out how you can marry my sister now—if you still want to."

"Darlene!" Andi said quickly. "Will you please go inside and tell—"

"No, wait," Greg interrupted. "I really want to marry her sister. I think I'd better hear this."

Darlene cast Andi her best "see-there" look and continued excitedly, "I've got it all worked out. You know Andi's qualifications, right?"

Even as Greg nodded, Andi saw immediately that her sister was about to recite from her checklist. "Darlene, really, don't—"

"It's okay," Greg said. "I already have a pretty good idea where I score on this list."

Darlene held up one finger. "Well, one, you're a member of the Church." She began to hold up a second finger, then lowered it cautiously. "You *do* have a temple recommend, don't you, Greg?"

"For baptism," he replied.

"Well, that's all *she* has," Darlene pointed out. "Andi can't expect you to be more committed to the gospel than she is, after all."

One side of Greg's lips rose in the beginning of a grin, even though he knew the going would get tougher as Darlene reached the last two qualifications.

Sure enough, the girl frowned. "I don't know about the *returned* part, Greg," she admitted slowly, "but after we heard you talk at that meeting-thing today, Dad told me that you were the best missionary *he'd* ever seen." She turned to her older sister hopefully. "You could count that for Rule Three, couldn't you, Andi?"

Nestling her head in the hollow of Greg's neck, Andi could only nod.

Darlene's little finger shot up now to complete the set. "And—if we ever do baptisms for the dead like that temple lady wants us to—Greg's gonna have *lots* of family, besides his mother, that are members of the Church." Darlene wiggled her four fingers triumphantly. "See there?"

"Darlene Reynolds," Greg said, looking up at her with a slow smile, "have I ever told you that I love you?"

"No," she said, "but you bought me a waffle cone once and that was even better."

"And I love you," Greg said, leaning over to kiss Clytie gently on the forehead. Then he cupped Andi's radiant face in his palms and raised it to his own. "And *you*, well . . ."

Darlene rolled her eyes as she clomped over to Clytie. "Come on, Clytie," she said, grasping her sister's sleeve with a sigh. "We'd better go tell the temple lady that it might be *forever* before these two come inside."

"Forever," Andi murmured as her lips met Greg's and a thousand new stars appeared in the deep velvet night behind her eyelids. She would spend forever and ever and ever with Greg and—perhaps—it would be just long enough.

ABOUT THE AUTHOR

A native of Arizona, Kerry currently lives in the Salt Lake City area with her husband, Gary, and two of their four children. Besides an avocation for family history, Kerry enjoys reading, speaking to women's and youth groups, and watching movies filmed before 1950. *The Heart Has Forever* is her second book with Covenant Communications. It is the sequel to *The Heart Has Its Reasons*.

Kerry loves to correspond with readers. You can write to her in care of Covenant Communications, Box 416, American Fork, Utah 84003-0416 or e-mail her at KerryLynnBlair@aol.com.

An excerpt from the soon-to-be released novel
by Marcie Anne Jenson

WHISPERS *of* HOPE

PROLOGUE

After calling 911, Ty Edwards left his car. Struggling against the wind, he stumbled down the cliffs, toward a small cove of pebbly sand, toward the incoming tide, toward his buddy who was somewhere in those waves. "THES!" he screamed at the churning sea. "THESEUS LAUTARO FLETCHER! THES!" A thought blew in his mind like a grenade. Theseus Lautaro Fletcher. His buddy's was a strange name for a newsflash, a headline, a tombstone.

Ty ran into the surf; the frigid water tugged at his tennis shoes, his socks, his jeans. He pictured Thes in his mind, the black hair and dark eyes. Ty swore at the ocean. He made bargains with God.

Ty knew Thes was a fighter. He was out there somewhere. Perhaps the ocean would throw Thes into his arms. Ty would drag his buddy out of the water to safety. He would pound his chest, and breathe into his blue lips, and life would return to those black, dark-lashed eyes. Ty prayed for a miracle. But no miracle came. The young man sobbed as he stared at the sea.

Then the image of Thes's younger sister, Dennie, rose in his mind. He saw the accusing glare she had thrown at him when she noticed the beer in the car before he and Thes left that morning.

Unbidden, his mind turned to a hot September day sixteen months ago, the day Dennie turned sixteen. After football practice, he remembered going home with Thes for a dip in the pool. Dennie had been swimming laps, her compact body cutting smoothly through the water, her long black hair streaming behind her.

She had stopped and pulled herself onto the side, her feet dangling in the blue. Ty and Thes dove off the board. Like an olympic judge, Dennie put up eight fingers for Thes's flip. Nine fingers for Ty's back dive. She had giggled as they argued about the scores.

"Den, watch out for Ty," Thes had said when he leapt from the pool and ran into the house to catch a phone call.

"What?" Ty remembered gesturing innocently, his wrists bending, and his hands in the air. Then, Ty had swum to where Dennie sat. He had teased her about turning sixteen, about her strict Mormon parents, her protective brother. "Sweet sixteen and never been kissed." He had laughed and tugged on her toes.

Dennie had jumped into the water and splashed him. He had grabbed her hands. Then, he had kissed her. Afterwards, her eyes had looked confused, but soft and beautiful, as if saying, *But this is my brother's best friend. But this is Ty.* He had felt a tremendous urge to hold her. Then, the slider door had opened and Dennie had jumped away. Thes had leapt into the pool, creating a splash that nearly suffocated them both.

A gull screeched overhead pulling Ty back into the present. "NO!" Ty's voice disappeared in the wind. He ducked his head and pounded his body forward, deeper into the waves. A wave covered him. Water blinded and numbed him. Then, strangers' arms were around him, gathering him to the shore.

Back on the coarse sand, away from the waves, he realized that the strange choking sounds were coming from himself. A uniformed man with a drenched mustache, who was an inch shorter than Ty and half Ty's breadth, locked his arms around Ty and held him until he could breathe again.

When Ty's breath came more evenly, he focused on the uniformed men, the ambulance, and the police cars. Then, Ty heard their questions and, swallowing, he told them the lie: that his buddy, Thes Fletcher, had drowned because he was trying to save the life of his best friend who had fallen off the rocks while fishing. "He died for me. He died trying to save me," Ty said. Then, he hung his head, half wishing he were in the water with his best friend, Theseus Lautaro Fletcher. At peace.

CHAPTER ONE
Black Clouds in a Turquoise Sky

Dennie Fletcher, seventeen years old and a junior in high school, looked out the window at California's deep-turquoise sky. The clouds hung black, and the sliver of moon shone like an arch cut from the sky. Dennie shivered and pulled her blue-green sweatshirt on over her black jeans. She lifted her black hair from the nape of the sweatshirt and shook it out. Her hair sloped past her shoulders, shiny and soft like a piece of ebony silk. She ran her fingers through it and felt its heaviness as it hung to her waist. She heard the lonely cry of a train whistle. The sound of the locomotive moving into the distance was like an echo of her sorrow.

Dennie sat down on the couch and reached for a photo album on the coffee table. It was brown leather with the raised gold letters *In Celebration of Your Life* printed on the front. For a moment, her fingers caressed the letters. Everything, the sky, the photo album, the very air she breathed reminded her of her brother, of the fact that he was gone forever, and of her relentless feeling of guilt, the whisper that she could have prevented his death.

Dennie opened the photo album. The first picture was taken twelve years ago on the day that Dennie and Thes, two orphans from Chile, had flown to the United States to meet their new parents. They were just two little kids, between the ages of five and seven, standing in an airport, holding a sign that said *Welcome Home.* In the photo, Dennie looked like she had just awakened. A dorky pink bow hung crookedly in her hair. But Thes's eyes shone bright like shiny black stones as if he were devising a way to steal all of the Cinnabons in the airport. Mounted below the picture, there was a poem written by Meryl Fletcher, Dennie and Thes's adoptive mother.

You
Thes Lautaro Fletcher
Came to us with Denizen
On airplane wings like magic
Dark-eyed orphan from Chile
With sun and storm in your gaze
Did you come that I might heal you?
Or did you heal
Me?

Dennie heard a knock. She shut the album and flipped off the lamp before opening the front door.

"O-lee-o," Aimy Tomlinson, Dennie's best friend and across-the-street neighbor, sliced into the darkening entryway. Aimy wove her fingers through her bangs, pushing her short, white-blonde hair back from her eyes. "Density, you need to turn some lights on. It's evening, in case you didn't notice." Aimy turned on the hall switch, and the artificial light made her pixie face appear even paler against the spattering of freckles. Her leather jacket hung over her arm and the neon words on her black T-shirt read: *DON'T INTERPRET THIS SMILE AS HAPPINESS, IT'S INSANITY.*

"In my family we turn off the lights when we leave. Saves electricity," Dennie said as she turned to flip the lights off again.

"Beware of intensity, Density," Aimy laughed. Before hitting the switch, Dennie caught her own image in the hallway mirror. Her eyes were wide set and so dark that the pupils were barely visible. The lids behind them were light and arched. Her cheeks were deep auburn, thanks to Cover Girl blush, her nose was larger and more prominent than she liked, and her lips were moist and full. Then, Dennie wondered the same thing she had wondered countless times over the past four weeks. *How could she look the same when her brother, Thes, was dead? How could she continue to exist now that the world was a tilting place, disjointed and obscure with dark holes that people could fall into at any moment?*

Twenty minutes later, Aimy and Dennie arrived at the Grantlin drag strip. They made their way to the bleachers where they spotted Blake Taylor, Dennie's uncle, sitting with his date, Karin Parker. Karin was in her early thirties and had moved to Grantlin three years ago. Blake and Karin stood up and enthusiastically swung their arms above their heads as if Aimy and Dennie were shipwrecked sailors whom they were motioning aboard to rescue.

Aimy crinkled her upturned nose as the girls mounted the bleachers. "Adults can be such dorks. I wish Sister Parker wasn't here. She drives me crazy. Her hair is *so* orange."

"They've been dating a lot lately," Dennie remarked as they neared a group of shirtless guys with their upper bodies painted green. The boys whistled and the air was rank with the sweetish stench of marijuana.

"We've got room," one of the guys invited.

"Sure thing!" Aimy grinned and acted like she was about to take a seat.

"She's kidding." Dennie grabbed Aimy's arm and steered her around the boys to the place where Blake and Karin were sitting.

"Hi." Blake Taylor squeezed Dennie's hand and kissed her cheek. Karin reached an arm around Aimy's angular shoulder. Aimy shook off the arm and dropped onto the bleacher in front of Blake.

Blake Taylor watched as Dennie sat down next to Aimy. His thoughts turned to both of the girls. How sharp and thin Aimy looked tonight! It had been two weeks since she had attended his seminary class. He hadn't seen her at church either. Blake hoped it wasn't because she was involved with Brak Meyers once more. Blake remembered a time, months ago, when Aimy had brought Brak to church. He was a handsome boy, tall with charcoal-black hair and alabaster skin. But he kept himself aloof, and coldly sluffed aside the missionaries' smiling overtures. Thes and Dennie's behavior towards Brak that Sunday bordered on rudeness. They hardly spoke to him. When Blake had asked them why, they had whispered that they hated the way he treated Aimy, and they were livid with Aimy for allowing it. But that was in the past.

Blake's thoughts turned to Dennie, his niece. By nature she was soft-spoken, intelligent and caring. Yet, since Thes's death she had become so quiet, so inward. It was as if her soul was folded away somewhere, deep inside. This worried him. Blake pushed his hand into his coat pocket and felt the journal he had purchased for her. He hoped it would help.

Blake's thoughts moved backwards in time to Thes's funeral. He had wanted to remain composed for Dennie, and for Meryl and Rick, his sister and brother-in-law. But instead he had sobbed, his eyes swollen like the ocean that had taken his nephew's life. And the emotion that had racked his body was not only for the loss of Thes but also for the stoic, silent way in which Dennie bore her grief—as if she were alone in the universe, with pain too terrible to permit her to weep.

"You both look *so* cute tonight," Karin's friendly voice scattered Blake's thoughts while it scratched like fingernails on Aimy's chalkboard nerves. "I was *so* excited when Blake told me you were coming," Karin went on. "I love your shoes, Dennie. Aimy, with your jacket unzipped, you remind me of my little Christopher. He doesn't seem to feel the cold! That T-shirt is a riot! Where did you get it?"

"The Gemini store," Aimy said shortly. Karin's chatter was driving her insane! Couldn't the woman just quit talking?

"That's such a unique place," Karin continued, unaware of Aimy's irritation. "Your mom does hair there, doesn't she? I walked by the store a few days ago and saw some cute things in the store window. I almost went in. I like how they do massages and hair. They have so many unique knickknacks. But then I thought about how they have a psychic there, telling fortunes. I decided not to go in. I don't think I would even *want* to know the future. Not only because we're Mormons and that kind of thing is taboo. It would be too scary. My everyday life teaching kindergarten and raising Chris is scary enough. Aimy, I admire your mom for her ability to raise you alone. What are her secrets?"

"Gemstone pendants." Aimy said, making her tone smooth and harmless as butter.

"Gemstone pendants?" Karin questioned. "What would gemstone pendants have to do with raising a child?"

"You know, gemstones—they have certain almost magical properties." Now Aimy became the knife cutting into the butter. "You should try them. Chrysocolla increases feminine qualities like communication and creativity. Not that you aren't feminine of course. But it might help you with communication—knowing when to talk and when to be quiet."

Karin's color heightened and her mouth formed a small *O*, like she wanted to say something but wasn't sure what it was. Aimy went on, "Then there's Tourmaline for the weak-hearted. It alleviates fear. Double-terminated clear quartz crystal gives energizing clarity. So you can make better choices. It might help you consider a different color for your hair, something less brassy. My mom could help you at the Gemini Store."

Dennie noticed Blake's arm tighten around Karin. Aimy's rudeness was getting to him. But Dennie knew her uncle. She knew he would be patient, that he wouldn't make a scene.

Karin took a breath and chose to let Aimy's hurtful comments slip from her, much like water sliding off a duck's back. Her cheerful voice shredded the uncomfortable silence. "Couldn't we all use energizing clarity? And look! The race is about to begin!"

A moment later the jet cars began to race. The horizon, formerly as black as Dennie's eyes, was dimmed by fire and smoke. Blake explained that the cars with the slowest dial times got a head start. A dial time was like a golf handicap.

"So the fastest cars give the slower cars a break. That's really nice," Karin grinned.

Dennie sat back down and gazed at the strange cars with their round, fat, back tires and their fronts like little vacuums. She saw the white smoke, the fire and light as they sped down the tracks. She heard the roar of the engines, smelled the rubber burning, watched the bright safety parachutes flare open slowing the speeding cars. She heard the crowd cheer.

But as Dennie watched, she shuddered. The chill air on her cheeks felt as cold as Thes's baby finger the day she slipped the CTR ring on it before they lowered the lid of his coffin.